J.T. HOWELL

Devour

Copyright © 2025 by J.T. Howell

All rights reserved. No part of this publication may be reproduced, stored, or transmitted in any form or by any means, electronic, mechanical, photocopying, recording, scanning, or otherwise without written permission from the publisher. It is illegal to copy this book, post it to a website, or distribute it by any other means without permission.

First edition

This book was professionally typeset on Reedsy.
Find out more at reedsy.com

Contents

 1 To Kill a God   1
 2 Interrogation   14
 3 A State of Mourning   26
 4 Proposition   41
 5 Execution   52
 6 The Emerald Pavilion   63
 7 A Hint of Vanilla   78
 8 The First Mark   92
 9 A Bad Branch   106
10 Dinner Guests   120
11 Fickle Desires   137
12 Respite   149
13 Lessons for a Ruler   165
14 Rats and Vipers   182
15 Fire Lilies   195
16 The Meridian   210
17 Home   225
18 The Winter Palace   240
19 Masquerade   254
20 Shattered   267
21 Solace   279
22 Ascension   294
23 Fox and Wolf   311
24 Freedom   326

1

To Kill a God

Assassinating the emperor was not as satisfying as Fenris had anticipated. After years of meticulous planning, rigorous training, and agonizing sacrifice, he cleaved the tyrant's head from his shoulders with a single, precise blow. The affair was swift, brutal, and anticlimactic; a victory achieved at a devastating cost.

He had assumed this moment would feel different, that he would revel in the death of the despot responsible for so much suffering and injustice. He should have been proud of liberating the people from such a cruel ruler and fulfilling the Meridian's mission. But as Fenris stood above the decapitated corpse of Claude Aleksandran, the forty-fifth god-emperor of the divine Xandrian Empire, he wept.

This somber reaction was unusual, as he had never cried for his previous targets. They had all deserved their bloody ends, none more so than the depraved emperor. Warmongers, human traffickers, murderers, oppressors, all enemies of the people and thus enemies of the Meridian. Regardless of their transgressions, their faces haunted Fenris, weighing on his conscience like innumerable anchors. He detested violence and resented the lethal skills he had gained from his years in the slums. Still, he would readily pay the price of a lifetime of nightmares in exchange for eliminating monsters.

His tears also fell for a second corpse crumpled against the far wall, his neck broken. Durian Mossebette, the Meridian's courageous leader and Fenris's mentor. He rescued Fenris from the slums, gave him a purpose, and taught him how to use his skills for the greater good.

Durian made the emperor's assassination possible and paid for it with his life. He infiltrated the palace alongside Fenris in hopes of overpowering the despot with their combined strength. But Emperor Claude resisted. The ruined bedchamber was proof of their deadly struggle.

Flames reduced the once magnificent furniture to smoldering piles of ash. Lightning and fire blackened and marred the silk carpet that once proudly displayed the emperor's great eagle seal. The walls and ceiling, however, remained untouched. The opulent tapestries of past Xandrian emperors and empresses, along with the ornate crystalline chandelier above, hung safely beyond the mystical veil Fenris conjured before the battle. Nothing had escaped the invisible ward, not his target, not their flaming projectiles, nor a single sound. The emperor had died in silence. As far as the palace was concerned, he remained fast asleep. Instead, his head lay at Fenris's feet, a few paces from his broken body.

Emperor Claude had a strong chin, high cheekbones, and a prominent, hook-shaped nose; his piercing eyes were glazed over in death.

Retrieving a pressed fire lily from his pocket, Fenris placed it delicately on the emperor's chest. Commonly grown in his homeland, the flower was said to help calm the souls of the departed. He left one with each victim as a token of respect for the life he took. And to quell his fathomless remorse. Using his blood-soaked sleeve as a brush, he painted his second token on the charred floor: a circle bisected with a curved line. The symbol of the Meridian. The realm would soon know who saved them from the emperor.

Fenris panted and dropped his shield, his tattered counterfeit livery barely covering his slight frame. Infiltrating the imperial palace was relatively simple; the lavish sprawl of gilded pavilions, towers, and gardens was a small, fortified city situated between the capital and the sea, home to thousands of servants, guards, and courtiers. Fenris and Durian entered unnoticed by disguising themselves as palace servants. Fenris's nondescript features and lithe build rendered him unassuming and forgettable, his greatest strength as an assassin. Though Durian's imposing presence was more difficult to hide, they managed to slip through the palace defenses undetected. Their newfound powers were only required once to enter the emperor's private chambers. Once inside, they merely had to wait for the opportune moment.

The emperor proved to be a ferocious opponent, which came as no surprise. The world considered the god-emperor of Xandria the most powerful being in existence, the only human imbued with the spirits' sacred power. The divine empire reserved such a practice, once considered taboo, for its leader. Whoever underwent the ritual became what the ancients once called a Tal'Rach. An emperor or empress was nearly impossible to defeat in direct combat, for no one else alive had the honor of becoming a living god.

No one except Fenris and Durian.

But unlike the emperor, they were newly forged Tal'Rach and untested in battle. Durian died instantly, though his sacrifice allowed Fenris to deliver the fatal blow. The entire altercation lasted less than a minute. Such was the incredible and terrifying strength of the Tal'Rach.

Blood and gristle covered Fenris's hands; the sight caused him to dry heave. He summoned an orb of water, which floated gracefully in the air. He plunged both of his hands into the clear liquid, which darkened to a red hue as it absorbed the emperor's lifeblood. He released the water, which fell to the charred carpet, bathing it in crimson. The process took precious time he did not have, but he could not escape the palace while resisting the urge to vomit.

Something clicked behind him, too quiet for human ears to detect. But Fenris wasn't a mere mortal. Not anymore.

A veiled figure crouched on the windowsill in black, lightweight clothing. Another assassin, likely sent by another master. But they were too late. The stranger must have arrived during the struggle and witnessed Fenris steal their bounty, unable to pierce the magical veil. Unlike Fenris, who killed out of principle and justice, most assassins only cared about the monetary reward. And an emperor's bounty would allow any assassin to live the rest of their days in luxury. Fenris would have chuckled at such a coincidence if he weren't so livid at his own carelessness. He had lowered the defensive veil before thoroughly checking his surroundings.

As he turned his head, the air in the room shimmered with a soft glow, a telltale sign of Animancy. Fenris cursed. Imperial law reserved such power for members of the royal family, the church, and Tal'Rach. This interloper was no ordinary assassin. The room glowed intensely. The figure at the window harnessed every spirit within reach. Fenris dropped to his stomach, pressing his face into the ruined carpet. A split second later, a searing beam of pure light tore through the room, incinerating the interior wall and tearing through the palace. The torrent of energy singed his back, missing him by a hairsbreadth. If he hadn't reacted so swiftly, the attack would have incinerated him.

The inferno subsided within a heartbeat, and darkness befell the bedchamber once more. Fenris would only have a moment to react before another assault. The air continued to glisten around him. His opponent maintained their connection to every spirit in reach, preventing anyone else from harnessing their power. But Fenris did not need the spirits around him, for he had countless surging within. He extended his hand and willed the cold night wind to surge through the window toward him.

The enemy assassin gasped as the tempest pulled them into the ruined room, drawing them toward Fenris. He reassumed his bestial form, a power only available to Tal'Rach. Black fur enveloped his skin, his hands replaced with claws, and his teeth with fangs. This form repulsed him, so he rarely adopted it, but it came with its advantages. He extended his claws as the black-clad assailant collided with him.

But the other assassin was ready, and summoned their own mystical shield, slamming into Fenris and knocking him backward. As he regained his balance, the assailant landed gracefully, brandishing a gleaming dagger in each hand. They were not only a powerful Animancer but also skilled in martial combat.

Sirens wailed from the courtyard outside. Fenris cursed. The assassin's devastating blast shattered the precious secrecy he and Durian had painstakingly maintained over the past few hours. Such an explosion must have awoken the entire palace, and soon the imperial guard would descend upon them. Escaping the fortress would prove to be a grueling feat.

But first, he had to contend with the assassin.

Fenris growled and lunged forward, claws extended. The pair engaged in a savage dance, daggers flashing in the moonlight. Fenris could admit the assassin was of a similar caliber. But they were not a Tal'Rach. Fenris was faster, stronger, and more ferocious. He dodged each strike, retaliating with his own. His lightning-fast swipes caught the assassin half a dozen times until they were heaving and covered in shallow cuts.

But the mysterious figure persisted, intent on dealing a death blow. Their strikes grew wilder with desperation.

And Fenris capitalized on their recklessness.

Dodging a frenzied melee, his claw shot forward, catching the assassin by the neck. Lifting them, he growled, shaking them until they dropped both daggers.

Fenris had only prepared himself for one death tonight; ending another life was almost too much for him to bear. But they left him with no other choice. He knew only too well that he could not reason or barter with an assassin.

He squeezed harder; his stomach twisted.

A bright flash grazed his shoulder and exploded against the outer wall. He growled in pain, releasing his grip. Half a dozen imperial soldiers poured in through the steaming hole left by the rogue assassin's attack, wielding metal crossbows. The weapons hissed, hurling bolts of energy toward Fenris. He lifted his hands instinctively, calling forth a shield of light. The energy bolts collided with the veil violently, but his defenses held.

Instinctively, he glanced to his right, prepared for another assault from the other assassin. A shadow disappeared around the window. The figure in black used the distraction to escape. Fenris sighed with relief. He would not need to end another life.

Holding his veil in place, Fenris hurled fire at the charging soldiers. Careful to avoid inflicting fatal hits, he aimed his volleys at their feet, creating a wall of fire. He had experienced enough death for one night and would not burden his conscience any further.

Unlike the rogue assassin, these soldiers were innocent, despite their murderous intent. They were all provincials, like Fenris, low-born citizens who hailed from lands conquered by the Xandrian Empire. They were victims of the corrupt world order, their agency and rights stripped away by the very oppressors who seized their homelands.

"Abomination!" they cried. A couple fled through the gap in horror. Fenris remained in his lupine form. From the soldiers' perspective, only one person alive could assume animalistic features. That man lay in pieces at Fenris's feet.

Fenris glanced at Durian once more, his stomach twisted in regret and shame. He hadn't been strong enough to save him. He wished he could return his mentor's body home, so their brothers and sisters of the Meridian could perform a proper burial. But he had no time.

His flames successfully deterred the soldiers, so he dropped his shield and retreated, diving through the closest window. He decided to maintain his lupine form, believing the fear it instilled could serve as an effective shield. A stealthy escape was out of the question.

He plummeted like a boulder to the courtyard below. A large bonsai broke his fall in a storm of splinters and leaves, disrupting the once serene private garden. Fenris ignored the wood piercing his flesh, scrambled to his feet, and frantically dashed across the courtyard.

The Golden Pavilion, the emperor's private residence, was nestled in the center of the sprawling palace complex, surrounded by four high walls. The one closest to Fenris held the only gate leading out, which was barred and closed. The parapets above were swarming with dozens of soldiers. Bolts of energy danced through the night air, illuminating the once sleepy garden in a deadly display of light. A few found their mark, but Fenris disregarded the excruciating pain as he bounded toward the blocked gate.

The soldiers above, though numerous, were a lesser threat compared to the group who rushed out of the Golden Pavilion behind him. Each of them was an officer, covered with insignis tattoos. The intricate ink adorning their skin not only marked them as pure-blooded Xandrians but also served as a weapon more fearsome than the crossbows wielded by the provincial guards. Fenris did not intend to witness the insignis tattoos in action.

He summoned another fierce gale, tearing the sturdy gate off its hinges, splintering the heavy wood as he crashed through it. A short tunnel lay beyond it, thankfully empty. Instead of running to the gate at the tunnel's opposite end, which would lead to another courtyard, Fenris stopped at a locked door carved into the wall. He tore it open with a sharp pull and bounded up the vacant stairs to the parapets above.

The palace was orderly and geometric, constructed in typical Xandrian fashion. Thick, high walls connected dozens of courtyards, each featuring its own lavish palace and surrounding garden. A guard tower rose at each intersection. Armed guards patrolled the extensive network of wide parapets, but it served as a convenient escape route for someone graced with Fenris's power.

Barreling through the ranks, Fenris tried his best to be as delicate as possible. He flung the guards into the short walls on either side, careful not to send them over the edge. A fall from such a height would prove fatal. And he would rather be riddled with bolts than bear the guilt of extinguishing another life.

Bolting across the high avenues, he navigated from the Golden Pavilion toward the palace's eastern perimeter. The farther he ran, the fewer soldiers blocked his way. He leaped over the corners to bypass the towers, where officers awaited him. Luckily, he avoided any encounter with the formidable Xandrian warriors and their insignis blades.

Despite the blaring sirens and the entire palace's defenses descending upon him, his escape proved easier than he had expected to the point that he questioned why he and Durian had bothered with stealth during their infiltration.

He reached the palace's far eastern wall, and the murky waters of the Cellicean Sea churned below. The chase would end once he dove into the treacherous waves. He could swim leagues in any direction without surfacing, making it impossible for his pursuers to follow.

The wall in front of him exploded.

He slammed into the short parapet behind him, and his lungs deflated. The explosion was far greater than any crossbow and twice as powerful as the beam unleashed by the rogue assassin; it annihilated the wall that once separated

Fenris from the sea.

Pulling himself to his feet, Fenris turned toward the origin of the blast—the nearest guard tower. A single figure stood at its apex. The air around him flickered with Animancy, his body covered in insignis tattoos, more than any officer pursuing Fenris. The odd tattoos roiled across his skin and poured outward, ink forming into liquid metal. The gleaming substance rippled around him, settling into the shape of heavy armor and a pair of long, curved swords. Fenris's wolf eyes could easily perceive the man's face in the night. He was handsome and nearing his middle years; age had not yet taken his beauty, but he had long since left the softness of youth. Piercing eyes were deeply set on either side of a beaked nose, burning with anger and hatred. Fenris would have gasped if any air remained in his lungs.

During his preparations, he had taken it upon himself to memorize the features of every prominent official in the palace. The identity of this man was unmistakable at first glance. Standing before him was High Lord Aludrien Aleksandran, the emperor's son and heir apparent to the Xandrian Empire. His reputation had preceded him: ruthless, cunning, cruel, and responsible for countless innocent deaths. Now that Fenris had slain Aludrien's father, he would soon take Claude's place as sovereign. He would undoubtedly be worse for the Imperium than his father could ever be.

Fenris and Durian's mission was clear. Assassinate the emperor and escape the palace while avoiding detection. No one else was to die. The rogue assassin had foiled the latter part of the plan. And if Aludrien assumed the throne, Fenris's despicable act and Durian's sacrifice would be for naught. The citizens of the Imperium would be in greater danger under his rule. The Meridian charged themselves to protect the realm from those who would harm it. Given that Fenris had removed Claude, Aludrien was the greatest threat to that goal.

Aludrien was not yet emperor and had not yet ascended to Tal'Rach. Xandrian law mandated a mourning period before the next ruler ascended—when the Meridian planned to strike again. And without the powers of a Tal'Rach, Aludrien would never again be as vulnerable or weak.

He glanced back at the dark waters below. Once Fenris leaped into the abyss, the whole ordeal would end, his mission complete. Regardless, he hesitated. A nagging sensation kept him from retreating into the safety of the sea.

Fenris looked into the cold eyes leering from the guard tower. Aludrien sneered arrogantly, and the sky around him gleamed as he prepared another blast.

Fenris inhaled deeply, asking himself if he could bear the weight of another murder. The answer up until this point had been a resounding no.

But that answer had changed in an instant.

He spun and charged at Aludrien.

His sudden movement prevented a flurry of lightning strikes from vaporizing him. The stone under his feet shuddered, crumbling beneath the might of the mystical assault. Fenris almost lost his balance as the outer palace wall behind him collapsed, giant pieces cascading into the sea. But he was already halfway to the guard tower as the last lightning bolt struck, propelled by inhuman speed.

The heir descended the steps and sprinted across the parapet toward him, brandishing a pair of vicious swords that shifted in his hand. Reaching out a claw, Fenris unleashed a ball of flame. It collided with Aludrien with a satisfying hiss. But the heir charged through the inferno as if it were mist, his gleaming insignis armor deflecting the attack with ease.

They collided.

Battling Claude was akin to fighting a storm; as a god-emperor, he was a force of nature. But after years as the most powerful being in existence, he had grown careless and overconfident. He believed he could smite both Fenris and Durian with pure strength, underestimating his opponents. Claude's arrogance proved to be his downfall.

High Lord Aludrien, however, had no such weakness. He fought like a true tactician, ever calculated and ruthless. He met every strike with a clever parry, instantly delivering a counter-strike. Within several heartbeats, Aludrien had landed several blows and remained untouched, his arrogant face contorted in a satisfied smirk. Fenris unleashed a pair of fireballs, but the heir's expertly placed wards rebuffed the flames. Aludrien was not only a world-class swordsman but also a world-class Animancer.

Fenris howled with frustration. He was the raging storm, and Aludrien a sly pack of vipers. Ever elusive, striking from every angle. His insignis blades warped and shifted into a dozen whip-like tendrils, slashing and stabbing Fenris with surgical precision. Fenris ignored the pain and pressed on, dagger-like claws seeking the soft flesh between helmet and chest plate. Aludrien was not a Tal'Rach and could not heal quickly. Fenris only needed one well-placed attack to finish the heir. But Aludrien was swift, and the evening's grueling events left Fenris fatigued and weary.

The only way Fenris could defeat Aludrien in his current condition was to sacrifice himself. He thought of the countless innocents he would save and lunged forward, forgoing any defenses.

A dozen metal ribbons impaled Fenris in the shoulder and thigh, but the gambit paid off; his claws struck the insignis armor, causing the heir to stumble backward. Aludrien grunted in surprise, and Fenris continued his onslaught, throwing his entire weight at the shocked heir.

Aludrien smiled.

In an instant, the metal tendrils constricted violently, restraining Fenris's limbs and tearing his flesh. The remaining tentacles fastened around him. If he moved, the sharp ribbons would cut him to pieces. He had incorrectly assumed he would have an advantage in close quarters. He had fallen for Aludrien's trap.

"Poor mutt," Aludrien jeered. The metal tightened. "You should have jumped."

With the butt of his sword, he savagely struck Fenris's temple, and the world faded.

2

Interrogation

Death did come for Fenris. Something far worse followed his defeat, a fate he dreaded more than anything.

Captivity.

He knew of the horrors that befell enemies detained by the empire, but experiencing a Xandrian cell firsthand was terrifying beyond comprehension. Fenris now understood how thousands of prisoners had broken under the weight of an imperial interrogation.

When Fenris first regained consciousness, he assumed he had died, floating in a pitch-black abyss. However, his circumstances became clearer when the dim lights flickered on. Six black surfaces formed an impenetrable cube, devoid of a single blemish, entrance, or window. He could only presume the walls were identical, as he hung suspended in the center of the cavernous room, immobilized. Barely able to turn his head, he recalled a Xandrian cell he had encountered on a job years ago when he assassinated a prominent general. A radiant cone of air held him fast, emanating from a metal circle on the cell floor.

Instinctively, he called upon the spirits within. Lightning, fire, and wind bounced uselessly off the mystical ward. Nothing he summoned could escape the glistening cone.

Luckily, he had remained in his bestial form while unconscious. The spirits inside him had healed his wounds before he woke, but he had not yet reverted to his natural state. He decided to retain his wolf-like features to intimidate his captors and conceal his identity. Though the empire could identify Durian's body and Fenris marked the scene with the Meridian's calling card, he feared revealing any further information that could jeopardize his comrades. He did not hide his identity for his own sake; Fenris understood he would die in this sterile cell.

Interrogations were his only way to measure time. Four grueling sessions passed, leading Fenris to deduce that four days had elapsed since his capture. Each session followed the same pattern: the lights illuminated his prison, an unseen door slid open, and a disembodied voice questioned him from far below.

"What is your name?"

"How did you enter the palace undetected?"

"Who were your associates?"

"Did someone in the palace hire you?"

"Who aided in your ascension?"

They were routine, mundane, and in Fenris's opinion, uninspired queries. He remained silent, refusing to disclose any information. For every non-answer, excruciating pain radiated from the dozen metal nodes his captors had affixed to his body. His skin burned as if a swarm of hornets was frantically stinging him from the inside, desperate to escape. He refused to cry out or acknowledge his captors, which only resulted in more pain.

Four unique voices, four separate interrogations, and endless pain, each concluding with the same result: a frustrated exit and a return to darkness.

The fifth session, however, deviated considerably from this routine.

Sudden illumination pulled Fenris from his fugue-like sleep, and he prepared himself for the coming onslaught. The familiar click of the exterior door echoed against the barren walls.

Instead of a single set of footsteps, a chorus of shuffling feet entered the cell, followed by hushed murmurs and horrified gasps. More than a dozen distinct voices filled the stale air, though he could not discern their exact words. This session, it seemed, would include an audience.

A few long moments passed as the crowd below shuffled into place, and something metallic scraped along the cell floor. The whispers subsided, quelled by the sharp snap of a heavy door sliding shut. Fenris stared forward, unsettled by the weight of dozens of eyes.

A crystalline, feminine voice broke the tense silence.

"How do you expect me to have a productive conversation when the prisoner cannot see me?"

Fenris's brow furrowed in confusion. Then he realized the voice was not addressing him.

"Ma'am," a gruff voice replied. "The precautions are necessary; we cannot underestimate a creature such as—"

"I care little for your recommendations, Lieutenant. There is no need to release him from his binds completely, but I would prefer to look him in the eye when I speak. Can you do that for me?" The words sounded casual and suggestive, but the tone was icy and commanding.

A mechanical buzz followed. The immense pressure immobilizing Fenris lessened. Breathing became easier, and he could move his head slightly, though the invisible restraints continued to hold him fast. His sore neck muscles screamed as he gingerly rolled his head, testing the limits of his new confinement. He lowered his chin to assess the situation below.

An entire squadron of soldiers surrounded the odd ring-shaped insignis engine, which emitted the cone of radiant light. Each guard aimed a crossbow directly at the floating prisoner. Off to the side, a man observed Fenris intently behind a control panel. The Lieutenant.

A score of courtiers clung to the far wall, faces obscured in shadow. Each adorned in black, somber attire, though the styles remained extravagant and outlandish. The court was in mourning. Three individuals sat between him and the crowd, calmly watching their captive from the comfort of their plush seats. Fenris recognized each one. Without the emperor, they were the three most powerful individuals in the entire empire. The appointed leaders of the church, military, and government. The three pillars of the realm, working at the throne's pleasure. In Xandria, nobles derived their station from divine appointments; outside the royal family, every courtier held a title associated with one of the three factions: ministers of the government, cardinals of the holy church, and generals of the armed forces. But the crown elevated three individuals above the rest, leading each branch of the glorious empire.

The woman on the left, Fenris assumed, was the one who had spoken earlier. Her practical black dress matched her tightly braided hair. She sat with a rigid posture, pursed lips, and narrowed eyes, scrutinizing the abomination before her without a trace of fear. Chancellor Vispin Vesper, the closest advisor to the late Emperor Claude, and the first low-born provincial appointed as the government's head. Like most bureaucrats, she had a reputation for being manipulative, duplicitous, and cunning. Unparalleled in these traits, she had clung to power for decades. According to intelligence from Durian's palace contacts, Emperor Claude trusted her above all others and considered her counsel as gospel.

"Pardon me if I skip the pleasantries," Vispin began, each word meticulously chosen. "But we have much to discuss, Fenris Vale of Belantine."

A cold chill ran through him, and his eyes widened in shock. He composed himself, attempting to conceal any further surprise, but his initial reaction had already betrayed him. The Chancellor's lips curled into a victorious grin. His identity must have been a matter of conjecture until he had subtly confirmed it. Vispin would prove to be a most formidable opponent.

"Ah, yes, I know who you are, as I am certain you are aware of my colleagues and me," the Chancellor gestured to the man and woman sitting beside her, who both remained silent. "Though it may surprise you that we have fewer questions than your previous inquisitors."

Fenris remained silent, refusing to respond to Vispin's obvious taunt. How the Chancellor had ascertained his name and birthplace made no difference to him. The three most powerful people in the Imperium sat before him. Such a spectacle made one thing clear: they desperately wanted to glean any information from him. But they would fail miserably. Nothing would force Fenris to betray the Meridian or those in the palace who had aided them.

After a tense silence, Vispin pursed her lips and proceeded.

"Fenris Vale of the Belantine plains, born twenty-eight years past in the eighth-hundred and fifty-second year of the glorious Xandrian Empire in a village called Trog. There, you were raised by shepherds, Senia and Philemon Vale, the second of four children. You were a shepherd until age nine, when Xandria judiciously assimilated Belantine. The rest of your relations, unfortunately, rebelled and did not survive the process. Despite your status as the child of dangerous insurgents, the empire graciously pardoned you of any crime and relocated you to the city of Kyriak. You promptly ran away from the Imperial orphanage, where an upstanding family could have adopted you. Instead, you found yourself at the mercy of the slums. Details remain murky until you joined the Meridian eight years ago, but I can assume it was not a delightful experience. Did I miss anything?"

A tongue of flame erupted from Fenris's claw, bouncing uselessly against the barrier. The courtiers below shrieked in horror and scurried to the rear wall. The soldiers fired crossbow bolts, but the cell's ward negated the blasts as it had with Fenris's attack. Only the three figures in the chairs remained unfazed.

Vispin tutted, like a teacher gently chiding a student.

"The crown prohibits the art of Animancy for any provincial not admitted into the clergy. According to Imperial law, only members of the holy church, the emperor, and the royal family have the right to practice Animancy. Am I correct, Your Eminence?"

She directed her question to the wizened gentleman who sat

in the rightmost chair. He wore billowing black priest's robes gilded in gold to mark his station. Insignis tattoos on his neck and forearms betrayed his purebred Xandrian lineage, though his features were too soft to be royal. Animancy, the sacred art of communing with departed souls and harnessing their energy, was the source of the empire's power. Artisans crafted weapons, shields, lights, and even common appliances using insignis engines powered by the spirits. Artisans shaped them, but priests and priestesses were responsible for imbuing them with spirits, using their Animancy. The church consolidated and maintained its power via the archaic practice. Though exceedingly rare, the empire considered provincials gifted in the mystical arts to be eligible for the highest rank, surpassing artisans, soldiers, and servants.

The Pontifex, highest in the holy church, received the title by appointment, but of course, they must be of the blood. Many considered Ignatius to be the most formidable Animancer in living memory, having served under two rulers during his tenure, both Claude and his mother, Empress Derulia. He was a constant counselor and, according to rumors, Vispin's bitter rival for the late emperor's favor.

His renowned kindness, however, was absent from his expression. He looked upon Fenris with only disgust and abhorrence.

"This is not Animancy, Chancellor. The abomination before you is much worse. Someone committed a cardinal sin, and a provincial has ascended to the station of Tal'Rach. Fusing countless spirits to a mortal's soul, granting them unimaginable power that eclipses normal Animancy. An honor only bestowed upon empresses and emperors."

Vispin bowed her head politely. "Thank you for the

clarification, Ignatius. The intricacies of Animancy have never been my expertise. But I do know such a task as ascension would require a dozen highly trained cardinals to perform. Am I correct?"

"I am afraid so, my child," Pontifex Ignatius replied, his voice tense as if the Chancellor had accused him of treason. "I assure you that I have launched extensive investigations into the matter, and I will root out any insurgency from the holy church."

"Your duty to the Imperium remains peerless," Vispin replied dryly.

"Although Imperial law strictly forbids the practice of Animancy to those outside the church and the royal family, it does not prevent the occasional provincial from learning the arts outside of the church's blessing," Ignatius said. "You of all people should be familiar with provincials disregarding centuries of precedent, Vispin."

The woman in the central chair finally spoke, her hand clenched in frustration. "Silence."

Vispin and Ignatius obeyed with absolute deference, visibly embarrassed by the public admonishment. The commanding woman in the center chair ignored them and turned to Fenris.

"We know who you are, child of insurgents. We know you hold no love for the empire, which explains your motivations behind my brother's death. We know you acted under the direction of Durian Mossebette and the Meridian. We also know this isn't the first murder you have committed for this terrorist organization; within hours, imperial investigators connected you to a score of notable assassinations in the past year alone. The fire lily you placed on the emperor's corpse betrayed you. The flower is native to the continent's central region, including the Belantine Plains. Imperial officers found them placed on numerous corpses of notable public figures, dignitaries, and nobles. It seems you are prolific, to the extent that investigators have named you 'the florist'. Finally, we know your meager band of rebels could not have possibly committed this act independently. The only information we require from you is: who created you, who aided your infiltration into the palace, and the identity of your accomplice who escaped. These unanswered questions are the only reason you still draw breath."

Grand Marshal Hestraea Aleksandran, the late emperor's sole sibling and commander of the Xandrian armed forces, spoke with curt authority. She wore her Insignis Armor, which expressed her station and obscured her hawk-like features. Under her relentless leadership, the Imperium's legions conquered more independent lands than any ruler in the empire's history, including Fenris's homeland. Though she was shrewd on the battlefield, her birthright as an Aleksandran allowed her more bluntness in the court than the other courtiers, who resorted to scheming to maintain power. Fenris resisted the urge to unleash another assault, grinding his teeth in frustration and unadulterated hatred.

"All we require is a name, Fenris," Vispin added, her tone almost compassionate. "Who turned you and Durian into Tal'Rach, or who aided your entrance to the palace, or your missing companion. One name, and this all will end."

Fenris resisted the urge to chuckle. The nobles' tactics may have caused him to lose his composure, but no amount of manipulation, grandstanding, or mind games would trick him into betraying his comrades.

"The Meridian acted alone," Fenris stated. The crowd below

murmured in surprise as he finally spoke. "We learned the rite of ascension and performed it ourselves. We killed for the people, to free them from tyranny. We have no friends within the palace."

He resumed his stony silence. There was nothing for him to reveal, regardless. Durian had managed the particulars with his secret contacts, keeping their identities hidden. Fenris knew nothing.

"My brother's funeral will start tomorrow, and according to our traditions, it will last for three days. Your execution will transpire the following day. Give us a single name, and I will allow you to wait in peace until your death. If you do not divulge the information we seek, your final days will not be pleasant."

"I only have one name to give," Fenris said. "The Meridian. Torture won't change the truth."

"Oh, you misunderstand me," Hestraea said. "I will ask you twice more. Once today and once in four days, before your execution. If you refuse, we will conclude our interrogation and leave you in isolation, with your pain receptors activated. You should also be aware that the inquisitors have previously used them at half strength. If you do not cooperate, you will experience them at their full capacity. Uninterrupted. For four days."

Fenris's stomach soured, recalling the excruciating hours of intense agony he had endured during his captivity. But the interrogators had used the cold metal receptors lodged in his body sparingly. The Grand Marshal threatened him with four days of unrelenting, mind-bending pain.

Vispin broke the silence.

"We have been so preoccupied with asking you for names

that I nearly forgot we have a list of our own. Maris Hutch. Ryland Baz. Parina Oberlon. Kass Prent."

Fenris balked, his body shaking. He knew each name intimately. The implications of the Chancellor uttering them sent a wave of panic through his body. Vispin noticed, grinning viciously.

"I have eleven more, if you want me to continue," Hestraea said. "We attempted to arrest your comrades in the Meridian, but I instructed my troops to respond to lethal force in kind. Unfortunately, each one of your compatriots decided to resist."

Fenris howled, tears streaming down his cheeks. Maris, Ryland, Parina, Kass, Durian. His family. Sixteen in total. All of them. He was the last of the Meridian. He summoned fire, lightning, and ice, but the barrier nullified them all.

"Someone betrayed your friends, Fenris. You have no one to protect. So I will ask you once more," Hestraea said. "Give us a name."

Jaw clenched, he strengthened his resolve. He knew the Grand Marshal was not bluffing; he understood the consequences of his defiance. Overly confident in their position, Vispin and Hestraea committed a fatal error. They had murdered their only bargaining chips. Without anyone to save, Fenris had no other recourse but to join his friends in death. Despite any fate awaiting him, only one possibility remained.

"The Meridian."

Several courtiers gasped, those who truly understood what Fenris was about to endure. The Pontifex paled; his fatherly disposition was too fragile for such a punishment. The Chancellor scowled, visibly upset by the Grand Marshal's ultimatum; Vispin would have undoubtedly spent hours attempting to manipulate Fenris into talking.

"You leave me no choice," Hestraea replied, seemingly pleased by his response. "I will return in four days."

The door opened, and the horrified courtiers filed out of the cell, followed by Ignatius and Vispin. Hestraea lingered, observing her soldiers' exit until only the Lieutenant behind the control panel remained. The poor man trembled; such an act of cruelty was unprecedented. However, Fenris had recently assassinated the emperor of Xandria, so the time for precedent was over.

"Do it," Hestraea commanded.

The Lieutenant complied.

Fenris howled.

The door sealed shut.

Darkness returned.

Only pain remained.

3

A State of Mourning

Emperor Claude Aleksandran's funeral lasted three days, in accordance with the traditions of mourning Xandria's sovereign. Each day honored one of the Core Triad of Virtues expected of any emperor who ascended to rule the Imperium.

The first day commemorated Valor, the first and most crucial Virtue. The morning began with a military procession through the capital, showcasing the realm's might. Thousands thronged the city streets to watch the body of their fallen emperor carried on a gilded palanquin, surrounded by the stoic members of the royal family. The parade concluded at the palace, where the assembled court enjoyed elaborate reenactments of the late emperor's martial victories. The empire had witnessed many triumphs during Claude's reign. However, most courtiers attributed the majority of the credit to Grand Marshal Hestraea: the Siege of Tearpa, the Battle of the Seven Sultans, and the Twilight Wars. The production continued late into the evening, though the performers omitted several of the emperor's conquests for the sake of time.

The second day, representing the Virtue of Divinity, was the most indulgent. The Pontifex and his clergy demonstrated the full power of Animancy. The sky above the royal capital sparkled with the spirits that fueled the empire's machinery, referred to as rach in the ancient tongue. Usually, the spirits of the ancestors remained invisible to the untrained eye, only perceptible as a brief shimmer when harnessed by a trained Animancer. In honor of the departed emperor, the spirits revealed their true nature in a spectacular display. Great specters of every shape and hue danced through the sky in intricate patterns: azure dragons, crimson birds, and vermilion serpents, all paying tribute to the late emperor. The evening concluded with a hedonistic ball, where the intoxicated courtiers feasted upon exotic food and drink from every corner of the realm.

The following morning, the haggard court ceased their dalliances and debauchery to attend the final ceremony hosted in the central courtyard. The third and most somber day honored the final Virtue: Wisdom. Delirious from the revelry of the previous evening, the hungover nobles sat in heavy silence, facing the funeral pyre of Emperor Claude Aleksandran, the forty-fifth god-emperor of Xandria.

High Lord Aludrien Aleksandran sat in the front row, intently observing the ceremony before him. Unlike his less disciplined peers, he had refrained from drinking excessively during the banquet and declined invitations to the gratuitous orgies that transpired after. Most of the audience hadn't slept the night prior, but Aludrien did not have the luxury of lowering his guard. He was the heir to the most powerful throne in existence—a position people would, and had, killed to possess. Countless reckless heirs had lost their lives in the days between the funeral and ascension. Aludrien would not allow himself to fail.

He scarcely registered Chancellor Vispin's droning, who had spent the last five hours recounting the Ancient History of Arachovia. She recited the entire Reginian Proverbs, written by Regina the Seventh, a renowned philosopher and scholar. Aludrien had memorized the text by his tenth birthday, shortly after his grandmother's funeral, when his father ascended and appointed him as heir apparent. He cared little for ancient and obsolete virtues such as temperance, empathy, and compassion. The imperial palace was no place for such weak and altruistic frivolities.

"Proverb six hundred and seventy-seven," Vispin said, her typically crisp voice frayed and strained by the impressively long recitation. "As a firm hand shatters the fragile orchid, so too does force steal all hope of fulfillment. What is meant to flourish will do so in its own season. Permit it to grow."

Aludrien sighed along with the surrounding courtiers as the Chancellor closed the heavy tome after finishing the final proverb. She vacated the stage, eventually replaced by Pontifex Ignatius.

The elderly man trundled up the steps and bowed to the giant casket at the dais' center. The emperor's pale corpse lay delicately on silken pillows, his head expertly sewn onto his body, though a giant ceremonial shroud obscured his features. The gilded coffin sat atop a mountain of furled tapestries, livery, and other relics the palace servants could gather, all embroidered with the golden eagle emblem. The era of Claude had ended; once Aludrien ascended, his lion sigil would replace his father's eagle, as was the tradition of Xandrian succession.

"Thus marks the end of the exalted and divine Emperor Claude Aleksandran XLV, may his legacy continue until eternity." Ignatius trundled off the stage with the help of two priestesses. They guided him to a vacant chair in the front row, next to the Chancellor.

As the Pontifex reached a safe distance, the edges of the circular dais glowed with Animancy. The metal platform rose from the courtyard's center, directly between the front gate and the steps leading to the central pavilion, which loomed over the palace grounds like a mountainous peak. The layout forced anyone entering the palace's central structure to circle the dais, which existed for a single purpose.

The gigantic insignis engine whirred to life, the entire surface illuminated with a blinding light. Aludrien shielded his eyes. A great beam of energy erupted from the stage, piercing the sky. The heat of the inferno was almost unbearable; if he were any closer, it would have singed his eyebrows clean off his face. A few of the younger courtiers gasped in horror and surprise.

After five heartbeats, the engine ceased, and the stage was empty, free of debris or even ash. The physical manifestation of Xandria's forty-fifth emperor had been completely incinerated; only his memory and legacy remained. The emperor's body returned to the heavens, completing the third and final day of the royal ceremony.

Aludrien blinked; the light of the funeral pyre was seared into his vision. The wake of the inferno cast the courtyard in reverent, stupefied silence. Save for the pained sobs of the hysterical man sitting directly to Aludrien's right. Several nobles murmured uncomfortably and dispersed quietly; the somber festivities had come to a close.

"Compose yourself, Basil," Aludrien hissed. "Such theatrics are unbecoming of a High Lord."

The words struck as deftly as a sword, efficiently terminating the man's incessant crying. Hatred swiftly replaced Basil's sorrow as he wiped the tears from his reddened cheeks and glared at Aludrien. He opened his mouth to retort, but quickly closed it. With a flourish, Basil vacated his seat and stalked away, followed by his dutiful husband, Lord Jareth, who held their sleeping daughter Magdolina. The pair glanced back as they disappeared into the milling crowd, undoubtedly cursing Aludrien in countless inventive ways.

The woman sitting to his left leaned over and spoke softly.

"You should consider a more tactful approach with your brother, Aludrien; you are not emperor yet."

"Half-brother," he corrected, earning him an annoyed scowl. "I highly doubt a sentimental word from me would mend our relationship. The bastard has loathed me since the day I was born. I find nothing more pitiful than petty jealousy."

"Careful with such barbs," she replied. The pair sat alone among the vacant chairs, but multiple courtiers lingered in the plaza, milling about and eagerly socializing after the monotonous ceremony. "Your father adopted High Lord Basil years ago, and many in this palace would rather see him on the throne over you. We have one hundred days of mourning before your ascension. Please try not to ruin it because of a childish rivalry."

"Should I expect such infinite wise counsel once I ascend, dearest aunt?" Aludrien asked dryly.

"If you expect to achieve half the legacy your father has, I'd suggest you take heed of my advice as he did," Grand Marshal Hestraea replied.

"Will you still consider me as merely your fledgling pupil when I become your emperor?" Aludrien asked. Few would dare speak to the heir apparent in such a way, which is why he respected his aunt above all others.

"Of course," Hestraea chuckled warmly. "You will always be the little boy who would sneak away from your wet nurse and steal chocolates from my study."

"Allegedly," Aludrien quipped.

Most wouldn't dare joke with the most fearsome and decorated military leader in Xandrian history, but she had nearly raised him after his mother had passed. She wasn't maternal, but she had taught Aludrien everything he knew: strategy, logic, the art of warfare, and the perilous game of daily politics in the imperial palace.

"Why did you miss the assassin's interrogation?" Hestraea asked. "As the one who apprehended him, I assumed you would be eager to attend. Even Basil was present."

"Did he reveal anything of value?" Aludrien asked.

"No."

"Precisely," Aludrien replied. "Our greatest inquisitors had their way with him for days. If they could not wring any information from him, I doubted you and the bickering court would. I did not want to waste my time."

"Who said I finished the interrogation?" Hestraea flashed a dangerous, chilling expression.

"I've heard whispers of what transpired, but I wasn't certain," Aludrien attempted to hide his horror. The Grand Marshal had accumulated a fearsome reputation, but he had thought his aunt operated above such unbelievable cruelty and malice.

"There will be a final audience tomorrow before the execution," Hestraea replied, her jaw clenched. "I encourage you to join. It would benefit you to witness the difficult decisions you will face as emperor."

"If your methods were as extreme as rumors suggest, then I doubt the bastard will be able to form a sentence, much less divulge the information you seek," Aludrien said.

"We shall see," Hestraea replied smoothly, almost too self-assured. "But the offer remains."

Aludrien sighed and rose. The courtyard was nearly empty, and the sun was about to set over the high palace walls.

"Preparing for my ascension is my main priority, dearest aunt. However, please notify me if you discover anything of note. How is the investigation regarding the Meridian progressing?"

"Easier than I originally predicted. We received multiple anonymous tips and dismantled their entire operation. They will no longer pose a threat."

"Have you uncovered the identities of the traitors in the palace?"

"Unfortunately not," Hestraea grimaced. "Without the prisoner's cooperation, we have no leads to the identity of the third assassin, nor those within the palace who colluded with the Meridian. We have only the guards' testimonies to rely on. No distinguishable features and no motive as to why the missing assailant fought with the prisoner after your father's death."

"Quite the mystery indeed. And an embarrassment to our house, allowing those involved with my father's murder to run free. Not to mention the implications of unsanctioned Tal'Rach. The Pontifex has much to explain for."

"No need to worry yourself with such matters. Your safety is my top priority."

"I don't doubt you, dear aunt. A pity no one else shares your opinion," Aludrien said, glancing at the lingering nobles. "By the looks I've received today, I presume everyone else in this palace wishes for my head on a spike."

Grand Marshal Hestraea's stoic expression softened. Having no children or spouse of her own, Aludrien had become her weakness. He smiled in return, bowed formally to his beloved aunt, and departed.

Six heavily armed guards surrounded him, falling into a tight formation, and escorted him out of the grand courtyard. There would be no feast, event, or celebration that evening, so the courtiers would slowly return to their quarters or private villas in the countryside. Half of the attendees would fly their airships home to their remote corners of the Imperium. Aludrien ignored them as he picked his way through the grounds, lingering glances and hushed whispers trailing in his wake.

Admiration, jealousy, hatred, Emperor Claude's son never had any trouble garnering strong emotions from those he encountered; regardless of their reaction, he thrived on their attention. He was the heir apparent, and in one hundred days, he would become the most powerful being alive.

If he survived.

His oversized entourage swiftly escorted him to the safety of his private quarters. The imperial builders had tucked the Emerald Pavilion in the southeast corner of the palace, strategically placing it far from the complex's main arteries. Aludrien's network of spies would alert him of anyone approaching long before they reached the front gate.

To his surprise, the security of the small palace had increased tenfold since he left earlier that morning. He counted nearly a hundred guards stationed along the walls and throughout the gardens. Giant crossbows perched atop each tower. A ghostly ward covered the entire complex.

His retinue of elite guards remained in their formation as he entered the pavilion. Fewer servants lined the halls, and he recognized each as his longest-serving and most loyal attendants. He marched to his private apartments, a series of lavish rooms spilling out onto a wide veranda. Nim had converted his foyer into a private study, and a large oak desk sat in front of a myriad of screens. Each depicted a different location within his pavilion; these devices were prototypes that used Animancy to project images from afar. A single individual stood beside his desk, dressed in tidy livery, inspecting the grounds through the screens.

"Busy day?" Aludrien asked, flashing a dangerous glance at his guard, who obediently remained in the hall, closing the door behind him.

"Correct, Your Grace," Nim said. "On top of tripling your security, I have received dozens of marriage proposals from lords and ladies from every backwater corner of the Empire."

"Reject them all. Such trivial matters are an inconsequential nuisance."

"A royal marriage may be in your best interest, Your Grace. It may strengthen your claim if you select the right spouse. I could create a short list, if you would like."

"No," Aludrien said sharply. "Focus your energy on more important matters. How are your investigations progressing?"

"I discovered two more murder plots this morning, which brings the total to nine." Aludrien's chamberlain bowed deeply as the heir sat behind his desk. Nim was a fastidious servant, if not borderline neurotic. They had served as Aludrien's head of household since he reached adulthood. He had almost dismissed them within the first week of service, annoyed by their overbearing nature, but eventually learned to appreciate such thoroughness. Nim's skills would prove indispensable in the days to come.

"I see. Have you discovered their origins?" Aludrien asked.

"I have identified the culprits of six assassination attempts, Your Grace. Three traced to distant cousins and minor nobles. I assume these perpetrators have targeted any individual close to the throne to cull the line of succession. Reports suggest thirteen low-ranking royals have fallen, none important enough for you to know by name. The other three attempts, however, are why I heightened security. I traced the poisoned bottle of wine to the household of your older brother, Basil."

"Half-brother," Aludrien corrected. "Such a play from the bastard comes as no surprise."

"Adopted *elder* brother, Your Grace," Nim countered. "Whose husband, Jareth, is a former general and the Vice Minister of War, and whose mother, Lady Ysuelt Seraphine, is the current Minister of Education, an influential conniver of the court, and loathes every member of your house. Although your father appointed you as his heir, many consider Basil as the better option with strong ties to the government and the military."

"Because the sniveling twat is soft and easy to manipulate," Aludrien spat. First Hestraea, now Nim. Aludrien was tired of being reminded of Basil's growing support. "Half the court favors a pliant emperor."

"You are correct, Your Grace, and a considerable number of minor royals and courtiers have already placed themselves firmly in his camp for that precise reason. And his legitimacy and his station as firstborn establish him as your greatest rival. You underestimate him at your peril."

"So you have expressed, every day since my father passed. We both knew Basil was a major player, so surely he wasn't the cause of this overzealous security."

"You assume correctly, Your Grace," Nim said gravely. "We traced the explosives detected underneath your bed to the Minister of Finance. I suspect the Chancellor herself to be responsible."

"Vispin the viper. That low-born has escaped reproach since my father appointed her as the leader of his government. I wonder if the rumors of her fucking her way into his good graces are true. I'm only surprised that you were able to implicate her."

"Only loosely," Nim said. "But the nobles in the bureaucracy have grown restless under the emperor's boot. And without your father, Vispin maintains total control of your government until your ascension. You should consider responding to her summons; she has sent an invitation for an audience every day since your father's death."

"To see if I will have the same vulnerability to her manipulations as my father," Aludrien said. "All she desires is to retain her seat as Chancellor once I ascend. Responding too hastily would be a show of weakness."

"You may want to evaluate that offer seriously, Your Grace," Nim said. "Vispin will pose a great threat to your reign, especially if she decides that Basil is more pliant."

"Valid, but having her as an ally may prove more deadly than as an opponent. She nearly ruined my father's credibility with her appointment and incessant scheming," Aludrien sighed.

He grew weary of politics and needed rest. "Go ahead and tell me the third, I just know you've reserved the juiciest morsel for last."

"The bath attendant who attempted to slit your throat," Nim said.

"Ah, the one with the big cock," Aludrien said wistfully. "Pity we had to dispose of such a specimen. I rather enjoyed him."

"He used to serve General Barrett," Nim said, gravely. "Multiple sources witnessed them meeting regularly before the attack."

"Who?" Aludrien asked. "Oh, Nim, you disappoint me. I was expecting some drama. I've never heard of a house Barrett, how could he pose a greater threat than Basil or Vispin?"

"But you do know him, Your Grace," Nim replied. "He has been a close friend to Grand Marshal Hestraea for years."

"Barry?" Aludrien chuckled. "My aunt's boy toy? He's been hopelessly pursuing her for years. I believe it's been eleven rejected proposals so far. Not that I'm counting."

"Nine, Your Grace. General Barrett is her lover, paramour, and most trusted confidant. I wouldn't take his influence over her lightly."

"Ridiculous. You think my aunt would want me dead? She has no desire for the throne."

"No," Nim admitted. "I doubt Hestraea knew of the scheme. But her intent is not what makes her dangerous, Your Grace. She is the late emperor's only sibling, the most decorated Grand Marshal in living memory, and beloved by the court. Many believe, and rightfully so, that she is the source of Claude's success."

"She was," Aludrien said. "And she will continue to serve

in the exact capacity under my reign; she may wield more power than she possessed with my father."

"The court does not know your intentions, and they fear what they cannot control. They fear you, Your Grace. They fear Hestraea as well, but she also has their respect and trust. Virtues you currently have not cultivated. General Barrett is a loyal, stalwart traditionalist and influential with the military faction. If he has already conspired against you, then we can infer he is not acting alone. You must consider her your rival, however reluctant she may be. But if she discovers how much support she truly has—"

"She will not move against me," Aludrien spat. Nim was beginning to overstep. They had a bad habit of forgetting their place. They were lucky they proved to be so useful.

"The allure of the throne is powerful, indeed. You have read the histories, Your Grace. How many emperors or empresses have murdered a loved one to ascend?"

"Officially dozens," Aludrien admitted. The gravity of his chamberlain's discovery dawned on him. "Unofficially, more than half. And I don't blame a single one. I only need to survive until my ascension."

"Survival is not your only worry, Your Grace. You know the laws," Nim said. "Any lord or lady with a majority support of the court is allowed to challenge the heir to mortal combat on the day of the ascension. It is one of the few democratic processes your ancestors haven't removed. You would be wise to remember that before you enrage the entire palace."

Aludrien grimaced. Cultivating friendships and allies was a tedious endeavor. Better to eliminate his opponents and avoid a fight to the death.

"You were wise to increase security. Double the interior

guard and divert the servants' attention to screen any object, edible or otherwise, that enters the Emerald Pavilion. Understood?"

"Yes, Your Grace." Nim bowed low.

"And what of the church?" Aludrien asked. "Are you unable to link the attempts on my life to them?"

"The Pontifex has more pressing matters than your ascension, Your Grace. Those who aided the Meridian in your father's murder are likely high-ranking cardinals or the Pontifex himself."

"The old bag of bones was never one for subtlety," Aludrien mused. "Though I can't imagine why he would want my father dead. He's too close to the grave to be ambitious."

"It would take more than a few powerful Animancers to create a pair of Tal'Rach without any detection. I would be wary of those connected to your father's murder, for their motivations remain unclear. And much like the court, I do not like what I do not know."

"So, almost every soul in this palace wishes me dead. Those who murdered my father, most of the royal family, plus a few whose identities remain a mystery. My two greatest threats are my beloved aunt and my sniveling bastard half-brother, both of whom possess substantial support and strong claims to the throne. And operatives in the church, military, and government conspire against me." Despite the adversity he faced, Aludrien smiled fiendishly. "And I almost thought these one hundred days were about to be dull. This will be most exciting."

"As you say, Your Grace," Nim said, though their face betrayed more trepidation. "Though it may be wiser to return to your residence in the Winter Palace. You would be substantially safer with a distance between you and the capital. Not to mention, it is near the ruins of Arachovia."

"And allow my rivals to scheme and gain power in my absence? I think not."

He should have been more fearful, but such a challenge ignited his blood. Life in the imperial palace had been dreadfully monotonous, and now, a nearly impossible task lay before him. His support dwindled, and, due to his brash nature, his popularity at court was middling at best. His chances for survival were slim.

A strange, audacious, nearly blasphemous idea formed in his mind. He grinned.

"Nim, before I retire for the evening, write to Grand Marshal Hestraea. There is an unclaimed piece on the board. And I must acquire it."

4

Proposition

Fenris inhaled deeply, filling his nostrils with the fresh aroma of the pampas grass as the warm breeze kissed his skin. The sky above was as violet as the flowers crushed beneath him. A herd of goats grazed along the hillside, their horns reflecting the sun's last rays. Nothing was more serene than dusk on the Belantine Plains.

A gentle plume of cooking smoke wafted into the sky from the village far below. Lights had already sprung to life between thatched roofs. His mother had nearly finished dinner, and Fenris hoped she had baked his favorite: huckleberry pie. The mere thought of the rich, fruity dessert made his mouth water with anticipation. She baked the treat only on special occasions, such as birthdays, the harvest festival, or Belantine week. Yet today was nothing special, for—

What day was it?

He shook the thought away and climbed to his feet. Yawning, he stretched lazily and retrieved his staff, descending toward his herd. The faint sounds of laughter echoed across the hillside, and he longed to join in.

A child darted from the tall grass, nearly knocking Fenris over.

Steadying himself, Fenris scanned the hillside. He called out for the child, but they were nowhere to be seen. The hillside was empty, save for the waving grass and milling goats.

Sharp laughter broke the silence.

Three women lingered on the hill's crest, their hair braided into long plaits that spilled down the backs of their gowns. Ladies such as these were out of place in a remote land like Belantine. Fenris cared little how they had come to be there, for they were entirely transparent.

They dissolved into mist.

Moments later, a mountainous warrior charged toward him, sword drawn. Fenris braced for an impact that never came. The ghostly apparition phased through his body, rampaging across the hillside before disappearing in a bright flash. His heart sank. He finally understood. He would never reach the village or taste his mother's huckleberry pie.

He was dreaming.

Since the night he ascended, the horde of spirits that he absorbed constantly plagued his every thought. During the day, he experienced a myriad of thoughts and emotions that were not his. Every so often, he would hear their voices loud and clear. At night, countless specters swarmed his dreams. He never witnessed the same figure twice, and they didn't linger long enough for Fenris to distinguish their faces. But he understood that each of them represented a rach, a spirit of the dead, residing within him. The concept made him sick.

But this dream was different from the rest.

The grass prickled his bare feet, the cool night breeze

rustled through his hair, and the bleating of goats drifted up the hill along with the savory aroma of the cooking fires in the village far below. It was unlike any dream he had ever experienced. He stood on the hillside, every detail impossibly real. But the specters' presence told him otherwise. He wasn't in the Belantine Plains. He was—

The world around him wavered, the ground and sky rippling as if a stone had dropped onto a pond's surface. The disturbance was fleeting, but long enough to allow something else to enter the dream.

Pain. Unimaginable pain.

The blood inside his veins boiled. He howled and doubled over. The soft images of his homeland faded.

Suspended in darkness, pain overwhelmed him. Captured and tortured. Deep within the Imperial Palace.

Specters materialized, flying frantically about and glowing brightly. They smoothed the wrinkles of the sky and earth, illuminating the surfaces as they flew. The pain subsided, the darkness faded.

Whatever this place was, it shielded him from reality. His memories swiftly returned. Killing the emperor, Durian's death, fending off a mysterious assassin, fighting the heir, lengthy interrogations, the destruction of the Meridian, and defying Grand Marshal Hestraea. And pain. Always pain.

So he sat along the tranquil hillside, admiring the infinite expanse of grass around him until he forgot once more.

Ages passed, and the majestic vista remained. The perpetual sunset painted its brilliant colors across the horizon. The laughter from the village returned, and he smiled. His father's bellowing chuckle echoed across the hillside, harmonizing with his mother's robust laughter.

Countless apparitions appeared and disappeared around him, but he paid them no heed and directed his attention to the scene below. Most spirits were silent, though a few would speak unintelligible words.

The voices grew louder.

Fenris scanned his surroundings, but the plains were empty. He was alone.

"…no use…" The words echoed through the valley like thunder.

The world rippled around him.

"…speak, or you will be…"

"…stop, Grand Marshal, there is…"

The veil around him faded, and the sheet of sky tore. Fenris peered through the tear.

Pain and darkness no longer lingered outside his spectral shield. Glaring lights illuminated his cell, and the receptors on his body lay dormant. A group had gathered below, but the door behind them was ajar as a steady trail of courtiers exited.

"It seems you overplayed your hand, Grand Marshal Hestraea. A catatonic prisoner makes for a poor informant. Practicing restraint will benefit you in the future," Chancellor Vispin said as she departed.

The Belantine Plains faded, and the hole in the sky grew. Fenris slowly returned to consciousness, fully inhabiting his body as his childhood home disappeared. His head lolled to the side, and his muzzle touched his fur-covered shoulder. He felt relieved to discover that his corporeal body remained in its bestial state.

The crowd below had dwindled to a handful of soldiers guarding a pair of figures. A man and a woman spoke in hushed tones. They fell still when Fenris stirred.

He crossed his eyes and kept his tongue hanging to the side. While his mind resided in the Belantine Plains, his body remained a useless husk. So he would play the part until his execution. Then he could die an honorable death and join his comrades. Soon, he would be with Durian.

Straining his ears, he eavesdropped on the pair below. Luckily, the tilt of his head was in the perfect position to survey the cell, despite his crossed eyes.

"How disappointing," the man drawled, his voice filled with contempt.

"I apologize for the anticlimactic interrogation, but I appreciate your presence," the woman said. Fenris recognized the stern voice as that of Grand Marshal Hestraea. She turned to the guards. "Dismissed."

The soldiers lowered their crossbows, saluted, and exited swiftly. The Grand Marshal followed. The man remained.

"Are you coming, Aludrien?" Hestraea asked, hesitated at the door. "The Pontifex will begin the prisoner's final rites shortly."

"In a moment, dear aunt," the man replied. His eyes bored into Fenris. "I would like a word with the man who murdered my father."

Hestraea sighed understandingly.

"I'll summon the guard."

"That will not be necessary. I bested the beast at his full strength. I can manage a drooling vegetable."

Hestraea opened her mouth to respond, but closed it in restraint. She departed, and the door closed behind her.

Aludrien smiled fiendishly.

"Your timing could not be more impeccable," he chuckled.

Fenris's hair stood on end. The heir was addressing him directly. He remained still, feigning his previous stupor. A battle of wills commenced, and Fenris refused to lose.

"Ah," the heir said, clicking his tongue. His footsteps echoed as he paced the cell floor, walking out of Fenris's field of vision. "I assumed you would have learned from our first encounter that challenging me is futile."

The footsteps stopped, followed by a mechanical click.

Fenris fell.

In a single heartbeat, the magical barrier evaporated, releasing its prisoner. He plunged downward. Before he collided with the floor, Fenris twisted his body, catching himself on all fours. His weak limbs screamed upon impact, his muscles nearly atrophied after a week of disuse. Lifting his head, his eyes locked with Aludrien's impudent stare. The heir stood behind the control panel.

With an enraged snarl, Fenris launched himself into the air, claws outstretched, summoning unearthly fire.

Click.

The barrier rematerialized before Fenris could travel three paces, quelling his flames and freezing him in place. Aludrien smiled wickedly.

"There you are. With all this deception behind us, we can finally hold a civilized conversation."

A lightning bolt violently struck the barrier. The heir ignored it.

"I am curious, though. Tell me, what is the mind palace like? You must have been inside it for the better part of three days. An impressive feat, I dare say. Though your predicament left you with no other choice."

Fenris furrowed his brow in confusion.

"Ah, I forgot. You may be a Tal'Rach, but you weren't properly trained and ascended in the shadows, unlawfully so. An abomination," Aludrien droned, his voice dripping with arrogance. "I'd wager you are not aware of the key differences between an Animancer and a Tal'Rach."

"Fuck you," Fenris snarled.

"An Animancer relies on the spirits around them," Aludrien lectured, ignoring Fenris. "They can guide spirits and harness them, but are limited by the amount of rach gathered in their immediate surroundings. A Tal'Rach, however, possesses the luxury of harnessing the rach that dwell inside to almost limitless potential. And what do you think a mind palace is?"

"I have no idea."

"Allow me to educate you," Aludrien said. "The mind palace is one of countless feats a Tal'Rach, blessed with the power of a legion of rach, can accomplish. It is an astral plane you create and control. With practice, you can host your consciousness within your realm, along with any other you choose. It's rather fascinating. The secrets of the Tal'Rach are passed orally from emperor to heir. Not even the Pontifex would know my aunt's brutal tactics would have little impact on you."

Aludrien's tone was casual, albeit condescending; an odd way to speak to the man who had murdered his father. The denizens of the palace were a vindictive, conniving lot. Fenris only wished he could have burned the palace to cinders when he had the chance.

"If you came for answers, you'll be disappointed," Fenris said defiantly.

"Oh, I'm not here to question you. I care little for why you killed my father or who helped you. In fact, I should thank you for it. Many emperors outlive their heirs, only to select a younger successor to carry on their legacy. If you hadn't done the deed, death could have taken me before my ascension."

"Rejoicing in your own father's murder?" Fenris seethed. "I've had enough of you, beast."

"Beast?" Aludrien exclaimed. "How dare you call the heir to the throne such a name, looking like that, all fangs and fur?"

"I'll tear your throat out."

"Well, you already had the chance. And you failed," Aludrien smirked. "But I am not here to gloat either. I have much more important matters to discuss."

"Spit it out," Fenris growled, exhausted by the theatrics.

"Not one for foreplay, I see," Aludrien chuckled chillingly. "I would like you to work for me."

"You're delusional."

"I would call myself pragmatic," Aludrien quipped. "My father's untimely demise has its benefits, namely my early ascension, but it presents several drawbacks. Many of my father's close blood relations remain, some with as strong a claim to the throne as I. Over a dozen have already fallen. I require a skilled assassin in my employ, and you have more than demonstrated your talents."

"You want me to murder your family?"

"No, I wish to assist you in eradicating those who wronged your people."

"You want me to murder your family."

"As I said, I'm a pragmatist."

Fenris chuckled grimly. The request was audacious. "Why would you think I would help a man like you ascend the throne? One so willing to kill his closest kin."

"You want to discover who betrayed your recently departed

friends," Aludrien said. "Whoever aided in your plot is most likely the same individual who provided my aunt with a list of every member of your organization. I'm unsure if you know the traitor, and frankly, I couldn't care less. But I'm certain you would like the chance to avenge your comrades. I can grant you that opportunity."

"You think petty vengeance will persuade me? You're more foolish than I thought."

"An idealist calling me a fool, that's rich," Aludrien said. "I already know the reason you murdered my father. You poor wretch, losing your family and homeland to the boot of the Imperium, raised in the slums, forced to become a weapon of death. You thought killing my father would rectify all of it; that you would save the world by killing one man, when the people in this palace are directly responsible for your miserable life. If the promise of vengeance doesn't sway you, then how about your ideals? Carry on the legacy of the Meridian. Purge the palace of rot."

"And allow you to ascend the throne?" Fenris spat, enraged at the heir's audacity. "If I wanted to rid the world of more monsters, I would start with you."

"You confuse my pragmatism with wickedness. And you have rejected my offer without hearing the payment."

"No amount of money would convince me to work for you. Leave. Let me have my final moments in peace."

"If you assist me until my ascension, foil the plots to take my life and cull my rivals in the process, I will allow you another chance to kill me," Aludrien said. Gone was the knowing smirk and the nonchalant attitude. The man was deathly serious. "If we are both alive on the eve of my ascension, I will allow you one final chance to kill me. A reprise of our previous fight, with both of us at full strength. You can either die today, and the Meridian dies with you, or live for a chance to continue your mission."

"What will stop me from killing you before the ascension?" Fenris asked.

"Nothing," Aludrien admitted. "Except you will lose the chance to remove greater threats to the realm. The high lords and ladies who swill wine and fornicate with abandon while children starve in the streets outside their high walls. I am not the only threat to the Imperium, and in my estimation, I've done far less harm by comparison."

"How can I trust that you will keep your promise and not kill me in my sleep once I do your dirty work?" Fenris remained in shock at the outlandish proposal.

"Oh, you can trust that I will kill you," Aludrien replied, coldly. "But you and I both know I do not need to rely on underhanded means to do so. You and I will reprise our battle, and I will have justice for my father's death."

"But my execution; I doubt even you could stop that."

"Correct, the guard will escort you from this place shortly, and then you will be incinerated before the entire court, as my father's body was yesterday. Feel honored, you will be the first peasant to die in this fashion. However, you are the first to kill a god."

"If you can't stop the execution, you are wasting your breath."

"I cannot prevent your execution. But I certainly can prevent your death." Aludrien's eyes glinted dangerously. "If you accept my offer, shield yourself during the blast."

"Do you think a flimsy Animancy ward could defend against an inferno?"

"For a few seconds, at least," the heir replied. "And that is all I require."

Before Fenris could respond, the cell door slid open. He stuck his tongue out and rolled his eyes back, resuming his stupefied facade. He wanted to avoid any further interrogation by additional parties. He merely wanted to die.

"Ah, Your Grace," an elderly male voice said. Fenris recognized it as Pontifex Ignatius. "My apologies, I assumed the interrogation had concluded."

"You are correct, Ignatius," Aludrien said. "The poor wretch remains unresponsive; the guards must carry him to his execution."

"Oh dear," Ignatius replied. "The sacred rites should not take too long."

"I will leave you to your duties, Pontifex, and take my place in the audience. I want a good seat for the execution. One second is all it takes."

After the final statement, obviously meant for Fenris, the heir apparent departed, leaving the prisoner alone with the Pontifex for the final rites.

5

Execution

The elderly man's shuffling footsteps grew louder as he crossed the cell toward the control panel. Fenris maintained his ruse, though it constrained his vision.

Click.

Fenris floated gently to the floor. He didn't need to open his eyes to know the Pontifex had disarmed the force field. Still, he remained supine, resting his aching limbs on the cold metal surface.

The sound of beleaguered breath grew louder until Ignatius loomed over him. Both men remained silent, neither moving a muscle. Fenris wished the Pontifex would perform the holy rites and leave. All he wanted was the end to come. But Ignatius waited. Fenris grew tired of the charade.

He opened his eyes and lunged.

Straight into a glowing ward.

"Ah, so you are awake, my dear boy," Ignatius crooned. The newly conjured shield pressed downward, grinding Fenris into the floor. "You and I must have a chat."

"I'll tell you what I told the others," Fenris sighed, tired of the court's constant scheming.

The ward pressed in, slowly crushing him. He resisted, but the Pontifex was too powerful. Ignatius was living up to his reputation as one of the empire's most skilled Animancers.

"Please do not lie to me, Fenris," Ignatius said. "A rabble of provincials could not possibly perform what only an elite group of cardinals is capable of."

"I assumed you orchestrated it all," Fenris said, truthfully. Durian hadn't disclosed his source within the palace. And the night they ascended, in a random warehouse beyond the slums, the cabal of priests who met them had hidden their faces behind oversized hoods. Fenris had nothing to tell. His interrogation and torture had been in vain.

Ignatius's eyes narrowed. His hands shook. He was nervous. Desperate. Ligaments popped as the ethereal shield compressed; Fenris called upon the spirits from within, but to no avail. After days of incarceration, he was weak and lethargic.

"And how did you come to that conclusion?" Ignatius asked. "One does not suspect the Pontifex of treason on a whim. Tell me exactly what Durian told you."

"Nothing," Fenris said. "But now I know for sure."

The ward faltered briefly; the Pontifex balked. His behavior was tantamount to an admission of guilt. Ignatius had not inquired about which cardinals had betrayed him, for he already knew who was involved with the ascension. He only cared about what Durian had divulged to the other members of the Meridian. Fenris was merely another loose end to tie up.

Fenris howled, bucking against his constraints. The man above him was responsible for his friends' deaths. He craved to sink his fangs into the traitor's neck. Fenris wanted to kill, yearned for it, with a ferocity he hadn't experienced before. Something in him had broken.

"It should have been you who died that day, you filthy scum," Ignatius seethed. The air around him shimmered.

The cell doors slid open. Ignatius jumped in surprise; his ward remained, but faded from the naked eye. Frenzied shouts and the hum of charging crossbows filled the air. The imperial soldiers were startled to discover the Pontifex of Xandria unguarded and undefended, with the beast who had murdered the emperor. Fenris kept his eyes open, staring at the far wall, feigning his stupor. Dozens of metal boots passed by as the soldiers surrounded him.

"Please calm yourselves, my children," Ignatius said, ignoring the guards' heated protests. "I was merely performing his last rites. The poor wretch's body remains, but his mind has gone; he is no longer a threat to anyone in this state."

The soldiers disengaged their weapons at their captain's behest, though a few studied Fenris warily. Releasing a prisoner without a guard was highly unusual, even for the most skilled Animancer in the empire.

"You must be here to fetch the prisoner. I performed his rites according to the divine customs, and he is ready to face judgment before the court. I presume the other preparations are complete?" Ignatius asked.

"Yes, Your Holiness," the captain replied.

"Excellent. I must depart. I entrust the prisoner to you, captain."

With a flourish of his robe and a click of the door, the Pontifex departed, leaving Fenris alone with the soldiers.

The ward disappeared. The guards were defenseless.

"Fetch a stretcher," the captain barked, and the door clicked once more as soldiers shuffled diligently out to obey their superior.

Tense silence hung over the cell. Not a single soldier spoke.

Fenris's claw twitched, ever so slightly, his body yearning to be free. But he doubted he could escape without killing or maiming the guards. Despite the atrocities they may have committed, they did so at the empire's behest; they were victims as much as Fenris.

Furthermore, Ignatius had intentionally released him. He wanted Fenris to kill the guards. To eliminate anyone who might have witnessed him speaking to the prisoner. If he couldn't kill Fenris himself, he would allow the guards to do it for him.

So Fenris stayed his hands.

Finally, the door opened once more. Footsteps shuffled closer. Inconsiderate hands roughly lifted Fenris and strapped him onto a narrow stretcher. He remained limp; any wrong move would betray his ruse and force him to murder everyone present. His stomach turned at the thought.

The soldiers formed around him, lifted the stretcher with labored grunts, and carried him out of the cell and through the palace. Emerging from the dungeons and into the barracks, Fenris watched the morbid procession through partially glazed eyes. Across manicured gardens, regal courtyards, and down ornate promenades, every step was one closer to his end.

He contemplated running, fleeing the capital, and living the rest of his life in the hinterlands, far from court politics. But a life without purpose, without those he cared for, was worse than death. So he remained motionless, resigned to his fate.

The palace grounds were nearly empty, for the execution was open to servants and soldiers, as well as every courtier. Few would dare miss such a historic event. The palace structures above him gave way to a bright blue sky. A wave of horrified gasps rippled through an unseen crowd. They had arrived.

Down the center aisle, his guard carried him past the murmurs of courtiers, servants, and soldiers alike. They climbed to a circular stage at the plaza's center. Fenris had only visited this place once, the night he murdered Claude. But the entire realm knew of its existence. The great dais on which every emperor and empress was laid to rest.

And Fenris would soon join them.

His escort tossed his limp body off the stretcher and lashed him to a vertical post erected in the center of the dais. Only then did he see the full extent of the crowd assembled to witness his death. Thousands, dressed in mourning black, glared at him; several screamed profanities, many wept. For most of them, they had never before beheld the monster who murdered their divine ruler.

One figure stood between him and the masses, clad head to toe in gleaming insignis armor, her back facing the pole. Grand Marshal Hestraea Aleksandran, commander of the Xandrian legions, sister to the late emperor, aunt to the heir, and Fenris's executioner.

"Fenris Vale of the Belantine plains," her deep voice echoed across the plaza, instantly silencing the crowd. "By the power divinely granted to me from the blood of Empress Aleksandra I, the mother of the glorious Xandrian Empire, flowing through my veins, with the court as my witness, I charge you with the crime of regicide. For the vicious murder of our beloved Emperor Claude Aleksandran XLV, I condemn you to death."

The crowd cheered, and the Grand Marshal paused dramatically. She wasn't speaking to Fenris at all, but to the legions of onlookers below. If the royal family possessed an innate talent, it was grandstanding.

"As this unprecedented and heinous murder is the first act of regicide committed in our empire's history, the Chancellor, the Pontifex, and I have unanimously agreed that death by incineration is a suitable punishment for your crime."

Fenris doubted anything poetic inspired the method of his execution; the incinerator was the only tested method capable of disposing of a Tal'Rach. He wondered if they had burned Durian's body similarly. Hestraea continued, drawing out the speech to create a spectacle. She needed to make Fenris an example before the entire court. He ignored the Grand Marshal and instead focused his attention on those in the front row.

Half a dozen royals, whose names he barely remembered, each sneered with smug satisfaction. Fenris doubted any of the monsters truly mourned the death of their emperor; in fact, they probably relished the chance to ascend to the throne. Any one of them would be as harmful to the Imperium as Claude, if not worse.

Ignatius sat on the end, face downcast, unable to view the spectacle. His hands shook, and his eyes nervously glanced around, stunned that Fenris had not taken the bait to eliminate the guards. Fenris seethed at the mere sight of him. Next to the Pontifex was Chancellor Vispin, her calculating eyes shifting over the royals around her, undoubtedly determining whose claim she would support. One individual, however, garnered his full attention.

High Lord Aludrien's jaw clenched, watching expectantly. His offer remained on the table. How the heir would save Fenris from his fate remained unclear. The man was vicious, cold, and power hungry. A civil war was on the verge of erupting in the palace, every High Lord and Lady of royal blood vying for the throne, and Aludrien was their primary target. The bastard wouldn't last a month.

Fenris had felt hollow since killing Claude, something he had desired for most of his life. Instead of feeling victorious or satisfied, he only endured more pain. More loss. In accomplishing his goal, he had lost everything. His friends, their mission, and most importantly, Durian. He had cut the head from the snake, and a thousand more vipers sprang forth. In the end, all his sacrifices were for naught.

But Aludrien's words sparked something within him. He could die an abject failure or live to further the Meridian's cause and remove more threats to the realm. And seek vengeance upon Ignatius.

Aludrien's callous actions, however, were hard to ignore. He was willing to murder his entire family to maintain his right to the throne. But the heir allowed Fenris access to the other monsters of the court and promised a chance to kill him once he completed his duty—a tempting offer.

"Witness the end of this abomination. Hail Xandria!"

The crowd echoed the chant as Hestraea stepped from the dais to safety. The time had come for Fenris's life to end.

The edges of the dais whirred to life, glowing with the power of Animancy, inching toward the center as the metal heated. The temperature rose with impossible speed, burning the flesh of his soles. Biting his tongue to avoid crying out in pain, Fenris looked out onto the crowd once more before the inferno consumed him.

All he saw was Aludrien's face.

His nostrils filled with the smell of burnt hair and flesh, his mind filled with uncertainty and doubt. The lights of the funeral pyre blinded him as the inferno erupted. The world vanished, replaced by blinding, blistering fire. A normal human would have disintegrated within a heartbeat, but Fenris was a Tal'Rach. Instead, his flesh burned, the spirits within screamed, desperate to heal, but the inferno was too great; it would consume him momentarily. The pole holding him melted away, but he was too far from the edges to escape.

But Aludrien's offer reminded him of his purpose: to carry out his mission for the sake of his fallen comrades. The last of the Meridian, he alone would honor their legacy and cull the empire of evil.

The voices in his head begged him to survive. To press on.

With Aludrien's petulant expression burned into his mind, his audacious request and instructions ringing in his ears, Fenris summoned the spirits within.

He formed a shield.

Immediate relief washed over him, his thin ward desperately holding the inferno at bay, wavering violently. His protection would only last a few heartbeats, then the fires would consume him once more.

Something below him clicked.

The floor fell away.

His body plummeted like a stone into darkness, flames licking from above until the trap door slid shut behind him. Losing concentration, he relinquished his protective shield and collided with the floor below, his legs breaking upon impact.

Lying in darkness, his skin and hair burning, bones broken, he breathed heavily. He was still alive.

"Apologies for the rough landing," a figure said, leering from the shadows. "I could not transport the proper padding on such short notice without drawing attention. I assume your capabilities as a Tal'Rach will mend any damage caused by the fall."

Fenris's eyes adjusted to the chamber's dim light, barely wider than the narrow hole he had fallen through. A servant stood above him, dressed in the neat gold and maroon livery of House Aleksandran. Raven hair tied in a neat androgynous top knot, revealing a stern face with alabaster skin. They were alone and unarmed—a foolish decision. The tingling sensation of reconstructing flesh and bone coursed through his body. He would be at fighting strength in moments.

"I suggest you refrain from violence," the servant said, steely eyes unfazed by the beast below them. "You could kill or subdue me with relative ease, true, but escaping the labyrinth situated around this chamber would not be an easy feat."

"Anyone can be a willing guide with a bit of pain," Fenris replied. He typically reserved violence for those who truly deserved it. Perhaps the palace was changing him.

The servant pulled a compact silver device from their pocket, and their thumb caressed the surface. The metal nodes in Fenris's body whirred to life, threatening to activate once more.

"Funny you should mention pain. I have certain contingencies in place to ensure my safety. However, I don't understand why you would resort to torturing an already willing guide," the servant said, lifting their thumb from the trigger. The receptors became dormant. "It seems as though you have healed faster than expected. I suggest you revert to your human form; the monster Fenris was incinerated above us moments ago, unless you would like the palace guard to capture and execute you again."

They tossed a large bundle on the ground next to Fenris. A rough set of nondescript clothing.

Killing or maiming this servant was less appealing than attacking the soldiers above. They were clearly present to aid Fenris's escape. Sighing, he reverted to his original form. Soft hands replaced claws, ruddy skin replaced fur, and unremarkable humanoid features replaced ferocious ones. Days had passed since he had inhabited his original body, and he exhaled deeply, delighting in the familiar sensations. The servant turned graciously, allowing Fenris privacy in his nakedness, calmly waiting for him to don the shabby outfit.

"Excellent. You possess at least a modicum of sense. Your presence here indicates you have accepted my master's offer to enter his employ. I am called Nim, chamberlain to his royal highness Aludrien Aleksandran. You will report directly to me as long as you remain in Aludrien's service, am I understood?"

Fenris grunted affirmatively, fastening the last buckle clumsily around his waist. Cloth felt foreign on his skin.

"We must depart; our lord will be eager to hear the wonderful news. Shall we?"

Nim hoisted a lantern, opened the rotting door at the end of the chamber, and led Fenris into the tunnel beyond. They hadn't been lying about the surrounding labyrinth. The chamberlain briskly navigated the chaotic tangle of tight tunnels deep below the palace. Fenris marveled at the complex; his infiltration would have been significantly easier had he known of their existence.

"These tunnels are old," he observed.

"Oh yes, their construction dates back to Empress Eugenia XXV. She constructed this complex to conceal the chamber from which we recently emerged. She had fallen in love with a serving girl, who was tragically of provincial birth. Despite her duty to the empire, Eugenia created these tunnels, complete with the trap door, and feigned her own death. I have never understood the sentimentality of others, but Aludrien assures me Eugenia's actions are considered romantic. Personally, I see nothing lovely about shirking one's duties and trading the throne for living in squalor in the outer Provinces. But as a lowly chamberlain, I am not one to judge."

"Clever," Fenris whispered, admiring the ingenuity of his escape. "Most would consider such a tale a legend. I doubt anyone else in the empire knows the truth besides the heir. Not even the Grand Marshal herself."

"Correct. Besides Aludrien and me, the entire empire believes you to be dead. We must make haste; we have much to accomplish."

6

The Emerald Pavilion

Despite the dramatic circumstances of his staged execution, joining Aludrien's service amounted to little more than Fenris trading one prison for another. His new accommodations, however, were a significant upgrade. Equipped with a bed, a wash bin, and regular food, his tenure under the heir's service began with a different form of incarceration, albeit a more comfortable one.

The indifferent chamberlain led Fenris out of the labyrinth and into a remote section of the capital, near the airship port but far from the palace. He could have disarmed Nim of the remote control and escaped into the hinterlands beyond the city's outskirts. But he did not evade execution only to live in exile for the rest of his days. His mission remained incomplete. Aludrien, Ignatius, and their ilk still drew breath.

Nim ushered him to a derelict boarding house filled with transients. This section of the city, nestled between the western gate and the airship port, housed thousands of souls who had traveled to the capital in search of a better life, most without a coin to their name. The filthy streets were a reminder of the slums where he had grown up. Without proper skills or trades to leverage a position in safer parts of the city, many resorted to petty crime or joined one of the multiple syndicates that called this place home.

The seedy neighborhood was the perfect place to hide the most notorious criminal in Xandria's history.

Nim escorted Fenris to an apartment in the flophouse's attic. To his surprise, crates lined the walls, filled with rations. The chamberlain promptly explained that Fenris must wait until preparations at the Emerald Pavilion, Aludrien's personal palace, were complete. Hiring a new servant the day of the execution would most certainly turn a few heads, and Nim had already reduced the heir's serving staff to a trusted few. They must practice patience in the coming days before introducing Fenris's new identity to the pavilion.

Nim removed the metal receptors embedded in Fenris's limbs with a wicked tool. The process was excruciating, as it involved extracting chunks of skin along with the devices, but the deep wounds rapidly healed. The chamberlain left a single node lodged in the base of Fenris's neck. They explained that the receptor would explode if it traveled too far from the palace or if he attempted to remove it. Even a Tal'Rach could not reattach a head. Emperor Claude was a prime example of that particular limitation.

When the chamberlain departed, the walls, ceiling, and floor shimmered with the familiar glow of an animancy shield. Fenris was trapped once more. The room was dim and cramped; a tiny window set high on the far wall was the only source of light or air. He found a crate filled with jugs of water and stale bread. Fenris promptly devoured a loaf. He hadn't eaten since before the assassination. The spirits within sustained him enough to go without food or water for lengthy periods, but they did little to curb the gnawing sensations of hunger and thirst. A separate washroom lay beyond the far door, complete with a sizable tub. The setup was rudimentary but an improvement compared to the grates at the bottom of his previous cell. It would be an uncomfortable stay, to say the least, but luxurious compared to the palace dungeons.

Nim did not return for fifteen days.

Fenris generally enjoyed solitude, but being idle was against his nature. And after days of total immobilization, he soon grew restless in his new, confined quarters. When he was inactive, all he could do was dwell on his fallen friends. Maris. Ryland. Durian. Their faces haunted his dreams, their loss weighing upon his soul. He had nothing left, save for an unquenchable hatred of Pontifex Ignatius.

He kept himself busy by rearranging the sparse furniture a dozen times, playing with a summoned ball of water, and spending hours grooming himself in the bath. When trivial activities lost their appeal, he resorted to more practical endeavors. Using leftover breadcrumbs, he created a diagram of the most important dignitaries and nobles in the palace, committing each to memory, especially those who posed a threat to Aludrien's ascension. He also practiced entering what the heir called the mind palace. The process proved awkward, as he had only achieved it previously under dire, painful circumstances. But Fenris was nothing if not persistent. Before the chamberlain returned, he could efficiently transport his consciousness to his artificial paradise at will.

"My apologies for the delay," the chamberlain said unapologetically. "We encountered a few…unforeseen obstacles."

"Fifteen days is long enough for your lord's enemies to close in on him," Fenris pointed out. "I am surprised that he's still alive."

"High Lord Aludrien is your master as well," Nim said. "I expect you to behave like a dutiful servant from now on. If anyone suspects you of being anything else, all of our lives will be forfeit."

"As you wish, my chamberlain."

Bowing deeply, Fenris shifted his posture expertly, his eyes downcast and his demeanor subservient, an easy act for someone of his quiet disposition to adopt. The obedient disguise, however, did not reach his voice, which retained a hint of defiance. Nim ignored his tone and nodded with curt approval.

"You will hereby be referred to as Pax of Garelina. You have been summoned to the palace by His Grace High Lord Aludrien to serve as his food taster. Your singular duty is to attend each of the heir's meals and sample his food and drink to detect any trace of poison before our High Lord consumes it. This position historically functions under the mistress of the kitchens, but as I have substantially reduced the staff, you will report directly to me."

"Sounds like a dangerous job," Fenris replied.

"The most hazardous in the pavilion. Even more so since the emperor's passing. As you may know, poison accounts for nine out of ten successful assassinations. The Emerald Pavilion has lost three food tasters since the royal funeral. Luckily, our fourth will be immune to such toxins, thanks to his supernatural abilities. Our enemies, unaware of your true nature, will mistake it for skill. And a long-lasting food taster deters future attempts."

"My new master is a savvy tactician," Fenris said. His

survival would confuse and intimidate Aludrien's enemies, while his daily duties would protect the heir from most assassination attempts.

"An understatement," Nim said. "Aludrien is a formidable opponent, as you discovered upon your first meeting. Every decision is made with the utmost foresight. Including harboring you here in the slums."

"I'm not the only servant here waiting to join the heir's service, am I? Will there be a significant turnover in the High Lord's staff today?" Fenris asked

Nim raised an eyebrow, their mouth twisting into an approving smile.

"There are twenty-two other servants lodged in this boarding house, all summoned to replace essential staff due to a security breach. The head valet attempted to slay the High Lord as he slept, allegedly at the behest of the Chancellor. He had served His Grace for the last decade. Given such a tragic turn of events, I took drastic measures to eliminate any remaining enemy agents from the Emerald Pavilion."

"A convenient story to disguise my arrival. And how did you discover the valet's connections?"

Nim avoided eye contact, confirming Fenris's suspicions. No conspiracy existed; the poor valet had become yet another victim in the escalating war of ascension. Aludrien was as ruthless as he was manipulative.

"You'll need servants from across the Imperium, without ties to the palace," Fenris conjectured, detecting an obvious flaw in the scheme. "But how will this new lot be more trustworthy than Aludrien's longest-serving vassals? What will prevent these new servants from betraying the heir?"

"Nothing," Nim admitted, jaw clenched. "I suspect most

would kill His Grace for a handful of coins. But the High Lord believes your presence outweighs the risk, and I do not question my master's immense intellect. We have lingered too long; the others may grow suspicious. We must depart."

The conversation concluded, and Nim left the apartment. At the chamberlain's request, Fenris waited before making his way to the boarding house's entrance. A fully armed battalion waited outside under the midday sun, casually flanking a nervous-looking group of misfits. Several carried worn rucksacks, but many possessed nothing but the clothes on their backs. The soldiers wore the lion insignia of the heir, but their loose formation and nonchalant demeanor made it apparent they were new to the High Lord's employ. Nim had refreshed the entire Emerald Pavilion, not only the servants.

Fenris joined the other transients; none paid him any attention. A few others joined soon after. Once they were twenty-three in number, Nim addressed the group briskly.

"From this point onward, you serve at the pleasure of His Grace High Lord Aludrien Aleksandran, heir to the throne and future emperor of the glorious Xandrian Empire. In eighty-four days, he will ascend to the throne, so I expect each of you to comport yourselves in a manner worthy of His Grace. You may address me as Nim or my chamberlain. Although I may be a lenient and understanding head of house, there will be no tolerance for disobedience, aggression, or most certainly, sloth. Step a toe out of line, and you will find yourselves back here, without another prospect for work. Am I understood?"

"Yes, my chamberlain," the crowd replied with gusto. Nim had skillfully instilled the precise amount of fear in their new subordinates.

"Excellent, your duties begin today, and we should not waste any more of our lord's precious time."

The journey from the boarding house to the palace was swift, efficient, and uneventful. Nim led the party from the twisted, derelict roads, through neatly manicured lanes, and into the massive gate looming over the city's western edge. The palace was its own miniature metropolis, separated from the sprawling capital by a deep moat and an enormous wall.

The Emerald Pavilion was a fortress unto itself, nestled in the southwest corner of the palace. Scores of soldiers lined the top of each wall, and the halls swarmed with armed guards positioned at each corner. The heir's defenses were ten times stronger than the emperor's had been the night Fenris slew him.

The chamberlain ushered the new arrivals to the servant baths at the rear of the sprawling complex. After cleaning the grime of the outer city from their bodies, each servant received a few sets of finely woven livery, complete with Aludrien's lion insignia.

It seemed Nim hadn't dismissed the entire staff. The veteran servants efficiently delegated the newcomers to their respective supervisors and assigned them to their living quarters.

A slight woman ushered Fenris to a modest room along with three others—two men and a woman. A pair of bunks clung to either side. The eldest, a woman with long raven hair and an indifferent expression, set her overstuffed bag on one of the lower bunks.

"Hopefully, none of you object," she drawled. "I'll be waking early with the rest of the kitchen staff and wouldn't want to disturb any of you."

"How considerate to think of us!" the younger of the two men exclaimed sincerely. Rail thin, he bounded into the room like an eager pup. "Can you believe the size of this place? We don't have buildings like this back in North Amberia. My ma told me stories, but I couldn't imagine anything like this. I'm Tipin by the way, it is so nice to—"

The third servant shoved Tipin aside aggressively with a brawny arm and threw his sack of belongings on the remaining lower bunk. He loomed above the others, his massive frame swallowing the room, assessing them like a predator. Fenris and the woman allowed him a wide berth, but Tipin bounded back to the man, unfazed.

"I don't mind the top bunk, mister. Actually, I prefer it. I always sleep better in smaller spaces. My pa would always find me napping in the hay loft on the farm. He would get so cross with me. What is your name?"

"Fuck off," the lumbering giant grunted.

"Fukov is an interesting name," Tipin said. He eyed the larger man's muscles, cheeks rosy. "What province does that come from? It sounds northern to me."

Fukov ignored the chipper young man and left the room with a grunt. Tipin, hopelessly oblivious, bounded out after him.

"That brute is going to eat poor Tipin alive, I fear. But we all learn the hard way," the woman chuckled as she watched the odd pair depart. Fenris cracked a smile. She reached out a hand. "You can call me Elzia. I'm one of the new cooks working under Belessia."

"Pleasure to meet you. I am Pax. The new food taster."
Elzia's smile fell.

"I see. We should report to the mistress of the kitchens,

though I don't suppose you have much to do before dinner."

The cook's demeanor became curt and detached. Fenris did not blame her. Elzia seemed a practical and savvy woman, one who wouldn't waste her time befriending someone whose days were limited. Under normal circumstances, Fenris wouldn't last a week. But he wasn't an ordinary food taster, and the cook would soon recognize that. Hopefully, she wasn't shrewd enough to become a complication in the future. Only time would tell.

They hardly spoke on their way to the kitchens, a series of sweltering rooms nestled in the center of the pavilion, directly behind the formal dining room. The mistress of the kitchens, Belessia, was a stern but kindly woman reaching her later years, with silver hair tucked into a neat bun. She appeared stressed, which was understandable since, including Elzia and herself, the entire kitchen staff totaled only six. Fenris estimated that a palace of this size would require at least three times that number to feed the heir and his servants.

The royal food taster reported directly to the chamberlain and performed a single official duty; these facts did not prevent Belessia from putting Fenris to work immediately, scrubbing the dirty dishes from lunch. He was grateful for the labor after remaining idle for so long. He was relieved to work with his hands once more. His position by the washbasin allowed him to monitor the kitchens before dinner, as they were the most likely place for treachery. Besides Belessia, the entire kitchen staff had turned over. If the heir's rivals wanted to place an operative in the Emerald Pavilion, the kitchens were the most strategic choice.

The cooks and scullery maids were a lively bunch, singing and laughing as they went about their chores, fueled by the nervous energy of a new work environment. Belessia did not seem to care as long as her staff completed the tasks. No one spoke to Fenris, which was perfectly fine with him, as he was preoccupied with cleaning and surveying his new surroundings. Luckily, he did not witness any suspicious behavior as the kitchen staff prepared the High Lord's meal.

Dinner, however, was more uneventful than expected. Aludrien dined alone, but his lack of dinner guests did not detract from the formality of the occasion. Four courses, each plated in the kitchens and served to the heir. The new staff, unfamiliar with the pavilion, blundered through the service the best they could, spurred on by tongue lashings from Belessia. Fortunately, no one made a significant mistake.

Fenris sat in a diminutive chamber between the kitchens and dining room, the chamberlain looming over him. As each course passed through, he would inspect the food closely and sample a tiny portion of each element directly from the plate. After ten minutes without experiencing adverse side effects, Fenris would send the course into the dining hall for the heir to enjoy. He repeated the process for the wine.

Food tasting was an archaic, yet practical process. Fenris did not envy Aludrien, who probably hadn't eaten a fully hot meal once in his life. No wonder the nobles seemed so miserable and petulant, for their suspicion and caution robbed them of life's culinary pleasures.

Soon, the fourth and final course, a honey-poached pear with clotted cream and walnut crumble, was sent into the dining chamber with a sliver removed. Fenris was grateful that none of the courses were tainted. Poison wouldn't kill a Tal'Rach like Fenris, but his divine nature did not shield him from experiencing pain.

The meal was exquisite, featuring the best food Fenris had ever tasted. However, the experience was difficult to appreciate, with the chamberlain breathing down his neck. Once his duties were complete, Nim dismissed him to eat his own late dinner alone in the servant halls; though not as intricate, the meal proved satisfactory.

The sun had long set, and the kitchens were empty when Fenris returned, so he retired to his quarters, where he found all of his roommates sound asleep. He had barely closed his eyes before someone shook him from his slumber.

"His Grace has requested a midnight snack," a young serving girl whispered. "Your presence is needed immediately."

Groaning, Fenris followed the youth to Aludrien's private chambers on the pavilion's highest floor. They passed through the heir's study, a gilded room featuring a giant desk that sat along a wall of paintings. Fenris eyed them suspiciously, realizing the images moved. Animancy was a strange and mysterious force indeed.

Aludrien sat along a wide veranda, which overlooked the moonlit Cellicean Sea beyond the palace's thick outer wall.

A chocolate tart sat on the table next to him, and he gazed across the glistening water, unbothered by the arrival of his servants, who both bowed.

"I am at your service, Your Grace," they said in unison. The girl's cheerful voice hid the petulance in Fenris's.

"Leave us," Aludrien commanded. The serving girl curtsied shakily and exited, leaving the two men alone in the cool night air.

The heir was isolated and unarmed, and Fenris was well-rested and fed. His hands twitched, eager to rid the world of another tyrant. But Aludrien's words hung in his mind. He was promised a final duel the night of the ascension, but first, he must cull the palace of the other monsters. The heir faced him, examining him intently.

"Your features are softer than I would have expected," Aludrien said, his expression indecipherable. "I would almost call them charming, albeit average. Neither tall nor short, neither attractive nor ugly, neither thin nor fat. Not a single feature of yours is remarkable. I would have forgotten you the instant you departed, had I not known your true identity."

Refraining from violence required most of Fenris's energy.

"Being ignored suits me fine. Anonymity is a valuable tool."

"Indeed," the heir's eyes narrowed. "Though it wasn't enough to protect you from me. Sit."

Fenris obeyed, somewhat reluctantly. Aludrien pushed the plate closer.

"My nightly snacks will be our only opportunity to converse freely. My new staff is unaware that I no longer fancy sweets as I did in my youth, so indulge if you like."

Fenris hesitated, eyeing both the tart and the heir warily, wondering if the offer was an odd test. But his love for chocolate trumped his better judgment, and he ate it, relishing the rich and decadent dessert. He found it impossible to contain his delight.

"Seems I have uncovered a weakness," Aludrien smirked.

"Hardly," he lied. "It's better than the stale bread you've been feeding me."

"At least I fed you. I see that gratitude is not one of your virtues."

"I'll give my regards to the chef. I reserve my appreciation for those who deserve it."

Aludrien's eyes gleamed, and his smile deepened. Fenris's

stomach twisted. The heir seemed to derive a sick pleasure from his barbs.

"We have much to discuss," Aludrien sighed. "Since my father's death, seven rebellions have erupted across the Imperium, and my aunt has returned to the field to quell them before my ascension. In Hestraea's absence, her lover, General Barrett, has consolidated a following within the military. Each day, more nobles turn to her or my bastard half-brother."

"Grand Marshal Hestraea would be a formidable opponent," Fenris interjected, ignoring Aludrien's scowl. "If General Barrett persuades enough nobles to join her cause, it could convince her to turn on you."

"And if General Barrett dies without justification, she will know I made a move against her. Murdering her lover would provoke her just the same," Aludrien spat. "You are a tool. Do not have the audacity to believe you are anything more. You are alive because you excel at killing. Not statecraft. In the coming days, I will provide you with a target, and you will eliminate it. Am I understood?"

"Who is the first mark?" Fenris asked. He severely regretted his decision to live. He added. "Your Grace."

"Don't be hasty, my dear assassin. Precisely eighty-four days remain until my ascension; you must learn patience and tact. I cannot simply dispatch you to each of my rivals one after the other; such a bold move, however convenient, would galvanize the other royals against me. You will continue to serve as my trusted food taster, keeping me safe."

"Inaction may provoke your rivals," Fenris suggested.

"Unlike you, I have not spent the last two weeks idly. And you will have more to do than taste my meals. I have identified the three who must die to ensure my ascension. In the coming days, you will stalk your prey, monitor their movements, associates, and defenses. Each night, you will relay your findings to me, and I will determine your first target once you have provided sufficient context. You were correct to assume General Barrett is one of the three. The buffoon is currently rallying support for my aunt. Hestraea harbors no wish to usurp me, but if she garners enough support, the temptation may prove too great. The second is Chancellor Vispin. She currently operates my government unilaterally and refuses to include me in any governance until I grant her a private audience. All she wants is an easily manipulated emperor to allow her to govern the Empire at her leisure. I doubt I would be her tenth choice if a weak spine is her prerequisite for an emperor. And the third is the greatest threat to my claim, and the one I suggest you begin with. My bastard half-brother. He has accumulated the support of nearly half the court. If any of my opponents gain a majority support, Imperial law allows them to challenge me to mortal combat on the day of ascension. I will not permit that to occur."

Fenris's stomach soured at the command. Aludrien displayed little emotion at the death of his father; in fact, he showed no qualms in working directly with his father's assassin. Now he wanted to murder his closest remaining relative to ascend to the throne. Basil wasn't the bastard; Aludrien was.

"Family must not matter much to—"

Fenris's retort was cut short by a stabbing pain in his stomach. Overcome with nausea, he fell off his chair. The excruciating sensation spider-webbed through his body, forcing him to convulse and foam at the mouth. His vision blurred.

The spirits within him awakened, filling his head with a

cacophony of voices.

Like a cooling spring, relief washed over him, cleansing his body of the strange sickness. He lay in a heap on the veranda, breathing laboriously. Aludrien stared at him, emotionless.

"It seems chocolate wasn't the only ingredient in that tart," he drawled. "You are not the only assassin who joined my household today."

7

A Hint of Vanilla

"Aye, I baked the tart myself like you asked, chamberlain. Nothing touches the High Lord's lips that isn't made in this here kitchen."

Belessia was a formidable woman. Her voice lilted with an Eastern Isles accent that enhanced her grit. Her imposing disposition, however, did not faze Nim, who proceeded with their interrogation of the mistress of the kitchens.

"And no one else touched the tart besides you?"

"Nay, 'sides the serving girl. She was the only one awake when I received the lord's request. So strange, he's never been one to gorge himself late at night, and I've been cooking for him since he was no taller than my knee. As I said before, I made the damned tart myself!"

"I understand," Nim said, nodding curtly and ignoring Belessia's aggravated outburst. "Could you please gather every ingredient you used to bake the tart? And ensure you provide the exact container you used for each component."

Belessia fell silent, her mouth hanging open incredulously.

"Are ye mad?" She puffed.

"The only deranged aspect about me is the lengths I will go to guarantee our Lord's safety," Nim replied. "And in that area, you can be assured that I am absolutely deranged. Fetch the ingredients."

The mistress of the kitchens glared daggers at the chamberlain but nodded and stormed off into the pantry, cursing under her breath. The door slammed shut, leaving Nim and Fenris alone in the dark, tasting room.

"She could bring different containers," Fenris observed.

"If Belessia is guilty of this crime, then she is the most conniving, deceptive spy in the history of the Empire. She's worked in these kitchens for longer than any of us has been alive. The crone wouldn't allow anything to prevent her from serving dinner, including murder."

"Fair enough."

They waited in silence until Belessia returned in a huff, hauling a heavy wooden tray filled with an assortment of jars, tubs, and flasks. She pointedly slammed it onto the table.

"Here ya go, chamberlain. Every jar I used to bake His Grace's chocolate tart, down to the salt."

"I appreciate the haste, Belessia," Nim replied.

The mistress nodded impatiently, eyeing the door behind her. The three stood awkwardly, the bustling sounds of the kitchens beyond penetrating the door.

"Do I have to stay?" Belessia asked haughtily. "Breakfast is in an hour and a half, and I've barely started. I still don't know how you expect me to run these kitchens with a handful of amateurs."

"My apologies, mistress," Nim said, unapologetically. "Please continue your duties. You are dismissed."

She departed dramatically, slamming the door. Nim gestured to the tray, and Fenris began his testing.

The chamberlain had awoken immediately following the poisoning. While Aludrien responded to the incident nonchalantly, retiring to his bed, Nim tore through the palace like a hurricane. Despite dozens of attempts in less than a month, the chamberlain behaved as though they were facing their first threat. Fenris was awake all night, accompanying the chamberlain on their myriad of interviews with anyone who glanced at the deadly tart. Their meticulous investigation inevitably led them to the kitchens.

Fenris started with the sugar, tasting a tiny portion with a silver spoon. They waited the customary ten minutes, but no pain followed. Although the poison from the tart was fast-acting, the chamberlain insisted they move slowly through the ingredients. The flour, butter, and cocoa powder were next, as they were the easiest substances to use to disguise a poison. One by one, they eliminated the ingredients.

The poison was in the vanilla.

The vial was small, as the extract was potent. Fenris only needed to taste a single drop. He knew the instant it touched his tongue. Instead of the overwhelming floral sweetness of vanilla, the liquid was sour. Within moments, the poison metabolized, and he doubled over in pain.

"Excellent," Nim said, ignoring Fenris's pained moans. "It shouldn't be too hard to trace its origins; vanilla is considered a luxury in this region. You've done well, Pax. Go rest before breakfast. You have a long day ahead of you."

Picking himself off the ground, his body healing from within, Fenris departed.

Like food and water, Fenris did not necessarily require sleep to survive, but the spirits' powers did not combat fatigue. His first day in Aludrien's employ had been a long and tiring one, and he yearned for rest.

He soon discovered he would not find sleep in his room.

Odd, muffled sounds echoed through the servants' hall, causing his cheeks to flush. When he opened the door, his suspicions were confirmed.

Tipin was bent over the lower bunk, clutching the wooden frame as it rocked against the wall. His clothes lay on the floor in a haphazard pile. His face was pressed into the mattress, muffling his high-pitched moans. Fukov mounted him, one hand gripping the top bunk, the other firmly around Tipin's waist. His muscular thighs flexed with each long thrust, shaking the bed as he slammed into the smaller servant. The enormous man cocked his head as Fenris entered and smiled devilishly, fucking Tipin harder. The thin servant squealed.

Fenris tensed, preparing to save the poor servant from Fukov.

The brute pulled Tipin's head from the mattress by his hair. A wide smile was plastered on his cherubic face, tongue lolling to the side. He was enjoying it. No longer constrained by cloth, Tipin's moans of ecstasy carried into the hall.

Fenris shut the door behind him, trapped inside with the lewd exhibition.

His face grew hot, and he could not look away.

Tipin gripped the mattress and bucked his hips backward, riding Fukov eagerly. The larger man's knees trembled, and he exhaled with a satisfied sigh, Tipin's ass slapping hard against his thighs. Thoroughly taunted, Fukov groaned and thrust harder, regaining control. Tipin yelped in delight, collapsing onto the bed, his back arched obediently. The carnal clapping of flesh against flesh intensified, their moans soaring. Fenris expected the pair to climax then and there. However, they persisted without any signs of stopping.

A part of Fenris wished to join them. But despite his growing lust, he contained himself and climbed into his own bed. He couldn't remember the last time he had enjoyed such pleasures with another man. He resigned himself to the fact that he may never experience such delights again.

Fenris slipped under the covers and closed his eyes, but the sounds emanating from across the room robbed him of sleep. He rolled to his side, deciding to enjoy the show.

Fukov leaned back on his bunk, thick legs sprawled over the side, giant hands firmly clutching Tipin's waist. The smaller servant expertly gyrated his hips, riding Fukov's cock with gleeful fervor. He quivered with each bounce, eyes rolled back. Tipin, it seemed, was not as innocent as he appeared.

Ignoring the sensual sounds, Fenris tried to sleep. He considered using his mind palace to escape the awkward situation. His presence encouraged the pair to grow louder, both excited by the audience. When they finished, the early sunlight streamed through the windows, and the morning bell rang softly through the corridors. The time for sleep had long passed.

Reluctantly, Fenris climbed out of bed and donned a fresh set of livery, ignored his dozing roommates, and returned to the kitchens.

Breakfast was delightfully uneventful. The hearty porridge, blueberry scones, and salmon bagels were free of poison. Nim was absent, preoccupied with uncovering the origins of the tainted vanilla. Belessia, too distracted and flustered by the morning's setbacks, dismissed Fenris before her staff had cleared the table.

Instead of returning to his room, he decided to venture out into the palace. With only a few hours until lunch, there wasn't sufficient time to sleep, and he had much to accomplish. He left the pavilion without issue, the heir's livery acting as his shield, allowing him to navigate the palace grounds unnoticed.

Security had increased substantially since the night Fenris had infiltrated the palace. However, having diligently studied the inner city's layout during his preparations for the emperor's assassination, Fenris knew precisely where to go.

The central pavilion loomed over all others; the massive structure set between the plaza and the emperor's Golden Pavilion housed most of the palace's courtiers, including all three of Aludrien's targets. Only the emperor and the heir lived in their own private pavilions. The rest of the court dwelled in smaller apartments in the hulking central tower, where Fenris would spend most of his days stalking his new prey.

He passed the central building entirely.

Aludrien's plans could wait another day; Fenris had more urgent matters to tend to. His destination lay on the far side of the complex near the northeast corner: a great golden spire reaching to the heavens. Security here was relatively scarce; only half a dozen guards milled about the tower's courtyard. They ignored Fenris as he entered the magnificent structure.

The interior was equally barren, though the inhabitants were unarmed and wore ornate robes. Several meditated along the walls or walked briskly around the giant columns. But the massive room seemed almost vacant. The air around him, however, teemed with spirits of every color, shape, and size. An azure peacock the size of a human, a lavender ram smaller than his fist, and a flock of seagulls in every hue of orange imaginable. The spirits of the departed, or rach, usually kept themselves hidden from the naked eye, but here they flaunted their ethereal beauty. Within the central temple, those born with the gift tended to them like shepherds to a flock.

Aludrien had been correct on one point: Fenris wanted vengeance upon the one who had betrayed the Meridian. What the heir was unaware of was the fact that Fenris already knew their identity. He had thought of little else but slaying Ignatius, and the first place he would find the Pontifex would be the central temple. Aludrien had not mentioned Ignatius on his list of adversaries, but Fenris only cared about one assassination. And he would execute it at the first opportunity he received.

He had imagined the center of the Empire's Animancy to be thriving and bustling, brimming with young priests and priestesses in training, the center of learning and discovery. Yet the temple was nearly deserted.

An elderly priestess materialized behind him.

"I'm afraid the morning service has concluded, my child," she said. "But feel free to return tomorrow."

"No evening ceremony?" Fenris asked, puzzled. Every church, regardless of its size, opened its doors to the public twice a day for a communal service of prayer, meditation, and paying tribute to the spirits, usually led by the head priest or priestess. Although the holy order was primarily a tool for the empire, harnessing the power of the rach into weapons and technology, it still retained its spiritual foundations.

"We are only capable of one service a day," she sighed. "I am so sorry for the inconvenience. As you can see, we are woefully understaffed."

If he wanted answers, he would have to acquire them from this priestess, lest he raise suspicion.

"I've never seen it so quiet before," Fenris commented, hoping the priestess possessed the hunger for conversation and connection that so many her age exhibited. He wanted to avoid asking questions or showing too much curiosity while obtaining the information he sought.

"These are dark times indeed. I was here when the soldiers came, you know. I half suspected they were here to arrest us all and start a holy war. Can you believe a dozen cardinals would want to kill our beloved emperor? It's a crock of lies, if you ask me."

"The Pontifex must be upset," Fenris said, glancing around the church grounds in hopes of catching a glimpse of Ignatius.

"Oh dear," she said. "That's putting it mildly. The poor man was beside himself. However, he respected the court's findings and allowed the guard to take the cardinals into custody. I believe he fears the Chancellor and Grand Marshal will turn on him next, enough that he left early to prepare for the ascension in Arachovia."

"Ignatius is gone?"

"I'm afraid so. Many of my brothers and sisters leaped at the chance to join His Eminence. I would have joined them, too, but alas, these old bones are too frail to weather a journey across the empire. If they had waited a few more days, I might have changed my mind. I haven't witnessed an ascension before, though I have visited the ruins of Arachovia. Three times."

Fenris nodded along, patiently waiting for the priestess to finish her rambling before departing respectfully. He would not find any more answers at the temple. Ignatius had fled the palace, allowing a handful of his pawns to take the fall and bringing the rest of his supporters with him. They would be safer in the ruins of Arachovia, far from the heart of the empire and those who questioned his connections to the disgraced cardinals arrested for aiding the Meridian in the emperor's murder.

He returned to the Emerald Pavilion for his lunchtime duties, not bothering to search the cathedral further.

The rest of the day passed quickly, with both lunch and dinner being served without a hitch. Aludrien entertained a few guests. Lower-ranking nobles from middling houses were invited to bolster his support against his rivals. And as he was unmarried, numerous lords and ladies offered their hands in marriage to become the future emperor's spouse; such a union would elevate any house for generations to come. With numerous opponents to his claim, the heir constantly engaged in politicking, promising titles, estates, and positions of power within his new regime. Such scheming twisted Fenris's stomach. He wondered which unlucky noble Aludrien would choose to wed. Whoever it was would surely get more than they bargained for.

Belessia remained in a state of frantic agitation, and Nim neglected to attend either meal. Fenris had ample leisure time outside his tasting duties, and his room was unoccupied between meals, allowing him to reclaim the sleep he had lost the previous night.

He was in particularly high spirits when summoned for the heir's nightly snack. He passed Fukov, who was exiting Aludrien's personal baths, carrying an empty bucket and towel. The brute's burly disposition did not particularly scream "bath attendant"; younger, more nimble servants typically performed such tedious duties. However, Fenris considered that the heir might require his chamber staff to be capable of combat in case of a direct assault.

"Eat," Aludrien ordered as Fenris entered the veranda, motioning to the treacle pudding on the side table. "For Nim's sake, I hope we don't have a repeat of last night's debacle. I'm not sure how many more investigations they can manage simultaneously. I've already lost count."

Fenris tasted the pudding, rich, creamy, and decadent, but the trauma of the tart prevented him from thoroughly enjoying it.

"You have been busy today, I hear," Aludrien drawled, observing Fenris with an acute curiosity. "I am told you spent a great deal of the morning on the palace grounds. Did you collect any useful information?"

"Nothing of use, I'm becoming familiar with my surroundings and learning the daily rhythms of the palace."

"Interesting," Aludrien mused. "I was unaware that any of your targets dwelled in the central temple."

Fenris nearly choked on the pudding.

"I enjoy meditation," he replied in a level tone, swallowing the pudding.

"Or you seek vengeance, after all," Aludrien said. "And here I thought you were above such base desires."

Fenris swallowed hard. "I don't know what you're talking about."

"Oh, spare me. Anyone in the palace with half a brain comprehends that Ignatius colluded with the Meridian to kill my father. I also know he had a little chat with you before your execution."

"He only performed my last rites. I didn't speak."

Fenris remained defiant, refusing to divulge more out of spite; the look of exasperation on the heir's face was its own reward.

"I'm sure," Aludrien drawled. "Anyways, in a strange turn of events, investigators found the names and contacts of twelve cardinals at a Meridian hideout. The exact number required to create a Tal'Rach. Each one admitted guilt before their swift execution. So the matter of my father's death has been officially laid to rest, though it seems too neat, in my opinion. And it turned out perfectly in the Pontifex's favor. This scheme may be why Ignatius wanted to speak with you."

"Funny how you forgot to mention that," Fenris said. "You wanted to see how I would act."

"And you marched straight to the cathedral at your first opportunity," Aludrien mused. "Exceedingly suspicious, if you ask me. Either you were trying to locate your allies in the church, or you sought vengeance against those who offered the Meridian on a silver platter. Regardless, it works to my advantage that Ignatius and his ilk fled to Arachovia. I can persuade the ambitious cardinals who remain with promises of appointing a new Pontifex. I will deal with Ignatius after my ascension."

"Seems like you have everything under control," Fenris said. "Though you resorted to begging the man who killed your father to protect you."

"I propositioned you. I do not grovel. And you agreed, though the reason remains to be seen. And you are incorrect. There is still much I do not know. Although your painfully sanctimonious and tragically naive reasons for killing my father are apparent, the circumstances of your ascension remain unclear. As is your reason for fighting your comrade after you bested the emperor, as the witnesses suggest."

Fenris furrowed his brow. "Do you mean the other assassin? They weren't with us."

Aludrien's eyes narrowed.

"Interesting," Aludrien mused. "Are you certain?"

"Yes," Fenris said. He had thought they had laid this to rest.

"And you fought them?"

"Yes."

"Why?"

"They attacked me," Fenris said. "After I killed your father."

"And why would they do that?" Aludrien asked. "If another assassin beat you to a mark, why would you confront them?"

"To claim the bounty," Fenris said. "If the other assassin isn't alive to tell the tale, then the truth is what I make it."

"Fair point," Aludrien said, hesitating.

"I thought you didn't care about who I was working with."

"Well, since you insist that you were not associated with them, I am curious about who else wanted my father dead, and where that assassin is. Someone of that caliber does not vanish into the ether."

"So you lied to me," Fenris said, grinning. "You faked disinterest before. But you want to know who aided in your father's death, why I visited the cathedral, and who I was looking for."

"I like to be aware of my enemies' identities," Aludrien said.

"Are you suggesting they remain in the palace?"

"Possibly. Whoever wanted my father dead will undoubtedly seek my head as well. However, you could be lying to protect your surviving associates. Or are they all dead?"

Fenris growled dangerously.

The door opened, and Nim rushed in, bowing briskly while maintaining their usual unflappable demeanor.

"Your Grace, I apologize for the intrusion, but I have garnered critical intelligence regarding your assassination attempt," Nim said.

"Which one?" Aludrien asked, amused.

"The most recent occurrence, the chocolate tart."

"You may continue; you haven't interrupted anything important."

"We analyzed the vial of vanilla and determined the glass to be a different hue than the others in our pantries. Belessia recorded seven vials in her ledgers, and we found seven in the pantries, including the poisoned one. I suspect someone within the pavilion swapped them."

"Any leads as to who might be culpable?" Aludrien inquired.

"That remains to be seen, though I would wager the missing vial of vanilla would betray them. But we made another discovery, one of greater importance. Your apothecary identified the poison laced in the vanilla. Belladonna. A rare nightshade only found in the southwest mountain groves. It is often used as a medicinal herb in local villages, though a potent dose, as found in the vanilla, is exceedingly toxic. I scoured the freight logs and only found a single shipment of belladonna in the last five years."

"Whose household was listed on the record?" Aludrien asked.

"A vassal house of the Seraphines. But the signature was Dyline Dercouix."

"And who the hell is that?"

"No one. Such a person does not exist."

"And how is this information helpful?"

"It is a common alias used by a prominent member of the court. Most chamberlains worth their salt would know immediately," Nim explained.

"Save me the suspense, Nim." Aludrien snapped. "Out with it."

"Dyline Dercouix is the alias commonly used by your half-brother, Basil."

Aludrien exhaled, eyes glistening. "How concrete is this evidence?"

"Damning, Your Grace."

"How swiftly can you spread this to other chamberlains?"

"I have already begun, Your Grace. The entire palace should know by sunrise."

"Excellent work, Nim. Such a devious play by Basil will justify a counterattack in the eyes of the court," Aludrien beamed, turning his attention to Fenris. "Forget the Chancellor and General Barrett. The bastard Basil will be your first target."

8

The First Mark

The rat's nest of the central pavilion proved harder to navigate than Fenris had previously assumed. As the oldest and most prominent building within the palace, it had been expanded by artisans over the centuries, with twelve unique structures melded into a disjointed blend of wood, mortar, and steel. The labyrinthine complex housed the most prominent nobles of the church, military, and government, and its halls teemed with vigilant servants experienced in espionage, subterfuge, and surveillance. Navigating such a space undetected proved nearly impossible.

As the heir's personal food taster, Fenris could roam the lower floors near the royal kitchens without arousing too much suspicion. High Lord Basil's apartments, however, were located in the south wing's eighth floor, and a servant wearing Aludrien's lion emblem would stick out like a beacon at midnight. Even if he wore a disguise, the veteran spies within the central pavilion would notice an unfamiliar face.

Fenris rectified this issue with a deft application of magic. Summoning the spirits within, Fenris cast a veil around his body to reflect the surrounding light. Invisible to the naked eye, he stalked the halls undeterred.

High-ranking nobles and courtiers had near limitless resources; layers of complex wards protected each apartment. Even with his invisibility, moving about the pavilion required the utmost care and patience.

But Fenris had infiltrated the palace once before; the patchwork defenses of dozens of feuding nobles were nothing compared to the iron shell that had once protected the late emperor. With months of careful planning, insider knowledge, and intelligence from Meridian agents, he and Durian had efficiently circumvented the Golden Pavilion's wards.

Fenris uncovered a path into Lord Basil's apartments within a day. He would have assassinated the High Lord immediately upon finding his way inside, but Aludrien insisted that Fenris first gather intelligence from Basil's household. Surveillance, in the heir's opinion, was essential to crafting a foolproof assassination. Aludrien demanded that he formulate the final plan himself once he had sufficient intelligence. Fenris was merely the tool.

After hours of careful surveillance between mealtimes, Fenris would end each day on the heir's veranda. Aludrien spent their late-night rendezvous peppering Fenris with countless questions about his half-brother's security and schedule. The following morning, the sounds of Fukov and Tipin's feral sexual escapades would wrench Fenris from his restless slumber, and he would repeat the process all over again.

Fenris continuously questioned his decision to live.

Aludrien, ever impatient and demanding, grew agitated

with each passing day, dissatisfied with Fenris's thorough intelligence. The heir ordered him to hide odd devices in each of Basil's rooms. Once they were in place, the paintings behind Aludrien's desk magically displayed the High Lord's chambers. Aludrien explained that they were a new device his engineers were testing, called cameras. They allowed the heir to see his brother's actions in real time. The strange machines unsettled Fenris.

After nine full days of reconnaissance, Fenris found himself in yet another meeting with the heir. Only seventy-four days remained until the ascension; over a quarter of the mourning period had passed, and all of Aludrien's enemies still drew breath.

Fenris grew restless and irritated by his new master's domineering and meticulous nature. In the Meridian, Durian had entrusted him with assassinations; Fenris determined the details of each mission, except for Claude's. In his experience, a perfect strategy existed only in theory; reality had a way of unraveling even the best-laid plans. The only truth one could rely on was uncertainty.

Aludrien disagreed.

"How many rooms do the apartments consist of?"

"Seven," Fenris replied. "A foyer, dining room, lounge, private baths, serving quarters, and two bedrooms. One for Basil and his husband Jareth, and the second for their daughter Magdolina."

"And the guards are under their employ?" Aludrien shot back.

"Twelve," Fenris sighed. Nine evenings had passed since he first broke into Basil's apartments, and nine times Aludrien had asked the same questions. "Four guards are stationed in eight-hour shifts. Two outside the exterior door, armed with crossbows. Two outside the bedroom doors, one officer equipped with insignis weapons and the other trained in Animancy."

"And the servants?"

"I've already told you—"

"Refresh my memory," Aludrien snapped.

"Fourteen. A chamberlain, a valet for each husband, and a governess for their daughter. The rest are low-ranking maids and footmen. From what I can tell, five are combat-trained, and three have allegiances to some other royals. I've observed each of them passing information in the hall when they suspect no one is watching."

"Any visitors today?"

"Only Basil's mother, Ysuelt. She has joined the family for most dinners."

"Did anyone accompany her?"

"Only her chamberlain and two guards. I already told you, her apartments are across the hall, so she comes alone. How many more times do I have to repeat myself?"

"Watch your tone," Aludrien said, exasperated. Fenris took pride in getting under his skin. The pompous brat wasn't accustomed to anyone speaking to him so flippantly without facing dire consequences. But Fenris did not care. Speaking to the conniving heir nightly and regularly consuming poison was punishment enough. In the last nine days, Fenris had foiled three more poisoning attempts. "Who else did Basil converse with today? Where did he venture in the palace?"

"No one. Your brother hasn't left his quarters. Though Magdolina entertained the children of seven lower-ranked nobles and their governesses."

"Did they speak of anything of importance or exchange anything that could contain a message?" Aludrien asked excitedly. "Tell me each of their names."

"Magdolina's playmates are all under five, and a few can't talk yet. They'd be terrible spies."

"You would be surprised how readily a noble would use their child," Aludrien said pointedly. "And what of the husband?"

"Jareth was the only member of the family to leave today," Fenris answered. "After meetings with the other ministers, he returned for dinner and fell asleep with his husband."

"What of their relationship?" Aludrien asked. It was the first new question he had presented tonight. "How do Basil and Jareth interact with one another?"

"Amicably," Fenris said. "In front of their daughter, at least. They are rarely alone together. I sense some tension between the two, though I'm not sure why."

"And how do they comport themselves behind closed doors?"

"I haven't entered their bedchamber at night. It's hard to escape once they retire."

"Regrettable. In the future, I expect your investigations to be more thorough. Is there anything else you can divulge regarding the two?"

"I've heard them raise their voices."

"Loud enough for the servants or guards to hear?" Aludrien asked, his interest considerably piqued.

"Definitely," Fenris said.

"Lovely," Aludrien's steely face broke into a vicious smile. "About how frequently do these squabbles occur?"

"Nightly."

"Excellent," Aludrien said.

The heir cleared his throat and rose. Fenris followed suit, expecting Aludrien to dismiss him. However, the heir passed him and exited the veranda with enigmatic haste.

Confused by the abrupt departure, Fenris cautiously followed him into the royal apartments. Aludrien had already arrived at his desk, busy rifling through the mahogany drawers. Fenris observed placidly, fascinated by the heir's uncharacteristically energetic behavior. Clicking his tongue, Aludrien lifted a glinting object from a drawer.

A dagger.

Bladed weapons were a rarity in the Empire, as provincials were forbidden from owning or wielding them. Imperial law only allowed pure-blooded Xandrians to own swords, axes, daggers, and other ancient armaments, which were exclusively crafted as Insignis weapons by Animancers. Aludrien's jewel-encrusted dagger gleamed in the soft light. Sliding it from the golden scabbard, the heir brandished the thin, bone-white blade, admiring the exquisite craftsmanship. This was no insignis weapon, but a piece of art.

"Empress Luxarene commissioned this ceremonial dagger to commemorate her ascension. Ever since, each emperor or empress has bestowed it on the heir as a symbol of trust and goodwill. My father gifted this to me when he appointed me as his heir."

"Royals are a sentimental lot," Fenris muttered.

"Guilty as charged," Aludrien said. "Which is why my father commanded me to gift the dagger to Basil after he publicly adopted him. He desired that I show the Empire my support for his decision and unify the royal family."

"Many might see that as passing the title of heir to Basil,"

Fenris mused.

"You are correct. Most that do currently support my brother's claim," Aludrien said, a quiet fury brewing behind the crystalline facade.

"Interesting that you have it, when you gifted it to your brother years ago."

"Half-brother," Aludrien corrected. "I ordered Nim to fetch it from the royal armory this morning, discreetly. Basil transferred it from his apartments for safekeeping after my father's death. No wonder, for this dagger is the only legitimate claim the bastard has to my throne."

"But not because he's your older brother?" Fenris asked wryly.

"Half-brother," Aludrien snapped, brandishing the gaudy blade. "His lineage is none of your concern, only his death."

"I'm sure the dagger is usually on full display," Fenris said, understanding Aludrien's intent. "Most outside his household wouldn't know he had moved it."

"Precisely," Aludrien said. "And you will use it tomorrow night to slit his throat. My dinner is scheduled an hour before his. Complete your duties here, infiltrate his apartments, and wait until Basil and his husband retire after dinner. Kill them both, stage it as a lover's quarrel, and escape undetected. I understand the final part is difficult for you, but I recommend you do so, since you are already aware of what type of suffering awaits you if the palace guard captures you."

"A bit too poetic, isn't it?" Fenris said. "Most of the court would suspect you."

"I expect them to," Aludrien replied proudly. "My enemies must understand the consequences of challenging me. Of course, there will be no concrete evidence to implicate me."

"And Magdolina?" Fenris asked.

"Is not to be touched," he said sternly. "I will not add infanticide to my conscience."

"But you're perfectly content with making her an orphan," Fenris pushed, satisfied by the anger his comment caused.

"She is a royal and will have a grandmother to look after her," Aludrien said, wincing as he realized he had fallen for Fenris's bait. The heir hadn't entertained his assassin's moral objections before, much less defended his own actions. Aludrien sheathed the dagger and thrust it into Fenris's hand. "Dismissed."

"Of course, Your Grace," Fenris bowed low, pleased by his small victory.

"And Pax," Aludrien said, pointedly enunciating his pseudonym like a slur. He brandished a silver remote, the same one connected to the remaining node lodged in Fenris's neck. Fenris hadn't seen it since his first day at the pavilion. "If you fail me, you will wish you had remained on the funeral pyre, am I understood? Your mind palace will not protect you from my wrath."

Fenris nodded, frozen by the bone-chilling threat. Regardless of his moral objections to his master's most recent order, he was certain Aludrien was not bluffing.

He retired to his chambers, thankful for a quiet room. Despite the lack of moaning and groaning from Fukov and Tipin, Fenris did not sleep at all. However, he never rested well the night before a kill. His conscience wouldn't allow it. Overcome with a mixture of guilt, nerves, and a healthy dose of fear, he stared at the ceiling until the sun's light peeked through the blinds.

The planning process was unlike any of his previous

assassinations, where Durian provided a detailed list of his target's sins and atrocities. The Meridian's leader had assured Fenris that his victims deserved death. In his mind, he saw it as a way to atone for the atrocities he committed in the slums before Durian found him.

But now, he was not certain if his mark truly deserved it. Yes, Basil was a hedonistic royal with more wealth than an entire province, and his husband Jareth had undoubtedly committed a crime or two as Vice Minister of War. Basil had even attempted to murder Aludrien first. However, Fenris could not shake the odd feeling bubbling deep inside. Uncertainty. Did these two men truly deserve the blade?

The following day, he carried out his duties for each of Aludrien's meals; thankfully, he did not ingest any more poison. The golden dagger hidden beneath his livery weighed on his mind like a lodestone. Finally, after dinner concluded, he retired to his empty room. He stuffed unused sets of uniforms under his blankets to simulate a sleeping body. To his roommates, he would appear sound asleep. He had nearly three hours before a maid would arrive to escort him to the heir's quarters for the nightly snack.

He would only require one.

Veiling himself, Fenris left the pavilion, padding softly past Aludrien's guard. He thought of how easy it would be for him to escape the palace entirely, leaving this world of shadows and conceit behind. But if he fled, no one else would prevent a monster from assuming the throne. And Ignatius, who had betrayed the Meridian, still drew breath. Not to mention the explosive node lodged in the base of his neck. He had no choice.

Basil's apartments were impossible to infiltrate from within, but the single ward protecting the windows was embarrassingly weak. Even if he dwelt on the eighth floor, the High Lord should have known an experienced assassin could scale the exterior wall and slip through a single ward undetected.

And Fenris did precisely that.

Basil's dinner had already begun when Fenris slipped inside the window of the servants' sleeping quarters. Within a few minutes, a young maid entered. Fenris danced past her, shifting on the balls of his feet, and entered the hall moments before the door shut behind him.

Sounds of intermittent, forced conversation floated in from the dining room, often interrupted by a child's laughter. The door to Basil and Jareth's bedchamber remained unguarded. Eventually, a valet entered the room, allowing Fenris inside.

There he waited. Clutching the dagger expectantly.

His marks arrived soon after.

Tall and thin, with soft features juxtaposed with a hooked nose, High Lord Basil entered first. He curtly dismissed his valet after changing from his formal attire to a silk evening robe. His famously upbeat and carefree attitude had soured of late, according to the gossip Fenris had overheard from the servants during his reconnaissance. Basil retired to the chaise lounge, scowling and staring out the window, lost in thought. Basil hardly acknowledged his husband, who joined him shortly afterward. Sturdy, stoic, and intense, Jareth lumbered into the chamber. Although a head shorter than his husband, the burly Minister outweighed Basil. Jareth possessed features common in the distant city of Kyriak: thick eyebrows, a full beard, and hairy forearms.

The room was silent until Jareth dismissed his valet. The Minister opened the bay window, allowing the cool night air to rush in, staring pensively out at the shadowy palace grounds below. Fenris lurked in the far corner, near the bed, clutching his dagger. He would strike the instant one of them raised their voice.

"We've waited long enough," Jareth's deep baritone broke the stalemate. "Magdolina leaves for the country estate. Tomorrow."

"Out of the question," Basil said, aggravated. "We have discussed this countless times, Jareth. She is safer here in the palace with both of us to look after her. She could be vulnerable in the country."

"We should leave with her."

"And what of your station? The Vice Minister of War is required in the palace."

"There are eleven Vice Ministers of War, Basil. You know as well as I that the title is ceremonial. I haven't done anything of importance since I left the military."

"You knew the price of loving me, of marrying a royal," Basil said stiffly. "You cannot resent me for it."

Jareth sighed with exasperation. Tonight was obviously not the first time the two had broached this sore topic.

"It's kept me by your side. By Magdolina's. Where I belong. Which is why we must leave. Tomorrow. Together."

"We simply cannot run away," Basil said. "I cannot have this conversation again. Mother-"

"To hell with that woman's opinion," Jareth snapped. "She's been filling your head with nonsense since your father died."

Fenris unsheathed the dagger, tensing his body.

"Is she wrong? You are well aware of what my brother is capable of. Do I need to remind you about all the horrors he put me through? He has despised me since the day he learned the meaning of the word. As long as I draw breath, he will consider me a threat."

"I know, my love," Jareth softened slightly. "Given what your mother's done, I wouldn't be surprised if it provokes him into action."

"She is trying to protect us! To keep our family safe!" Basil exclaimed.

Fenris padded softly toward Jareth.

"I am trying to keep our family safe!" Jareth bellowed. "And your mother has endangered us all with her scheming. Sending assassins after Aludrien, conspiring with her associates to champion your claim to the throne. Every day, your brother's agents grow closer. After your mother's stunt last week, it's only a matter of time until he retaliates. Please, Basil. Come with me, before it's too late."

"There is no point in running," Basil said adamantly. "Aludrien will find me anywhere. The best chance we have is to trust Mother."

"Basil, do you wish to be emperor?"

Fenris stopped, three paces from Jareth, glancing in Basil's direction. Basil recoiled as if Jareth had slapped him.

He burst into laughter.

"Of course not!" Basil chortled. "Could you imagine? I can hardly decide what to wear for dinner."

Fenris sheathed his dagger.

"Why are you entertaining the old bat? Publicly support Aludrien's claim and be done with it!"

"Ah, there it is," Basil said. "Every single night, the same foolhardy argument. I have told you repeatedly, and yet you still won't heed my words. I have spent my entire life trying to win Aludrien's affection, desperately trying to quell his ire.

There is not one word, action, or miracle that will douse the flame of his hatred. I could proclaim to the entire world that I do not desire the throne, fly us across the Dragon's Teeth until his ascension, and still, he would not trust me. I am not suited for this deadly game, but my mother is. She will navigate us out of this mess. Trust me. Please, my love."

Basil rose, inching toward his husband with every word, until their foreheads touched. They remained in silence, both exhausted and overwhelmed.

"Trust is no longer enough, Basil," Jareth said, pulling away. "Love is not a shield. It cannot repel an arrow or cure poison. If it were only my life in jeopardy, that would be a different matter. But yours? Magdolina's? I cannot idly sit by and watch my family be destroyed."

"Neither can I, my love," Basil replied. "But running is not the answer."

"I hope you're right. For our daughter's sake."

Jareth retired to the bed, and Basil lingered by the window, tears welling in his eyes, before joining his husband. The lights turned off.

Fenris lurked deathly quiet in the darkness, knees trembling, overcome with emotion. He could not kill these men who shared such a love. He would not.

Basil wasn't a threat to Aludrien; he was a prisoner in the game of succession. Used as a pawn by his mother, Ysuelt. She was the true mastermind behind the poisoning attempt, undoubtedly striving to set her easily manipulated son on the throne. Fenris would rather face Aludrien's wrath than spill the blood of two innocents.

He waited until Jareth's snoring began before slipping out the bay window.

The palace grounds were barren so late at night, save for intermittent patrols. The Emerald Pavilion's gates were closed, so Fenris scaled the wall and swiftly snuck to the safety of his bed. His roommates were already fast asleep, and none had discovered his decoy. It wasn't long before a serving girl entered to summon him to Aludrien's chambers.

"Well? Is it finished?" the heir asked, lounging at his usual place on the veranda.

Fenris pulled the dagger from his robes.

Aludrien's eyes narrowed. "Explain."

Fenris obliged and recounted the entire conversation he had overheard, not neglecting a single detail. Ysuelt was the driving force behind Basil's claim, responsible for at least one assassination attempt. Basil merely wished to coexist with his brother, as did his husband. Surprisingly, Aludrien allowed him to speak without interruption, listening intently with a neutral expression.

"Basil has never been your enemy," Fenris concluded. "He would be more useful endorsing your claim. It's his mother, Ysuelt, you should be concerned with."

Fenris's suggestion prompted a long silence. Aludrien waited to ensure he had finished before speaking.

"I see."

Aludrien pulled something from his pocket—the silver remote.

He pressed the button.

Pain blossomed from the metal node lodged in Fenris's neck.

9

A Bad Branch

"Enter."

The door of Aludrien's greenhouse opened, and Nim promptly sauntered inside, bowing deeply. Aludrien, preoccupied with the painstaking task of trimming his prized bonsai, did not lift his head. Hundreds of rare plants and flowers flourished upon every available surface within the muggy interior garden. Moonstone lilies from the southern jungles, a pair of lava orchids from the Dragon's Teeth, and even a row of precious golden helianths. A dozen bonsai clustered together on a side table, wisteria, azalea, and juniper, all forming a miniature forest. However, none were as precious as the elm that he had cared for since he was ten.

"Speak," Aludrien commanded, punctuated by the click of his shears, expertly severing an unwanted branch from his tree.

Nim cleared their throat rather impetuously. Aludrien would remember the infraction for later. "General Cassius and Vice Minister Impelios have agreed to dine with you tomorrow evening, Your Grace. Impelios maintains considerable influence within the government, which will be imperative to exploit. Cassius is in league with General Barrett and your aunt's coalition. He has plainly agreed to join in the hopes of gathering information. However, I believe we can purchase his support. His gambling habits have left him financially vulnerable. Your royal cousins, the Thraxius twins, have politely declined your invitation to tomorrow's luncheon, which confirms my fears. They have aligned with your half-brother."

"What is the status of your search for a new food taster?" Aludrien asked, culling a slightly withered bough with a decisive strike.

"Inconclusive. However, it has only been three days since you relieved Pax of his station. I will continue his duties in the interim."

Aludrien clicked his tongue in disapproval. "You are far too useful to lose over a poisoned scone."

"Please do not concern yourself, Your Grace. Detecting toxins is merely one of the countless required skills for a royal chamberlain. You won't lose me that easily."

Aludrien chortled. Others had labeled him as detached and icy his entire life, but his dutiful chamberlain had steel running through their veins. Sometimes he wondered if they were human. Nim awaited a response, oddly shifting back and forth, lips pursed scrupulously. An expression Aludrien knew too well.

"If you have any qualms, speak them now. Otherwise, you are dismissed."

"My personal misgivings are not what worry me, Your Grace," Nim's voice wavered, betraying a rare hint of emotion. "I have been your chamberlain since your aunt gifted you that tree. Though you spend much of your time within this garden, I have only witnessed you prune that particular bonsai when you are most perturbed."

The metal shears clattered to the floor.

"I saved his life for one purpose. I clothed him, fed him, and asked for only one condition in return. What assassin refuses to kill their mark?"

"One with good judgment, Your Grace."

"So you agree with the wretch?" Aludrien asked, his voice falling to a whisper.

Nim inhaled sharply, understanding they were treading on dangerous ground. When Aludrien lost his temper, survivors were rare. His chamberlain hesitated, carefully crafting a response.

"Do you have any reason to believe the assassin's report to be false?" Nim asked.

"No."

"Then we can assume Lady Ysuelt is the rotten branch in that household. Not your half-brother."

"She is not a contender to the throne. The bastard is. He must not survive to see the ascension."

Nim paused, once more displaying that irksome expression of apprehension. They retrieved the fallen shears and placed them gingerly on the tabletop.

"May I speak candidly, Your Grace?"

"When haven't you?" Aludrien sighed.

"Valid. Based on my astute observations over the years, it is my humble opinion that Basil is a fool incapable of opening a door without his valet, much less leading a successful coup. I must admit, I suspected his husband, not his mother, to be the mastermind behind the vanilla incident. Despite your deserved disdain for the lout, your half-brother has been visibly desperate for your affection since you could string two words together."

"He loathes me."

"He fears you."

"He refuses to submit to my authority."

"Incorrect evaluation, Your Grace. You used to torture the poor boy."

"Ridiculous, the bastard made my life a living hell."

"You used to drop electric eels in his bath."

"Because he ratted me out to Father for pilfering the geraniums from the central gardens."

"You stuffed cow dung in his mattress."

"He tripped me!" Aludrien caught himself, recognizing the immaturity of his words. Was his blood feud with his bastard brother so trivial? He flushed with embarrassment, fueled by Nim's stern expression. "What is your recommendation?"

The question came reluctantly and tasted bitter in his mouth.

"Well, as I continue to repeat, I recommend we return to the safety of the Winter Palace," Nim said. "But since you insist on remaining in the viper's nest of the capital. I suggest you heed your assassin's recommendations."

A toxic pit of dread roiled in Aludrien's stomach. He had long since prepared himself mentally and emotionally for the horrors required of him to ascend the throne. Such actions were inevitable for an heir. But nothing disgusted him more than the depths he was about to descend to.

"Send an invitation to Basil and his entire household. I will host them for dinner tomorrow night. I shall take care of the rest."

"Shall I rescind Cassius and Impelios's invitations?" Nim asked.

"Yes," Aludrien said. "This dinner is far above their station. But my plan requires witnesses. I would like you to extend an invitation to two others."

"And who might those be, Your Grace?"

"Why, there are only two options," Aludrien grinned mischievously. "General Barrett and Chancellor Vispin."

Nim paled. "Are you certain they would accept? Barrett is borderline hostile to your claim, and you have rejected Vispin's numerous requests for a private audience. She may not take a group invitation so kindly."

"They will accept if they wish to retain the court's respect. And I am confident their curiosity will trump their caution. It is high time I gathered all the players to my table. You are dismissed."

"As you command, Your Grace," Nim replied, bowing deeply.

"Wait," Aludrien said.

The chamberlain paused obediently. "Yes, Your Grace?"

"I am curious. What narrative did you leak to the staff regarding the other night's events?"

"That your food taster was apprehended and is currently under arrest in the cellars, which is true, for the crime of making eye contact with the heir. His incarceration is indefinite, awaiting the judgment of Your Grace."

"Devilish," Aludrien grinned. "The staff may not sleep at night."

"Ensuring your servants' obedience is one of my highest priorities. The rumor should suffice for a while."

"If a serving girl spills wine on me with a trembling hand,

I'll know who to blame."

"And I will accept whatever punishment my master deems fit." The chamberlain bowed graciously. "Though I must ask, have you decided how I should proceed with Pax?"

"No," Aludrien snapped. The mere mention of the insubordinate ingrate made his blood boil. Why couldn't he be as pliant and effective as Nim? The useless assassin questioned his every thought, ignored every order, and completely disregarded his authority. "I must deal with my sniveling half-brother first. Then I can focus on the rogue assassin contaminating my cellar. Leave me."

"Of course, Your Grace."

The door closed, and Aludrien refocused his attention on his bonsai. He cleaved a thin branch that was crowding another. Scanning the miniature canopy, he found no other blemishes in his masterpiece. Plants were simple if you took the time to understand them. Apply the correct care, soil, water, and light, and you could mold any to your will. Humans, with their vices, chaos, and infuriating need for free will, were trickier to mold. Of course, the obvious motivators were money, sex, and power. If those failed, emotions such as rage and fear were efficient alternatives. His position and title were also practical tools. Aludrien prided himself on controlling situations and people with the ease with which he shaped his bonsai.

But Fenris proved to be an outlier.

The infuriating cretin seemed not to care for power, or wealth, or glory. He was too stubborn to intimidate, too intelligent to deceive, and too virtuous to corrupt. On top of that, he had an impulsive wildness that was impossible to predict. Even his motivations were suspect. True, Fenris murdered his father in a feckless attempt to free the empire of a tyrant, then he risked capture to save the empire from another possible oppressor. Aludrien. But why did the assassin choose to live? It wasn't for self-preservation. Aludrien knew a martyr when he saw one. He assumed Fenris's motivation was to kill every royal in the palace, to further the Meridian's goals, and save the empire from those he deemed villainous. But after Fenris refused to murder Basil and his husband, Aludrien was perplexed. The mystery unsettled him.

Although he understood enlisting the wildcard was a risky gambit, Aludrien was bitter at the unfortunate outcome. Fenris's third incarceration could finally break him, though he highly doubted it. Otherwise, the only recourse for a useless tool was to dispose of it.

He cursed, slamming his shears on the tabletop, aggravated by the hours he wasted dwelling on the damned insubordinate swine. Devising a plan to deal with his fool of a half-brother, Basil, should be his priority. The fact that sparing his brother was Fenris's idea burned him hotter than a searing iron. He had an impulse to rush over and murder his bastard half-brother himself.

But Nim's reasoning was sound.

Basil feared him. And he could use fear to his advantage. The chamberlain also spoke of the man's desire to be accepted by Aludrien.

A plan rapidly formed.

# # #

Ignatius was not an ostentatious man. His quarters in

Arachovia were a testament to that; a cramped, nondescript room furnished with only a simple desk and a firm pallet in the corner. The Pontifex hailed from the Lilias family, a proud line of cardinals and priests tracing its origins back to the era of Empress Alexandra I. Four of his ancestors held the title of Pontifex before him. As a result, his parents instilled in him the virtues of humility and piety from an early age. His gaudy ceremonial robes were the most luxurious items he owned.

He hunched over his desk, a tiny puddle of wax pooled on the worn wood around the waning candle. Sighing, Ignatius looked out the window and admired the ancient ruins outside. Unlike other courtiers, who luxuriated in the lavish Winter Palace or other outlying estates during their sojourn to the homeland, church officials stayed within the ruins themselves. Ignatius relished his time here. A grounding, humbling experience that provided him with a proper perspective. The impressive stone monuments harkened back to an ancient civilization that lived in harmony with the spirits.

An age before the Tal'Rach. Before the empire conquered half the known world.

The tranquil night was interrupted by a sharp rap at the door.

"Enter, my child," Ignatius said.

Cardinal Rylia opened the door, as brazenly as ever. She was a passionate, loyal, and reliable servant. Ignatius would never sire children, though, if he had, he would hope they would have grown into half the woman Rylia was.

"Good evening, your Eminence," Rylia said. She did not bow, for she knew Ignatius privately detested the pageantry of his station. However, that fact did not quell her respect or reverence.

"And what a fine evening it is, my child," Ignatius said. "How is your work progressing in the amphitheater?"

"Slowly," Rylia said. "Our task is ambitious. I'm thankful you had the foresight to journey here so early. If not, I doubt we would be sufficiently prepared for the ascension."

"I have more than enough faith in you, Rylia," Ignatius said. "Though if there is no hindrance in our preparations, then why do I have the pleasure of speaking with you at this late hour?"

Rylia shifted her feet and bit her lip, a telltale sign of trepidation. She had commonly adopted the expression since the emperor's death. The Cardinal, unfortunately, proved to have a weaker constitution than Ignatius had hoped.

"Reports from our churches in the northern territories have arrived," Rylia said, her voice wavering.

"Which is where Grand Marshal Hestraea deployed her legion, correct?"

"Yes. The citizens of the region have launched a sizable rebellion."

"The estimated death toll?"

"At least ten thousand," Rylia said. "And the fighting along the crystal coasts has produced double that number."

Ignatius sighed. He considered himself a pragmatist, which is why he had gone to such lengths to save the empire from itself. But even he could not shake the cost of his choices. Nevertheless, they must persist. Their work was far from complete.

"A travesty. Alert the cardinals in Kyriak and Raephina. They have enough reserves to send aid. It isn't much, but it is the least we can do."

"Thank you, Your Eminence. I will send word to them immediately," Rylia said, but her eyes continued to wander.

"What is worrying you so?"

"I—" Rylia began. "I did not know it would be like this."

"Rest easy, my child," Ignatius said. "This nasty business will soon end."

"Are you certain?"

"We will save millions of lives if our mission succeeds, my child," Ignatius said, trying to conceal his frustration. He did not need his subordinates to lose their grit at this stage. "Any news from the palace?"

"The court remains split between Basil, Aludrien, and Hestraea. I fear the war for ascension will turn bloody."

"That is unavoidable, but we should not concern ourselves with court politics. I care little for who reaches ascension," Ignatius said. "And what of our other problem within the palace?"

"We have confirmed the loose end remains active, Your Eminence. And I have reason to believe the situation has created another liability."

"We must take a more direct approach," Ignatius said sternly. "Resolve this crisis before the ascension; we cannot risk failure."

"Y-yes, Your Eminence," Rylia said.

"Good evening, my child."

Rylia departed, visibly disturbed by her mentor's sudden curtness. He regretted the words, but he could not afford to be soft at this critical juncture. Not after everything he sacrificed.

If he executed his plan perfectly, the world would finally know peace.

\# \# \#

The cellars beneath the Emerald Pavilion were dim and dank. Legends spoke of a general who constructed the palace, the cruel and sadistic daughter of Empress Eugenia. Rumors said she used her personal dungeons to punish her servants in brutal, inventive ways. Multiple alcoves remained outfitted with rusted iron bars and chain rings, the only remnants of the ancient prison. Subsequent heirs had repurposed the dungeon *as* storage, save for the cell where Fenris sat.

Better than his first, worse than his second, his third incarceration was a middling experience of boredom and frustration. Chains reinforced with Animancy fastened him to the wall; the metal node lodged in his neck hummed ominously, emitting an annoying level of pain. Strong enough to prevent Fenris from focusing, but weak enough to keep him from retreating to his mind palace. These measures were the feeblest yet, but Fenris remained, grudgingly, reminded of the Meridian's goal, not to mention the explosive lodged near his brain that would detonate if he left the palace.

Interestingly, his detention uncovered an unexpected ally. Nim had revealed their support during the fallout three days earlier. They took every measure to maintain Fenris's cover during his arrest, even creating a false infraction to justify his punishment. The chamberlain could have allowed Aludrien to kill Fenris on the spot, as the heir had initially intended. They could have taken Fenris to a more secure prison, removing him from Aludrien's staff indefinitely. Instead, they spirited him to the cellars with a believable narrative to await judgment. Nim had every intention of releasing Fenris and returning him to his duties.

The doors to the kitchens opened, and Elzia descended the steps, holding a tray.

"Didn't peg you as the rebellious type the way you scurry about the palace like a good little mouse."

"I forgot myself," he said, as meekly as possible, deciding to play along with the chamberlain's ruse. "This is my first position with a master of High Lord Aludrien's station. I won't make the mistake again."

Elzia chuckled. "Oh, you poor thing. I was merely teasing."

Fenris blushed in embarrassment. He hadn't spent much time with his bunkmate since their employment began and hadn't recognized her dry sense of humor.

Sliding the tray into the cell, Elzia sighed and leaned against the bars. Instead of the cold bowls of gruel from breakfast and lunch, the tray held a steaming hot plate of glazed hen, roasted potatoes, fresh greens, and a pair of rolls, along with a bowl of chocolate pudding.

"Is this from the master's dinner?" he asked incredulously.

"What the chamberlain doesn't know won't hurt them," Elzia said brightly. "Can't have my roommate starve to death down here, can I?"

"You're too kind," Fenris said, digging into his meal. "Though I'm not sure if you can continue smuggling Belessia's prized dishes without getting caught."

"Oh, they won't hold you here much longer," she said. "The heir is obviously using you as an example to whip his new staff into shape. I've seen this plenty of times before. Pick a servant at random, typically one who is quieter, charge them with a fake crime, and discipline them with an excessive punishment. With such a high turnover in the Emerald Pavilion, it was inevitable. So sorry it had to be you."

"Thank you," Fenris said with a mouthful of chicken. He had eaten so well in recent weeks that the cold gruel was the most challenging aspect of his punishment. "Who did they replace me with?"

"No one."

"But the High Lord needs a food taster."

"The chamberlain is completing your duties," Elzia explained. "As I said, you are meant to be an example. If they wanted you sacked or executed, they would have hired another food taster before breakfast. They may reinstate you before tomorrow evening, given the current circumstances. The chamberlain has had their hands full."

"With what?" Fenris asked, trying his best to avoid sounding overly concerned or curious.

"His Grace has invited his brother, Lord Basil, and his entire household for dinner tomorrow, along with the Chancellor and a famous general. The entire pavilion is abuzz. I heard the pair have been feuding since they were boys. I wish I were a serving girl; the dinner is bound to be dramatic."

"I see," Fenris said, his mind reeling.

Aludrien could not be that brash, could he? The heir wished for the court to know he was responsible for his brother's death. Without a skilled assassin, it would be impossible to strike promptly, and with his foes closing in on all sides, Aludrien was becoming desperate. Basil could not possibly decline a royal invitation, not if he valued his reputation.

With the greatest threats to his ascension in attendance, Aludrien could wipe out Basil, Barrett, and Vispin in a single blow. Such a ruthless and bold move would discourage any others from defying him. Brilliant. Heartless. Fenris thought Aludrien to be more cautious than this, but perhaps the pressure of the looming ascension had forced him to act out of character.

"I must return before Belessia drags me up herself," Elzia sighed. "Hopefully, you'll sleep more down here than in our harem of a room."

"You would think Tipin would run out of energy," Fenris chuckled.

"Oh, to be young and insatiable again," Elzia said wistfully as she departed.

Fenris sat alone in the dark, belly full of warm food, body wracked with dull pain, and head filled with the unspeakable. Aludrien was too monstrous to be allowed to live any longer. Given the chance for mercy and leniency, the heir chose violence and treachery. He did not deserve Fenris's protection, and he did not deserve life. If he acted fast enough, he could save Basil, whom he believed to be a better choice for emperor than Aludrien.

Sitting in silence, Fenris planned. He would finally accomplish what he had initially stayed in the palace for. He wouldn't wait any longer.

He would kill Aludrien and save the empire from another sadistic ruler.

10

Dinner Guests

Aludrien remained in his nursery for the rest of the evening and the better part of the following day. He pored over every variable of his scheme, devising contingencies for every possible scenario. Neurotic. Obsessive. Controlling. These were all traits his first tutor had used to describe him; she was currently teaching in a backwater orphanage in the southern wastes as punishment for her insolence. She wasn't incorrect, however, and Aludrien used these tendencies to remain ten steps ahead of his enemies.

With less than twenty-four hours to plan the first major battle of his ascension, he lost himself among the manicured flora. Only Nim was allowed entrance, strictly to deliver him meals and intel about the impending dinner with Basil. He stayed up late into the evening, his overactive mind depriving him of sleep.

His half-brother promptly accepted the invitation within hours, declaring that he, his mother, husband, and daughter would be delighted to dine with the heir. Vispin and Barrett responded with their acceptance letters soon after. The pieces were steadily falling into place.

The hours before dinner were a blur of preparations for the main event. Nim dutifully executed each of Aludrien's odd requests without question, wise enough not to challenge his authority.

Soon, night had fallen, and Aludrien donned an outfit fitting the occasion. Fine silk robes of maroon and gold flowed off his frame with abundant opulence. The extravagant fabric bore his lion insignia on almost every available inch. The final touch was the silver crown affixed to his head; he hadn't even worn it at his father's funeral.

He kept his guests waiting for twenty minutes before making his grand entrance, sweeping into the dining room with dramatic flair. The dinner guests promptly rose upon his arrival, although begrudgingly. They were clearly agitated by his tardiness. Frustration clouded judgment and weakened opponents. This dinner was a battle, one he intended to win.

"It delights me to host such an array of illustrious personalities such as yourselves," Aludrien said, taking his place at the head of the table. He waited a long, excruciating moment before signaling the others to take their seats.

The cupbearers promptly strode from their places along the walls and served the lords and ladies a rich Talus wine, Basil's least favorite. Chancellor Vispin, General Barrett, and Basil each brought their own cupbearer and food taster to the Emerald Pavilion, as was customary for such events.

General Barrett, a barrel-chested man with a ruddy face and a jovial smile, sat near the end of the table on Aludrien's left and raised his glass.

"A toast to our gracious host, heir to the throne of Xandria, Aludrien Aleksandran, may his reign be long and glorious,"

General Barrett proclaimed, although his tone was a little too arrogant for Aludrien's taste.

"May his reign be long and glorious," the others parroted.

Aludrien smiled and drank deeply, watching the others take tentative sips. Basil, who sat directly to his right, barely lifted the goblet to his lips, regarding Aludrien with an expression he once mistook for hatred. He now understood it as overwhelming terror.

The only guest who did not partake in the libations was young Magdolina, who was far too young to be served alcohol. Aged five or six, Aludrien wasn't sure and frankly didn't care; she was the epitome of a young royal. Back straight, hands folded neatly in her lap, chin held high and quiet as a mouse in her bright pink gown. Bitter memories of Aludrien's etiquette lessons flooded back to him, where a severe old hag of a tutor had beaten the whimsy and individuality out of him. Poor Magdolina's eyes squinted as she struggled to maintain her composure.

Aludrien broke the terse silence. As host, he was obligated to facilitate the conversation, and most of his guests were burdened by trepidation and confusion at the spontaneity of their invitations.

"I appreciate the sentiment, General Barrett," Aludrien said. "I hear you recently purchased an estate near Arachovia?"

"It's a magnificent property, Your Grace," Barrett said proudly, hesitating before adding the honorific. The confounding man had wormed his way into Hestraea's graces during Aludrien's childhood and never missed an opportunity to be condescending. "You are more than welcome to visit whenever you like. It will be helpful for you to see how an estate is properly managed."

"I am sure you are an excellent instructor. Though I wonder if you must obtain approval from my dear aunt before hosting guests."

Barrett clutched his goblet so tightly that his knuckles turned white. Aludrien hadn't intended to verbally spar with his aunt's vexing fuck puppet, but he found it immensely satisfying.

"No need. The last I checked, the surname on the estate is Barrett, not Aleksandran," Barrett said tersely.

Only the most ancient or most influential houses possessed estates in the homeland. The former inherited the land while the latter purchased or built villas outright. Maintaining an estate near Arachovia was impractical, as it lay at the far western edge of the empire; owning one was merely a symbol of status and power.

"The estate has an interesting history," Aludrien mused.

"Ah, yes," Vispin said, sitting directly across from General Barrett. Her lips upturned slightly, taking Aludrien's bait. "You purchased the villa from the Lady Seraphine. You must be ecstatic to claim one of the oldest mansions in the region."

Barrett clenched his jaw, and Ysuelt Seraphine glared at Vispin, barely containing her indignation. Aludrien studied the Chancellor, curious as to why she was so quick to side with him over the general. Perhaps she sought to curry Aludrien's favor.

According to palace gossip, House Seraphine had significantly fallen in recent years, hemorrhaging its fortune. Ysuelt's ill-fated affair with the emperor was only the beginning. Basil's adoption did little to rectify their low standing. The sale of their ancient seat of power to an upstart house was yet another testament to the Seraphines' decline.

"You are correct, Chancellor," General Barrett said. "Though the Lady Seraphine is always welcome."

"My son carries the surname Aleksandran, General Barrett," Ysuelt said icily, sitting tensely to Aludrien's right. "My place is at the Winter Palace."

"You are welcome to visit when you travel west for the ascension; we are a short airship ride away, as you know," General Barrett said smoothly.

Despite his proclivity for Hestraea, Barrett had earned a reputation as a philanderer. Aludrien considered it rather impetuous to be so forward in front of his lover's beloved nephew. Ysuelt's smile faltered slightly, and she nodded curtly.

"A lovely prospect, General Barrett, though I must first check my schedule for an invitation so far in the future," she said, noncommittally. Barrett deflated at the apparent rebuff.

"The ascension is in precisely sixty-nine days," Jareth offered. Aludrien raised an eyebrow, equally impressed and concerned that the answer had come to his brother-in-law with such ease. He thought he was the only one who obsessively dwelt on the timeline of his ascension.

Aludrien clapped his hands, signaling the first course, smoked trout with herb butter on a toasted brioche. The nobles ate delicately. General Barrett rambled on about various conquests on the battlefield with Lord Jareth, who sat stoically between him and Ysuelt. Jareth listened politely, though his eyes darted across the table to his husband. Normally, the life of any party, Basil ate in silence, shoulders hunched and despondent.

The main course came and went: roast venison with red wine and blackberry sauce, root vegetable purée, and buttered asparagus. Aludrien relied on his guests to continue the conversation, only speaking when asked a direct question. Vispin and Barrett grew restless as the night drew on, both expecting to hear Aludrien plead for their support. There would be no such conversation tonight. He reveled in the growing discomfort his silence created, leaving each of his guests to wonder the actual reason behind the invitation. Emotionally, he had positioned them exactly where he wanted. Soon, he would strike.

Finally, the third course arrived: a honey-and-almond tart with fresh berries and whipped cream. Predictably, Magdolina briefly forgot herself and tore into the sugary treat. Children were easy to manipulate. The brat cleaned the plate before the others had taken two bites. The adults ate with more trepidation, mouths twisted in a poor attempt to hide their aversion to the overly sweet dessert.

Aludrien didn't touch his plate.

"General Barrett, how do you like my tart?" Aludrien asked pointedly.

"Adequate, Your Grace," he said after a reluctant mouthful. Lie. "The cream is…unusual, though I cannot place the flavor. Must be some rare ingredient from the northern provinces. What is it called?"

"Vanilla."

Aludrien set an empty vial on the table with a snap. His guests furrowed their brows in confusion. His head swiveled to Ysuelt, who met his gaze. Her eyes darted from the vial to Aludrien's untouched plate to Magdolina's empty one.

Ysuelt gasped in sheer horror and leaped from her chair.

"You monster!" Ysuelt screeched, her face ruby red with rage.

"What is the meaning of this, Your Grace?" Vispin asked

incredulously.

The air around Ysuelt brightened with Animancy.

"Mother!" Basil cried.

Aludrien clapped his hands.

The doors behind him flew open, and a squadron of guards marched in, crossbows charged. Magdolina screamed. Jareth leaped to his feet, an insignis sword flowing from his forearm.

"I suggest you all sit, before we do or say anything we regret," Aludrien said.

This juncture was the crux of his scheme, with the highest potential for catastrophe. Magdolina and Jareth had the sense to sit; Ysuelt remained standing, though the air ceased its shimmer as she released her hold on the surrounding spirits.

"Lady Seraphine, I must say your outburst is entirely disrespectful. Please explain yourself," Aludrien said.

"Basil!" Ysuelt cried. "The charcoal! Magdolina needs it! It is in the vanilla!"

Basil wheezed, finally understanding Ysuelt's reaction.

Aludrien clapped his hands once more.

The vestibule door opened.

Nim led three servants from the antechamber, the guests' food tasters. All four bowed, keeping their heads lowered.

"Your lord asks you an imperative question. The penalty for lying to a royal is death. Do you understand?" Aludrien asked.

"Yes, Your Grace," they said in unison.

"Did you each taste from your masters' tarts?"

"Yes, Your Grace."

"How can we believe their testimony when you have weapons drawn on them?" Ysuelt screeched. "Moreover, you did not touch the dessert!"

"I selected this tart for our dear Magdolina, despite my distaste for almond and vanilla, but as a host, I prioritize my guests," Aludrien drawled. He brandished his spoon, cleaved a large portion, and swallowed it in one bite. He struggled to keep a straight face as the disgusting slop slid down his throat. "I hope this dispels any notion you may have of foul play, Lady Seraphine."

Ysuelt remained standing.

"You could have had a separate tart prepared."

"Help yourself to a charcoal pill if you'd like." Aludrien snapped his fingers, and Nim presented a silver tray with half a dozen obsidian pills. "Though please use my washroom if you do, I would rather not have you vomit on my rug."

"Lady Seraphine," Barrett said evenly. "What makes you so certain our host has poisoned us?"

"Yes, Ysuelt, I am curious to hear the reasoning behind such a bold and insulting accusation," Aludrien added.

Ysuelt remained silent; instead, she pointed to the empty vial on the table.

"Interesting," Aludrien mused. "For those of you who are unaware, this vial was involved in a recent assassination attempt against me. It once held a potent poison disguised as vanilla."

"Why present this now, Your Grace?" Jareth asked cautiously.

"The poison in question, as Lady Seraphine knows well, was belladonna," Aludrien explained. "And according to court records, your household, Jareth, ordered an alarming amount nearly two weeks ago."

"You bastard," Ysuelt seethed. Aludrien was surprised she hadn't attacked yet. Was it her refinement and high-quality breeding that prevented her from acting impulsively? Or was it the crossbows aimed directly at her, her son, and her granddaughter?

"Nim, how long has it been since you served the third course?" Aludrien asked.

"Approximately five minutes, Your Grace," the chamberlain responded.

"Ysuelt, tell the room how long it takes for belladonna to activate."

"I…I do not know such matters," Ysuelt stuttered, but the relief in her eyes betrayed her. Aludrien wasn't the only one who noticed.

"Mother," Basil hissed. "Stop lying, please. You're making matters worse."

"You must understand, my son," Ysuelt pleaded. Basil's apparent disgust caused her to falter and finally sit. "I only want what is best for you."

"Basil," Barrett said. "You were aware of these events, too?"

"No!" Ysuelt exclaimed. "Leave my son out of this. He had nothing to do with it. Only me."

"Lady Seraphine," Vispin said evenly, having remained still during the entire ordeal, observing the guests with an aloof curiosity. "Your words sound remarkably like treason."

"Enough!" Aludrien snapped, immensely satisfied by the admission. Before the night ended, the entire palace would know of Ysuelt's guilt. "Calm yourselves, no one has been poisoned this evening. Despite my desire to resolve the mystery of my assassination attempt, I invited you all here to celebrate."

"And what is the occasion, Your Grace?" Jareth asked.

Pulling out the second object hidden within his silken

pockets, Aludrien placed the ceremonial dagger on the table. A hush fell over the dining room.

"I apologize for the theft, Basil, but I took the liberty of obtaining this from your storeroom. I would have sent a formal request to your chamberlain, but I wished to surprise you. As I am to take my father's place, someone must become my heir. And though I cannot officially appoint one until my ascension, I will convey my intentions and symbolically regift this dagger to my intended heir: Magdolina Aleksandran."

A shocked silence befell his guests, and Magdolina's eyes bulged in surprise. Nim collected the dagger and gingerly presented it to her.

"Why?" Basil broke the silence.

"To repair the long-standing rift in our family, dear brother," Aludrien lied. "And of all the royals, Magdolina is the most auspicious choice for the future Empress."

"Lies!" Ysuelt hissed. "You are a liar, exactly like your father."

"Please do not judge me based on your former lover's actions," Aludrien said. He clapped once more, and Nim produced a scroll, which they handed to Basil, who cautiously inspected it. "My intentions are marked clearly in writing and reinforced with my seal and signature. When I ascend, Magdolina will become my heir apparent."

"Basil, do not—"

"Silence, mother! You have done enough," Basil shouted, turning to Aludrien apprehensively. "And how can I be assured this will not endanger my daughter further? How can I trust that you will not have us killed the moment we leave here tonight?"

"If I desired you and your family dead, you would have ingested a belladonna-laced tart. However, fratricide is particularly frowned upon, and my claim is stronger with you as an ally. And if all of this is not enough, I hereby promise to appoint your husband, Jareth Aleksandran, to the position of commander of my guard. With his military experience, he will be an excellent addition to my council. If it does not interfere with his duties as Vice Minister, of course."

Basil's mouth opened in disbelief. He remained silent momentarily, considering the shocking volley of Aludrien's revelations. He glanced at his husband, who returned his gaze with a short nod.

"I accept your terms," Basil said. "You have my full support. I will release an official statement tomorrow."

"Excellent," Aludrien beamed. The evening could not have gone any better.

"You foolish boy!" Ysuelt screamed. "I have given you everything, and still you throw yourself at the feet of that monster. He will swallow your entire family whole."

"You are the unreasonable one, mother," Basil said defiantly. "Your scheming endangered us in the first place."

Ysuelt shrieked and stalked toward the door, and Aludrien's guard raised their crossbows.

"Allow her to depart," Aludrien ordered. The door slammed behind Ysuelt. "I must report her crimes, though I will refrain until the morning as a courtesy to you to put your affairs in order."

"I appreciate that…brother," Basil said, eyes filled with hope. "I appreciate everything you have said this evening, more than you could know."

"Of course…dear brother," Aludrien said, the words tasted worse than the ruined tart, but the bastard must believe his sincerity. "This is what Father would have wanted."

That was the final blow. The last strike to seal the deal. Basil erupted into tears, and Jareth rushed to his side. Magdolina held the golden dagger in awe. Vispin and Barrett gaped.

With a single dinner, the greatest threat to his ascension was defeated, without a drop of blood spilled.

Satisfied, he dismissed his guests. Vispin and Barrett departed first, whispering to each other. They set out into the palace to fulfill the purpose of their invitation. Gossip. Before the sun rose, every royal and noble worth their salt would know Claude's sons had accomplished the impossible and settled their long-standing feud. With Aludrien's claim strengthened, many would flee to the hinterlands or fall in line as Basil had.

Only the Chancellor and his aunt's lapdog would attempt to gather Basil's hemorrhaging supporters, but it wouldn't matter. They would soon fall. He had briefly considered poisoning all of his guests, removing every obstacle in his path with a single stroke. But the court was sensitive; such a rash approach would only create martyrs and increase his enemies' hostility. No, he must proceed carefully in the days ahead.

"Magdolina, please thank High Lord Aludrien," Basil gently bade his daughter.

The child glided around the table and presented an immaculate curtsy. "Many thanks for the gracious invitation to your illustrious home and the delectable meal you shared. I am truly honored by your decision to name me heir. I will do my utmost to earn your respect and fulfill my duties."

Hearing such regal words come from such a juvenile source was jarring. Still, Aludrien's newly appointed successor was the height of nobility, having received the most rigorous training and education in the land.

"You will make me proud, Lady Magdolina," Aludrien said, not fully disbelieving his words. She would make a suitable pawn during his reign, a moldable sponge to protect his position of power.

"You have my thanks, as well, Your Grace," Jareth said. He bowed and shot him a smile that did not reach his eyes. The Minister was renowned for his steadfast nature and straightforward approach; if anything, the subterfuge of the evening had increased his distrust of Aludrien. "And I am honored to be at your service."

"Excellent," Aludrien said curtly. He did not deem it necessary to feign familiarity with the man. Both men knew the position was strictly political. "You may report to me starting tomorrow morning. We have much to do in the coming months."

"Yes, Your Grace," Jareth bowed, ushering his daughter from the dining room, leaving Aludrien and his half-brother alone.

"Thank you, Aludrien, truthfully. I knew my mother had her machinations, but I did not condone them. I have always desired to be friends, to support you in your ascension. I—"

Aludrien raised his hand. He needed to quell the bastard's desire for a meaningful connection.

"Remember that you serve at my pleasure. As quickly as I extended mercy to you and your family, I can take it away," Aludrien whispered. Basil's smile fell. "Am I understood?"

"Yes…Your Grace," Basil said stiffly. He bowed and exited swiftly.

Aludrien sighed in relief, finally alone. Completely elated. He had never had such an entertaining evening in his life. With Nim busy in the kitchens, he decided to retire for the evening. Further planning could wait until tomorrow. Tonight, he could rest easy, knowing he was one step closer to becoming a god.

Lounging in his favorite spot on the veranda, he stared out at the dark sea beyond, listening to the faint sound of powerful waves crashing onto the cliffs below the palace wall. Since he was a child, the water had soothed his nerves and comforted his overactive mind. Scanning the dark horizon, he marveled at the countless possibilities that hid in its depths. The veranda and the nursery were the only places of solace he found in his otherwise hectic and demanding life.

He had barely calmed his mind when a decisive knock at the door disturbed his musings. He sighed.

"Enter," he called, rising to meet Nim, who waited calmly in his chambers.

"My apologies for disturbing your respite, Your Grace," the chamberlain said, head hung low.

"If you were so regretful, you wouldn't have bothered me in the first place," Aludrien countered. "Speak. I assume whatever it is, it could not wait until the morning."

"Indeed, Your Grace," Nim said, revealing a thick stack of ornate envelopes. "Since your dinner concluded, we have received twenty-seven missives from various royals, nobles, ministers, and generals. I have taken the liberty of screening them for you."

"Positive or negative?" Aludrien asked.

"Overwhelmingly positive, Your Grace," the chamberlain beamed. "Most are requests for personal audiences, but a few are outright declarations of fealty. Three marriage proposals, too. Each petitioner was either a known supporter of your brother's claim or suspected of such. I presume we will receive ten times as many before first light."

"Gossip travels fast in this palace," Aludrien chuckled. "Faster than even I could have predicted."

"It is fully attributed to your complete victory, Your Grace. With Basil out of the picture, his staunch supporters have nowhere else to turn but your mercy. And with Lady Seraphine fully rebuffed, there is no one to rally the extremists."

"I assume Ysuelt has already fled the capital?"

"Of course. And three other families of note, far fewer than anticipated, though we shall see who else makes an unexpected departure in the coming days."

"Keep a close eye on Ysuelt. Tonight, I tore her family from her, which will make her dangerous."

"As you wish, Your Grace. Without your half-brother to sponsor, she is less significant, though I am curious to see who she will throw in with."

"As am I," Aludrien mused. "Her hatred extends to the entire house of Aleksandran, including my aunt, so I would presume she would turn to Chancellor Vispin. She has a penchant for collecting strays. We should eliminate her next. But for now, we must focus on solidifying my newfound support. Wait to respond to the letters until tomorrow; we do not want to seem too desperate to our new allies."

"Of course, Your Grace," Nim said. They hesitated, lips pursed apprehensively. "There is the matter of your food taster. He cannot rot in your cellars for much longer."

Aludrien scowled. Nim adopted a knowing expression that irritated him endlessly. Only one person could claim responsibility for this evening's absolute victory. Aludrien wouldn't have given such a strategy a second thought without

Fenris's recommendation. If Aludrien had his way, Basil would have become a martyr, galvanizing his most staunch devotees against him. Fear was an intense yet ephemeral motivator, only effective on the weak. Aludrien's claim to the throne was strengthened tenfold by listening to his deranged assassin. It made his stomach churn.

For the first time in his life, he had to admit to himself that he was wrong. That his strategy was not the most superior.

He loathed to admit it, but his path to success would include the volatile, overly sentimental Fenris.

"You are right, Nim," Aludrien said. "Have the insubordinate food taster, Pax, brought to me at once. I shall deal with him tonight."

"As you command, so I shall obey, Your Grace," Nim said apprehensively. Aludrien relished the look of trepidation on the chamberlain's face. He did not want to confess his appreciation of Fenris yet.

Aludrien carried the letters to his desk and examined them closely, writing each name in his ledger. He kept notes of every ally, enemy, and free agent in the war of ascension.

A door closed softly, and he looked up.

Fenris lurked near the veranda's entrance. His expression was placid, unreadable, and disturbingly calm.

"That was quick," Aludrien tutted. "Nim has been overeager as of late."

"Your chamberlain did not send me," Fenris said.

The walls surrounding them glowed brightly.

"Ah," Aludrien clenched his jaw and slowly stood. Fenris had entered from the veranda, not the hall. He had been here the entire time. "I loathe eavesdroppers."

"Congratulations on finally murdering your brother," Fenris hissed. His fingernails elongated into sharp claws. "One step closer to the throne without his claim, as you said. You must be elated."

"Misguided fool," Aludrien cackled, calling upon his insignis blades. The intricate tattoos on his arms roiled and pooled at his hands, pouring out and shaping into swords.

The simple misunderstanding was laughable, but conversation did not alleviate the murderous intent in Fenris's eyes.

Fenris pounced, claws outstretched.

11

Fickle Desires

Fenris waited until the beginning of dinner service to escape his cell, using his enhanced hearing to listen for Belessia's cue. The chains snapped, and the bars bent like butter. Rendering himself invisible, he crept through the pavilion. Aludrien's guards surged into the dining room, crossbows raised.

Ignoring his conscience, Fenris resisted the urge to charge in after them. He could not save Basil, but he would avenge him. So he made his way to the rear garden and climbed the exterior wall to the heir's veranda and waited.

And waited.

Nervous energy nearly overwhelmed him; his hands shook with anticipation when the door opened. Aludrien Aleksandran strode to the railing, smugly looking out over the inky expanse of water.

Fenris stalked toward him, prepared to strike. The heir's smile faded, revealing a strange expression of child-like wonderment. Aludrien, the epitome of poise and pompousness, marveled at the roiling sea as if he were a different person. More innocent, more idealistic, more...

Someone knocked at the door.

"Enter," Aludrien called, rising to greet his guest

Fenris hopped backward to avoid colliding with Aludrien as he glided across the veranda. Nim had already entered the royal apartment before the heir reached the door. Fenris stayed his hand; he wanted to avoid unnecessary casualties, especially the dutiful chamberlain.

So he waited, listening to their conversation intently through the glass. Their words only confirmed what Fenris had already suspected: Aludrien had eliminated Basil. His entire family was likely caught in the crossfire, including the innocent child, Magdolina.

Fenris's blood boiled.

Finally, Nim departed, and Aludrien retired to his desk. Hands trembling with rage, Fenris entered.

Aludrien looked up, unfazed by his arrival. The heir was nothing if not unflappable. Fenris constructed a veil around the room, as he had done before attacking the late emperor. No one would come to Aludrien's aid.

"Misguided fool," Aludrien spat, summoning his insignis blades.

Fenris charged the heir, claws drawn.

Aludrien's mystical swords twisted and stretched, deadly tendrils whipping through the air to strike at Fenris, but he dodged most of them with ease. Several found their mark, drawing blood, but did little to hinder Fenris's momentum. Within moments, he broke through the heir's defenses, his claws reaching for Aludrien's neck.

A ball of wind punched Fenris in the gut, sending him flying backward into his own ward. He fell to the floor, catching himself on all fours.

The moment he touched the ground, Aludrien unleashed a pillar of hot white flame. Calling upon the spirits within, Fenris summoned a second ward, narrowly shielding him from incineration. The attack persisted, and flames licked the thin barrier. Fenris groaned, blood trickling from the wound on his forearm. The spirits were too preoccupied with his pair of shields to heal his injuries.

Most Animancers could only focus the rach to complete one task at a time, and while Fenris could manage two summons simultaneously, three was beyond him. If he wanted to heal himself, he must either drop the outer ward and risk discovery or drop his inner ward and risk death.

But he did not need healing. Not yet. Nevertheless, he extinguished the smaller ward, dropping to the ground and rolling to the side. The beam of deadly light narrowly missed him and struck the outer ward.

Fenris launched his own gale, hitting Aludrien from the side; the heir stumbled backward and lost his footing. The blazing inferno evaporated.

Fenris lurched forward, using the distraction to close the gap. He was three paces from the heir before Aludrien regained his balance. The pair of insignis blades reformed into curved scimitars; Fenris's claws clashed against the solid metal, igniting sparks. The heir parried and retreated a few steps, but Fenris continued his onslaught, slashing with his vicious claws.

Their second fight was unlike their first. Fenris was faster, stronger, and angrier. Aludrien, conversely, seemed unwilling to land critical strikes. He parried and dodged, but offered no counterattacks. Which only enraged Fenris further.

Roaring, he struck at Aludrien's face, which one sword

easily blocked. In the same heartbeat, he savagely swiped the heir's other hand. With a surprised yelp, the blade flew across the room and clattered to the floor.

Lurching forward, Fenris tackled the heir to the ground, pinning his wrist with one claw and placing the other on his neck. He snarled victoriously, his nails drawing a rivulet of blood.

Aludrien smiled widely. He relaxed, relinquishing his grip on his remaining sword. He was enjoying himself.

Fenris pressed his claws harder, and more blood flowed. The smile widened.

"Have you accepted your fate?" Fenris asked. "Are you ready to face absolution?"

"Whatever for, Fenris?" Aludrien chuckled knowingly.

"Besides murdering your brother in cold blood? You will be more dangerous to the Xandrian people than even your father."

"You fool, I did not kill my half-brother."

"Liar," Fenris said. He had grown tired of the manipulative cretin.

"See for yourself," Aludrien nodded to the array of screens affixed to the wall.

Most displayed odd, choppy images of the dark palace grounds, but multiple showed Basil's private quarters.

Fenris exhaled sharply.

In the top left corner, Basil and Jareth leaned against their bed. Basil laughed as Jareth pulled him closer for a kiss. They were alive. But was this some trick of Animancy?

Aludrien struck.

A violent gust shoved Fenris aside. The heir grappled him and twisted savagely; his insignis blade poured over Fenris's wrists and punctured the floor beneath him, pinning his arms to the ground. Aludrien's fallen sword rattled and flew across the room, landing safely in his hand. He twisted the blade, laying the edge against Fenris's neck.

Fenris resisted, but Aludrien pressed his weight down, holding him in place. He leaned forward so that their faces were a hairsbreadth apart, and he smiled.

Once again, the heir had bested Fenris in combat.

Indignation fueled his rage, his heart pounded, his hatred blossomed, and the desire to tear into Aludrien's flesh overcame him. So strong it nearly scared him. The voices in his head screamed with unyielding fury. He had never felt so intensely about any of his targets before. The heir's hot, sweaty skin was inches from him, covering the large, tense muscles that held him in place.

Panting with exhaustion, Fenris stared into Aludrien's calculating eyes. The heir's calm gaze penetrated Fenris.

Fenris flushed slightly.

His rage had shifted into something he couldn't fully comprehend. It burned with passion, but it reminded him of lying in bed listening to Fukov and Tipin. It reminded him of the same feeling he had when he thought of Durian.

"If you weren't so rude, you would have known that I had sent Nim to fetch you moments ago, not to punish you. But to thank you," Aludrien said.

"What for?"

"For proving me wrong. Basil was never a threat. And he is more valuable to me alive than dead."

Fenris relaxed, his claws retracting. In response, the insignis blade that pinned his wrists loosened slightly.

Aludrien continued.

"At dinner, I exposed Ysuelt for her treachery, made amends with Basil by naming his daughter my heir, and asked his husband to be the head of my security. He willingly accepted. You were right."

Fenris stared upward, dumbstruck, unable to process the heir's story. For all the outrageous events Aludrien had revealed, what surprised Fenris the most was the sincere acknowledgment that the heir had taken his advice. He glanced back at the screen, which depicted Basil and Jareth undressing. The heir could be telling the truth.

"You—"

The desk behind them exploded.

Instinctively, Fenris broke from Aludrien's hold and twisted his body so he was on top of the heir. He sprawled over Aludrien, using himself as a shield. Flame consumed them, scorching his back. Aludrien screamed as the fire licked the top of his head. Fenris summoned the spirits within and swiftly constructed a ward around them, protecting them from the inferno. The air shimmered violently as the blast swept over them.

When the flames subsided, he dropped his second ward and examined Aludrien. His hair was singed, but he was still alive. Fenris had taken the brunt of the explosion, but his charred skin was already healing.

Dropping his outer ward, Fenris rolled off of Aludrien and collapsed on the floor beside him. Something clattered on the wood beneath him, and a sharp object dug into the fresh, sensitive skin on his shoulder. He caught his breath when he realized what the object was: the final pain receptor, dislodged from his neck by the explosion. He lay down on it, careful to keep it hidden from the heir.

His exterior ward had contained the blast within the study; the remnants of the desk littered the blackened room in ashen heaps.

Aludrien gazed over with a peculiar expression, and the odd heat returned to Fenris's cheeks.

"You are a fickle creature, Fenris," Aludrien panted. "You wish to kill me, protect me, kill me again, then save me. Which will it be tomorrow?"

"Depends," Fenris smiled. "On how much of an asshole you are."

"In that case, I'd better have Nim arrange my funeral," Aludrien chuckled.

Fenris laughed with him. His body had made the choice his mind could not. When Aludrien's life was at stake, he had instinctively decided to save it. Aludrien had admitted his faults moments before and eventually listened to reason. Fenris might have misjudged him, after all.

"And why the hell are the two of you laughing?"

Nim entered through the open doorway, flanked by a pair of distressed soldiers. The chamberlain placidly surveyed the ruined foyer, betraying only a hint of annoyance as they glanced between the ruined desk and Fenris.

The pair climbed to their feet, and Fenris snatched the charred receptor from the floor as he rose. In a fluid motion, he pocketed the device in his ruined robes, hoping neither Nim nor Aludrien would notice.

"Pax and I are merely relieved that we have survived another assassination attempt," Aludrien said. "Someone concealed explosives in my desk. Luckily, I managed to shield myself and my food taster. Guards, alert your captain and seal the gates. The perpetrator may still be on the premises."

The guards saluted and departed expeditiously, apparently too overwhelmed to realize they hadn't admitted Fenris into the heir's chambers that evening. Hopefully, they would forget or be wise enough not to pry further.

Nim remained, eyeing Fenris carefully. "So the two of you have made amends?"

"Our dear Fenris is not the assassin in this pavilion you should be worried about," Aludrien said, brushing the soot from his tattered robes. "Reinstate him as my personal food taster and focus your talents on uncovering the mysteries of this explosion."

"Of course, Your Grace," Nim said briskly. If they harbored any misgivings, they kept them concealed.

"You are dismissed," Aludrien said, turning to Fenris. His cold demeanor had melted slightly. "As are you. You should sleep; we have considerable work ahead of us if I am to survive until my ascension."

"Yes, Your Grace," Fenris bowed, his tone slightly less defiant than usual.

# # #

Standing impatiently outside her carriage, Lady Ysuelt stared at the palace's high spires, shining brilliantly in the distance. The waves crashed against the cliffs far below the country road, the carriage driver's lantern casting long shadows along the forest's edge.

The elk that drew the carriage unsettled Ysuelt. Such an antiquated mode of travel was beneath her, but she was in no position to complain. Her abrupt departure from the palace had prevented her from procuring passage on an airship.

Nothing could have prepared her for the sheer loss she suffered that evening. Her social standing in the court, her family's safety, and most bitterly, her son's trust. The scum Aludrien had outmaneuvered her most spectacularly; she would have been impressed if an uncontrollable rage hadn't consumed her every thought. Her son was Claude's firstborn and the rightful heir to the throne. Claude had promised her. He had made numerous promises and broken every last one. They were supposed to marry, she and Claude, a month before Basil was born. To join the ancient houses of Seraphine and Aleksandran.

Until that bitch arrived and stole Ysuelt's lover away.

Lady Jellia, Aludrien's mother. All hips and wit and grace. Within four days of arriving at court, the tramp stole Claude's affections entirely. Jellia robbed Ysuelt of her triumph and her goal of restoring honor to her house. Moreover, Basil's birth generated more scandal. A lady with a tarnished reputation and her bastard boy were sent to live out their days in the shadow of a radiant, legitimate heir.

Thankfully, Ysuelt did not have to wait long to seek her vengeance on Jellia; the upstart bitch was far too trusting and succumbed to belladonna. The rare poison had become Ysuelt's preferred method of removing obstacles from her path.

But the heir proved more shrewd than his mother, thwarting attempt after attempt. She had thought her newly hired assassin would finally succeed, but again, the cruel fates were ever against her and the Seraphine name.

"Did you receive any correspondence before our departure?" Ysuelt asked her chamberlain, a neurotic, wiry man who was positively trembling after tonight's events.

"Yes, My Lady," he said. "Chancellor Vispin sends her regards. I suspect she will arrange to speak with you once you have settled at the country estate."

"Desperate for more allies, I see," Ysuelt said. "Ever the opportunist, that one. However, I am not one to talk, given my current position. Any others?"

The chamberlain hesitated, eyes darting nervously into the shadowy forest. "No, My Lady, no others. And if you will forgive me, but I believe we should be on our way. These roads are not safe."

"Not yet," Ysuelt snapped.

Her chamberlain recoiled and joined the driver atop the carriage, leaving Ysuelt alone by the forest, anxiously waiting.

Hours had passed since her swift departure, and news of her crimes had undoubtedly reached the proper authorities. Every official within fifty leagues of the capital would be combing the countryside searching for her. If they caught her, they would arrest her, torture her, and execute her at the leisure of the wretched House Aleksandran. But she could not leave the capital before she attended to certain matters.

She knew this particular cliffside alcove well, only a league south of the capital. As the road was treacherous and ill-kept, merchants and migrants preferred the pristine highway half a league to the west. Few would be foolish enough to traverse such a perilous route in the dark of night. A perfect venue for a clandestine rendezvous.

A figure materialized from the darkness, features obscured by a billowing cloak. The elk grunted nervously, pawing the dirt with their hooves.

"What news of the Emerald Pavilion?" Ysuelt asked, disregarding pleasantries. Haste superseded politeness.

"The heir still lives," the figure said quietly, lingering at the forest's edge.

Ysuelt cursed.

"You have failed yet again," she snapped. "I fear I have paid you more than you are worth. How did Aludrien survive the explosion?"

"I believe someone is protecting him," the assassin said.

"Of course they are, you dolt!" Ysuelt scoffed. "Aludrien Aleksandran has the tightest security in the Imperium. You have worked there for weeks; you should have deduced that by now."

"You misunderstand me. I suspect there is another in the pavilion under the heir's control. One trained in the arts of death dealing. Their presence has impeded my efforts considerably."

"Ah, well, you are one of the most expensive killers this side of the Dragon's Teeth. I would assume a bit of competition wouldn't be difficult for you to overcome," Ysuelt said. "Were you seen leaving tonight?"

"Of course not," the assassin said indignantly. Ysuelt had struck a nerve.

"At least you have done something right this evening. Return to the Emerald Pavilion; your mission is not yet complete. I will be absent from the palace for the foreseeable future, but my associates will ensure your payments continue. Do not stop until Aludrien is dead."

The assassin nodded and stepped forward.

"You are dismissed," Ysuelt said. She sighed, dreading the arduous journey ahead.

The assassin took another step.

"Have you lost your hearing? You are dismissed!"

The cloaked figure continued their approach. A thin blade in the assassin's hand caught the moonlight.

Ysuelt called upon her insignis steel. A petty assassin was no match for a skilled fighter such as herself.

Her arms froze, held in place by an invisible force.

The night air gleamed around the assassin; any spirit within reach was under their control. She turned to call upon her chamberlain and driver, but both slumped over, throats slashed.

"You dare defy one of the blood?" She cried. "You are my servant! I am your mistress! I have already paid you a fortune!"

"Employer, yes. But you are not my true master," the assassin said. "Some things are more important than coin."

The last thing Ysuelt saw was a flash of silver as the kitchen knife plunged into her throat.

12

Respite

The height of summer had finally reached the capital, gripping the palace in a sweltering embrace. The swift pace of court life slowed to a lethargic halt. Courtiers wore silken garments and lounged in shaded alcoves in the gardens. Servants hurried along at their masters' sides, wrestling with absurdly oversized fans, trying to keep pace while producing a slight breeze. The central baths became a popular destination, where nobles lounged in calm pools of water, sipping refreshing iced wine and grazing on an array of frozen treats.

Chancellor Vispin spent most of her summer days soaking in the central baths' crystalline waters, her skin too fair to risk excessive sun exposure. Northerners melted in the capital's humid summers, and the emperor's chief bureaucrat was no different. She frequented a private pool, tucked away in a nook behind a pair of heavy pillars. The rest of the court granted her a wide berth out of a combination of respect and fear. Most days, she would arrive at her pool shortly after breakfast and soak until nearly dinnertime, conducting her business from the cool confines of the grotto.

Her guards defended the alcove, half a dozen strong, glaring at the half-naked bathers as they passed by. The air quivered slightly around them, betraying the telltale signs of defensive wards.

Fenris effortlessly evaded the feeble defenses.

He crouched in the far corner on the narrow marble lip separating the wall from the pool, observing his prey.

"Grand Marshal Hestraea has already decimated the insurgents in the northern territories and is quelling the rebellions on the crystal coast as we speak." General Barrett said. Surprisingly, the bear of a man was one of the Chancellor's most regular guests. He spent most of their meetings trying to convince her to support Hestraea's claim. But Vispin was savvy and not so easily swayed. She listened and asked questions, but remained neutral, still considering her options.

The gossip around the palace suggested their blossoming friendship began after Aludrien's dinner party. A fact that enraged the heir. His two greatest threats joining forces would prove disastrous.

"The barbarians are of little concern to me," Vispin said, leaning against the pool's edge. "Open rebellion is not difficult to suppress. The whispers coming from the eastern cities, however..."

"Ah, you mean Raephina, Kyriak, and Lapis?"

"Their governors have met seven times since the royal funeral," Vispin said, her tongue flicking across her thin lips in irritation. The nervous tic explained why she had earned the moniker "viper."

"Oh, they would sooner invade one another before aligning against the Imperium," Barrett scoffed. "Their people have been warring for centuries."

"A power vacuum is a potent motivator to disregard an ancient foe," Vispin countered. "If the three decide to merge their military might, the surrounding cities would be sure to surrender. An independent nation could form overnight, so close to Arachovia. A terrifying possibility."

"Which candidate do they support?" Barrett asked. In private, the general dropped the boisterous facade to reveal a much more cunning demeanor.

"Unclear, though I am certain their allegiance will come to light before the ascension."

"Any news from Lady Seraphine? I haven't heard a single whisper."

"Unfortunately not," Vispin said. "My sources say she never reached her country estate. It is safe to assume Aludrien has exacted his revenge sooner than expected."

"Which would complicate his tenuous relationship with Basil. Can you believe the boy dared to promote Jareth to the head of his security?"

"It is genius," Vispin said. "Unifying the royal family and consolidating support from members of my government. Aludrien is more shrewd than I gave him credit for; his scheme has been more effective than if he had placed Basil's entire family under house arrest. It is safe to conclude Claude's firstborn son will remain out of play."

"Indeed. Which leaves only two credible candidates," Barrett said.

"Hestraea has publicly denied any interest in the throne," Vispin said.

"Most of the military is already behind her," Barrett said eagerly. "She would certainly change her tune if she gained the government's support."

"Hestraea's recent victories are strengthening her standing," Vispin admitted. "While the heir schemes and remains hidden within the confines of the Emerald Pavilion, the Grand Marshal is on the front lines, maintaining peace and order. But I believe her virtue is too pure to turn on her beloved nephew."

"Fifty-two days until the ascension," Barrett said. "Ample time for the winds to shift. We both know which direction is preferable. And I don't know about you, but I would rather there be a single option on the day of the ascension, for the good of the empire."

"You may have a point," Vispin said. "It would provide a smoother, more peaceful transition."

"And I can personally assure you that Hestraea would have no intention of replacing you as Chancellor. Something I can't say about Aludrien. Hasn't he rejected every request for a private audience, even while you hold the reins to his government? That does not seem promising for your future in the court."

Vispin bristled.

"And your motivations for supporting Hestraea's claim are entirely noble and have nothing to do with the fact that an Empress needs an official spouse by Imperial law, and you just so happen to be her bedfellow. How many times have you proposed to the Grand Marshal? Six?"

Barrett glowered, his face crimson.

"Watch yourself, Vispin. My personal feelings for Hestraea are completely separate from my confidence in her future leadership."

"Your station, pedigree, and intimate relationship with

the would-be empress would undoubtedly make you the most logical and auspicious choice. I would call the gesture romantic if it didn't result in you becoming one of the most powerful players at court, inches from the throne. With your faint Aleksandran blood, you could very well have a strong claim to the throne if anything should tragically befall Hestraea."

"I didn't know you thought so poorly of me, Vispin. That I would kill the woman I love?"

"Your integrity is not on trial. I am merely discussing my observations and potential scenarios; that is all. Do you deny considering that possibility?"

Barrett's expression grew dark.

"If you insist on speaking of choices, would you rather have me, or that petulant brat on the throne?"

"I cannot fault your logic," Vispin said.

Barrett beamed fiendishly and pulled himself from the water, flopping onto his towel, and promptly wrapped himself to cover his nudity. "I knew you would see my side, eventually. In that case, we should accelerate my agenda."

"We must tread carefully, General Barrett," Vispin warned. "I have not survived this long by acting brashly. I only strike when I know I can hit my target. And I must still consider the Imperium's options."

Barrett glowered, unable to mask his growing frustration at Vispin's apprehension.

"The longer you wait to make a decision, the greater the chance someone else will make it for you. Remember that Vispin."

The Chancellor sighed and fully submerged in the water as the lord departed. Fenris observed her do so after more tense conversations, but out of every meeting he had spied upon, this was by far the most incendiary. Most of her audiences were uneventful, filled with pleasantries, subtleties, and empty promises.

Barrett wanted Aludrien dead, and soon. And Vispin was leaning in his direction.

Fenris resisted the urge to dispatch a lightning bolt into the pool or dive in to slit her throat. Such an act would be too conspicuous, and he desperately wanted to avoid a fourth incarceration. Besides, he preferred to relay the crucial information to Aludrien before acting rashly. It was odd to ignore his innate instincts. His time in the palace had taught him patience and tact while significantly curbing his natural impulses. The heir's tendencies were rubbing off on him. The thought made him sick.

However, his working relationship with Aludrien had improved substantially since Fenris saved his life, though the heir's innate desire for control remained. Fenris still loathed the pompous brat and everything he represented, but at least the heir had ceased being actively hostile to Fenris. Small victories.

Before Vispin resurfaced, Fenris crept out of the grotto, maintaining his invisibility. Tiptoeing past the useless guards and wards, he ducked into the main baths.

A sizable crowd had gathered in the furthest pool, laughing boisterously. General Barrett was floating at its center, telling some off-color joke. The suave, brawny man was the epitome of a socialite, filling his days with luncheons, tea, parties, and lavish balls. His hectic and fluid schedule made him unpredictable and difficult to stalk. Gregarious and infectious, the general effortlessly swayed courtiers to join his cause, even in Hestraea's absence. According to Aludrien, Barrett acted without his aunt's blessing. Fenris was not so sure.

Returning to the Emerald Pavilion as the sun set below the high palace walls, Fenris completed his dinnertime duties. The heir's meal was free of poison, as every meal for the past seventeen days had been. Aludrien's victory over his brother had awarded him some respite from the bevy of assassination attempts. It also allowed Fenris more time to investigate his enemies.

Fenris's instinctive reaction to save Aludrien from the explosion was a turning point in his perception of the heir. Behind the domineering facade lay a more understanding and reasonable individual, one capable of leading the empire into a new, peaceful era. He had entered the heir's chambers that night under the assumption that he had murdered his brother in cold blood, realizing that Aludrien had listened to reason had changed everything.

The night of the explosion, Fenris had snuck to the outer wall, under the veil of invisibility, and looked out onto the dark, roiling Cellicean Sea. Without the pain receptor, he could jump into its waves and flee, far from the backstabbing court. For a moment, the prospect tempted him, as did the louder voices in his head. Standing above the sea for a second time, his freedom within his grasp. And yet again, he chose to remain. Tossing the broken receptor off the ledge, he returned to his quarters, adamant in his resolve to fulfill the Meridian's goal and cull the empire of any ruler that would harm it.

He would remain at the heir's side until the ascension and eliminate any threat to the masses. Aludrien granted him access to purge the palace of corruption, and he could not refuse it. And once they reached the ascension, he could deal with Aludrien as promised.

When Fenris was summoned for the heir's nighttime snack, the stifling humidity had broken into a torrential downpour. Heavy droplets pattered on the rooftops, cascaded off the eaves, and pooled into the gardens below. Servants ran between covered walkways, clothes drenched by the downpour. Fenris found the summer storm oddly calming.

The newly refurbished foyer was empty when Fenris arrived, as was the soaked veranda beyond, though the windows were open to allow in the cool, wet breeze. Fenris waited for a few silent moments before entering Aludrien's bedchamber. Since the storms had begun, the heir had taken his nightly snack there. A berry tart sat on the table near the window, but Aludrien was nowhere to be seen. Regardless, Fenris sat by the window and awkwardly waited.

Then he heard it.

At first, the noise was muffled, coming from behind the bathroom door. Fenris focused his hearing with curiosity. A voice, distinctively Aludrien's, cried out in pain. Fenris sprang to his feet, heart racing.

He traveled two paces before he stopped in his tracks. His face flushed.

Aludrien was not distressed; quite the opposite. Moans of pleasure echoed from the baths. The lewd sounds grew louder. Aludrien was surprisingly high-pitched; his cries sounded hungry, insatiable, and borderline submissive. His groans synced with the familiar clapping of flesh against flesh. The pace quickened.

Fenris backed away, embarrassed, his face on fire. He hadn't thought the heir capable of such sounds. They were ravenous and compliant, which strangely excited Fenris.

A deep grunting echoed from the bath. He was intimately familiar with the second voice, as it woke him nearly every morning. Fukov.

An odd sensation rose from his chest. Jealousy.

The carnal sounds grew to a crescendo, and Fenris tried everything in his power to focus on the rain outside. He thought he was desensitized by the sounds of fucking, though for some reason he could not control his lust as he eavesdropped on Aludrien being plowed by his servant. He was repressed after months of celibacy.

Finally, Aludrien cried out, a high, sweet sound that made Fenris's heart stop. Silence. Eventually, the door opened, and Fukov exited, his livery disheveled. Fenris gawked, incredulous. How did the man retain his stamina after fucking Tipin multiple times a day?

Fenris finally understood why Aludrien hired such a burly specimen as his bath attendant. His roommate possessed talents that transcended cleaning, which Fenris seriously doubted Fukov ever performed.

Fukov smirked smugly as he departed, and Fenris was strangely overcome with the desire to tear out his throat.

Aludrien exited shortly after, fresh-faced and beaming with satisfaction, his chest exposed through his silken robe. His intricate insignis tattoos obscured his otherwise smooth skin.

"Apologies for the tardiness," Aludrien said, joining Fenris at the table. "Alexei was a bit more thorough this evening."

"No worries," Fenris stammered, staring awkwardly at the tart.

Aludrien paused and examined Fenris. Such deference was out of the ordinary, and the heir's greatest skill was sensing weakness in others and extorting it.

"Ah," Aludrien said, his gaze lingering on Fenris's flushed cheeks. "Does such lewdness make you uncomfortable?"

"I've seen my fair share of cock, if that's what you mean," Fenris said, deciding bluntness was the best way to diffuse the tension. "I'm simply not used to them being flaunted so frivolously like they are in the capital."

"So you are simply a prude?" Aludrien teased.

Fenris bristled. "No. I find certain activities more enjoyable when they stay private. But it seems like you wanted the entire palace to hear, the way you were shrieking like a dying cat."

"So you are a romantic at heart?"

"Is that so bad?"

"A sentimental and soft heart is destined to be broken."

"At least I have one."

Aludrien's smile widened, and Fenris immediately regretted his response. The more he insulted the heir, the happier Aludrien became. Fenris suspected ridicule was how he received and showed affection. Fenris would have to restrain himself in the future, lest he appease the spoiled brat too much.

"I shall remember to be more mindful of the noise in the future. Or would you like to join us?"

Fenris choked. Aludrien regarded him with an indistinct expression. Fenris wasn't sure if the invitation was sincere or a way to provoke him. He held his gaze, refusing to glance at the heir's exposed chest. He found it rather impressive.

Thankfully, Aludrien broke the silence.

"Discussing my sexual proclivities is not the reason for this audience. What news do you bring from the central pavilion?"

Fenris swallowed, thankful for the change in subject. He

detailed his findings meticulously, careful to include every last detail, as the heir preferred. Aludrien listened patiently, hanging onto his every word with intense interest. He nearly lost his composure when Barrett's personal machinations for the throne came to light. Once the report was complete, the heir paused briefly before speaking to ensure Fenris had expunged every morsel of information.

"So," he said. "Our respite is finally over. When do you estimate Barrett will strike?"

Fenris hesitated. After two weeks, the respect the heir displayed surprised him. It had become clear that saving his life had softened Aludrien's hard edges, and after the success with Basil, he valued Fenris's insight and opinion.

"Soon, I fear," he said. "Barrett already has schemes in motion, and Vispin is on the verge of falling in his direction."

"And how do you suggest we continue?" Aludrien asked.

"We strike first. Vispin will be a difficult target, but not impossible. Her apartment's security vastly outmatches Basil's. I still haven't been able to infiltrate it, so I suggest another approach. She is most vulnerable in the baths. However, the method presents an issue. I could poison the water, but the baths are drained daily and inspected; moreover, that would require multiple exposures over a long period, which we do not have. I could use Animancy, but her guard would detect me."

"And it must be impossible to implicate me," Aludrien added. "Any royal or noble is fair game in this war, but if anyone discovers that the heir to the throne murdered the Chancellor? That could mark the end of my dynasty."

"We could start with Barrett," Fenris suggested. "He threatens both you and your aunt. Vispin remains neutral and is less of an immediate threat. If the Grand Marshal garners the government's favor, it would solidify her claim. But if you removed Barrett from the equation, Vispin would be easier to persuade. She's already sent invitations for a private audience with you. He's more careless and less guarded than the Chancellor and drinks too much; I could stop his heart, and most would believe it to be by natural causes."

Fenris was reluctant to cause more casualties, but after weeks of surveillance, General Barrett made many of Fenris's previous targets seem virtuous in comparison. The Imperium would be safer without a man like that. Eliminating monsters was his goal, after all.

"Such a move would cause Vispin's security to double, as she would remain my only threat," Aludrien countered. "Though you might be on the right track with Barrett. We could sway Vispin, but the general is too stubborn to relinquish support for my aunt. Not if he ultimately desires the throne for himself. The Chancellor is an opportunist. It is easy to manipulate such a person. We could use his death to weaken Vispin."

"Or use him as a scapegoat," Fenris suggested.

Aludrien smiled. "I like the way you think."

Fenris's stomach flipped slightly, ashamed by how much he enjoyed receiving such praise. Was the heir corrupting him?

"So I should start with Barrett?"

Aludrien shook his head. "Continue to spy on both Barrett and Vispin until we devise our next course of action. I must converse with Nim."

"As you wish," Fenris said, fidgeting nervously. Patience wasn't his strong suit, and that virtue was next to godliness in the Emerald Pavilion. "Now that you mention Nim, have they gained any ground on their investigation?"

"Ah, yes," Aludrien smiled. "I almost forgot. The explosive device was created in the palace, tracing back to Ysuelt. Nim believes that whichever servant was responsible for the vanilla incident is also connected to the explosion."

"That's a disturbing theory."

"Quite. And it is only the tip of the spear, I'm afraid," Aludrien sighed. "Whoever planted the explosives managed to circumnavigate powerful wards. We fear they may be an Animancer of remarkable skill who rivals your own."

The heir punctuated the sentence with a deliberate pause. Fenris waited for him to continue before realizing the insinuation.

"The rogue assassin," Fenris said. "I told you I did not know them."

"And I did not suggest you did," Aludrien said, suspiciously. "Ysuelt wished my father dead more than anyone in the capital. She may have hired the other assailant the night of my father's death and installed that very person in my staff. However, this is all conjecture."

"Has anyone gone missing since that night?" Fenris asked.

"No," Aludrien grimaced. "This assassin remains in our midst. An unsettling prospect."

"I can try to uncover the culprit," Fenris offered.

Aludrien shook his head. "No, that isn't necessary. Ysuelt is dead. Without a mistress, her minion will not strike until they find another master. Nim is handling the investigation, and I require your full attention on my living adversaries. Though I am curious to know who killed Ysuelt."

"Vispin suspects you were responsible."

"Of that I am painfully aware. I have lost a great deal of

support due to that theory. And I fear it may fracture my truce with Basil."

"Minister Jareth seems to be a great addition to your council," Fenris offered.

"Someone in that household had to be competent," Aludrien scoffed. "But you are correct, he has proven to be an asset. He seems to enjoy the work, too."

"Small blessings, I suppose."

"Indeed."

A curt knock on the door halted their conversation.

"Enter, Nim," Aludrien called.

The chamberlain bowed graciously upon their arrival, scowling upon seeing Fenris. Unfortunately, the trajectory of his favor with the chamberlain starkly contrasted with Aludrien's. Nim seemed irritated at Fenris's presence, seemingly indignant that a lowly assassin was quickly becoming a trusted advisor to their master. Fenris smiled graciously, for he had no wish to incur the wrath of the chamberlain. Nim would prove to be a terrifying foe.

"If you will forgive me, Your Grace," the chamberlain began. "But the news I bring is sensitive."

"Fenris will stay," Aludrien said sternly. Fenris swallowed hard, ignoring Nim's annoyed expression. "In fact, I am glad I have you both. Fenris informed me of some fascinating news. Barrett is on the move. I believe he will strike within the week. I am increasingly concerned that Vispin is aligning herself with my aunt's claim. However, I want you to assess her connection with Barrett and determine if she has any weaknesses that can be exploited or leveraged. She may prove to be a more useful ally than an enemy. Use whatever means necessary, as you usually do. By tomorrow, I want to know if we can drive a wedge between them. Am I understood?"

Nim's lips twisted, resisting another scowl.

"May I speak freely, Your Grace?"

"If you must."

"I must," Nim said. "Vispin may be the most dangerous individual in the Imperium. I would not underestimate her lightly."

"The chamberlain may have a point," Fenris said, producing a slight scowl from Aludrien and a raised eyebrow from Nim.

"Moments ago, you said she would be easier to persuade. I am exploring this option based on your recommendation," Aludrien said skeptically.

Fenris swallowed hard. In his spontaneous attempt to support Nim, he ended up contradicting himself.

"Compared to Barrett, perhaps. But I've seen how she operates. She's almost as ruthless as you, so I'd be careful if you want to bring her into the fold."

"Thank you both for your candor," Aludrien said, rubbing his temples in irritation. "I still expect your report tomorrow evening, Nim."

"As you wish, Your Grace," Nim bowed, regarding Fenris with a softer expression. Fenris hoped his open support would keep him in the chamberlain's good graces.

"I haven't forgotten that you came here with news. What is it?"

"Of course, Your Grace. How foolish of me. I received a missive this evening that requires your immediate attention," Nim said. They revealed an envelope, seal already broken, and presented it to Aludrien.

The heir hesitantly opened the letter, reading its contents methodically. A grimace marred his otherwise handsome face. He reread it, gripping the paper.

"Are you certain this letter is not a forgery?" he asked in a whisper.

"Yes, Your Grace."

"Lovely," Aludrien groaned. "This complicates matters."

"And how would you like me to respond, Your Grace?" Nim asked delicately. They knew better than to test the heir's temper.

"Obviously in the affirmative. I dare not decline," Aludrien snapped, reading the letter once more. "Disregard my previous orders, respond immediately, and begin preparations."

"Of course, Your Grace," the chamberlain bowed and scurried away.

Fenris waited in silence as Aludrien read the letter a fourth time; a smirk formed.

"Do I dare ask what fresh hell this letter has brought us?" Fenris finally asked, realizing the heir wouldn't answer without prompting.

"A most formidable opponent has forced my hand," Aludrien replied. "Chancellor Vispin has invited me for a luncheon three days hence."

"How is this different from her other daily invitations?" Fenris asked, perplexed.

"This one includes a threat," Aludrien said grimly. "One I cannot ignore. We must prepare for our audience with the Chancellor."

13

Lessons for a Ruler

Aludrien sighed and leaned back in his chair, staring at the empty wall behind his new desk. His chief engineer had assured him that the state-of-the-art surveillance screens would take months to replicate. Time that he did not have. With only forty-nine days until his ascension, more than halfway to the grand ceremony, time quickened as surely as his enemies multiplied.

"Do you have an update on the rat skulking about my pavilion?" Aludrien asked.

"Nothing new, I'm afraid," Nim replied, stationed near the window, stiff as a rod. "I still have my suspicions that Lady Ysuelt's assassin was not only responsible for both the vanilla and explosive incidents, but remains under your employ."

"So you have said, repeatedly," Aludrien sighed. "But with their mistress missing and presumed deceased, what would keep them here? Without payment, I would assume any assassin worth their salt would be halfway across the empire by now."

"An agent of such a caliber placed in a critical position would not be in want of another generous donor. I suspect their employment has transferred to another rival or one of Ysuelt's associates."

"Do you still believe they could be the same assailant spotted in my father's chambers? Was Ysuelt the other party who had wanted my father dead?"

"A strong possibility, Your Grace," Nim said. "But without Ysuelt to question, the truth of such matters will prove difficult to uncover."

"What say you, Lord Jareth?" Aludrien glanced at the far wall where his newly appointed commander was stationed. "You were intimately involved in your late mother-in-law's social life."

"Basil has inquired with her network, Your Grace. Anyone of note or means has either fled the capital or enthusiastically announced support for you and your new heir. Though I doubt any of them are capable of maintaining an assassin, I'll send your chamberlain a list by this evening," Jareth replied evenly.

"I am happy to give you and your husband something to discuss," Aludrien quipped. "I understand marriages of your length tend to grow stale."

He waited for a reaction, but none came. Jareth remained at his station, his expression neutral.

Aludrien clenched his jaw in frustration. The decorated general and vice minister was a consummate professional; no matter which button Aludrien pushed, Jareth ignored it and carried on. Even as Aludrien dredged up Ysuelt's death, Jareth remained unflappable. Aludrien prided himself on his innate ability to find anyone's weakness and get under their skin. But Jareth was nearly impenetrable. He was such a bore.

"Very well," Aludrien said, deciding to end his efforts at provoking Jareth. "Though I find myself agreeing with your assessment. Whoever hired Ysuelt's agent must be an important player. And if they are possibly responsible for her disappearance, you and your family may be in danger as well."

"Basil has tripled our apartment's security, Your Grace," Jareth said. "Your heir is protected, I assure you."

"Though you must be concerned with most of your time spent here," Aludrien said. Jareth had quickly proven to be an invaluable asset, almost as efficient as Nim. During his short tenure, the former general had thwarted half a dozen assassination attempts before they reached the pavilion. Satisfying him was essential. "Would you consider moving your family to the Emerald Pavilion?"

"We wouldn't dream of imposing in such a manner, Your Grace," Jareth said, his eye twitching slightly.

Aludrien smiled, finally victorious at eliciting a response.

"Nonsense," Aludrien scoffed. "You are family. And more importantly, this pavilion belongs to Magdolina after I ascend. It may ease the transition for your daughter."

"With all due respect," Jareth said, his fist clenched ever so slightly. "This is the last place I would want my daughter to live. Especially with a known assassin masquerading as a servant or guard."

Aludrien balked. Ironically, he had finally provoked Jareth while attempting to placate him. The man's greatest weakness was his daughter. Aludrien would make sure to remember that for later.

"Of course, how foolish of me," Aludrien said hastily. "I merely mentioned it so you could be closer to your family. We can discuss it later, when we have routed out the rat."

"As you wish, Your Grace," Jareth said, bowing deeply.

Nim raised an eyebrow. Aludrien didn't blame them; he wasn't known for being so amenable. Was he growing soft?

"Speaking of rats," Aludrien said, sharply turning to Nim. "Three days have passed without much word. What have you discovered about General Barrett and Vispin's relationship?"

"As I suspect, the general was secretly instrumental in Vispin's rise to power," Nim said. "And in turn, she has been most generous to him and his interests since becoming Chancellor. I sincerely doubt he would ever turn on her."

"If Vispin supports him, nothing will stop my aunt from becoming Empress. She is a devout traditionalist and would marry Barrett to retain our family's honor. Little will prevent him from murdering her for a chance at the throne," Aludrien said.

"We have scouted his private quarters and thoroughly observed his daily patterns. We can execute an operation at your word," Nim said, intentionally leaving out Fenris's name. Jareth did not need to know Aludrien's food taster was also a skilled assassin. Avoiding unnecessary questions would be best for all parties.

"Excellent," Aludrien said. "Hold off until after today's luncheon. I have yet to decide who is a greater threat between Vispin and Barrett."

"As you wish, Your Grace," Nim said, hesitating.

"Speak your mind," Aludrien said.

"Is it wise to have accepted her invitation?" Nim asked. "If she is as dangerous as you suspect, what would prevent her from striking when you are in her domain?"

"I agree with the chamberlain, Your Grace," Jareth interjected. "Such an occasion seems particularly treacherous.

Even if Vispin has not laid a trap, word of your luncheon has spread through the palace. You haven't left the Emerald Pavilion since your father's funeral. Your enemies may use this opportunity to strike."

"Your concerns are appreciated, but unnecessary," Aludrien said, standing. "I welcome any overt challenge. It presents me with the opportunity to retaliate justifiably. I hope some of my enemies rear their heads today so I can cull the herd."

He waved his hand, concluding the audience, and retired to his chambers to prepare for the luncheon.

Soon, Aludrien left the Emerald Pavilion with his entire retinue in tow. Jareth on his right, Nim on his left, a dozen servants, including Fenris, trailing behind. Three dozen guards surrounded the procession, heavily armed and marching perfectly in sync.

With his crown affixed to his head and his most expensive robe glinting in the sunlight, he strode into the palace. Inhaling deeply, he marched through the trimmed gardens with a satisfied grin. Courtiers and servants halted in their tracks, falling on their knees in reverence. Excited whispers followed him as he went; since his guard obscured his view, he could only imagine the look of awe on their faces. The very thought exhilarated him. Over a month had passed since he left the confines of his home, and he had sorely missed the attention.

Although Chancellor Vispin dwelt within the central pavilion with the other courtiers, her quarters rivaled the Emerald Pavilion in their splendor. The leader of the empire's government inhabited an entire wing, complete with an expansive inner courtyard.

Upon arrival, the Chancellor's staff escorted Aludrien and

his entourage through her home directly to the lavish garden. A central dining pavilion sat in the center of an elegant array of topiaries and fountains. The table was already occupied. Aludrien smiled as he strode to meet his host, who sat impatiently at the table's center. Oddly enough, she was alone. Aludrien had assumed several of her more trusted ministers would attend such a momentous meeting. However, the Chancellor had intended the luncheon to be a private affair. Curious, indeed.

He had intentionally arrived three-quarters of an hour late, using the same tactic he deployed at his banquet. Vispin's expression remained placid as she rose and bowed, but her twitching eye betrayed the rage she all but expertly concealed. She was livid with his tardiness.

"High Lord Aludrien Aleksandran, you honor me and my house. I serve at your pleasure," Vispin said, mirthlessly. Although the greeting was perfectly acceptable, her tone lacked any of the hospitality her words promised.

"Vispin," Aludrien said, unceremoniously sprawling into the nearest chair. As heir, he outranked her and thus could greet her however he saw fit. His lack of respect was intended to cut deep, and judging by the throbbing vein on the Chancellor's forehead, he had succeeded.

He tried his best not to smile. Oh, how he enjoyed this game.

"It is unorthodox for an heir to refuse a chancellor's summons. One would think an heir would have a vested interest in the governing of their empire," Vispin said. "I must admit, I was surprised to hear you responded to my latest invitation, much less positively, after so many rejections."

"More important matters required my concentration, and

with them sorted, I can finally give you the attention you deserve," Aludrien lied. They both knew why Aludrien had finally come. But he needed to lay more groundwork before discussing the threat.

"When did you leave the safety of your pavilion last? Your father's funeral?" Vispin asked.

"Astute observation," Aludrien said, amused by the pitiful attempt to rattle him. The Chancellor was unaware of the disdain he harbored toward his late father. She would have to do better than this to best him. "Have you been stalking me, Vispin?"

"As the leader of the government, I have a vested interest in the future ruler of the Imperium. Whoever that may be. Succession is such a volatile affair, and there are so many qualified candidates this time around."

"Fewer by the day," Aludrien noted, glancing at Jareth.

Vispin followed his gaze, her lips curling into a cruel smile. "Ah, you must be referring to poor Ysuelt. How odd that she disappeared the night of your dinner. The same night that you declared her granddaughter your heir and her son-in-law as your head of security. Do you find that strange, Lord Jareth?"

Aludrien held his breath, unsure of how the man would respond. Vispin would smell blood in the water if Jareth's allegiance faltered even slightly. He currently held the position of Vice Minister of War, after all, with supposed allegiance to the Chancellor. She could twist his words into rumors that would shatter Aludrien's tenuous alliance with his half-brother in a matter of days.

"I have a mind for the battlefield, Your Imminence," Jareth replied. "Virtues such as scheming, plotting, and backstabbing are best left to politicians, such as yourself."

"Family is of the utmost importance, Vispin," Aludrien said. "As a provincial who clawed her way to the top, I would not expect you to understand."

The insult was a cheap shot, lacking originality or flair, but it proved effective nonetheless. Inch by inch, he dismantled her meticulous facade.

"Your candor is appreciated, Your Grace," Vispin said, her voice quivering ever so slightly. "In the spirit of honesty, I am surprised an impertinent brat who creates an enemy every time he opens his petulant mouth has survived this long."

Aludrien grabbed the empty chalice in front of him and brandished it at Vispin.

"My throat is parched," he said. "I must say, your talents for entertaining leave much to be desired."

Vispin's eyes narrowed.

"No matter, I brought my own wine," Aludrien clapped, and a serving boy trotted over with a filled chalice. He took a long sip and smacked his lips. "And my own cup. My mistrust of vipers such as yourself is the reason I have—how did you put it? Survived this long."

He hoped his performance would provoke a stronger response; he wasn't afraid of an attack. Fenris skulked along the perimeter, prepared to foil any strike. The misguided fool had proven himself refreshingly resourceful.

Despite his enjoyment of taunting the Chancellor, his brazen actions served a purpose. Vispin was renowned for her ruthlessness and cunning, which he intended to dull with rage. Verbal sparring with such an opponent could last days, and he intended to expedite their conversation. His opening gambit proved exceptionally fruitful, as her face had darkened to a shade of ruby.

She clapped her hands forcefully. "Shall we begin?"

A contingent of servants materialized from the garden, carrying silver trays of miniature sandwiches, confections, and fruit. They set them on the table and began service, but Aludrien waved them away.

He smiled at the food in front of him, relishing in the slight imperfections, for the meal had sat out for longer than intended, losing its polished splendor.

"How gracious of you to provide such an elegant array, but alas, I have brought my own meal to enjoy. I hope you don't mind."

Before the words left his lips, one of his servants placed a covered plate in front of him, revealing a steaming hot meal. Belessia had prepared a lavish lunch before they left the Emerald Pavilion. He devoured the food, smiling. Insulting a host in such a manner was unheard of, and Vispin's hand shook as she attempted to consume a melted pastry.

"So," Aludrien said between mouthfuls of braised hen. "You wish to resurrect the Senate?"

"Correction," Vispin said. "I have already begun the process. If you had accepted any of my previous invitations, you would have been privy to this information from the start."

Aludrien gritted his teeth; ignoring the Chancellor for so long had backfired. He should have known to keep better tabs on the one controlling his government. A Chancellor only reported to an Emperor, not an heir. These one hundred days were when Vispin was at her most powerful, with no one to answer to but herself.

"The Senate was abolished hundreds of years ago by Imperial decree, Vispin. As the chief lawmaker in the empire, you should understand that the only way to change a royal decree is with the power of the throne itself. You have no authority to reestablish the Senate."

"Correct," Vispin said. "Which is why I wanted to discuss my offer."

"And what could you possibly have to leverage?"

Vispin snapped her fingers, and a servant appeared with a scroll and quill. A contract.

"Pledge that you will authorize the return of a democratically elected Senate to legislate laws on behalf of the people of Xandria, and I will officially endorse your claim to the throne."

Aludrien's blood turned to ice.

"It is the emperor's divine right to select their heir. My claim is irrefutable," Aludrien stated, attempting to keep his rage in check.

"You are correct on all accounts, Your Grace, though you neglect a crucial tenet of power," Vispin said evenly. "A ruler cannot exist without their subjects, and a wise ruler understands that their right to rule does not come from divinity, but from the blessing of their subjects. If you lose the hearts of the people, you lose the right to rule. And the Senate is the will of the people. Restore their freedom, and you win their hearts."

"Be exceedingly cautious with the words you choose next, Vispin," Aludrien said. "You suggest I weaken the power of my birthright. To transfer control of my government to an elected group of fools."

"A wise ruler understands that they cannot accomplish anything on their own. When was the last time you left these walls, Aludrien? Do you know how your subjects live from day to day? How can you lead people you know nothing of?"

"I have been preparing my entire life!" Aludrien hit the table with his fist, and the porcelain plates rattled violently. "There doesn't exist another soul in the Imperium who understands the people better than I."

"A ruler who stands alone does not stand for long. Your father understood this truth."

"My father is dead! The fool allowed himself to be murdered! What does he know?"

"I am not saying he was a perfect ruler, or even an effective one," Vispin said, her tone softening considerably. "If he had left the Empire better than he had found it, your aunt wouldn't be fighting dozens of rebellions as we speak."

"Watch yourself, Vispin," Aludrien hissed. "You rapidly approach treason."

"I am merely stating the truth, Your Grace," Vispin said, her patronizing tone grating like hot irons on his skin. "The Empire will not survive another god-tyrant who rejects the will of the people."

"So you know better than I? You presume to be a champion for the people, but we both know who would lead the Senate. It is the easiest way for you to consolidate power and to strip it from my bloodline."

"On the contrary, Your Grace. I would intend to relinquish it, for the good of the realm. Sacrifice is another crucial component of leadership, one you do not seem to grasp yet."

"And you do not yet grasp the extent of my wrath," Aludrien said.

"I comprehend your cruel tendencies, Your Grace, which is why I am not surprised by the sheer number of attempts on your life these past months. It may, in fact, be a record."

"Jealousy is a powerful motivator, as is power."

"In my opinion, it is fear," Vispin said. "Fear of the ruler you may become, enough to drive them to poison vanilla or hide explosives in your desk."

Aludrien paled.

Nim stifled a gasp behind him.

Vispin smiled smugly.

"I believe I have overstayed my welcome," Aludrien said. "I bid you farewell, Chancellor."

"The pleasure has been all mine, Aludrien," Vispin said. Her eyes bore into him as he briskly departed the dining pavilion.

His entourage in tow, he stalked through the palace, ignoring the whispers as his procession passed, preoccupied by his anger.

He ignored his chamberlain's questions during the return journey. He remained silent when entering the mammoth gate of the Emerald Pavilion. He waved for Jareth and Nim to follow, dismissing the rest, save for a modest escort. Instead of retiring to his chambers, he circled the gardens and sought refuge in his greenhouse. Only when the door was closed did he speak to his two advisors.

"Nim, how easily can you trace the leak?" Aludrien asked.

"I'm not certain, Your Grace," Nim replied, their voice wavering uncharacteristically. Vispin's revelation had upset Nim more than Aludrien. "Whereas specifics of the vanilla incident were widely known, especially in the kitchens, the location of the explosives was known only by me, you, Jareth, and your food taster."

"Jareth, have you spoken to your husband about that night?" Aludrien asked. Jareth shook his head. "If that is true, we can only assume the information came directly from the assassin.

"We shouldn't jump to any conclusions," Jareth said. "She could simply maintain a spy in your pavilion. What about your food taster?"

Aludrien prepared to shake his head when Nim interjected.

"Good point, Your Grace. Pax also knew about the vanilla. I will question him thoroughly."

"Excellent," Aludrien said, thankful for Nim's quick thinking. His emotions were clouding his judgment; he needed to calm himself before committing any critical mistakes. "Jareth, question the guards posted outside my apartments that night. I want this spy found. You are dismissed."

"Yes, Your Grace," Jareth said. He bowed and departed.

"What do you think of our newest addition?" Aludrien asked once the door closed. "He seems to be flourishing after years of complacency with a useless title."

"He's effective and intelligent, though I believe his presence is superfluous," Nim said brusquely.

"No worries, I have no intention of replacing you," Aludrien chuckled. "Jareth's position is merely part of the game. With his assistance, you might sleep more than an hour a night."

"My personal life should not be a factor, Your Grace. Can we trust him?"

"Probably not," Aludrien admitted. "But I must use every tool at my disposal. Vispin has become a greater threat than even I first suspected. This Senate scheme appears to have been years in the making and may have been a plausible motive for removing the emperor. Vispin may have colluded with Ignatius and the Meridian."

"That is a strong possibility," Nim said. "What of dinner, Your Grace?"

The windows of the greenhouse had grown dark; the day

had slipped by.

"Cancel it," he said. "I have no appetite. Do not disturb me until tomorrow."

"Of course, Your Grace. But what of your evening snack?"

"Ah." He had almost forgotten. "Send Fenris here, I would like to speak to him."

"As you wish," Nim replied, hesitating as if contemplating what to say next.

"If you mention the Winter Palace once more," Aludrien warned, brandishing his shears.

"The ascension rapidly approaches, Your Grace. It is House Aleksandran's privilege to host a ball a few days before the sacred event. And as the new head of the house, the responsibility falls to you. It would be perfectly acceptable in the eyes of the court if you travel west to begin your preparations."

"And allow Vispin and Barrett to have full rein of my palace? Not to mention that I would trade my enemies here for Ignatius and his ilk who lurk in the ruins of Arachovia. Each of them is a more powerful Animancer than I. Do you truly believe I would be safer there?"

"Unquestionably."

"Leave me," Aludrien barked.

Nim scampered away.

Ignoring their departure, Aludrien turned his attention to his prized bonsai, focusing on the intricate foliage and immaculate design that he had spent half his life curating.

His breath slowed, his vision sharpened, and his emotions ebbed slightly. Tending his garden calmed him.

But the Chancellor's words still echoed in his mind, stoking the smoldering fires of his anger.

Who was she to lecture him about his birthright? She knew nothing of what Aludrien had done to prepare himself. He had sacrificed his entire childhood for his destiny.

The door opened once more. Fenris entered, holding a steaming pie and gawking at Aludrien's prized collection. The food taster had never been invited into the greenhouse before.

"I forgot you were called the florist before you entered my employ," Aludrien said, amused by Fenris's stupefied grin. "You must appreciate this place more than anyone."

"My sister tended the garden," Fenris said, setting the pie down absentmindedly, gazing at the row of star orchids with particular interest. "I was too busy in the pasture with the flock. I always envied her."

"Don't be. It's a tedious, thankless habit," Aludrien said. "Though I do find myself ensnared by it."

"I would consider beauty such as this its own reward," Fenris said. "I'm surprised that you enjoy caring for other living things."

Aludrien smiled; he had grown fond of the assassin's barbs. No one else would dare tease him in such a way.

"Even a tyrant such as myself can contain multitudes. Though I'm sure the Chancellor would disagree. Did you glean what you needed from today's luncheon?"

"Yes," Fenris said. "I discovered a weak spot in her wards. Directly above the courtyard. If you would like, I could test them tomorrow."

"No, we must wait," Aludrien interjected. "But when you do enter, it will not be for reconnaissance."

"Vispin's words upset you that much?"

"I believe she is the new mistress of Ysuelt's assassin, and potentially the mastermind behind her plot. She is a threat that must be dealt with swiftly. Her poor attempt at lecturing me about the virtues of leadership is meaningless."

"I found myself agreeing with her, for the most part," Fenris said.

"And what could you possibly know about ruling?" Aludrien said, resisting the urge to stab Fenris with his shears. "My life has had a singular purpose: to prepare to replace my father. I have studied with the greatest generals, philosophers, and historians the world has ever known. As a student of strategy and diplomacy, I have memorized each major battle, rebellion, and ruler in the empire's history. I am familiar with all vassal states and fluent in all languages. No one is more qualified to lead the Imperium than me."

"And yet you know little of its people," Fenris said. "Do you know why I killed your father?"

"Simply your foolish attempt to murder someone you thought was a tyrant."

"And why do you suppose I considered him a tyrant?" Fenris asked. Aludrien remained silent, unable to answer. "The outside world is not as neat and peaceful as your palace."

"I have seen battle, if that is what you mean," Aludrien said. "Of course, I know strife exists."

"Have you seen children starving to death on the streets? Have you experienced the plagues that wreak havoc on a newly conquered province? Have you seen soldiers rape and pillage?"

"I have witnessed the chaos of the lawless lands beyond our borders," Aludrien said. "And I can assure you, their circumstances are much worse."

"I grew up in a land outside your borders. I wouldn't have

called it chaotic. Until the Imperium invaded."

Aludrien groaned, exasperated. "So what would you have me do? Give Vispin the power she craves and reinstate the Senate?"

"I am not one for politics," Fenris admitted. "And though I don't trust Vispin in the slightest, I do agree that no one can rule alone."

"We can leave the murdering to you, and the thinking to me," Aludrien said, aggravated. "Dismissed."

Fenris bowed his head slightly and retreated, leaving Aludrien alone with his plants. He breathed deeply, calmed by the pleasant aromas.

He continued his pruning, though another knock at the door interrupted his concentration.

"Nim," he growled. "I told you not to disturb me until tomorrow."

The door opened.

It wasn't the chamberlain, but Fenris.

The assassin entered, his eyes wide and his face ashen.

"I have no wish to continue our discussion. Unless you wish me to stab you numerous times. Leave—" the words hung in his mouth. Fenris clutched a tiny object.

"Is that—?"

Fenris nodded. He presented a glass vial; the word 'vanilla' was scrawled on the label.

"Where did you find that?"

"Underneath a floorboard," Fenris explained. "Hidden in my bedchamber."

14

Rats and Vipers

Clinging to wet shingles, Fenris peered over the roof at the shadowy alley below. A cloaked figure stepped carefully around the puddles and through the tight space between outbuildings. This section of the palace was a tangle of warehouses tucked into the northwest corner, far from the Emerald Pavilion and central kitchens—an odd place for a cook like Elzia to venture.

She disappeared around a corner, and Fenris leaped across the alley to the adjacent roof, careful to land silently. He continued to stalk his quarry from above, his invisible veil protecting him from unwanted eyes.

For the past week, he had spent every waking moment observing his three roommates' movements. His discovery on the night of Vispin's luncheon had shifted Aludrien's priorities toward uncovering the Chancellor's mole. According to the heir's logic, if they could connect Vispin's informant to the string of assassination attempts, they could neutralize her threat more efficiently than simply killing her. Fenris was pleased that Aludrien had chosen diplomacy over brute force for a second time. Perhaps it was Fenris who was changing Aludrien, not the other way around.

Finding the vial had been a stroke of blind luck. After Fenris's odd conversation with Aludrien in the greenhouse, he returned to his quarters. He hadn't seen that side of the heir before, vulnerable, uncertain, and contemplative. The Chancellor's harsh words had jarred the typically composed and self-assured aristocrat. But the oddest part was that Aludrien had taken them to heart, especially when Fenris repeated them in the greenhouse.

The heir's secret hobby also came as a shock. Fenris had assumed the man cared for nothing but himself, but the vibrant and lush private garden told a different story. Fenris could rest easy if only Aludrien cared about his subjects as he did his plants.

After his dismissal, Fenris returned to his quarters but found himself pacing, lost in thought. When he was idle, his mind often drifted to unwanted places, Aludrien in particular. He recalled the sounds the heir made in the baths with Fukov and remembered how it felt to have the heir's body weight pressing down upon him the night of the explosion. He found it impossible to even look at the heir without those memories resurfacing, quickening his heartbeat, and causing his cheeks to flush.

Luckily, Fukov and Tipin had already finished their nightly dalliance and were fast asleep. He trod carefully across the floor so as not to wake the others, trying to think of anything but Aludrien's impressive chest. But a floorboard creaked louder than the rest. After several passes, Fenris noticed a slight gap between the plank and the others. Curious, he knelt to investigate.

That was where he found it: the vial of vanilla.

It was no coincidence. Such a rare ingredient was hard to come by, and all vials were accounted for, except the one stolen by Ysuelt's assassin. Fenris rarely spent time in his room besides sleeping, though he found it odd that he hadn't come across it before.

Aludrien was convinced that one of Fenris's roommates was the culprit. His plans for Vispin's immediate death had all but vanished. Instead, he had charged Fenris with uncovering the assassin's identity.

Fenris started with Fukov. He was convinced that the man was the most nefarious due to his hostile disposition, not because the loathsome brute had stolen countless hours of sleep from him. And certainly not because he was Aludrien's secret lover.

But Fukov spent most of his days fucking Aludrien in the bath, fucking Tipin in their room, and sleeping. He rarely deviated from his daily rituals. Fenris was jealous of the simplicity. Had he been reincarnated as a muscular idiot with a fat cock, life would be so much simpler.

He switched to observing Tipin, whose schedule was more complex than Fukov's. As a junior servant, Tipin was stationed in almost every corner of the pavilion, scrubbing floors, carrying boxes of supplies, washing clothes, and performing countless menial tasks. Despite hours of hard labor, Tipin remained perpetually bubbly and enthusiastic. His sheer energy impressed Fenris, though the lad was anything but subtle. The boy never shut his mouth, talking to whoever would listen. Fenris found it hard to believe such a pesky novice could go about unnoticed.

That left Elzia.

Fenris loathed considering that his favorite roommate could be a skilled assassin hellbent on killing the heir. As she was the only one of the three he had a relationship with, stalking her weighed on his conscience. They had spent a great deal of time together in the kitchens, joking and casually chatting.

Once Fenris began observing her, Elzia's behavior proved to be the most suspicious.

Though their quarters were close to the kitchens, Elzia often meandered between the two, winding through remote parts of the pavilion. She never loitered or skulked, but she traveled slowly and methodically. To the untrained eye, she was a weary servant trudging to or from a shift, but to Fenris, the behavior was alarming. It resembled his own demeanor when he wished to gather information undetected.

Since the kitchen was grossly understaffed, Belessia often sent her subordinates to the central kitchens for supplies. As the most senior kitchen servant, Belessia commonly chose Elzia for these runs. But the younger servants gossiped, complaining about the length of her trips. A handful dared to suggest she had taken a lover in the central pavilion.

But Fenris reached a more nefarious conclusion.

His suspicions were confirmed on the seventh day, when he stalked Elzia as she journeyed to the central kitchens. Cloaked in invisibility, he leaped from roof to roof as she calmly padded toward the center of the palace grounds. No one paid her any heed as she walked with her head bowed and an empty basket strapped to her back. Like all servants, she could move about the palace virtually unnoticed. Instead of entering the central pavilion, she turned sharply into an alley leading to the secluded warehouses in the northwest corner.

Fenris almost lost her as she navigated the maze of vacant buildings. She never changed her pace or faltered, taking each turn deliberately like someone trained to evade a shadow.

But Fenris wasn't easy to lose.

He followed her closely as she picked her way through the alleys, carefully monitoring her movements. If she were, in fact, Ysuelt's former assassin, this would be the perfect place to rendezvous with her new master.

She turned a corner into a covered alley, a narrow walkway wedged between two tall warehouses, disappearing into the shadows. Fenris followed, padding across the roof, mimicking her speed. When he reached the end of the tunnel, he stopped.

The street beyond was empty.

He strained his ears, expecting the soft sounds of footsteps, but only heard the rushing wind. Elzia must have entered one of the buildings. Fenris cursed. Both warehouses were massive and would take too long to search; if he chose the wrong one, she could escape through the other.

A trio of female voices rang out in his head. The spirits within. They sang a slow, calm melody.

Fenris felt the urge to stay, believing that the meeting would take place here.

The alleyway might hold a clue.

He dropped to the pavers below, his feet hitting the stone silently.

Elzia nearly walked straight into him.

Fenris rolled backward to avoid a collision. Elzia exited the tunnel and turned right, missing Fenris by a hairsbreadth.

Heart racing, he lay on the ground, deathly still, holding his breath. Elzia continued down the street and turned another corner with careful determination. He exhaled with relief. She hadn't noticed him.

Climbing to his feet, he pursued. Halting, he glanced back at the alley.

Elzia had stopped here deliberately. Had she dropped a message? If he were wrong, she would escape, and he would learn nothing. But his intuition told him to stay.

He crept into the darkened alleyway, senses heightened, prepared to strike. The narrow, covered path was scarcely wide enough for a single person to walk abreast. Stalking forward, he drew his claws, prepared to confront Elzia's master.

The alley was vacant.

No windows, no doors, no plants, nothing out of the ordinary. Fenris walked its length a dozen more times. If Elzia had left something, she had hidden it expertly. Or his intuition was wrong, and pausing in the alley was merely a tactic to throw off anyone following her. In that case, she succeeded. She would be impossible to find now.

Stubbornly, Fenris waited. If Elzia had dropped a parcel here, someone would come by soon to collect it. He climbed to the rafters above and perched on an ancient wooden beam.

He waited. And waited.

Hours passed. The alley grew darker. Still, Fenris waited. He was in danger of missing dinner, which would raise suspicion. But he remained.

Footsteps approached.

A man entered the alley. An elderly gentleman who smelled sickly sweet and wheezed as he breathed. As he approached, his features became clearer. Fenris had never seen him before. He passed Fenris's hiding spot and continued a few more paces before halting. Kneeling, his trembling hands caressed the paving stones methodically.

Fenris held his breath. He had been correct.

Finding his prize, the elderly fellow lifted a paving stone and pulled an object from underneath it. Through the dim light, Fenris's inhuman eyesight could clearly see a tiny scroll. Elzia had left a message.

Whoever this man was, he was much less cautious than Elzia. He trundled through the palace grounds, coughing and wheezing. Taking no detour, he headed straight toward the central pavilion. Because he wore the fine clothes of a low-ranking noble, guards passed him by with little thought. Fenris did not recognize him, but was sure to memorize every minute detail to report to Aludrien.

He stalked the gentleman to the lavish central gardens. The sun had already set, and many courtiers were retiring for dinner, but a few still milled about the fountains and topiaries. The elderly man found a bench near the center to marvel at the landscape. Perched in an orange tree directly above him, Fenris waited.

An hour passed, and the moon cast its silver light upon the palace grounds. Aludrien would forgive him for missing dinner, and Nim would certainly contrive a reasonable explanation for his absence. But only if he retrieved vital information.

So he waited.

Finally, a young servant girl rushed down the garden path. In a smooth flurry of motion, the elderly noble held out the scroll, and the girl snatched it. If Fenris weren't watching from above, he would have missed the split-second interaction.

Two separate couriers. Whoever the note was intended for certainly valued discretion. Fenris wouldn't have been surprised if the note had been transferred through at least one other hand. But it was not. The girl hurried straight to her master, Fenris in tow.

The recipient's identity was clear the instant they entered the baths. The girl obtained a towel, stuffed the note inside, and hurried past the changing rooms. The half-dozen soldiers who guarded the main chamber allowed the girl to pass. Fenris slipped in behind her.

The baths were empty, except for Vispin, who lounged in her favorite grotto. It was a perfect place to receive a clandestine letter from one of her operatives, far from prying eyes, even her guards, who waited outside. Fenris hadn't been able to scout during dinner because of his other duties. Of course, that was precisely when the Chancellor was the least guarded.

The girl placed the towel next to another already neatly folded on the pool's edge, where Vispin rested her head.

"Much appreciated," Vispin said as the courier departed.

Retrieving the scroll, Vispin unfurled it, inspecting its contents closely, her brow furrowed in concentration. The voices inside his head buzzed furiously, and Fenris was overcome with an impulse to slay the Chancellor; there wouldn't be a better opportunity to strike. She was cruel, calculating, and a threat to the Xandrian people. According to the Meridian's beliefs, he must eliminate her. Fenris padded closer, his claws extended. With one blow, he could remove Aludrien's greatest threat. But he had proof that Elzia was the Chancellor's agent. Elzia had access to the kitchens, where she could swap out the vanilla. Vispin was pulling Ysuelt's strings. If she were captured and confessed, the guard would arrest Vispin for treason. He lowered his claws, thankful he did not have to shed blood.

"It is embarrassing what passes as Animancy these days."

Something dark swirled along Vispin's arm. A metal spear erupted from her hand—an insignis blade. Fenris howled as it impaled him, piercing his chest. He fell to his knees. The ribbon of metal wrapped around him, lashing his arms together.

"I may not be a trained Animancer, but I'm smart enough to recognize a sloppy veil when I see one."

She pulled herself from the pool and wrapped the towel around her torso. Fenris released his invisibility, allowing the spirits within to focus on healing the giant hole in his chest. They howled and raged, but the insignis blade lodged inside prevented them from fully mending the wound. He growled and resisted, but the more he moved, the more the blade tore into his flesh. The blasted maneuver was precisely how Aludrien had subdued him.

Fenris hadn't expected this from her. Despite her station, she was still a provincial, and insignis weapons were reserved for the blood. He had never noticed a tattoo, realizing she must have kept it hidden. She was truly a cunning foe.

The Chancellor inched closer, eyes locked onto his. An arrogant smile blossomed.

"Ah, so you are the rat who has been noisily scuttling around these past weeks. I know you. I never forget a face. You are Aludrien's food taster. I am surprised the brute hasn't come for my head sooner."

"He is only retaliating against your threats," Fenris said, his voice strained.

"I am not sure what you are insinuating," Vispin said. Her gaze flicked to his claws. Her smile faded. Her eyes widened as Fenris's true identity became clear. "I must admit, I am not often surprised, but this is unexpected, Fenris Vale."

"Pleasure to see you again, Chancellor," Fenris said.

"Aludrien's depravity must know no bounds," Vispin said. "Enlisting the monster who murdered his father."

"I am not sure you're in a position to judge him," Fenris said through gritted teeth.

"The real question is why a zealot such as yourself willingly works for a man such as Aludrien," Vispin mused. "I thought the Meridian's goal was to rid the Empire of tyranny. It makes one wonder how their sole survivor works for the future tyrant."

"You know nothing of my mission," Fenris seethed.

"Oh, I know more of your pathetic, defunct organization than you do," Vispin said. "Have you ever wondered how a rebel leader, Durian, managed to collude with high-ranking cardinals? Or how easily we rooted out your entire network? Have you ever stopped to think why another assassin was in place to attack you seconds after you completed your mission? You cannot be that foolish."

"Keep his name out of your mouth," Fenris seethed, enraged by what the Chancellor implied. "You have no idea who that man was."

"Do I know him any better than you did?" Vispin asked. "Any better than you know Aludrien? It seems like you have a penchant for following men who hide their true motives. How pitiful."

"Better to be a fool than a conniving viper waiting in the shadows, ready to topple the Imperium to satisfy your own hunger for power. I know about Elzia and how she tried to poison the heir, how she hid explosives in his desk per Ysuelt's orders. How you directed her to kill Ysuelt and purchased her contract."

As he spoke, he called upon the spirits within; they screamed and howled, writhing and burning him from the inside. The Chancellor was talented with her blade, but her strength paled compared to the might of a Tal'Rach. But he needed more time.

"Oh, Fenris," Vispin said. "I am not sure which is more tragic. Your complete and total ignorance of the true nature of the Meridian, or how misguided and incorrect you are about mine."

"What are you implying?" Fenris asked.

"Durian, my dear," Vispin began. "Are you aware—"

A crossbow bolt hit Vispin between the eyes, leaving a smoking hole in her skull. She crumpled to the ground, lifeless.

Fenris fell after her, the insignis blade dissolving into a thick, black liquid.

A hooded figure with a slight frame crouched across the main pool, crossbow in hand. Their dark cloak shifted, revealing the gold and maroon livery of House Aleksandran.

Elzia.

Face obscured by her hood, she tossed the crossbow aside and disappeared through the far doorway.

Soldiers poured in from the nearest entrance, shouting furiously with crossbows drawn.

Struggling to his feet, Fenris released his pent-up energy, sending the guards flying with a violent torrent of air. He sprinted across the baths, running on the water as if it were solid stone. Before he reached the doorway, he reconstructed his veil of invisibility. The guards may have caught a glimpse of him, but he wanted to keep the witnesses to a minimum.

The guards stationed by the far door lay in bloody piles. Elzia must have dispatched them silently before entering the baths.

The moonlit palace was empty, save for a few guards on patrol, holding lanterns high. A figure disappeared over the nearest wall. Fenris dashed in pursuit. He wouldn't allow Elzia to escape.

With a single bound, he reached the top of the wall, narrowly avoiding a passing guard, oblivious to the chase transpiring before her. He crouched on the wall's edge, scanning the sleeping palace. Fenris thought he had lost her. Abruptly, a shadow moved across the furthest rooftop, a black cloak illuminated by the moonlight.

Catapulting himself forward, Fenris collided with the nearest roof, the sound echoing through the palace. The cloaked figure, who had reached the far wall, stopped and whirled toward the loud noise. Fenris sped across the roof, capitalizing on his prey's hesitation. It only lasted a few heartbeats, but it was enough.

When Elzia dropped from the wall, Fenris was only a dozen paces behind. The chase continued across the palace, around the lavish gardens and private pavilions, and over dozens of high walls.

Elzia was fast, but Fenris was faster, propelled by the inhuman speed of a Tal'Rach. She would tire long before Fenris. If he persisted, he would inevitably catch her. Her inability to perceive her pursuer did not prevent her from flying across the rooftops with great haste. He would have been impressed if he hadn't been consumed by adrenaline.

Bells chimed from behind, followed by a series of alarmed shouts. The Chancellor's body had been found. Soon, the entire palace would be swarming with soldiers eager to capture her murderer.

Fenris needed to end this chase. And fast.

Summoning a gust of wind, he launched himself into the air, hurtling toward his target, who had climbed to the top of a guard tower. She stopped briefly to take in her surroundings.

Fenris had her.

He reached out, claws extended, bracing for the impact.

Elzia dropped into the darkness.

Without a body to impede his flight, Fenris sailed over the tower and into the courtyard beyond. He crashed into a topiary in the center of a garden, sending a pair of sleeping doves fluttering away in annoyance.

A gruff voice shouted, and a pair of heavy boots stampeded across the pathway. Fenris darted into the safety of the hedges, narrowly evading detection. Another guard joined the first, and they searched the garden, but Fenris was already on the move, scouring the grounds for Elzia.

She was nowhere to be seen. But that was to be expected, given their location—the Emerald Pavilion. The chase was over. And Elzia was undoubtedly retreating to their room.

Someone had murdered the Chancellor, and Fenris was without an alibi.

15

Fire Lilies

Fenris awakened in the infirmary, the pungent smell of incense stinging his nose. The wizened apothecary clattered loudly with his instruments, humming an ancient tune. The old man had served the Emerald Pavilion long before Emperor Claude's birth.

"Good morning, young one," he said, shuffling over, clasping a large stone bowl. "I see the color has returned to your cheeks. After five days, I feared the poison had gotten the better of you."

"It's been three," Fenris said groggily.

"Ah, my mistake," the apothecary said, placing the bowl beside Fenris. "Time does seem to lose meaning at my age."

"I hope I live long enough to understand that," Fenris lied.

"You will, if you drink my juniper soup," the apothecary said, gesturing to the bowl with a shriveled hand.

Fenris paled. The liquid inside was bright red.

"Drink up, drink up," he said, pushing the bowl closer.

Begrudgingly, Fenris accepted the vessel and drank. The liquid tasted sickly sour and stung as he swallowed. The fool had used yew berries again, his failing eyesight mistaking them for juniper. A juniper brew would help alleviate pain, but yew berries were notoriously toxic. His stomach churned violently as the spirits within battled the poison.

"Thank you, I feel much better," Fenris said, but the apothecary had already returned to his station, out of earshot.

Fenris sighed and stared at the ceiling, his foot tapping restlessly against the footboard. Feigning illness for three days had proved a strenuous task; luckily, no one dared enter the infirmary and risk the wrath of the ancient apothecary. Fenris didn't blame them. He wondered why the delirious oaf remained employed.

However, it proved a fantastic alibi, crafted by the wily chamberlain. When Fenris hadn't appeared for dinner, Nim had told the staff that the heir's food taster had fallen ill after lunch and was resting with the apothecary. The story was believable, since food tasters commonly died from poisoning. Fenris had outlived the average life expectancy by weeks, to the point where the kitchen staff had begun to grow suspicious.

The elderly apothecary was already showing signs of dementia, so he wouldn't recall when Fenris first came under his care if anyone were to ask—a brilliant move.

Since arriving at the palace, Fenris had grown accustomed to days of immobilization due to his series of incarcerations. Yet that did not prevent him from becoming agitated with boredom and anxiety. For all he knew, Elzia remained on the loose, hunting Aludrien. And he was powerless to stop her. But he must wait until the apothecary deemed him fit for duty; otherwise, his ruse would be for naught.

The door opened, and Fenris's heart soared.

The chamberlain entered, smiling sheepishly.

"Nam, it is so good to see you," the apothecary said, trundling over, holding a steaming mug filled with a putrid concoction. "How many years has it been since we last saw each other? Would you like some soup? Oh, how I've missed my old friend."

"Good morning, Elridge," Nim said, ignoring the mispronunciation of their name and eyeing the mug as if it were a giant scorpion. "I am full from lunch, but thank you for your hospitality. I am here to check on your patient."

"Ah, right," Elridge said. "Pox here is on the mend, but he will need a few days to recover. Yew is a nasty poison to treat."

"I believe the patient has fully recovered and is ready to be discharged," Nim said.

"Oh dear me, he has fully recovered?" Elridge asked, laying a shaky hand on Fenris's forehead. "I could have sworn that Pux was at death's door only a moment ago."

"You called me here yourself, Elridge. Your letter stated that the food taster is in full health," Nim lied.

"Oh, did I? That must have slipped my mind. If I sent for you, then the patient must be ready to leave my care."

"Excellent," Nim said. "We shall be leaving immediately so Pax can return to his duties. Thank you so much for all that you do, Elridge."

"My pleasure, Nam," the apothecary said. Rifling through his robes, he produced a piece of chocolate and handed it to the chamberlain. "Please give this to young Aludrien. And don't tell his father."

"Our lord will be extremely pleased," Nim said, wrapping the melting sweet in their handkerchief.

Fenris hastily gathered himself and donned the fresh livery

Nim had brought. He bowed graciously and followed the chamberlain into the hallway.

The pair walked closely together. Nim relaxed a bit in Fenris's presence, which greatly relieved him. He had spent the better part of his tenure ingratiating himself with the chamberlain, and luckily, his deference had paid off despite his growing bond with Aludrien. Though not exactly friends, he could tell Nim viewed him with neutrality. Which was all he could ask for.

"Why haven't you sacked that pile of bones?" Fenris asked quietly. "He nearly killed me a dozen times."

"Elridge has served the Aleksandrans for decades. He helped deliver Emperor Claude," Nim explained. "Aludrien tends to be sentimental around such matters and has refused my numerous requests to fire him."

"I feel sorry for your staff if that is the level of care they receive. How many poor souls have you lost to Elridge?"

"None," Nim replied with a grin. "The central infirmary functions adequately."

Fenris suppressed a laugh. The chamberlain was the epitome of efficiency; it must have aggravated them to send the sick servants to the central infirmary when they could replace Elridge with a more competent apothecary. Aludrien was much softer than Fenris gave him credit for.

"How has the heir fared in my absence?"

"With the grace and stoicism typical of House Aleksandran. Though he has been as concerned with your well-being as you appear to be with his," Nim said, their lips curling into a wry smile.

Fenris's cheeks flushed slightly before he could compose himself, horrified by what the chamberlain alluded to.

"What of Elzia?" he asked hastily.

"We found her sleeping in your quarters and promptly arrested her," Nim explained. The pavilion gardens outside the infirmary were vacant, and the chamberlain seemed comfortable speaking freely. "She remains captive in the cellars. Aludrien has spent the last few days extracting information from her."

"What have you learned?"

"Nothing useful. While Elzia admits to working for the Chancellor by gathering information within the Emerald Pavilion, she denies any involvement with Vispin's death, or the attempts on Aludrien's life."

"I saw her livery in the baths," Fenris said.

"So you explained. But Elzia insists that she was fast asleep. Unfortunately for her, neither of your roommates can corroborate her story. Tipin was sleeping, and Alexei was with Aludrien when the murder occurred."

"And how has the palace reacted to Vispin's death?" Fenris desperately wanted to change the topic of conversation; anything to avoid imagining Fukov and Aludrien naked in a bath. The mere thought of them fucking irritated Fenris to no end.

"Fallen into chaos," Nim said. "The government is leaderless, fractured into a dozen ministries. General Barrett has capitalized on the situation, claiming the palace would be safer under Hestraea's rule. Most blame Aludrien for the murder, and many are calling for a trial. Luckily, there is little evidence, but that hasn't prevented his supporters from hemorrhaging."

"But there is one less viper in the garden," Fenris offered.

"I didn't consider you an optimist," Nim said, grinning.

"You may be correct, but I fear our lord's position is more precarious than ever. And the ascension rapidly approaches. Only thirty-nine days remain."

"Are you taking me to him?"

"No, he currently resides in his private garden and will not be disturbed. He instructed me to bring you to the captive."

"Why?" Fenris asked, incredulous.

"Our place is not to question His Grace," Nim said.

They fell silent and entered the pavilion's central structure, passing into the kitchens. Servants rushed by, their gazes lingering on Fenris and the chamberlain. He sincerely hoped his time in the infirmary did not attract too much attention, for he thrived in anonymity. However, he had abruptly fallen ill the evening of Vispin's murder, which must have drawn some speculation, especially since the heir had incarcerated Fenris's roommate in the cellar.

Elzia sat placidly behind iron bars, chained to the wall, eyes affixed to the floor. Fenris was morbidly familiar with the makeshift dungeon and had little desire to revisit it.

"Good day to you, Elzia," Nim said. "Our lord was unable to join us, but I would like to discuss various matters."

"I have told you all that I know, chamberlain." Elzia looked up, and her eyes narrowed. "What is Pax doing here?"

"He is merely observing; pay him no heed."

"I wondered why you spent so much time in the heir's private quarters. I assumed Aludrien wasn't fully satisfied with Fukov. I've heard he has a voracious appetite."

"Fukov?" Nim asked.

"Our name for Alexei," Fenris said, his cheeks flushing with rage at the mere thought of the brute.

"Ah."

"But I should have known you were one of his pawns," Elzia said. "Was it you who followed me to the warehouse? I thought I heard footsteps on the roofs."

"Stop pretending," Fenris snapped. "You saw me in the baths."

"Baths?" Elzia furrowed her brow.

"I shall be asking the questions," Nim said, raising a hand. "When did you enter Vispin's employ?"

"Years ago," Elzia said. "Long before arriving here. I already told High Lord Aludrien."

"So you were the Chancellor's trusted agent?"

"Never met the woman. Discretion is my livelihood, and distance from my employer results in success," Elzia said.

"Tell me more about this 'livelihood'. Have you ever murdered someone?"

Elzia scoffed. "Do I look like an assassin to you? I deal in secrets, not death."

"You seemed a pretty accurate shot to me," Fenris said.

"Please stop talking in riddles, Pax," Elzia said. "Kill me now, chamberlain. Because I can't tell you what you want to hear."

She was an extraordinary actress; Fenris almost believed her. She possessed the perfect combination of exasperation, confusion, and apathy. But she could not fool Fenris.

"What are the names of your associates?" Nim asked calmly.

"I've never dealt with anyone face-to-face. And if I had, they would have used an alias. Like Pax. I would think you would be more familiar with the art of subterfuge, chamberlain."

"I have one final question," Nim said. "Why have you been so forthcoming about your employment with Vispin?"

"Because true loyalty is a fantasy," Elzia said. "A captured spy is a dead spy. My life is forfeit. And if what you say is true and someone murdered Chancellor Vispin, then I have no one to be loyal to. But I would not be so foolish as to bite the hand that feeds me. Isn't that right, Pax? I believe you ended up in this exact cell for doing the same."

"Enough," Nim said, raising their hand once more. "Our conversation has ended. Thank you for your time, Elzia."

"Pleasure," she replied, her voice dripping with venom.

Fenris waited until they were safely in the vacant halls above before speaking.

"She is talented," Fenris said. "She's maintaining the facade until the bitter end, like any assassin worth their salt."

"I'm not sure if I fully agree with you. Elzia seemed surprised to see you. And betrayed."

"So that is why you brought me along," Fenris said. "To see how she would react. But someone with her talent wouldn't fall for such a blatant trick."

"Time will tell," Nim said. "For now, retire to your room. Someone will fetch you for lunch."

Fenris bowed and departed; Tipin and Fukov were thankfully working, so his quarters were empty. He paced across the floor, unable to sit still after lying supine for three excruciating days. Every so often, his foot found the loose floorboard, causing him to dwell on his traitorous roommate and the deceased Chancellor.

Both Elzia and Vispin claimed they had nothing to do with Ysuelt's plots, yet neither could be trusted. But the Chancellor's mention of Durian unsettled him the most; how a rebel leader could collude with the highest-ranking priests in the empire. She implied that Durian was involved in the Meridian's betrayal and hired the third assassin specifically to kill Fenris. But that was nonsense. Fenris knew Durian. He was unyielding in his integrity and cared for every member of the Meridian, handpicking most of them himself. A man like that could not act so callously as Vispin was suggesting. The mere notion that Durian could be involved was incredibly upsetting.

The sun had reached its peak when a guard fetched Fenris for lunch, which transpired in the heir's greenhouse instead of the formal dining room. The soldier mentioned that Aludrien had spent most of his time within his greenhouse since Fenris fell ill.

The air inside the conservatory was humid, and a shirtless Aludrien toiled in a fresh flowerbed along the left-hand wall. A large platter prepared by Belessia sat abandoned in the corner.

Aludrien smiled as Fenris entered, streaks of dirt covering his sweaty body. Fenris found it difficult not to admire the taut, gleaming muscles beneath the dark insignis tattoos. He rather enjoyed this unkempt version of Aludrien, finding it particularly flattering.

"It is good to see that you have recovered," Aludrien said, waving him over. "I feared we had lost a capable food taster."

"Luckily, I found myself in the skillful hands of your master apothecary," Fenris said. He froze.

Aludrien was planting fire lilies.

Moreover, the large pot brimmed with azaleas, coral bells, hydrangeas, and even Hakone grass. All native plants of the Belantine Plains. His home.

Aludrien resumed his work, gingerly placing the exotic flowers in the soil. When the heir was within the greenhouse, he shed the facade of the ruthless, icy aristocrat and became a calmer, gentler version of himself. This new disposition was equally refreshing as it was jarring.

"Hand me that bag of soil," Aludrien said. Fenris obeyed, eyes affixed on the flowers. The heir grabbed the sack and carefully sprinkled the fresh earth into an empty corner of the flowerbed. "Do you like my newest additions? They arrived this morning."

"They are lovely, though I'm not sure why you're planting flowers from the Belantine Plains."

"I was inspired by the flower you left on my father's corpse. I must say, your homeland contains some of the most beautiful flora I have ever worked with."

"Why do you speak so casually about your father's death?" Fenris asked. "It almost seems like you hated the man."

"Not as much as you, it seems," Aludrien said. "It is rather difficult to maintain an intimate relationship with the leader of the empire. My father was less of a parental figure and more like an ideal. Something to strive to be."

"So you have always desired to be a tyrant?"

"You did not know him," Aludrien snapped. "And your mind has been poisoned by the Meridian's doctrine. Do you think it is easy to run the entire world? That one does not make mistakes? He was a cold man, yes. But he did his best. Up until the end."

"You've never cared that I'm the one who killed him."

"Do you blame a shovel for disrupting the earth or a pair of scissors for cutting a dress? Frankly, you were merely a tool. Blaming you would be as foolish as blaming a sword for killing a soldier. I reserve my anger for my father's death for the one who ordered it."

Fenris bristled

"But I wanted the emperor dead," Fenris said. "I tried to kill you. Multiple times."

"You merely followed your convictions, however misguided they were," Aludrien said. "At first, I found it foolish. Following an ideal so blindly, committing countless murders for it. But I have grown to admire it."

Fenris blinked. Aludrien never complimented anyone. Save for Nim on occasion. However, his praise was certainly backhanded.

"So you no longer think me an idiot?"

"Oh, I still do, but an infectious one. I have grown to appreciate your presence."

"You only say that because I saved your life."

"It certainly helps your cause," Aludrien said with a grin.

Fenris found himself smiling, too, staring into the heir's eyes. They were rather remarkable, catching the diffused light of the greenhouse.

"I forgot to mention something Vispin said before she died," Fenris said. His curiosity overcame his caution. "What do you know about the Meridian and its leader, Durian Mossebette?"

Aludrien furrowed his brow. "Is that what has you reminiscing about the night of my father's death? What did Vispin say about him?"

"She mentioned him in passing," Fenris lied. He cursed himself. He had desperately tried to keep his past hidden from Aludrien, but now that Fenris had piqued his interest, there would be no stopping him.

"Well, I can't say I know more about Durian than you," Aludrien said. "Tell me about him."

"Stoic, unrelenting, but kind," Fenris said, his eyes becoming misty. "He could be bull-headed, but I haven't met another soul who cared for others as much as he. We met years ago, when I was still living in the slums. He was passing through, on a mission for the Meridian. Durian stuck out like a sore thumb, and I mistook him for an easy target. I tried stealing from him, and he knocked me on my ass. Instead of kicking me or calling the authorities, he helped me to my feet and offered me a meal. I hadn't experienced such kindness since the empire invaded my home. So I followed him ever since. He was the most selfless and honorable man I will ever have the fortune of knowing."

"And you loved him," Aludrien said. The statement sounded like an accusation.

"He saved me," Fenris said. "I was merely a street urchin with a knack for slitting throats when he found me. Durian fed me, clothed me, and gave me a new purpose. He found a way to use my skills so no other child would suffer as I had."

"Extraordinarily noble of him," Aludrien said, his lips pursed in a peculiar expression. Fenris's story irritated the heir. "So he was only your mentor? You never fucked?"

Fenris bristled.

"Ah, unrequited love, pining after your savior. Well, he sounds like he was an exemplary man, to have this effect on you," Aludrien said wryly. "But why would Vispin mention his name? Seems strange."

"I believe she attempted to use his memory as leverage against me," Fenris said hastily. "Which is why I forgot to mention it in my report. Probably nothing significant."

"No, I'll have Nim look into it," Aludrien said. "The Chancellor's death has…reduced my support in the palace, and I will utilize anything to turn the tide."

"I thought removing Vispin would improve your claim."

"So did I," Aludrien sighed. "But it seems General Barrett

has twisted the narrative in his favor. And with the government in disarray, the houses aligned with the military have regained their influence. And most favor my aunt. I cannot allow that cretin to succeed; my aunt's life would be forfeit."

"You still have plenty of time to turn the tide," Fenris said.

"My ascension is rapidly approaching," Aludrien said. "Though I have been meaning to ask you, what is it like?"

"I'm not sure what you mean."

"The ascension," Aludrien said. "As a Tal'Rach, you are the only person alive who has experienced the event. What can I expect?"

Fenris shuddered, experiencing a visceral reaction as he recalled his own ascension.

"Are you sure you want to know?"

"Of course."

"Imagine a swarm of bees descends upon you, plunging down your throat. When they reach your stomach, each one stings you. No. Imagine they burrow into you, ripping your insides apart. Your soul burns with each, compounding on top of one another until you feel as if you have transformed into a bonfire."

"Fairly grotesque imagery," Aludrien said. "I have lost my appetite."

"You insisted."

"Fair point. Continue."

"But it is more than the pain. The rach provide you with more than mere power. Each one used to be a human, complete with a lifetime of memories, fears, and desires. Their voices, their personalities, their memories, it all becomes a part of you."

"No wonder most of my ancestors descended into madness,"

Aludrien said. "How do you cope with them?"

"At first, the entire horde screamed at me every moment of the day. I almost threw myself off a cliff. But then I stopped fighting them," Fenris said. "They are a part of me. Most are content with residing in my dreams. But others are more persistent. Instead of fighting them, I listen. Call it an enhanced intuition. The words I say, the decisions I make, you may find me chaotic or unpredictable, but that is the nature of a Tal'Rach."

"Explains your infuriating tendencies, for certain," Aludrien said. "So instead of commanding their power, you submit?"

"I know it sounds like an impossible feat for you," Fenris teased. "But the rach are like a storm, you will drive yourself insane trying to assert dominance."

"I will take your word for it," Aludrien said, wiping dirt from his forehead, which only smeared it further. "Plenty for me to think about when the time comes, but we must first focus on reaching my ascension. The ministers may be fractured, but they are united in one goal. Finding the late Chancellor's murderer. And I am at the top of that list. This entire pavilion will be upended during their investigation, jeopardizing my security. Barrett and his ilk could launch an assault at any time."

"How will you respond?"

"By giving the ministers what they desire. A scapegoat. I will offer them Elzia and retreat to the Winter Palace until the ascension."

"Wouldn't that implicate you further?" Fenris asked. "And empower Barrett?"

"My residence there is more defensible," Aludrien explained. "And it is where I sent my most trusted servants. The rabble

I hired, along with you, can stay here. I'm sure Elzia was not the only spy. A grand ball is scheduled two days before the ascension, which the heir historically hosts at the Winter Palace. Most of the court, including my aunt and General Barrett, will be in attendance, and I will have a few weeks' advantage to set my traps."

"You have thought of everything," Fenris said.

"As I always do," Aludrien smirked. "You are dismissed. We have plenty of packing to do."

16

The Meridian

The following week slipped by in a chaotic haze as the entire Emerald Pavilion was upended to facilitate the heir's transition to the Winter Palace. Nim departed the day after Aludrien's announcement to prepare the estate for the heir's impending arrival. The chamberlain's absence was keenly felt; without their deft delegation, the responsibilities for packing fell to the department heads, who coordinated as well as a dozen rats trapped in a bucket.

Dozens of crates littered the halls, half-filled and unmarked. Fenris was stunned by how many of the heir's belongings Aludrien insisted on bringing along. Servants carried every tapestry, silver tray, and odd piece of furniture to the growing pile in the courtyard. Belessia's shouts echoed across the pavilion as she barked instructions at her kitchen staff. Cooking three square meals a day while packing her entire inventory was a demanding undertaking.

Instead of delegating to his servants, Aludrien preoccupied himself with dismantling his greenhouse. To Fenris's horror, the heir intended to transport his garden to the Winter Palace.

The tedious process was precisely why the heir had postponed his journey rather than fleeing with his chamberlain.

With his supporters abandoning him by the day, calls for his arrest growing louder, and his aunt's claim to the throne gaining momentum, Fenris couldn't understand why Aludrien was more concerned with the packaging of his prized bonsai than with salvaging his collapsing support. Only thirty-two days remained until the ascension, and the time to regain ground was rapidly evaporating.

"If I didn't know any better, I'd say you're admitting defeat," Fenris said, peering over Aludrien's private veranda at the half-dismantled greenhouse below.

"Which is precisely the point," Aludrien said. "When emboldened, enemies are prone to missteps. They will prove easier to exploit."

"Or it will finally convince your aunt to move against you."

"I will speak with her at the Winter Palace. She wrote to me the other day, proclaiming her intent to attend the ascension masquerade."

"The wars in the far provinces must be going well."

"Which comes as no surprise. Thankfully, that suggests Hestraea will be in high spirits."

"And her followers will have more reason to support her. The victorious war hero, returning from the battlefield. And arguably the best swordsman alive."

"She will support her beloved nephew and serve as his trusted Grand Marshal, as she did for his father. She wouldn't challenge me to a trial by combat, even if she had majority support," Aludrien said sharply.

Fenris wondered which of them the heir was trying to convince.

Jareth passed by the courtyard below, a dozen soldiers in tow. The austere man barked a few orders, and his subordinates hurried to obey. The head of Aludrien's security had the aggravating task of maintaining the defenses during the transition.

"He has adjusted nicely," Fenris said.

"Indeed, I thought he would resent me for pulling him from his ceremonial duties as Vice Minister of War. It seems he is more suited for leading than pushing papers."

"He may want to extend his service past the ascension."

"It is a vast Imperium," Aludrien said. "One cannot have too many competent servants. Speaking of which, he and Basil are content with the venue change. They agreed to join us on the airship tomorrow with my heir."

"Bet that took some convincing," Fenris said.

"I simply offered Basil the honor of hosting the masquerade. He has always enjoyed such frivolities."

"Valid. But I don't believe you summoned me here in the middle of the day, outside of a mealtime, to discuss politics."

Aludrien hesitated, his jaw clenched.

"Please sit."

Fenris's stomach soured at the grave tone.

Reluctantly, Fenris sat on the only remaining couch. Aludrien remained standing, staring out onto the garden pensively.

"There is a matter regarding my father's death that I would like to discuss. And you must be truthful," Aludrien finally said.

"Alright," Fenris replied, swallowing hard. The heir still held a grudge after all. "I have nothing to hide."

"Were you, or have you ever been a priest?"

"Excuse me?"

"Answer the question," Aludrien snapped.

"I'm not a priest," Fenris said.

"Where did you meet Durian?"

Fenris stared at him blankly. He instantly regretted mentioning his mentor to Aludrien.

"As I said before, he found me in the slums. Or weren't you listening?"

"Fenris," Aludrien said. His insignis tattoos on his forearm shifted slightly. "Do not insult me. You were deeply involved with the Meridian and had an intimate relationship with its leader; that much is clear. But I must know. What do you know of Durian's past?"

"Am I detecting jealousy?" Fenris asked.

Aludrien lunged forward, summoning his blade. He pinned Fenris to the couch, holding the steel to his neck. Fenris did not resist.

"Fenris, please," Aludrien said desperately.

In the short time they had known each other, the heir hadn't once apologized, shown weakness, or begged for anything.

"He never spoke of his past," Fenris said.

"There is nothing you can say that I do not already know," Aludrien said. "Jareth sent me a full report this morning. You know how resourceful he is. Tell me, what is the true nature of the Meridian?"

"You already know the answer," Fenris said, confused by the line of questioning.

The blade pressed in, drawing blood.

"Answer my question," Aludrien hissed. "What is the Meridian?"

"A rebellion!" Fenris yelled. "The Meridian is my cause.

Before Durian recruited me, I had no reason for living. But because of him, I gained a new one: to fight your corrupt dynasty. I have culled countless lives from this earth: murderers, warmongers, human traffickers. I did what your family could not do to keep the common people safe. But your empire destroyed it all. Only I remain."

The sword retracted. Aludrien stalked away to the railing, his back turned.

"Fenris," Aludrien said slowly. "That is not what Jareth discovered. What Vispin attempted to tell you before she died is that Durian was a priest."

"Impossible."

"Durian Mossebette wasn't even his name," Aludrien said. "Hestraea and Vispin were so distracted by the two assassins who survived my father's death that they neglected to investigate the one who died thoroughly. His name was Sayd Balin, a devout priest of Kyriak."

"I don't believe you."

"Your cause wasn't a revolution, but a church-funded insurgency," Aludrien said. "Your fallen comrades may have believed in the cause like you, but Durian exploited your altruism and naivety and turned you into a tool. A way to sow discord in the empire and eliminate their enemies. Including my father. When you fulfilled your purpose, they disposed of you. Or tried to, at least."

"No," Fenris said, shaking his head. "He cared about the people. He cared about me!"

"Why did he turn you into a monster?" Aludrien asked.

"He used my skills!" Fenris said. "Focused them into righteousness. He saved me."

"I saved you," Aludrien whispered.

Fenris blinked, taken aback by the sincerity. Indignation and disgust replaced his surprise.

"Do not pretend that you rescued me out of the goodness of your heart. You only view me as a tool. You've told me as much!"

"As you were a tool for the church," Aludrien said. "But tell me, how many innocents have you killed under my direction?"

"None, but that was of my doing," Fenris said.

"When will you drop my brother? I already apologized for my mistake."

"No, you actually haven't."

"Well, consider this my apology. You haven't murdered a single soul since you joined, have you? Not a particularly effective assassin."

"But I saved your life," Fenris countered.

"You do function better as a protector. Pity your former mentor disagreed."

"He found a use for my rage, directing it toward those who would hurt the innocent."

"The bastard twisted you into his tool, Fenris! You weren't killing the wicked. You were killing the church's enemies, like the other misguided members of the Meridian."

"He would never do that," Fenris said, standing. An unmitigated rage coursed inside of him. "Do you think your lies will cause me to turn against my mission?"

"When have I ever lied to you?" Aludrien asked. Sincerity was unusual for the heir, which further confused Fenris. "What do I have to gain from telling you this? Vispin brought it to your attention. Your curiosity sparked mine. I am merely filling in the pieces."

"No," Fenris said, tears welling in his eyes. "I don't believe you."

"Fenris," Aludrien said, drawing closer. "I am truly sorry."

Fenris recoiled and stormed to the door, overwhelmed.

"I haven't dismissed you yet. Where are you going?" Aludrien called after him.

"To think."

If the heir responded, he did not hear it. The world around him blurred, a whirl of objects and distant voices. One moment, he was on the veranda; the next, he was lying in his bed.

Durian wasn't capable of the manipulation Aludrien suggested. And if it were true, then Fenris was truly a monster. He believed himself a weapon for justice and peace. Not a tool for a corrupt church. He knew Durian better than most. The man only desired the betterment of the realm.

He lay staring at the ceiling, unable to move, unable to digest, unable to believe the horrors Aludrien had suggested.

So he escaped.

Closing his eyes, he drew himself into his mind palace. For the first time since arriving at the Emerald Pavilion, he entered his astral hideaway with relative ease.

The long grass rustled in the wind, like the surface of a brilliant green ocean. A bright plume of smoke rose from the village below. Jovial sounds of laughter echoed across the plains.

He closed his eyes, reveling in the sweet kiss of the gentle breeze, the smell of fire lilies filling his nostrils. His goats bleated softly, grazing upon the nearby knoll.

Exhaling, he expelled his dark thoughts until nothing remained. Only him and the Belantine Plains. Opening his eyes, he marveled at the nearly untouched nature.

He was safe.

He was home.

A spectral woman in a flowing gown pirouetted around him before dissolving in the wind. A rotund boy giggled with glee as he rolled down the hill, out of sight. Several more came and went silently; none would dare disturb him in his sanctum. He'd hear their voices throughout the day, feel their fleeting emotions, but within his mind palace, he was truly alone.

Reveling in the tranquility, he lounged in the long grass. Nothing else mattered here. He would worry about his troubles later.

Something tickled his neck.

The odd sensation persisted, and drops of water trickled down to his chest. He raised his palm to wipe it. When he pulled it away, his hand was crimson.

Pain followed. Excruciating, blinding pain, as if an invisible blade slashed his neck. He clutched his throat, but the blood poured from his wound like a scarlet waterfall. He rose to his feet, but faltered and tumbled down the hill.

The world around him shuddered, threatening to break. The pain increased tenfold.

Fenris opened his eyes, extinguishing his mind palace and returning to his bed. The room was dim. Night had fallen. A shadowy figure knelt on his chest. A long dagger dug into his throat.

Roaring, he summoned beastly strength and tossed the assailant across the room. They grunted as they collided with the far wall.

Leaping off his bunk, he gripped his neck. The wound was deep, and blood drenched his body. The injury would have killed a normal human, but he was a Tal'Rach.

Before his bare feet touched the ground, the dark figure had already risen, brandishing the bloody blade. They stepped forward, the soft moonlight illuminating their face.

"Tipin," he rasped. Blood poured from his mouth as he spoke.

"Why the fuck aren't you dead yet?" the petite servant hissed, eyes narrowed.

Fenris's neck tingled; the spirits within were already mending his torn throat. Within a few heartbeats, they would fully heal the wound, and he could engage Tipin with his entire strength. He needed to stall the assassin until the spirits finished. Then he could produce a lightning bolt and slay Tipin. The spirits within required more time.

"Elzia almost took the blame for all the attempts on the heir's life. For Vispin's murder. You are Ysuelt's assassin," Fenris croaked.

"Oh, you misunderstand the situation, Fenris," Tipin said. Fenris paled at the mention of his name. "Aludrien has never been my target."

Fenris furrowed his brow. "How is that possible? The vanilla."

"Aludrien does not like sweets. The tart was for you, with enough belladonna to kill a grown bull. But I should have known a Tal'Rach like you would be resistant."

"You seem familiar with the heir's inner workings."

"Aludrien is loose-lipped while getting fucked. And so is Fukov," Tipin said. "He was such a treasure trove of information. You would have never thought it by looking at him. A valuable asset."

"If you were responsible for the vanilla, then you must have rigged the explosives as well."

"Who do you think weakened your cell's defenses for you to escape?" Tipin said. "I knew you would rush to Aludrien's quarters to confront him, while he was safe at the dinner party. I wired the explosives to the device lodged in your neck. I noticed it while you were sleeping. You needed to step close for the bomb to activate. I did not foresee that you would stay on the veranda. My mistake."

A second dagger appeared from his sleeve, gleaming in the soft light. Tipin crouched into an expert position; it seemed familiar in a way. The air shimmered around him. He was an Animancer.

"You," Fenris gasped. "In Claude's chambers. You were the other assassin who tried to kill the emperor that night."

"Close, but once again you are misguided," Tipin said, inching closer. "You were my only mark, Fenris. I came to kill you."

"If I were your target, then why murder Vispin?" Fenris asked. The pieces were slowly falling into place, but Tipin's motives remained unclear. Why would Ysuelt's assassin want Fenris dead? How did she even know who Fenris was?

"I was aiming for you," Tipin shrugged, taking another step forward while assessing his opponent carefully. This fight wasn't his first. "Crossbows are not my weapon of choice. The Chancellor was an unfortunate mistake, which cost me a tongue-lashing from my master. I'll remove your tongue in retribution."

Blood continued to flow freely, though Fenris could breathe more easily; the wound hadn't healed and required all of his energy.

"But Ysuelt was already dead."

"Ysuelt Seraphine wasn't my true master," Tipin said. "Though she thought she was. I used her to gain access to the Emerald Pavilion. But she was becoming a nuisance, and my master ordered me to cleave any loose ends. So I disposed of her."

Fenris's head spun; none of Tipin's story made sense.

"You joined the Emerald Pavilion when I did. How could you have known?

"I'm an excellent hunter, which is why my master charged me with this divine mission. I was in your cell. I heard your conversation with Aludrien. I was at your execution, Fenris. I paid close attention. You summoned a shield moments before the blast."

"You had every opportunity to kill me while I slept," Fenris said in a desperate attempt to buy himself some time. "Why did you wait so long?"

"I tried every night," Tipin said. "But the spirits protected you with a veil during your slumber. Slaying a Tal'Rach is a bothersome endeavor. My master has been growing most impatient. Though it seems the rach have forsaken you today. Lucky for me."

"Your master," Fenris said, grinding his teeth. There could be only one who knew Fenris's identity and would go to such lengths to silence him. "Ignatius."

"I serve the church, Fenris."

Fenris exhaled sharply. The mind palace. He hadn't previously accessed it during his stay in the Emerald Pavilion. The assassin was intimately familiar with the nature of the rach and spoke of divinity. Fenris's stomach lurched. Tipin was a provincial and an Animancer. Only one institution taught commoners the sacred arts of the spirits. Tipin was a priest.

"Who sent you to kill me?"

"Which time?" Tipin spat.

"In Claude's chambers. Who sent you to kill Durian and me after we slew the emperor?"

"Oh, Fenris," Tipin cackled. "Ignatius only sent me there for you. Unfortunately, I was not anticipating facing you one-on-one. I was expecting help."

"Liar," Fenris hissed. His blood boiled. Durian wouldn't betray him like this.

"You served the church so brilliantly, Fenris. Made the people fear you, loathe you, shudder at the name of Tal'Rach. And you killed a brutal tyrant and enemy of everything the church holds dear. But you failed in one aspect. A single act you refuse to commit. One that you must achieve today. You have to fucking die already."

Tipin lunged. He was fast.

Fenris attempted to block with his free hand, but Tipin twisted his body expertly, and the knife soared through his defenses, sinking deep into his shoulder. Fenris roared in pain.

He torqued his body sharply, kicking Tipin away, who lost his grip on the dagger and rolled to a safe distance. The sharp blade remained lodged in Fenris's shoulder. He ripped the knife from his flesh, ignoring the pain.

The assassin struck with speed and precision. He sliced at Fenris's arms and legs, leaving a dozen wounds while evading his opponent's thrashing strikes. The spirits within howled, overwhelmed by the task of mending so much torn flesh. Fenris retreated, pressing his shoulders against the window. Tipin brandished his blades and crept closer, a deranged smile plastered on his face.

Tipin lunged, propelled forward with inhuman strength and swiftness.

Fenris was ready.

Growling, he commanded the spirits within, compelling them to cease their healing. Blood flowed freely from dozens of deep wounds. With a blood-curdling cry, he summoned his remaining strength to his right hand. Tipin was upon him, bloody daggers inches from his flesh.

Fenris summoned a bolt of lightning.

Tipin squeaked. His concentration was focused on strengthening his attack; his defenses were wide open. Unlike Fenris, he could only command the spirits to complete one task at a time. The air quivered slightly as he focused the rach into a shield.

The boy was quick, but he wasn't faster than lightning.

The torrent of energy hit him square in the chest, propelling him across the room with the speed of a howling storm. His body hit the far wall with a sickening snap. His slight frame crumpled to the ground, lifeless.

Fenris hobbled across the room. The spirits had returned to their work, though much weaker than before. Blood continued to flow.

He passed by the other bunk, noticing a massive form lying on the mattress. Fenris was surprised the frenzied battle hadn't awoken Fukov. The entire pavilion must have heard; faint shouts echoed through the wall. Aludrien's guard would descend upon the room within moments.

As he neared the bunk, Fenris stopped. His stomach curdled.

Fukov looked up at him with sightless eyes, his throat

slashed cruelly. The sadistic Tipin was probably planning to frame yet another roommate and stage a fight between Fenris and Fukov before disappearing.

He reached Tipin's broken body. He hadn't ended a life since Claude. Despite the carnage and chaos he had caused, killing Tipin did not hurt any less. True, he was a cold and calculated murderer. But was Fenris any better? The pair had more in common than most. Both tools of death. He recognized the righteous rage in the other man's eyes.

Something small had fallen out of Tipin's pocket during the violent exchange, sitting in a puddle of blood. Once he was certain his foe was truly dead, Fenris knelt and retrieved the object.

His heart nearly stopped.

A scroll, tightly wound and smaller than his thumb. It looked oddly familiar. Fenris unfurled it, his stomach threatening to empty.

Two words were scrawled on the yellowed parchment, written by a familiar hand.

Fenris Vale.

He had held a similar parchment countless times. Each contained the name of a target, sometimes with specific instructions or valuable information. But this one was simple. A single name. Written by the same hand that had authored every scroll Fenris had ever received since joining the Meridian.

Durian.

Fenris's mentor. The same man who saved Fenris from a meaningless life wanted him dead. Tipin had been truthful, after all. At Ignatius's behest, Durian created the Meridian to kill Claude, and once that mission succeeded, they planned

to dispose of all the loose ends, including Fenris.
He vomited.

17

Home

The airship's hull rattled, stirring Fenris from his slumber. He cursed and rolled over in his cot, shielding his eyes from the morning sunlight filtering in through the tiny cabin's porthole. Three days had passed since they departed, and Fenris had yet to sleep through the night. Rest had eluded his troubled mind.

Aludrien postponed his journey to the Winter Palace after the debacle in the servants' quarters. The court had countless questions about the dead assassin in his employ. Without a pontifex, chancellor, or grand marshal present in the capital, the investigation was disjointed and haphazard. Luckily, the heir used the chaos and division to his advantage and left the capital four days after Tipin's death.

Fenris hardly spoke; he barely ate and merely existed, trying his best to avoid any thoughts that might lead him down a rabbit hole of anguish and misery. He was a murderer. A political tool. Not a freedom fighter. Part of him thought it best to throw himself off the airship and rid the world of his menace.

But he remained and joined Aludrien on the airship bound for the Winter Palace. Partly because Ignatius waited among the ruins of Arachovia, and he could take his revenge.

The trip had been relatively quiet, as Aludrien insisted on using his private airship. A massive imperial freighter ferried the majority of his belongings and staff, along with Basil and his family. Only the heir, Fenris, a handful of guards, and servants boarded the smaller aircraft.

Although spacious, Fenris's quarters were stowed in the ship's bowels. He only left during mealtimes to perform his food-tasting duties. He was silent in Aludrien's presence, ignoring the heir's obvious taunts and refusing to look him in the eye.

The last full conversation they shared transpired over Tipin's corpse. Aludrien was thrilled that Fenris slew the perpetrator, remarking that he could stage the death to appear like a foiled assassination attempt.

Fenris, however, could not look Aludrien in the eye. His voice was flat, his eyes hollow, and his usual fire doused. He was a shell of himself. He relayed the altercation with surprising detail, even including the realization that Durian ordered Tipin to kill Fenris.

Before they left the city, Aludrien turned over Tipin's body. Without Vispin, the government conducted a brief, sloppy investigation, linking the boy to Ysuelt. The official story was that a rogue assassin killed his master and proceeded with a zealous rampage through the capital to slay the heads of state. The compelling tale alleviated considerable pressure, though many of Aludrien's staunch adversaries continued to believe it a fabrication and blamed him.

Aludrien's mood soured on the airship, likely because he had no one to fuck him after Fukov's death. But Fenris cared little for the heir's sex life. He cared for nothing, for that matter. He numbed himself to it all, his best coping mechanism after realizing his life with the Meridian had been a lie.

Aludrien began the trip with surprising patience, allowing Fenris to process. It seemed that he understood that such a revelation could provoke a fair bit of emotion. But the silence continued, and with each passing day, Fenris's sullen demeanor bothered Aludrien more and more until he snapped. On one occasion, Aludrien cursed him, throwing a chalice at the wall, but nothing elicited a response, fueling his growing frustration.

Footsteps echoed outside Fenris's cabin with a flurry of motion. The airship shuddered, jolted violently, and fell still.

They had landed.

Fenris furrowed his brow. He had thought it would take five whole days to reach Arachovia by airship. But it had only been three. Fenris had lost track of time.

The door opened, revealing Aludrien. Fenris blinked in confusion at his abrupt arrival.

"Come," Aludrien barked, stalking down the hall without waiting for a response.

Hurrying after the heir, Fenris caught up to him moments before they reached the ship's exit. Blinding light poured in from the opening; the metal ramp extended. Without turning, Aludrien strode down the plank, footsteps echoing against the metal.

Fenris followed him outside and gasped.

He was expecting to be bombarded with the sounds and smells of the Winter Palace's airship port. Instead, a familiar scent filled his nostrils.

All that surrounded the airship was a rolling plain of endless green. The wind coursed gently through the tall grass, and wildflowers danced in its wake, their fluorescent bodies catching the mid-morning sun.

He was home—the Belantine Plains.

Aludrien halted at the end of the ramp and spun sharply; Fenris almost crashed into him. Jaw clenched, the heir stared at him, regarding him with an odd expression.

"Why haven't you run away yet?" Aludrien asked.

Fenris gaped blankly, unable to form a coherent thought. Since they left the capital, he had suppressed most of his emotions. He spent most nights inside his mind palace, finding it the best way to numb the pain and quell the voices inside his head. He was unable to confront the truth.

He wasn't a force for justice or liberation as he had once thought. He was a mass murderer—a villain who ended countless lives for the sake of a corrupt church.

Durian. Fenris's skin burned whenever the fake rebel leader surfaced in his mind, fueling an anger stronger than he thought possible. He had trusted the man, considered him a mentor. However, the training he received was merely indoctrination, corrupting Fenris into a tool of death. And he wasn't the only one. Tipin. Countless others. Durian and Ignatius were the monsters that Fenris had once thought Aludrien to be.

The heir towered over him. The man whose father he slew at the behest of a madman. Was Claude truly the tyrant Durian led him to believe? While the Imperium's inequality was evident, Claude might have been actively trying to address it. Aludrien proved to possess several redeeming qualities, so Claude could be another number on Fenris's endless list of victims that did not deserve their ends.

"I'll repeat myself once more," Aludrien said. "You have not looked at me twice since we departed the capital. Why do you still serve me? Why haven't you escaped into the night when you had the chance?"

"I could not leave," Fenris lied, for he did not know the answer. "You told me you'd detonate the remaining node if I ran away."

Aludrien pulled the silver remote from his pocket and pressed the button.

Nothing happened.

"Fenris Vale," he said, his voice smothered with phony pomp. "Your services as my royal food taster and my personal assassin are hereby terminated. You are discharged from my service and are a free man. I bid you farewell."

"What?"

"You heard me. You have your freedom. Now leave."

Fenris froze in place, indignant at the dismissal.

"And the ascension?"

"I can manage without a single assassin."

"What happened to doing whatever it takes to claim the throne?"

"Well, it seems that we have discovered my limits now, haven't we?"

Fenris gaped, staring out into the fields, the same ones previously accessible solely through his mind palace. Now he was here, in the flesh, in the homeland that he missed so desperately. All he needed to do was step forward and run into the vast wilderness, leaving everything behind. He could find a new life, a new name, a new purpose.

The voices of the rach grew louder, but their sentiments

were split. Half pleaded with Fenris to flee down the hill and never look back. The others implored him to stay.

Aludrien was freely giving him his freedom, allowing the man who murdered his father to escape into the wilds. The heir appeared apprehensive and unsure of his decision. It wasn't a test. It was a lifeline.

But the Fenris Vale of the Belantine Plains was dead, as was his family. A beast like him did not belong here. This place was paradise, and Fenris deserved hell. He could not find the strength to step forward, to leave the ramp and set foot on the blessed ground. And the more Aludrien pushed him to go, the more he desired to stay.

"I...I cannot accept," Fenris said, the words like knives scraping against his tongue. "I want to accompany you to Arachovia."

In a flash of gold and maroon, Aludrien rushed forward and grabbed Fenris by the nape of his neck. He glared at Fenris, who remained motionless; he wouldn't resist. His conscience wouldn't let him; he had done enough to ruin Aludrien's life.

"Do not lie to me again, or you will wish the node hadn't burned off in the explosion," Aludrien said. "Tell me, why didn't you leave once it was destroyed? And why haven't you tried to kill me since?"

"Because I believed the Meridian wouldn't want me to," Fenris croaked. "And to stay and kill your rivals until the ascension. To free Xandria of tyranny."

Aludrien's eyes narrowed.

"Ah, yes," he mused. "You still want me to hold up my end of our bargain and face you in a battle to the death?"

Fenris blinked. In all the commotion, he had thought little of their original agreement. Killing Aludrien did not appeal to him much since Tipin's revelations.

"I-I don't think I do."

"So what keeps you here?" Aludrien asked. "Now that you've realized your former mentor's treachery, why do you insist on remaining in my employ when your home lies before you?"

"I don't know!" Fenris shouted, tears welling in his eyes. "I do not know who I am anymore. What I am. Except that I'm a monster who deserves death. You should have let me burn for killing your father."

"You possess numerous attributes, Fenris Vale," Aludrien said, their faces inches apart, his breath hot and sweet. "Woefully naive, inanely impulsive, frustratingly insubordinate, and a pain in my ass. But you are not a monster. You may be the most caring individual I have ever met. You are not a natural-born killer, and I have seen my fair share. It isn't in your blood. You believed you were saving the realm when you killed my father, as you did with all of those others. You are principled, kind, and desire the best for the world."

A tear streamed down Fenris's cheek. No one had ever given him such a compliment before, not even his parents. Not even Durian.

"You're softer now," Fenris said. "The heir I first met wouldn't stoop so low as to console his servant."

"Seems like you have corrupted me. I could punish you for such an offense. Make an example out of you," Aludrien smirked. His lips looked plump, inviting, his hand firmly grasping the nape of Fenris's neck.

Fenris found himself leaning forward, realizing precisely why he decided to stay with Aludrien.

The heir withdrew, releasing his hold. Fenris recoiled in

embarrassment. Aludrien merely studied him with an odd expression.

"Do you still wish to kill me, Fenris?"

"No."

"Do you believe I am the best candidate for ascension?"

Fenris hesitated, considering the man before him, whom he once considered a self-serving beast. A man who moments ago jeopardized his lifelong dreams to grant Fenris what he desired most. His freedom.

"Yes."

"And will you kill one last person to help me do so?"

"Are you asking me or commanding me?"

"Consider it a request," Aludrien said. "After what you have experienced, I cannot force you to take another life."

"I'm your assassin after all," Fenris admitted. "Although I haven't performed up to my usual standards."

"You haven't successfully eliminated a single target, have you? Except for Tipin, who wasn't technically a threat to me, it turns out. You have proven to be a lousy assassin," Aludrien grinned. "I should find another to finish the job."

"Oh, shut up," Fenris said, pushing him playfully.

"Truthfully, you have kept me alive this far," Aludrien said, his tone growing serious. "And helped me retain my dignity. If I make it to my ascension, I promise you that I will personally ensure Ignatius faces justice."

"No," Fenris growled. "If anyone is going to face him, it will be me."

"Excellent," Aludrien said, skipping up the airship's ramp with renewed vigor. "Seems we have struck an accord. Come, we have much to prepare. My ascension is only twenty-five days away, not that I'm counting."

Fenris sighed, glancing back once more at the place that was no longer his home. He was as foreign to it as the Xandrian airship. He belonged on that craft, hurtling toward his demise.

# # #

"Are you certain, Your Grace?" Nim asked, their face hidden behind a long cowl.

"Would you prefer to spend the night in the desert?" Aludrien replied dryly, motioning to the dusty edge of the airship port.

"That is not what I meant, and you know it," Nim whispered, following closely as they pushed their way through the dirty crowd.

Aludrien chuckled and continued to the entrance. The sprawling city of New Arachovia loomed beyond the gate, the faint outlines of bulky buildings obscured by the hazy air.

He had visited Xandrian's historic capital throughout his childhood. Of course, he spent the vast majority of his time in the Winter Palace, situated on the outskirts of the northern ruins. The insufferably hot climate caused every breath to chap his lips further. Aludrien hated his trips here.

He had almost forgotten that an entire city had sprung from the desert along the southern edges of the ancient seat of power. The great lake flooded much of the southern reaches of the ancient city, creating an oasis that attracted numerous settlers from the arid region. Since it lay on the opposite side of Lake Arachovia from the ruins, the royal family had little reason to visit the bustling desert metropolis.

Which is why he ordered his private airship to drop him off here upon his arrival before heading across the lake to the Winter Palace. Despite each of his advisors' strong objections, he wanted the chance to see the city through his subjects' eyes before he ascended the throne. Fenris had constantly hyperbolized the dire state of the Imperium, so he thought it best to experience it with his own eyes.

Nim had insisted upon meeting him upon his arrival and nearly doubled over when they learned Aludrien had come without any guard, only Fenris. His soldiers would merely interfere. Besides, an all-powerful Tal'Rach would be more than enough to repel a few ruffians.

Weaving through the crowd, Aludrien and Nim finally arrived at the garish, rusty city gate. A short, cloaked figure loitered patiently off to the side.

Nim sent Fenris to the wharf to secure passage across the lake. After a short tour of the city, the trio would take a vessel to the northeastern shores, then walk to the Winter Palace. Such an adventure was thrilling after months trapped in the capital.

Fenris smiled as they approached; his spirits had lifted significantly since Aludrien's ultimatum. The heir sympathized with what Fenris had suffered, but he remained a crucial asset on his path to the throne. He needed to ensure his assassin was fully committed to his cause. So he offered what Fenris had always sought. Freedom. And still, the assassin stayed. Aludrien still did not fully understand why Fenris's choice to remain elated him so.

Aludrien approached Fenris swiftly, clasping him on the shoulder in a casual greeting. Nim awkwardly followed suit.

"Do we have our route set?" Aludrien asked.

"More or less," Fenris said.

Nim groaned.

"Why are we standing here out in the dust?" Aludrien asked

haughtily. "Lead the way, Pax."

The other two exchanged a worried glance.

"What is it now?" Aludrien groaned, his patience wearing thin. His throat rasped, crying out for water.

"Well—" Nim said, staring at their feet, shifting awkwardly.

"You need to know what you're about to walk into," Fenris said. "This isn't like the royal palace."

"You both are idiots," Aludrien groaned. "Do you believe me to be so sheltered?"

"Yes," Fenris said, a tad too quickly.

"Have I not spent the last few days cramped in an airship with you? Did I complain once?"

"Almost constantly," Fenris said. "There is a big difference between a luxury ship and a slum."

"Oh, get over yourselves," Aludrien said, pushing past Fenris and into the city beyond.

The smells of New Arachovia, however, nearly halted him in his tracks. His nostrils burned, and his eyes watered with the malignant cocktail of feces, trash, and dirty bodies swirling around the air. The stifling environment nearly incapacitated him.

The sounds were worse.

A cacophony of deafening noises filled the narrow, confined street. Children cried, their emaciated bodies sprawling against crumbling walls. Beggars pleaded for scraps, clawed at his cloak, and rattled off heart-wrenching stories to support their dire case. Bloodcurdling screeches emitted from the darkened windows, sounds of people being attacked—or worse.

A street urchin collided with him, almost pushing him over. Fenris materialized next to Aludrien, steadying him and grabbing the young girl by the shirt. She shrieked, flailing her hands. No one came to her aid. She held a leather pouch in her hand. Aludrien's coin purse. Cursing, he snatched it from her. Fenris released the wretch, and she scampered away.

A pair of grizzled men soon replaced her. They glared at him hungrily, daggers slipping into their hands. Fenris confronted them before they took another step, tripping one with a swipe of his leg. The other lunged forward to stab him, but the assassin dodged with ease, grabbing the brigand by the wrist, twisting him violently, and wrenching the dagger from his clutch.

They had taken two dozen steps into the city.

A third assailant materialized from the crowd, rusty knife aimed at Aludrien's neck. Fenris lunged to intercept, throwing himself between him and the assailant. In a fluid motion, the assassin pushed Aludrien back into the wall, holding him in place and shielding him from the assault. The rusty knife plunged into Fenris's shoulder. Unfazed, the assassin punched the assailant with supernatural force. The thin man's head jolted back as his nose broke. Relinquishing the knife, the terrified man scampered off into the city.

Fenris tore the small blade from his shoulder and discarded it. Instead of tending to his own wound, he inspected Aludrien thoroughly with wild eyes. The smaller man pressed the heir against the wall with surprising strength and tenderness.

"Were you cut?"

"No."

Aludrien swallowed hard, regarding Fenris closely. He had experienced this instinctive assertiveness once before: the explosion in his study. Fenris adopted the same intense expression as he had before, pressing into Aludrien with his immense strength. Despite their precarious circumstances, he felt safe and secure. Nothing could harm him as long as Fenris was by his side.

Aludrien flushed, resisting the urge to lean down.

"Stay close," Fenris hissed, releasing his grip. "Lower your gaze and hunch your shoulders. You look like a noble."

"I am a noble," Aludrien protested.

Fenris cursed, looking around nervously. "You'll lose your head if you speak like that. Follow my lead."

Obeying others wasn't Aludrien's strong suit, but after witnessing Fenris in action, he willingly heeded his advice, allowing him to lead the group through the putrid hellscape.

His shoulders ached from the unnaturally slouched posture, but it proved surprisingly effective. The assaults decreased in frequency as Fenris guided them through the chaotic masses. Despite his best efforts to fix his eyes on the dirt path, Aludrien witnessed a few dozen more unspeakable horrors that would haunt his dreams for the rest of his life.

After an eternity, the roads widened, the crowds dispersed, and the putrid smells lessened, though they did not entirely dissipate. Trash still piled in heaps in the alleyway, and rogue children continued to scamper about, shirtless and rail-thin. Dozens of wretches lay along the boulevard, staring hopelessly into the smoggy sky.

"Well, at least we survived the slums," Nim said.

"What do you mean? Are these not the slums?" Aludrien asked, glancing at a disgruntled couple screaming at each other in front of a dilapidated fruit stand.

Fenris and Nim shared another infuriating look.

"No," Fenris said. "Welcome to the Harbor District of New Arachovia. The pearl of the city."

Aludrien gaped.

"Our vessel is this way," Fenris said, ignoring his incredulous expression. "Keep close. A pair of pickpockets is stalking us."

Aludrien obeyed, following Fenris forward, the briny, pungent smell of fish added to the ensemble of foul odors.

The road spilled out onto a sprawling harbor where fishing boats rocked against the tide. Fishmongers cried above the din as citizens milled about the piers.

Lake Arachovia spread out before them, light blue contrasting against the hazy, orange sky. The water was relatively shallow, but an excellent source of fish. Thousands of white sails dotted the horizon. Beyond them, giant monoliths loomed on the far shore. Barely visible, the ancient city of Arachovia sat along the far bank. He hadn't seen the ruins from this angle before and found himself marveling at their mysterious grandeur. They certainly seemed more impressive from afar.

In a few short weeks, he would be among those pillars, receiving his birthright. He nearly shook with anticipation.

Their journey ended at a run-down dock near the harbor's eastern edge. Fenris led them to a wooden rowboat that lay low in the water. He helped Nim into the stern before extending a hand to Aludrien, who eyed the derelict watercraft apprehensively.

Groaning, he climbed into the vessel and sat next to Nim. If he could spend an hour in the slums, he could survive a short, precarious boat ride. Fenris loosed the thick rope from the dock and began paddling them out of the harbor, northward toward the ruins of Arachovia. In twenty-three days, he would enter the ancient amphitheater in the center of the old city and finally ascend to his rightful place as Emperor. Assuming he survived that long.

"We tried to warn you," Fenris said.

"Next time, try harder."

"It's nearly impossible to convince you of anything," Fenris said coyly.

"Slap me if you must," Aludrien said. "Though I am not sure anything would have prepared me for that."

"The slums here are a paradise compared to the ones in your capital. And you could not begin to imagine what freshly conquered provinces are like."

Aludrien stared at Fenris, the reality of his words finally sinking in. As the heir, he was privileged to travel to the far corners of the Imperium, but he spent his time in palaces, manors, and manicured inner cities, far away from the public. They had walked the entire city's length from end to end, and every inch was a nest of poverty, starvation, and crime. The hell he witnessed was daily life for the vast majority of his subjects.

The epiphany was enough for him to nearly wretch. He had previously reduced Fenris's motivations for killing his father to mere misguided naivety. Now he understood it wasn't Fenris who was naive.

"Well, Vispin may have been on to something," Aludrien mused.

Fenris smiled widely at this, though Aludrien didn't understand what made him so happy.

18

The Winter Palace

"Silver sconces! Have you lost your mind? What do you think we are preparing, a provincial potluck? Fetch the gold!"

An abashed servant scurried out of the courtyard as half a dozen others set about dismantling the ornate braziers from the stone walls. The entire Winter Palace was abuzz with activity as an army of servants cleaned every square inch, adorning every possible surface with priceless sculptures, ancient tapestries, and intricate bouquets of exotic flowers. Basil stood in the center of the courtyard, commanding his legions of servants like a seasoned general.

"You would think the masquerade was tomorrow, not in seven days," Aludrien mused, watching his half-brother scamper about from a balcony high above.

Rough outlines of ruined towers peeked above the palace's outer walls; the ancient city of Arachovia lay on the other side of the oasis.

"He simply wishes to impress you," Nim suggested, standing behind him dutifully. "You did spare his family a bloody end, after all."

"He acts out of fear, nothing more," Aludrien said. "He still believes I murdered his mother."

"It seems to me as if he is enjoying himself," Nim said, smirking.

"He certainly has an odd sense of what constitutes entertainment," Aludrien said. "You and he may have more in common than I previously thought, mistaking stress for pleasure."

"We all have our vices, Your Grace," Nim said. "Though I do believe his anxiety has heightened today due to your aunt's imminent arrival. You appear tense yourself."

"It is a momentous day. We must receive Grand Marshal Hestraea with a banquet worthy of a war hero. She has successfully quelled every rebellion, clearing the way for my ascension. There is much to celebrate. And much to discuss before General Barrett worms his way into her ear."

"We did not have to send him an invitation," Nim said.

"No, excluding Barrett would have seemed suspicious," Aludrien said. "He has already moved into his winter estate. The banquet tonight is to commemorate a military victory; it would be odd if we snubbed a decorated general."

"True," Nim said. "Though this particular general has been busy as of late. I have already uncovered half a dozen of his spies in the Winter Palace. Along with a few dozen hired by his associates. I fear they will strike at the masquerade."

"All the more reason for us to prepare a counterstrike."

"Agreed, Your Grace. Speaking of invitations. The guest list includes a few noticeable absences."

"Allow me to guess," Aludrien said, staring at the ruins through the hazy sky. "Ignatius and his cohort? I have wondered what nefarious schemes they have been hatching while lurking in the ruins."

"Correct, not a single priest or priestess will be attending the festivities," Nim said. "The common excuse is incapacitation due to preparations for the upcoming ascension. Though I must say their absence will be appreciated."

"I cannot say I disagree. I would not want Fenris tearing throats out during my grand celebration."

"Funny you should mention him. The two of you have spent a lot of time together since you arrived at the Winter Palace. Have you found a permanent replacement for Alexei?"

Aludrien scowled.

Nim flinched.

"You are becoming too comfortable with yourself, Nim," Aludrien growled, his cheeks flushing.

"Forgive me for the intrusion. I am merely asking a question, Your Grace," Nim said, a wry smile blooming on their face. "It seems as though your ultimatum on the Belantine Plains has brought him to heel. He is in high spirits, all things considered."

"What are you insinuating, Nim?" he asked, dangerously quiet. The chamberlain was seriously testing his tolerance and mercy.

"Simply conveying my humble observations," Nim said nonchalantly. "As is my duty. Your mood has brightened as well."

"It could be due to my approaching ascension, or the warmer weather," Aludrien said, oddly flustered by Nim's insinuation.

"You detest the heat, and your position at court lies on a razor's edge," Nim countered. "Yet I have never seen you so...content. I particularly enjoy it."

"Do not preoccupy yourself with my demeanor," Aludrien

snapped.

"It is my obligation, Your Grace," Nim said, their voice lowering. "But I advise you to tread carefully. Your ascension looms, and such a distraction, however pleasant, could prove fatal at this juncture. Especially if this distraction is an invaluable asset."

"Point taken," Aludrien said. He did not want to betray himself any further than he already had. "You are dismissed. I must prepare for Grand Marshal Hestraea's arrival. Her airship should be landing momentarily."

"Of course, Your Grace."

Lingering after the chamberlain's departure, Aludrien observed his half-brother below and chuckled. He descended the steps, inhaling the dry air laced with the sweet musk of tropical plants, dabbing the beading sweat on his forehead with his linen sleeve in disgust. He had wasted much of his childhood in this godforsaken place; Aludrien loathed every second, longing for the more temperate climate of the capital.

His airship had arrived in New Arachovia two weeks prior, and he had spent every waking moment lamenting the swampy heat and planning his final moves before the ascension.

Centuries ago, after she established the new capital in the east, Empress Luxarene constructed the Winter Palace near the ancient Arachovia, a lush oasis amid the dusty plains. Tropical birds of every color roosted in the rafters, warbling their sweet melodies. The western region's dry season coincided with the capital's winter, and Luxarene famously despised the cold, stating the Aleksandran bloodline was forged in an arid land and wilted in lower temperatures. For generations after her, it became commonplace for the royal family to migrate westward for the winter and rule the Imperium from the warm luxuries of the Winter Palace.

Luckily for Aludrien, his father wasn't one for tradition and seldom traveled westward. However, Claude deemed it essential for his son to spend a few months each year studying near the ancient ruins to learn the history of their dynasty firsthand.

Aludrien loathed every moment of it. The sweat, the chapped lips, the heat, the boredom. The bugs. Even in the cooler months, the Winter Palace was far too hot for his liking; he could handle the short, humid summers of the capital, but the constant ungodly temperatures around Arachovia drove him to lethargy. He craved the cool nights of the capital, for he valued efficiency and productivity above all. One could hardly develop a thought in the blistering heat, let alone lead an empire. Since reaching adulthood, Aludrien had avoided the Winter Palace. He had remained in the east with other like-minded nobles who preferred to conduct their business in the capital and deal with the changing seasons.

Swatting a fly, he padded into the water gardens, passing by a horde of anxious servants. Sunlight filtered in from the canopy above, and birds of paradise trotted across marble pathways. Lilies of all shades and sizes floated atop crystalline waters, and vibrant fish danced within their depths. Thousands of flowers lined the path, filling the air with a calming fragrance.

Admittedly, this was the birthplace of Aludrien's passion for gardening, the Winter Palace's saving grace. He spotted several flowers he did not recognize, making a mental note to ask the master of the gardens for their names and origins. He desired to add them to his collection.

The water gardens lay at the center of the complex, separating the palace's public and private spaces. The former held the grand ballroom, courtyard, and guest lodgings, while the latter served as the private estate for House Aleksandran. The Winter Palace was markedly smaller than the palace in the capital, as were its guest quarters. The lack of space prompted more affluent nobles, such as General Barrett, to build or acquire nearby estates for better access to the royal family during the winter months. Like a swarm of locusts circling a fresh crop, their airships would soon fill the skies over Arachovia.

The private Aleksandran estate, though larger than the Emerald Pavilion, consisted of a charming cluster of villas hidden behind the water gardens. Tall walls separated the well-fortified villa from the rest of the property.

Exhibiting astonishing foresight, Nim had transferred Aludrien's most trusted servants to the Winter Palace during the upheaval after his father's funeral. The only staff from the Emerald Pavilion who joined the journey were Nim, Belessia, Elridge, Fenris, and a handful of others.

When Aludrien's airship arrived, Nim had fully prepared the estate, along with his greenhouse, constructed in the corner, nearest his quarters.

He exited the gardens and entered the private villa. Magdolina squealed from a balcony and waved. He smiled slightly and returned the gesture. He had insisted that Basil and his family stay in the spacious villa; he needed to keep his heir safe from the conniving clutches of visiting courtiers.

Unsurprisingly, Jareth had been resistant to the idea; however, Aludrien won the argument.

A cook bowed as he passed; he shot her a knowing grin.

Nim had almost quit in outrage when Aludrien decided to bring Elzia along. Exonerated of her crimes, the heir decided her skills of espionage would be helpful in the coming days. He had a penchant for collecting dangerous tools, but ultimately, he was nothing if not a pragmatist. Of course, he paid the spy triple what she claimed the Chancellor had, which was already an overestimate. The coin would ensure Elzia's loyalty.

A dark figure appeared around the corner as he climbed the steps to his chambers. Fenris.

"You look a mess," Fenris jibed as he approached, grinning mischievously. "If this is your homeland, then why do you sweat like a pig?"

Aludrien's cheeks grew hot with irritation, recalling Nim's words. Was he that obvious?

"Watch your tone, Pax," Aludrien snapped, immediately regretting his words when Fenris wrinkled his brow in confusion.

"Apologies, Your Grace," Fenris said stiffly. "Would you like me to fetch a guard for your daily walk?"

"That will not be necessary. I must begin preparations for this evening's feast."

"This early? Ah, I forgot Hestraea is arriving tonight. Explains the prickly attitude. Well, pricklier than usual, that is."

"I informed you of the celebration last night. How can I trust a servant who cannot remember a simple piece of information?" Aludrien asked, resisting a smirk.

"And what happened to you doing the thinking for both of us?"

"Silly of me to assume you could manage a single independent thought without supervision."

Aludrien stepped closer, his face flushing. It annoyed him to admit that he deeply enjoyed his nightly conversations with the man who had killed his father. He found the food taster's blunt speech surprisingly refreshing. No one else dared speak so candidly, as if he weren't the most powerful person in the realm, including Nim.

"And you think too much," Fenris said. "She's still your aunt, despite her relationship with Barrett. She'll listen to you when you tell her about his treachery."

"Perhaps I should have you eliminate Barrett after dinner. It would make my life much easier."

"And what about the melodramatic scheme you've been devising for the masquerade?"

"I suppose you are right," Aludrien sighed. "It is not in my nature to act rashly."

"That's my area of expertise," Fenris chuckled. "I should leave you to your preparations; it may take a while to clean all that sweat without Alexei's help."

"You are dismissed," Aludrien said, watching Fenris closely as he bounded off.

After the confrontation at the Belantine Plains and the trip to the slums, the air between the two men had shifted considerably, as if a veil had been lifted. They continued to spar verbally, which pleased Aludrien, but he also felt more comfortable lowering his guard around the assassin. He had never experienced such a sensation with anyone before.

However, Aludrien wasn't so foolish as to think Fenris had remained out of loyalty. Ignatius was in the ruins of Arachovia, mere leagues from the Winter Palace. Fenris wanted justice, and the only way to achieve that was to follow

Aludrien. He was only surprised that Fenris did not run to the ruins of the ancient city the moment they arrived at the Winter Palace.

He shook the thought from his head; he must prepare for Hestraea's arrival. Only nine days remained until the ascension. One week until his ascension masquerade, followed by a day of rest before the grand ceremony. Barrett remained in play. The general's support was at an all-time high, at levels that would be difficult for even a virtuous and dutiful veteran like his aunt to ignore.

But Aludrien hadn't spent his days in the Winter Palace lounging by a pool. He had crafted a meticulous and foolproof plan. One narrow, treacherous path lay between him and ascension. The following days would determine success or failure. And Fenris was an integral piece.

His anxieties only grew as he busied himself in his quarters, bathing, grooming, and donning a garish costume that was much too heavy for the climate. As the sun set, Nim entered his quarters to announce Hestraea's arrival. Readying himself in the mirror, he carefully adjusted his robes. His aunt was a particular woman whom he admired deeply, and someone he found himself desperate to impress.

Brass horns echoed through the windows, signaling Hestraea's arrival. Rushing out the door, he nearly tripped over himself. She prized punctuality above all else. He could not keep her waiting.

When he arrived at his private villa's entrance, his lion emblem, with the maroon and gold of House Aleksandran, was draped across every surface, illuminated by golden braziers. His soldiers and servants stood attentively in a neat formation. He assumed his position next to Basil, Jareth, and

Magdolina. Basil drooped with fatigue, eyes darting across the plaza, ensuring every detail was perfect. Selecting him as the master of festivities was one of Aludrien's better choices in recent memory.

"Cutting it rather close, my brother," Basil said.

"Half-brother," Aludrien snapped, his feet tapping in irritation.

"You seem nervous, Your Grace," Jareth said, loud enough for only him and Basil to hear. "I assumed you and your aunt were close."

Aludrien shot the couple a glare that wiped the mischievous grins off their faces.

"She may be my beloved aunt," Aludrien hissed. "But she is currently my greatest rival to the throne. Treat her as such."

His subordinates had grown too relaxed with him lately. Had he grown soft? Should he execute one to regain their respect? Though that would most likely provoke Fenris to attack. He was particularly sensitive to tyrannical behavior.

Scowling, he shoved the infuriating menace from his mind.

He composed himself as the great gates opened onto the water gardens, revealing a small contingent.

Grand Marshal Hestraea Aleksandran strode through the entrance of her ancestral home with her usual intimidating presence. She had summoned her insignis armor, which gleamed in the firelight. Half a dozen prominent generals trailed behind, along with a few overly eager sycophants who had journeyed south early to see the returning Grand Marshal.

General Barrett was not among them.

Aludrien elegantly descended the steps, assuming the role of gracious host, one of many masks instilled in him at a young age, though one he preferred to leave to fools like Basil.

"I, Lord Aludrien Aleksandran, son of Claude Aleksandran, the forty-fifth emperor of the Xandrian Empire, heir to the throne, welcome you to my home," he said, ensuring his voice was loud enough to echo through the palace. "It humbles me to welcome you, my esteemed and resplendent aunt. Victorious in battle and hero of the realm."

He met Hestraea at the base of the stairs, bowing deeply. When he rose, he shot his aunt a cheeky smile.

She returned a cold, aloof stare.

"The pleasure is all mine, Your Grace," Hestraea replied stoically, bowing deeper than Aludrien had, holding it for a few moments.

The public etiquette of the royal house was stiff and formal, even with close relatives. Though more relaxed behind closed doors, Aleksandrans were expected to conduct themselves with a ceremonial demeanor befitting their station. However strict, Hestraea despised the pomp and circumstance of her position. During his youth, she would often pull the mask away enough for Aludrien to see behind it. It calmed him, reminding him that his loving aunt remained beneath the guise of the greatest general in Xandrian history.

Today, he could not afford such a luxury. He swallowed hard.

"Greetings to my other honorable guests. We shall retire to the dining room for libations and sustenance. As your host, I have prepared a feast for such a joyous occasion."

Offering his arm to Hestraea, he ushered her up the stairs and into the villa, trailed by their respective entourages. Basil was preparing the great hall at the front of the palace for the masquerade, so the arrival banquet would take place in the villa's private dining room. It was ample enough for such a gathering and, in his opinion, a generous gesture to celebrate in an otherwise intimate space.

"I've missed you these past months," Aludrien whispered. Thankful for a brief moment to converse privately. He wished to speak with her promptly after her airship landed, but tradition required the reception to take place in public. "We have much to discuss."

"Indeed."

He inhaled sharply at the terse reply.

The dinner guests assumed their places at the table, Hestraea to his right, Basil and his family to his left. The courtiers fortunate enough to receive an invitation filled the rest of the long dining table. Cupbearers poured the wine, followed by a long series of toasts praising the general's victorious campaign and contribution to the realm. Course after course of sumptuous plates followed, exquisitely prepared by Belessia. The dinner conversation was lively. Hestraea and her generals regaled the guests with elaborate, thrilling stories of the campaign. They were clearly rehearsed and whitewashed the gruesome realities of war, but their audience consisted of sheltered and privileged nobles who hadn't once set foot on a battlefield.

He barely paid attention, focusing on Hestraea, dissecting her every word, expression, and movement. Something was amiss; he was sure of it. Toward the end of the dinner, as the table splintered into dozens of side conversations, Basil piped up.

"I presumed General Barrett would be joining us this evening," Basil said, gesturing to the empty chair near the end of the table. "Has he not recently purchased an estate nearby?"

"Yes," Hestraea said. "I find it as lovely as when it belonged to your mother, Basil. May her soul rest."

Basil trembled slightly at the mention of his mother. Jareth placed a calming hand on his shoulder.

"So you have been there?" Jareth asked. "I was under the impression that he purchased it only months ago."

"Yes, I journeyed from there today. General Barrett was generous enough to host me for a few nights after my long voyage. He decided to remain at his estate a while longer, but you will see him at the masquerade. I'm sure he'll love to tell you all about the menagerie of peacocks he purchased."

If Jareth or Basil responded, Aludrien did not hear it. He clutched his fork so hard he almost bled. She had visited the bastard first. Hestraea was fully aware of the amount of support backing her claim to the throne, corrupted by General Barrett's influence. That explained her aloofness. But if Grand Marshal Hestraea wanted the throne, she wouldn't be here sitting at dinner so casually. Her entrance would have been a coup. He could still sway her, convince his aunt to remain loyal, and avoid being corrupted by power. If he told her of Barrett's desire to use and dispose of her to gain the crown, then she might see reason.

After dinner concluded and conversation dried, Aludrien stood, marking the end of the banquet. Escorting Hestraea from the dining hall, he turned toward her private quarters, which he had Nim diligently prepare for her return.

Hestraea halted.

"I have arranged accommodations in the front palace for the evening," she said, her tone remaining formal despite their relative privacy.

"You are an Aleksandran; your place is here. With your family," Aludrien insisted. "Not that bastard Barrett. You cannot trust him."

"I do not wish to disturb you as you prepare for your ascension. My guest quarters will serve me adequately. I will be traveling before the masquerade. It's been months since I attended court, and I have received numerous invitations to dine at various winter homes before your ascension."

"But we must talk, dear aunt," Aludrien said, frustrated by her indifferent demeanor and cryptic words. Was she admitting to conspiring for the throne? Could she be that bold?

"I understand," Hestraea sighed, her facade briefly fading. "But I have traveled long and need rest. Have your chamberlain speak with mine and schedule a meeting. I apologize that we cannot speak as soon as you'd like, but I promise we will discuss everything in due time. Try to enjoy your final party before your ascension, dear nephew."

She bowed deeply and walked off into the night, leaving Aludrien alone, speechless. His aunt might be too far gone, but he was certain of a singular truth.

General Barrett must die.

19

Masquerade

"What in the fresh hell is this?" Fenris asked incredulously, tossing the garish bundle of clothing onto the bed in disgust.

"Expensive. Do be careful with it," Nim snapped, cradling the garment like a delicate relic. "This costume cost a fortune to construct, tailored exclusively for you."

The mid-afternoon sun bathed the heir's private chambers in warm light while the courtyard below bustled with servants preparing for the impending masquerade.

"I'm not sure why I would need something so flashy," Fenris said. "Wouldn't it make more sense to maintain my disguise as your food taster?"

"Not if you have been officially invited to my masquerade ball as a guest," Aludrien said, placing a heavy golden mask in Fenris's hands. "A mysterious lord is far more inconspicuous than a bumbling servant."

Inspecting the mask, Fenris admired the intricate carvings and delicate craftsmanship. Nim hadn't been exaggerating about the sheer cost of the ensemble. Fenris groaned when he recognized the shape of the mask—a howling wolf.

"A bit literal, isn't it?" Fenris said blankly.

"Scores of other lords will wear a similar guise," Aludrien explained. "Wolves are a popular costume for these events. Especially among bloodthirsty and ambitious men."

"Is that what you think of me?" Fenris asked, smiling cheekily.

Nim cleared their throat, revealing a long decorative pin.

"Ah, thank you, Nim." Aludrien gingerly collected the long needle and presented it to Fenris. "Fasten it to your sleeve; such a decoration is the fashion in the northern provinces. However, this particular pin is coated in a lethal toxin. Though the effects will not manifest for at least a day."

"Giving General Barrett enough time to return to the comforts of his villa," Fenris said. "Allowing you to claim innocence."

"That will not deter my enemies from accusing me, of course," Aludrien sighed. "But such complications are unavoidable."

"And what of my target?" Fenris asked.

"He arrived early this morning, eager to conspire with the courtiers residing in the guest quarters. Elzia has provided me with a detailed report," Nim said, hesitating before adding. "Grand Marshal Hestraea accompanied the general's retinue."

Aludrien grimaced.

"Have you spoken to her since the banquet?" Fenris asked.

"Of course not," Aludrien snapped. "She hasn't returned to the Winter Palace since. Too busy cavorting with Barrett's ilk."

"Are you certain that killing Barrett will discourage her supporters?" Fenris asked. "We are only two days from the ascension, after all."

"I will not murder my aunt!" Aludrien spat, glowering. "And that is the last I will hear of the sort. She will hear reason once the toxic Barrett stops spewing nonsense in her ear and she learns of his treachery. I am sure of it."

Fenris opened his mouth to retort, but thought better of it.

"According to Elzia," Nim said. "General Barrett will be wearing a boar's mask."

"Fitting," Aludrien said. "A pig disguised as a pig."

"I am sure he will be one of the first to arrive at the gala," Nim resumed, ignoring their master's barbs. "A single prick with this needle will suffice, anywhere on the body. Ensure you finish the deed before High Lord Aludrien's arrival, which will be fashionably late. The palace defenses will double once the heir arrives. By then, your mission will be complete."

"If you're planning an attack, we can assume Barrett will do the same," Fenris said.

"Do not concern yourself with my safety, Fenris. Only focus on your target," Aludrien said. "Though in another life, you would have made an excellent bodyguard. Regardless, I have taken the necessary precautions. Jareth is aware of our scheme and is managing my security for the evening."

"But I will finish before you arrive," Fenris insisted. "The least I can do is eliminate potential threats."

"You are free to slip away upon my arrival," Aludrien said. "Unless you want to indulge in the festivities."

"Masquerades were scarce on the Belantine Plains," Fenris said. "So I may have to take you up on that offer."

Aludrien smiled devilishly.

"Your Grace," Nim interjected, pursing their lips. The chamberlain seized the mask from Fenris and delicately placed it in a bag along with his robes. "We must prepare you for the gala. The costume you have selected is painfully intricate."

"I suppose you are right," Aludrien sighed, turning to Fenris. "Are we clear?"

"Yes, Your Grace."

Aludrien smiled, seizing the bag from Nim and handing it to Fenris. "Good luck."

Bowing, Fenris ignored Nim's groans and exited the bedroom. The past week had flown by, filled with late-night discussions in the garden and surveillance missions in the guest quarters as the pinnacle of society arrived at the Winter Palace. Between Nim, Elzia, and Fenris, the entire guest list had been thoroughly dissected and vetted. A makeshift diagram lay on Aludrien's bedroom floor, detailing the allegiance of every known lord and lady, like the musings of a madman. Over half supported Hestraea's claim, while the rest remained faithful to Aludrien.

Barrett's death would hopefully tip the scales in the heir's favor. Aludrien's spirits rose with each passing day. Fenris eagerly anticipated their nightly rendezvous in the private greenhouse. The heir had softened toward Fenris since the Belantine Plains. Behind his icy facade lay an intelligent, eager, and humorous tactician. One that Fenris had grown to care for.

Which was why he stayed. Aludrien was correct; Fenris could have escaped after he learned Durian had deceived him. He no longer had a stake in the ascension. But he still cared about the realm's future. And Aludrien would be the best emperor in generations.

He nearly collided with Elzia on his way to the far wall; they exchanged knowing smiles as they passed. He had no time to stop and chat; too many wandering eyes watched in such a public place.

Aludrien saving Elzia was a testament to his graciousness. And Fenris enjoyed having another friendly face in the Winter Palace. He did not blame her for working for Vispin; he understood that she was merely trying to survive. The pair met often to exchange vital information.

The sun was waning, and airships dotted the horizon. The masquerade would begin shortly.

Slipping behind Aludrien's greenhouse, Fenris cloaked himself in invisibility. The private garden occupied a narrow space wedged between the villa and the outer wall. The ancient stone was remarkably easy to scale; its deep grooves provided ample footholds. Within a heartbeat, Fenris propelled himself to the top, narrowly dodging a patrol.

Leaping over the outer battlements, he plummeted to the ground, landing on all fours. The impact vibrated through his body. Recovering, he sped into the oasis's thick tangle of trees. Drawn by his body heat, a swarm of gnats followed him as he skulked through the undergrowth. Snakes slithered below, and odd noises echoed off the mossy tree trunks. Fenris did not mind; he missed the freedom of the wilds after months of palace life.

The journey was slow and painstaking, but soon he reached a large glade, filled with dozens of airships, their metal glinting in the setting sun. He crouched behind a vacant ship furthest from the main entrance and expanded his veil.

He slipped on his costume, a rich purple cloak that billowed over his regular clothes, satin gloves, and pristine leather boots. He attached the pin to his sleeve, careful not to prick himself in the process.

Once he fastened the mask, Fenris dropped the veil and strode confidently toward the palace.

A pair of guards stopped him near the gate; his invitation was already in hand. Lord Maruc Tyrelian of Tybalt—an outlandish name, but the grunts wouldn't scrutinize it beyond the official seal. Fenris had infiltrated numerous parties in his day, but none hosted by his employer. Access was effortless.

The courtyard beyond nearly took his breath away. Basil had converted it into a curated jungle. Golden braziers illuminated sculptures constructed entirely of exotic flowers: bears, eagles, fish, and a dozen other elaborate shapes.

Musicians played lilting music from a dais built in the far corner, filling the courtyard with an upbeat melody. Dozens of lords and ladies milled around, casually conversing with the new arrivals as they filtered in from the airstrip.

Servants passed by with silver trays filled with hors d'oeuvres, scrumptious bites prepared by Belessia and her staff. Fenris was unsure how the woman had remained standing after weeks of cooking for the massive event. To his dismay, most of the nobles ignored or declined the offerings of food and drink, opting to partake of their personal chalices, held by their doting servants, who trailed in their wake.

Fenris ignored them and climbed the stairs on the left. Although every guest in the courtyard wore a mask similar to his, he did not want to loiter too long, lest he risk unwanted attention. Small talk wasn't a core strength, and he preferred to avoid any questions about the fictional Maruc Tyrelian of Tybalt.

Royals, nobles, ministers, and officers, the height of Xandrian society was on full display. Invitations for the royal ball were coveted almost more than the ascension itself. The only group noticeably absent was the church, which was for the best, for Fenris wouldn't have been able to contain himself if he encountered Ignatius at the party. It took every ounce of his energy to remain in the Winter Palace and not march over to the ruins to take vengeance upon the individual who had orchestrated the Meridian's creation and its subsequent destruction.

Weaving through the palace foyer, he entered the lavish ballroom. Two curved staircases descended to the giant dance floor. Extravagant chandeliers illuminated the cavernous room from above, as did the floor-to-ceiling windows along the far wall, which peered out into the glorious water garden.

A band played from a platform along the far wall, accompanying the lively dance in the room's center. The sun had yet to set, but the dance floor was already full, with more nobles streaming down the steps.

Leaning casually against the railing, Fenris accepted a champagne flute from a passing servant and surveyed the ballroom. Sipping his drink, he scanned the crowd.

Basil and Jareth were already on the dance floor, wearing matching masks adorned with radiant peacock feathers. The pair twirled gracefully around, Jareth leading with decisive strength. They looked at each other with such love and admiration that it moved Fenris. He had never experienced such a connection as theirs. And probably never would.

He turned from the dance floor and resumed observing the crowd. He had until sunset to complete his mission. According to his intel, General Barrett preferred drinking over dancing, so Fenris began his search along the room's fringe. Remembering the lord's behavior in the baths, he started with the largest and most rambunctious groups.

There, in the center of the third-largest gathering, a bulky man with a silver boar mask talked fervently with his hands. The nobles around him roared with laughter, undoubtedly at some off-color joke.

General Barrett was unmistakable, even in this crowd.

Fenris descended the stairs, careful to avoid eye contact with the other guests. He weaved through the party, narrowly avoiding the already drunken nobles and their anxious servants. He methodically traversed the crowd and found himself at the edge of Barrett's group. He circled it slowly, observing it out of the corner of his eye.

Barrett vanished.

Frantic, Fenris scanned the party, weaving around the outer edge. He could not attract too much attention, but he needed to find a better vantage point.

And then he saw it. The silver boar. Across the dance floor, next to the band. Chatting with a tall woman in a golden puma mask. Grand Marshal Hestraea.

Fixated on the silver, Fenris weaved through the crowd, which had grown significantly larger as more guests flooded in from the courtyard. The orange light of sunset poured in from the giant windows. He did not have much time left.

Grand Marshal Hestraea had taken her leave, replaced by a dozen courtiers, but Barrett remained in place.

Someone grabbed his arm.

"May I have this dance?" A tall lady in a seafoam ball gown and matching swan mask curtsied elegantly.

Before he could respond, she pulled him onto the dance floor, swirling in the sea of silk and gold. Having never danced before, Fenris awkwardly followed the lady's lead, who quickly assessed the skill level of her new dance partner and graciously obliged.

But she led him further from Barrett.

The song changed to an upbeat jig, and the swan swept him into the center of the fray. Despite her delicate frame, her grip resembled iron, and she kept Fenris from stepping too far out of line.

Following the swan's lead, he memorized the steps, gaining confidence as the music swelled. He glanced over to the far corner. Thankfully, Barrett remained in his group, on the perimeter of the dance floor.

The swan spun them to the right, in the opposite direction, but Fenris firmed his grip and flipped around. He swept his partner into the center and out the other end. His movements were clunky at first, but soon he found his stride and worked his way toward the far end.

"You are a fast learner," the swan said.

"Thank you, m-" Fenris said. He stopped himself, remembering that nobles did not use honorifics with each other. "I had an excellent teacher."

The swan blushed and followed his lead, excited by this new surge of confidence. The elegant lady allowed herself to surrender to the moment and trust her partner's lead. Soaring across the dance floor, Fenris twirled her around, straight into General Barrett.

The swan shrieked and nearly fell over. But the boar was sturdy and quick, and caught the falling noblewoman with ease.

Pulled by the swan, Fenris leaned into Barrett. Right before impact, he pulled the pin from his sleeve with his free hand and wedged it firmly between his fingers. When his palm clasped Barrett's shoulder, the needle found its mark, piercing through fabric and puncturing skin. Barrett did not notice, distracted by the woman who had crashed into him.

"My apologies," Fenris said, slurring his words intentionally. "This dance is foreign to me."

"Ah, no worries," Barrett said, pulling the swan to her feet. "I used to be known for my two left feet back in the day, nothing to be ashamed of."

"I need to stop choosing men half my age," the swan said, eyeing General Barrett expectantly.

"A pristine lady such as yourself deserves a more…mature dance partner," Barrett replied, turning to Fenris. "Sorry, my boy, but I will take it from here."

Fenris bowed, feigning embarrassment as the boar and the swan twirled into the throng.

He succeeded. Barrett would be dead within the day. And Aludrien's path to ascension would be clearer than ever before.

The song ended, and trumpets sounded from the stairs. The crowd halted, turning to the entrance. A hush fell over the party as they craned their necks expectantly.

"Introducing your illustrious host for this evening," a crier announced from the apex of the stairs. "His majesty, High Lord Aludrien Aleksandran, son of Claude Aleksandran and heir to the Xandrian Empire."

A vision of maroon and gold, Aludrien entered the ballroom, his giant, golden lion mask covering his face entirely, its intricate mane pluming behind him. A walking sculpture, he glided down the steps with ease. Fenris could not help but marvel at him.

"He looks amazing, doesn't he?" a voice whispered.

Fenris whirled, coming face to face with a tall, broad-shouldered man in a black robe and bronze fox mask. He smiled knowingly.

The voice was unmistakable, as was the smell. Fenris was well acquainted with both.

"It's unlike you to avoid public adoration," Fenris muttered.

"Can we not evolve?" Aludrien asked. "Besides, I would rather witness your handiwork up close. Excellent work with Lady Schima."

"Who?"

"The swan," Aludrien said, trembling with giddy energy.

"Who is the impostor?" Fenris asked, glancing at the grand staircase.

"Nim, of course."

"They're a head shorter than you."

"Stilts," Aludrien grinned mischievously. "Such is the marvel of modern engineering. We created the costume to hold Nim, but to portray my exact measurements."

"And wouldn't you want to take this opportunity to garner more support from your subjects?"

"Nim is much better at kissing ass than I. And their voice is sufficiently muffled by the garish mask that anyone would mistake it for mine."

The fake Aludrien disappeared into the crowd, and the band resumed playing a lively jig. The lords and ladies paired up around them, swirling to the music.

"Well, I shouldn't attract any more attention by standing around," Fenris said. "I will take my leave. Enjoy your party."

The heir reached out a hand.

"Why don't we have a dance before you depart?"

Fenris gaped at Aludrien, befuddled by the invitation. A passing lord elbowed him in the ribs. They were in the center of the dance floor; it would look suspicious if they did not join. Reluctantly, he grasped the heir's hand.

Aludrien pulled him into a tight embrace. Fenris had witnessed Aludrien's strength firsthand on numerous occasions, but he hadn't experienced it in such a tender manner before.

One hand intertwined with his, the other placed on the small of Fenris's back, Aludrien led the pair into the swirling tempest of the dance. The tune was frenetic and upbeat, Fenris's heart pounded faster and faster as they quickened their pace.

Their eyes locked, and the world faded until only the fox and the wolf remained, surrounded by a myriad of colors and sounds. Fenris fell into step, much more in sync than he was with the swan. Aludrien's arms felt natural wrapped around him. Comfortable.

The song ended, and Fenris's heart sank. He did not want it to end.

Aludrien did not break away.

A new song began, much slower. The couples around them adjusted their holds, embracing each other tightly.

Aludrien pulled Fenris closer, wrapping both arms around his waist. Left without a choice, Fenris threw his arms around Aludrien's neck, gazing into the eyes hidden behind the fox mask.

They swayed gently to the soft music, together as one.

"You were trying to kiss me when I confronted you in the Belantine Plains," Aludrien said.

"No," Fenris countered. "It was you who almost kissed me in the slums, after I saved your ass."

"If you wanted to fuck, you should have told me," Aludrien mused. "I must admit that I have been craving it ever since

Tipin murdered Alexei."

"It's not like that," Fenris snapped indignantly. "I have no desire to be your doting bed servant."

"Ah, I see," Aludrien said. "In that case…"

He dipped Fenris low. Holding him tightly, Aludrien stared down longingly.

Gently, he placed his lips upon Fenris's.

They were soft, warm, and inviting. Fenris lost himself in them. He relaxed, held by strong arms, overtaken by desire. Aludrien's lips moved, and Fenris opened his mouth, allowing a skilled tongue to enter and touch his. As their passions grew, he ran his fingers through Aludrien's hair, caressing his cheek, relishing the softness of his skin.

For the first time since his ascension, the spirits within were completely still; the only voice inside his head was his own.

To those around them, they were a wistful pair of lords overcome by the emotions of the song. Not the heir to the Xandrian Empire and the assassin who killed his father.

But to them, they were simply Aludrien and Fenris. Nothing else existed. Fenris did not want anything else to exist.

A lady screamed.

Followed by dozens of others.

The music stopped abruptly.

The crowd around them surged, breaking their embrace. Irritated, Fenris regained his footing and pivoted toward the stairs, where everyone else was looking. Through the crowd, he could see a clearing. A figure lay on the ground, a great golden lion's mane splayed along the marble, a dagger protruding from their chest.

Nim.

20

Shattered

Fenris rushed forward instinctively, but an iron grip halted his advance. Aludrien grimly shook his head as the crowd scattered in panic.

"Careful," he whispered. "A pair of random lords rushing to the heir would appear suspicious."

Composing himself, Fenris heeded the advice. The throng parted slightly, providing a better view of the scene. Basil and Jareth crouched next to Nim's prostrate body, which was still disguised as Aludrien. A dozen guards had already assembled around them, crossbows raised. Grand Marshal Hestraea rushed to the scene, discarding her puma mask and summoning her blades as she barked orders to the soldiers.

"The heir is dead!" a lord screamed.

Courtiers stampeded up the stairs, desperate to escape. Fenris pulled Aludrien into the chaos. The pair would look suspicious if they lingered and gawked.

As would the assassin.

Scanning the crowd, Fenris searched for predatory activity. Anyone who moved too calmly, too erratically, hid their hands in a pocket, or was also scrutinizing the ballroom as he was.

He lost count after twelve.

A lady in a mesh veil stalked the perimeter of the dance floor, her hands hidden beneath the folds of her gown. A violinist surveyed the crowd as he leisurely vacated the stage, gripping his instrument tightly; his fellow musicians had already evacuated the platform in a panic. A pair of brawny men loitered placidly by the side door leading to the kitchens, standing immovable as nobles surged by. A slight woman in an ill-fitting dress frantically shoved her way up the stairs, glancing at the heir, as if to ensure he had indeed perished. Another, clad in a revealing golden dress, her hair held in a bun by two long pins, perched at the top of the stairs and locked eyes with Fenris.

Cursing, he dropped his gaze and steered Aludrien away, hoping the other assassins hadn't noticed his scrutiny. He skirted the veiled woman and led Aludrien toward the stairs.

"We have a full party," Fenris warned, trying his best to mimic the behavior of a frantic lord.

They had nearly arrived at the stairs when he detected movement to his right. The violinist weaved through the masses, stalking toward them. His hand pulled a tuning peg from the instrument, revealing a slender blade.

Pivoting, Fenris put himself between Aludrien and the assassin. The blade grazed his waist, tearing his tunic. Fenris elbowed the violinist in the temple, sending him to the floor, stunned.

"We may have another rat in our midst," the heir whispered, eyes wide.

"I'm not so sure," Fenris said, motioning toward a limp body near the stairs. A tall lord stared sightlessly at the chandelier above, his throat cut. "Our uninvited guests are a contingency in case you used a decoy. Whoever planned this is a cunning tactician."

The woman in gold, who had spotted them earlier, descended the stairs with her hair flowing and pins in hand. Fenris tugged Aludrien backward, toward the kitchen.

"Not that way," Aludrien hissed.

The contingent of soldiers carried Nim's limp body toward the kitchens where the pair of burly men had engaged them. One already lay lifeless on the floor. Jareth fought off the other, a bloody insignis blade in hand.

"What do you suggest?" Fenris asked, motioning to the stairs. One was blocked by the woman in gold, the other by a group of soldiers.

"Follow my lead."

Aludrien pulled right, away from the kitchens and back toward the stairs. Fenris resisted at first, but soon fell in line, knowing better than to contradict the heir once his mind was set. The lady in gold had almost reached the bottom of the stairs. The crowd had already thinned, escaping into the courtyard above, leaving half a dozen young men dead on the marble. Whoever orchestrated this attack had no qualms about slaughtering innocent bystanders. Anyone who remotely looked like the heir was a target.

Aludrien continued toward the curved, vacant alcove formed by the double staircases. Without a crowd to impede them, they dashed forward and collided with the wall. To Fenris's surprise, the marble panel gave way and swiveled, ushering them into an unlit tunnel. The secret door flipped back into place, leaving them in pitch darkness.

A blue ball of light appeared in Aludrien's palm, and an

insignis blade materialized in the other. Fenris tried to pull forward into the tunnel, but the heir stood his ground.

"Wait," he hissed. "One of those bastards was sure to see our escape. I'd prefer it if no one followed us."

Fenris nodded, his fingernails already lengthening into claws.

The pair lingered in tense silence, focused on the trap door. Sure enough, the stone panel gradually opened, grinding against the floor. A golden dress gleamed in the blue light. Fenris lurched forward, seizing the woman by the throat and plunging his claws into her skin. He pulled her into the tunnel as the panel slammed shut, driving her straight into Aludrien's blade. Her corpse slumped to the floor, throat crushed and chest impaled.

His stomach twisted, but he pushed away the regret and focused on protecting Aludrien.

They cautiously monitored the door, in case another assassin had witnessed the first entering the secret tunnel. But no one came. The chaotic sounds of the ballroom carried through the trapdoor, but the marble remained closed.

"We should be safe now," Aludrien said. "This tunnel leads out to the water gardens. We can join Jareth and the others at the villa. Hopefully, they have arrived there safely."

"Poor Nim," Fenris said.

"They knew the risks," Aludrien said. His voice wavered, betraying his true feelings. The chamberlain had served as the heir's closest confidant for years, and Fenris considered Nim more of a loyal companion and friend than a mere servant. But they could not dwell on the tragedy yet; he had to escort Aludrien to safety.

They proceeded in silence, following the winding tunnel.

Fenris insisted on leading, peering around each bend as if an assassin were waiting in the shadows. Finally, they reached the end, a sheer marble wall, like the entrance to the ballroom.

Carefully, Fenris pushed the secret door open and stepped out into the muggy evening air.

A crossbow bolt slammed into his chest.

Falling backward into the tunnel, Fenris called upon the spirits within and summoned a ward to cover the entrance. A half-dozen bolts of energy collided violently with the shield.

"Are you alright?" Aludrien asked, crouching as his body became covered in insignis armor.

"I'll survive," Fenris groaned. The steaming wound on his chest was a mixture of burned skin and fabric. It would have killed an ordinary person, but unfortunately for Fenris, he would have to endure the blinding pain until the spirits repaired the flesh. The process moved more slowly than usual, with most of his strength focused on shielding the entrance.

Outside the tunnel, dark figures appeared from the shadows, steadily advancing. The shield wavered, pummeled by volley after volley of projectiles.

"This won't do," Aludrien growled, raising his hands high.

The sky outside shimmered, illuminating the gardens and the small host of assassins, disguised in masquerade costumes. The sky erupted, claps of thunder echoed against the stone walls, and bolts of lightning struck the ground, sending up a cloud of stone, dirt, and burned flesh.

Moments after the last strike, Aludrien cried, "Release the shield!"

Fenris obeyed as the heir lurched forward, slamming the trap door shut.

His chest tingled as the spirits healed his charred flesh. The ethereal voices screamed in agony. Aludrien leaned against the door. The wound wasn't deep, so Fenris hoped it would fully recover before the enemy could regroup.

Something bashed against the marble, and the door shifted slightly.

"So much for a secret passage," Fenris groaned.

"Quiet," Aludrien snapped, straining against the increasing force applied against the door. "How much longer do you require?"

"Move," Fenris growled. The wound still stung, but he felt strong enough to continue fighting.

Aludrien obliged, ducking behind Fenris. The door snapped open, and a trio of assassins spilled in. Fenris summoned a violent maelstrom to greet them. It ripped the stone door from its hinges, shattering it into pieces. Rubble and bodies flew across the garden, breaking against the path beyond.

Aludrien dashed from the tunnel, insignis blades flashing in the moonlight. Fenris followed on his heels, claws outstretched. More assassins materialized from the shadows, drawn by Aludrien's display. The sheer magnitude and coordination of the attack were staggering. Such an undertaking was more than a single lord's doing; it must have taken the concentrated effort of every single one of Aludrien's enemies.

But thankfully, none of these assassins were Animancers or insignis bearers. Apparently, the nobles did not want to dirty their own hands.

Aludrien and Fenris fought back-to-back. Blade and claw. Like their dance in the ballroom, they moved in unison. Aludrien's calculated precision combined with Fenris's instinctive wildness proved the perfect combination. The lowly provincial assassins, though dozens in number, were no match for the heir and the Tal'Rach. Before long, the pair stood in the center of a field of corpses, panting laboriously.

A fireball erupted from the shadows, blasting into Aludrien's back. It glanced harmlessly off his armor but sent him careening to the ground. Fenris raised his shield, fending off another flaming projectile.

A man materialized from the shadows, the night air shimmering dangerously around him. His body was covered in insignis armor, and a silver boar mask obscured his face.

"Good evening, Lord Aludrien," General Barrett said, his voice booming. His eyes shifted to Fenris's claws, and his smug expression twisted into one of surprise and indignant rage. "Fighting alongside the monster who murdered your father. I knew you to be a bastard, Aludrien, and ill fit for the throne, but I never believed you to be evil. Was it you who ordered your father's death?"

"Silence, you pathetic pig," Aludrien snapped, climbing to his feet. "Why would I explain myself to the walking dead?"

Fenris pulled the pin from his sleeve and brandished it. "You stole my dance partner."

"You," Barrett growled, gripping his insignis blade. He relaxed his shoulders and laughed. His chest heaved with the boisterous sound. "Well, I had a good run. I'll take you with me."

He lurched forward, his blade shaping into an ax. The mystical weapon cleaved the shield slightly, forming a crack wide enough for tendrils of metal to sneak through. Aludrien and Fenris scattered to avoid the spears.

Dropping the shield, Fenris unleashed a fireball at the general, which bounced off his armor. But the distraction was enough for Aludrien to close in, his blades forming into deadly whips.

Standing back, claws at the ready, Fenris watched the two Xandrians engage in a savage contest. He hadn't witnessed a pair of insignis wielders battle before. It was a true sight to behold. Metal flowed through the air like water, both graceful and deadly. Aludrien possessed two blades to Barrett's one, marking his higher station. He was faster, stronger, and possessed more stamina, but Barrett was more seasoned, tactical, and had nothing to lose. The elder drew first blood, leaving a shallow cut on Aludrien's calf. The heir cried out in pain.

Fenris growled, stepping forward. But he stopped himself. Aludrien and Barrett were too close for Fenris to intervene without risking injury to the heir. So he waited, feeling powerless.

Spurned by anger, Aludrien responded with a series of rapid strikes, pushing Barrett backward. The veteran parried the barrage expertly, but he rapidly lost stamina. Each strike was slower than the last. Soon, Aludrien would have him.

Barrett lowered his blade.

Aludrien's whips found their mark, impaling the lord in both shoulders. Barrett smiled viciously.

Fenris understood. Barrett's life was already forfeit; he didn't mean to survive the encounter.

Fenris screamed a warning. The metal of Barrett's breastplate shifted and swirled around Aludrien's blades, holding them fast. With a roar, the veteran charged forward, ax outstretched. The blade connected with an Animancy shield, but the force of the charge pushed Aludrien backward. He stumbled and tripped over a corpse and fell to the ground, Barrett crashing on top of him. The shield shattered.

Fenris saw red.

Throwing his mask aside, a real wolf's snout replaced the fake one. His clothes tore and shredded as he shifted into his lupine form. Loping across the ruined garden grounds, he only saw Barrett. He crashed into the thick man in a collision of metal and flesh. His bones shattered, but he ignored the pain. Only Aludrien's safety mattered.

Barrett lay beneath him, eyes wide with terror and rage. The cold sting of metal tore through Fenris's ribcage. His claws and teeth craved to rend flesh. The metal shell proved a challenge, but with the sheer strength of a Tal'Rach, he tore the breastplate off and tossed it aside, exposing Barrett's chest.

Fenris howled in victory, bleeding from multiple wounds. But he had experienced worse pain. The voices in his head urged him to kill. His claws tore into flesh, bone, and organs. He continued his frenzied attack until the metal ax slipped out of his body. General Barrett lay in pieces below him. For the first time in his life, he did not mourn the death of a victim. The bastard dared to harm Aludrien.

A lightning bolt crashed into him, searing his flesh and throwing him into a nearby tree. A small group appeared through the darkness. A woman in insignis armor stood at the forefront. Basil and Jareth flanked her, followed by the half dozen soldiers who carried Nim's limp body. They looked on in horror and disgust. They had only witnessed the end of the battle, but that was enough. Basil doubled over and vomited into a nearby pool.

"Aludrien, back away!" Hestraea cried. Flame bloomed from her hands.

Already on his feet, Aludrien frantically raised his hands and rushed between his aunt and Fenris.

"Stop," he said. "You do not understand! He will not hurt us, he was merely defending—"

"Aludrien," Jareth said. "If I am not mistaken…that creature looks remarkably like—"

His voice trailed off, his eyes widening in surprise and revulsion.

Hestraea extinguished her flames, mouth agape. She finally understood. Her jaw clenched, eyes hardening.

"So Barrett was correct about you from the start," Hestraea said. "You ordered your father's death, not the cardinals. What for, Aludrien? The throne was already yours. All you needed was to be patient!"

"You misunderstand. Barrett was going to kill you once—"

"I defended you!" Hestraea bellowed. "For all these months, half the Imperium begged me to turn on you, to take the throne for myself, and I refused, for I believed the man I helped raise was virtuous and just. Oh, how wrong I was."

"Stood by me? You ignored me! We haven't properly spoken since Father's funeral! You abandoned me to fend for myself!"

"I was preoccupied. Rebellion tends to take some energy to quell, I thought you could handle yourself in the meantime."

"You've had a week to speak with me; instead, you spent your days consorting with my enemies. The same ones who tried to kill me tonight."

"Oh, you foolish boy! You impetuous, silly child," Hestraea said. "And why do you suppose I spent so much time with Barrett and his ilk? To convince them to yield and support your claim."

"Seems like you failed in that," Aludrien said dryly.

"Seems like I shouldn't have tried in the first place," Hestraea spat.

"You don't mean that."

Hestraea summoned more flame. "I do."

"I will not fight you, dear aunt," Aludrien said. The metal protecting his body roiled and receded, reshaping into the benign tattoos that covered his body. He extended his arms, chest exposed. "I cannot."

Hestraea glared at him, flames roiling. She yelled in frustration, extinguishing them in an instant and retracting her own blade.

"I will offer this one kindness, not for you, but for your father. Despite your treachery, Claude loved you more than life itself. But you must leave this place tonight. I never want to see you again. And if you so much as set foot in Arachovia, I will kill you myself."

"So you plan to usurp my birthright," Aludrien hissed. "How can I be sure this wasn't your plan all along?"

"I'm not the one who is commanding the beast that slew your father, Aludrien. You broke my allegiance all by yourself. I have no desire to be empress, but I will sacrifice for the Imperium if it means keeping one such as you from the throne. Now step aside as I deal with your father's murderer."

"I will leave," Aludrien begged. "Tonight. But spare Fenris. He was following orders. I take full responsibility for his actions."

Hestraea cackled.

"Oh, you foolish, foolish boy," she said. Sighing, she turned to leave, and the others followed.

"Leave my chamberlain," Aludrien said desperately.

Hestraea raised an eyebrow. "Very well." She gestured to her soldiers, and they gingerly set Nim on the stone pathway. "Remember what I said, boy. If I see your face again, I will end your life."

The Grand Marshal turned and disappeared into the night. Basil and Jareth followed, shooting Aludrien scornful looks.

The heir rushed over to Nim's prostrate body, removing the mask gingerly. Fenris climbed to his feet to join them. The chamberlain's face was gaunt, but their chest still rose and fell slightly. They were alive.

"Fenris, hurry," Aludrien said. "They still breathe. Please, heal them."

21

Solace

Fenris gazed through the airship window, watching the spectacular sunset cast a golden glow upon the lake's placid surface. Barely visible silhouettes of vast buildings rose from the far side of Lake Arachovia. Unblinking, he stared across the water intently. Ignatius waited somewhere in those ruins. Fenris's mood soured at the mere thought of the Pontifex. With Durian already dead, killing Ignatius might be the only way for Fenris to atone for his countless sins and avenge his fallen friends.

Months ago, Fenris had sacrificed his freedom for a chance to kill the heir. Now, on the eve of the ascension, he would do almost anything to ensure that Aludrien would become the next emperor. Funny how circumstances had changed.

Durian's betrayal had weighed heavily on his mind, as everything the Meridian fought for was ultimately a lie. But Aludrien provided Fenris with what he had lost—something he desperately needed: a cause to fight for.

Shaking his foot impatiently, he turned to the bed beside him where Nim slept, their chest rising with shallow breaths.

The chamberlain's survival surprised him, but they had proved resilient.

After Barrett's attack, Fenris had carried Nim to safety in the heir's private airship. He spent the rest of the evening exhausting the spirits within to heal the chamberlain. While he was busy harnessing the power of the rach, Aludrien had flown his airship from the Winter Palace to the southern banks of Lake Arachovia, near the outskirts of the new city's wharf. The journey was rough, as Aludrien had rarely captained a vessel of such a size. No other guard or servant had joined the heir in his exile. And Fenris did not blame them, not after the grisly events of the masquerade.

They waited along the remote shore all night and through an excruciatingly long day, subsisting off the airship's limited pantry. Aludrien insisted on staying near the ruins until his ascension. The heir remained steadfast and undeterred in his ambitions, undeterred by the catastrophic series of events that would have dissuaded the average man. But Aludrien was anything but ordinary.

Fenris anticipated Hestraea would send her guards after them. However, she neglected their presence on the lake's edge: the disgraced heir, the severely injured chamberlain, and the most reviled assassin in Xandria's history.

After ensuring that Nim still drew breath, Fenris departed and climbed to Aludrien's suite situated at the ship's bow. Without knocking, he entered. Aludrien paced across the plush carpet, pausing at the massive windows to stare at the tranquil lake.

His bedchamber was cozy, complete with a personal bath in the far corner, full and steaming. Fenris had drawn it himself before checking on Nim. Without his staff, it appeared that

Aludrien was almost entirely incapable of taking care of himself. Fenris found it oddly endearing, and he had no qualms about performing tedious tasks. He enjoyed mundane chores; they kept him active and busy.

"Are you prepared for tomorrow?" Fenris asked as he approached.

"And why shouldn't I be?" Aludrien snapped. "I know you would rather me tuck my tail between my legs and flee to the far reaches of the Imperium to live out my days in shame. But I will not renounce my divine right to rule. I shall not."

"I wasn't suggesting that, Aludrien." Fenris paused. Both men noticed Fenris calling the heir by his first name. Surprisingly, Aludrien reacted indifferently to the slight. "I merely wanted to ensure you've thought everything through."

"Have my plans ever led us astray?"

"Yes. Almost always."

Aludrien chuckled. "I cannot disagree with that. Many errors have been made since you came into my employ, but trust me."

"I do," Fenris said sincerely. "It's...I am ready to face Ignatius tomorrow. To kill him. Are you willing to do the same with Hestraea? She will challenge your claim. There will be a fight to the death."

"I—"

Aludrien behaved strangely. His shoulders hunched, and his breathing became erratic. His face contorted into an expression dangerously close to worry.

"I'm sure you will do fine," Fenris said. Their eyes lingered on each other for several heartbeats.

"You know, I am not so sure if I believe that anymore," Aludrien said, his face downcast. It was the eve of his ascension, the day he had been yearning for his entire life. Now that it had arrived, the heir no longer projected his usual overconfidence; an anxious demeanor replaced it.

"What's wrong?"

"The truth," Aludrien said somberly. "My aunt held a mirror to my behavior. I'm a monster, and I suspect I have been since birth. I have committed unspeakable acts since my father's passing. I might become the tyrant you feared me to be."

Fenris grabbed Aludrien by the shoulder, forcing the heir to face him and stare him directly in the eye. The pitiful words sounded foreign on Aludrien's lips, which agitated Fenris.

"Enough," Fenris snapped. Aludrien's eyes widened. "You've made mistakes, sure. You've killed, yes. But that doesn't make you a monster."

"Why did I order you to murder Barrett?"

"Self-defense. The general was bound to attack you regardless of Hestraea's wishes. And to protect your aunt from his betrayal."

"And Vispin?"

"Similar reasons, but in the end, it wasn't us who killed her."

"Basil," Aludrien said. Fenris opened his mouth to retort, but he could not find the words. "I wanted my brother dead, and I wouldn't have lost sleep. You forced me to see reason and reconcile with Basil. That is the difference between you and me. I ask others to kill for my benefit; you kill for the sake of others. You are the only reason I've made it so far with my soul intact."

Fenris shook his head, his shame blooming. "I have only made your life more difficult. The only reason you're spending the night before your ascension exiled on your airship, and not in the Winter Palace where you belong, is because you chose to save me."

"You are a peculiar creature, Fenris," Aludrien said. "One who cannot see himself for who he truly is. It is my actions that have led us here, not yours."

"No. If you had allowed Hestraea to strike me down, you would be feasting in the palace as we speak, the entire court behind you, with the biggest stain on your reputation wiped clean. Instead, you saved me and implicated yourself in your father's murder."

"Fenris," he said. "I could not allow you to die."

"Why?"

"I—," Aludrien caught himself, studying Fenris closely. "How could I rule with a clear conscience if I sacrificed the life of a trusted confidant?"

"I remember you stating you would do whatever it takes to fulfill your destiny. What's changed?"

"I met you. It seems like you have corrupted me, after all," Aludrien chuckled.

"A conscience is cumbersome, isn't it?"

"Is that why you stayed with me?" Aludrien asked. "After Tipin's death. You remained in my service when you could have gone. Did you know I would lead you to Ignatius? So you could clear your conscience with his death?"

"That's what I said. But that was merely a half-truth. Like the one you gave me. Why did you save me?"

"Why did you stay?" Aludrien's face split into an irritating grin.

"Idiot," Fenris groaned.

Grabbing him by the hair, he pulled Aludrien close, kissing him savagely. His soft lips opened eagerly, allowing Fenris's tongue to enter, probing the warm recesses in earnest. Their lips intertwined effortlessly, recreating their dalliance at the masquerade with a searing, carnal fire that threatened to consume them both. Aludrien proved surprisingly pliant, his mouth eagerly responding to Fenris's movements. The voices in his head fell completely silent once more, just as they had at the masquerade. It was an intoxicating feeling.

They moved toward the bed until Fenris straddled Aludrien, one hand grasping his hair while the other gripped his neck tightly. Soft whimpers escaped the heir's lips, muffled by Fenris's tongue. The seductive sound spurred Fenris on, his body reacting instinctively. Firming his grip, he gently bit Aludrien's lip, grazing his teeth against the soft flesh. It produced a moan that reverberated in his chest. Repeating it with more pressure, Fenris growled softly, nibbling the heir's lip.

Overcome with lust, Fenris leaned forward, forcing Aludrien onto the bed, pinning him in place. His hands held Aludrien's wrists, and he locked eyes with him. The icy facade had melted, revealing soft, delicate features filled with longing and desire. Aludrien looked up expectantly, waiting for Fenris to take control once more. Gone was the domineering and self-assured aristocrat, and in his place was a delicate and eager man, waiting to be ravaged.

"There he is," Fenris said.

Their shirts flew off in a flurry of motion, accompanied by the sharp sound of tearing fabric. Neither minded, for the time for gentleness had ended. Fenris admired Aludrien's torso—the tight muscles and delicately soft skin. He traced the spirals of the insignis tattoo with his fingers, satisfied when Aludrien trembled at his touch. Lowering himself, Fenris inhaled, enjoying the musky scent. He growled and extended his tongue, licking an erect nipple. Aludrien whimpered.

Teasing the heir and holding him in place, Fenris explored the body that had been out of reach for so long. He traced his tongue along the folds of his muscles, relishing the taste and discovering sensitive spots that made Aludrien squirm in pleasure. His nipples were a particular hot spot, producing an enticing moan when Fenris gently nibbled them.

Working his way down, he grabbed Aludrien's pants with his teeth, pulling them off as he gradually slipped off the bed to kneel on the floor. The heir lay on his back, eyes closed, chest heaving, his pants around his ankles, and fully erect. Fenris smiled, admiring his handiwork.

Gently pushing Aludrien's knees apart, Fenris kissed his inner thigh, working his tongue upward while massaging the other thigh firmly with his free hand.

Higher and higher he kissed, until he traced his tongue up the side of Aludrien's cock. The moans grew louder until Fenris could no longer resist.

Taking Aludrien in his mouth, Fenris sucked, exploring every inch with fervor, which pleased the heir immensely, whose moans grew louder with every flick of the tongue.

It had been ages since Fenris had taken such a pleasure, so he made sure to savor every moment.

Reaching up, Fenris traced his fingers across Aludrien's taut torso, up his neck, and into his open mouth. Two fingers plunged inside, and the heir's lips enclosed them eagerly, sucking with such skill that Fenris grew harder. Working his fingers down his throat, Fenris waited until the saliva sufficiently lubricated his digits before removing them.

In one fluid motion, Fenris lifted Aludrien's legs and

positioned his feet on his shoulders, revealing his ultimate prize. Placing his wet fingers on the heir's hole, he massaged it gently, loosening the tight muscles until they welcomed him in. Aludrien moaned, inspiring Fenris to push deeper. The warm muscles melted at his touch.

Working his way inside, Fenris pumped faster and faster, stretching Aludrien open. The heir whimpered, moaned, and shuddered in ecstasy, which only made Fenris's lust grow. Before he could contain himself, he ripped off his trousers, spat on his cock, and pushed Aludrien's ankles over his head. The heir was surprisingly flexible.

"Do you want me inside of you, Your Grace?" Fenris asked hotly.

"Please," Aludrien whimpered.

Fenris obliged. Steadily pressing in. A sense of warmth covered his entire body as he slipped inside, as if he had always belonged here. Aludrien loosened expertly, eyes rolled back, and eagerly awaited more.

Fenris gave it to him.

With long, slow strokes, Fenris panted in heat, taking immense pleasure in each thrust. Aludrien melted into the bed, his tongue lolling to the side as Fenris fucked.

"Harder," Aludrien begged.

Fenris stopped.

The heir opened his eyes in surprise.

"What did you say?" Fenris growled.

"Please," Aludrien begged. "Please fuck me harder."

Fenris smiled, plunging back inside and thrusting forcefully. Aludrien gasped. At first, Fenris believed he had hurt the heir, but a wild smile bloomed on the flushed face. He thrust again.

His rhythm quickened, faster and faster. His cock glided

in and out of Aludrien, hitting his prostate with each pump. The heir's moans rose into wild cries of pleasure, begging for more. Fenris obliged, using his leverage to fuck as hard as he could without relying on the spirits within.

He leaned over and kissed Aludrien, fucking him soundly and muffling his cries with his tongue. The heir wrapped his thick arms and legs around him, pulling him closer, clinging to him desperately. The heir was insatiable; however forcefully Fenris fucked, he still begged for more.

Pulling out, Fenris gruffly grabbed Aludrien by the waist and flipped him around. The heir happily obeyed, landing on his hands and knees, back arched, looking back expectantly.

Clutching his hips, Fenris reentered Aludrien savagely. The heir cried out in pleasure. In this new position, Fenris could go deeper. He watched Aludrien's ass bounce with every thrust.

Reaching around, he grabbed Aludrien's cock and stroked rapidly, feeling the hot precum flow over his hand.

It didn't take long for Aludrien's moans to turn high-pitched, his hole clenched, and he cried out, climaxing into the sheets.

With muscles tightening around his cock, Fenris bellowed as he joined Aludrien, his body overcome with pleasure as he released.

The pair collapsed onto the bed, Fenris still inside, lying on Aludrien and kissing his neck softly.

"You made a mess," Aludrien said.

"That's what the bath is for," Fenris replied.

Aludrien sighed deeply, but made no indication of moving. They lay there in silence, enjoying each other's heat, breathing in unison. Finally, Fenris pulled out and climbed off, heading to the bath.

He called upon the spirits within and focused on the tepid water, imagining a flame within its depths. Gradually, the surface began to roil and bubble. When steam billowed from the tub, Fenris stuck his finger in to test the temperature, delighted by the warmth.

"It's ready," he called, and was met with a lazy groan.

Aludrien remained still, face down on the bed. Groaning, Fenris marched over and pulled Aludrien from his supine position. Remarkably, he did not resist, following Fenris to the bath obediently. He had never seen Aludrien so compliant. He would have to fuck him more often.

Slipping into the steaming pool, the heir sank until his shoulders were submerged, sighing in pleasure. Fenris smiled and approached the bed. He had much to clean.

"Are you not going to join me?" Aludrien asked, the question was not so much a demand as an eager plea.

Fenris smiled and entered the tub, large enough for two, but Aludrien was considerably taller than he was, and their legs intertwined beneath the water. They stared at each other for a short while. Aludrien remained soft, his cold facade permanently melted, regarding Fenris with a peculiar expression.

"Anything you wish to say?" Fenris asked, curious to understand what was going on in the recesses of Aludrien's mind.

"Can you tell me more about your mind palace?"

Fenris blinked. It took a few moments for the question to register.

"It's like a dream, but different. You can smell and taste and touch, but it isn't like reality, exactly," Fenris crinkled his nose as he searched for the correct words. "It is difficult to describe."

"Can I see it for myself?" Aludrien asked. "If you don't mind."

"Is that possible?"

"So I have been told. As long as you are touching another, you can bring their consciousness when you enter, though I must admit there are no recorded instances."

Aludrien was surprisingly coy. Of course, he was curious about the nature of the Tal'Rach, for if he were to succeed tomorrow, he would become one.

"Take my hand," Fenris said, reaching out. "Sit up straight, we don't want you to slip beneath the water and drown."

"Are you certain?"

"Of course."

Their hands touched. Fenris concentrated intently, imagining the Belantine Plains, and the spirits within hummed in response. The tub and the cabin vanished, but Aludrien's hand remained. Within a few moments, the pair stood naked along the familiar knoll above Fenris's village, the long grass waving in the warm breeze.

Aludrien gazed upon the scene with childlike wonder, marveling at the majesty around him. Taking a few steps, he caressed the long grass, breathing deeply, and testing each of his senses. Fenris found it surprisingly endearing. The heir gawked at the half-dozen rach who appeared and disappeared around him, exhilarated.

Looking down at his nakedness, his face split into a cheeky grin.

"Oh, Fenris, you degenerate, imagining the heir to the Xandrian Empire in such a salacious state."

"I can summon you some clothes, if you'd like," Fenris

offered.

"No need. I prefer it this way."

He playfully pushed Fenris, who fell over, taken by surprise, and rolled down the hill, cackling in delight. Pulling himself to his feet, Fenris chased him, feeling like a child again. Once he reached Aludrien, he tackled him into the grass, and they rolled together, laughing as they went. They halted with Aludrien on top, lips close together, faces hot.

"It is remarkable how closely this place resembles the real Belantine Plains," Aludrien said, staring at the sleepy village below. "So this was your home?"

"For my early childhood, yes," Fenris said. "Before—"

"Before my family invaded," Aludrien finished. "I'm beginning to understand your hatred of the throne. If someone had taken my childhood home in such a way, I—"

"We should go," Fenris said, swallowing hard. The haunting images of the invasion soured his delight.

"Oh, yes. Of course," Aludrien said. "Thank you for bringing me here."

Fenris looked away. He resisted dwelling on the past, for it pained him too greatly.

The Plains faded, and they returned to the tub; thankfully, neither had submerged while they were unconscious.

The pair sat in the warm water in awkward silence.

"Can you pass the soap?" Aludrien said, motioning toward the bottle and brush sitting on the tub's ledge behind Fenris.

Nodding, Fenris rose to grab them. A pair of strong hands grabbed him by the hips. He nearly tumbled over the side, but caught himself, sitting on the tub's edge.

Aludrien was already upon him, pushing his knees apart and taking Fenris's soft cock in his mouth. He should have known the heir was exceptionally talented by how he sucked his fingers earlier, but experiencing it firsthand was an entirely different story.

Hungrily, Aludrien bobbed up and down, swirling his tongue and stroking the shaft until Fenris was fully erect. He threw his head back, moans erupting from his throat, melting at his lover's touch. Aludrien looked up with ravenous eyes, cheeks flushed, and back arched.

Gripping the side of the tub, Fenris panted, allowing the heir to have his way. Eventually, his hands found their way to Aludrien's wet hair, guiding his head onto his cock. The heir moaned in delight and resumed his task.

Without warning, Aludrien erupted from the tub, sending waves cascading over the side. Turning around, he presented his bottom, reddened from earlier. Fenris guided Aludrien as he sat on his lap, entering him once more. Aludrien descended, his hands on top of Fenris's until his rear touched Fenris's thighs.

He looked at Fenris mischievously, towering over him. The muscles squeezed, constricting around Fenris's member. Toes curling underwater, Fenris shook in pleasure, but the larger man kept him still.

The muscles in Aludrien's thighs tensed as he raised himself, right before Fenris fell out of him. He dropped with a satisfying smack. Fenris growled, softly biting Aludrien's arm. The heir ignored him, repeating the movement. He rode faster and harder, taking Fenris fully and bucking savagely. Euphoria overtook Fenris, his moans harmonizing with Aludrien's.

The heir pleasured himself, tugging wildly as he bounced on Fenris, his head thrown back.

Fenris took this opportunity to regain control.

Using his newly freed arm, he wrapped it around Aludrien's waist and thrust upward, using the leverage of the tub to deliver deft strokes. The heir howled, leaning onto Fenris, his back sticking to his chest.

Fenris continued, finding this particular angle especially pleasurable, and increased his speed until Aludrien could not hold out any longer. The heir screamed, and he climaxed again. His hole clenched around Fenris, and he rode it once more. Fenris intended to continue, but the heir had other plans. Toes curled, Fenris cried as he came again. The wave of ecstasy was more substantial the second time; it reverberated through his body, and his legs spasmed wildly. He clung to Aludrien, arms wrapped around him as they rode the orgasm together.

Panting, the pair slipped into the warm pool, thoroughly exhausted. They lounged in silence, trading flirtatious glances, but neither had the strength for conversation. They eventually began bathing, scrubbing their bodies with soap, and taking turns cleaning each other. Although fully depleted, they still exchanged cheeky kisses, exploring each other further with their hands. Fenris summoned more water to rinse the suds from their bodies.

The evening continued in contented silence as they dried off and ate their dinner. They spoke of small things, gently teasing each other. At first, Fenris suspected the heir's change in demeanor was circumstantial, that he would raise his walls and order Fenris about once the lust wore off. But Aludrien remained soft, deferential, and affectionate.

The pair slipped into the unsoiled side of the bed they hadn't used for sex. It wasn't discussed whether they would share a bed; they wrapped around each other immediately, Fenris holding Aludrien.

They lay for a while, but neither could sleep. Fenris could feel Aludrien's heart racing.

"It will be fine," Fenris said. "You're still recognized as the heir. And Hestraea would be a fool to stand in your way."

"But the court considers me a monster," Aludrien said. "How can I hope to lead if I have lost all of their respect?"

"They'll see through the lies," Fenris said, tightening his grip. "And we'll expose Ignatius for his treachery."

Aludrien's breathing slowed, as did his heartbeat. He believed the sentiment, though Fenris did not.

Aludrien must confront his aunt in single combat—one of the most skilled warriors in the Imperium. If he survived the ascension, the entire Imperium would resent him for killing his father. And Fenris was to blame.

He waited until Aludrien fell asleep, his chest rising and falling. He disentangled their bodies, careful not to wake him, and edged off the bed.

Only one thing would ensure Aludrien's ascension and a successful reign. A few voices within spoke of various courses of action. But Fenris knew what he had to do; he wished he could survive to see Aludrien become emperor.

He slipped on his clothes, kissed Aludrien gently on the forehead, and departed.

22

Ascension

Aludrien awoke smiling to the sound of hungry gulls, dawn's light shining in his eyes. He had awaited this day his entire life, the one promised to him since childhood. Never had he imagined that the night before his ascension would be the best of his life.

Lovers had come and gone throughout his life, mostly servants or ambitious lords. He had never lacked bedfellows, but last night was unlike any other. What transpired between him and Fenris was different. They had made love.

He had not found the assassin particularly appealing at first, but as they became more acquainted, his attraction grew stronger. He had developed an unspoken affinity for Fenris, but he'd dismissed it as a mixture of lust and respect. He never imagined experiencing such intensity as when Fenris pushed him onto the bed.

Today, he would achieve his destiny with Fenris by his side.

Opening his eyes, he reached over longingly, only to discover an empty bed. Sitting up, he looked around the room. Fenris had vanished, and so had his clothes. Confused, he waited, assuming the assassin had gone to check on Nim before their journey across the lake.

But the longer he waited, the more a foreboding sensation grew in his chest. The sun rose high above the horizon before Aludrien finally dressed, his apprehension turning to icy cold dread.

Fenris wasn't returning.

A primal scream tore from his throat. He overturned the side table, sending it clattering to the floor. His insignis tattoos roiled, and he nearly summoned his blades, yearning to tear the room to shreds. Anything to destroy the memory of last night, to sear it from his brain.

Everything that bastard had said was a lie. The day Aludrien needed him most, Fenris abandoned him. Did he not feel the same last night? Why would he leave?

His mind racing with the countless possibilities, he left his room, nearly tearing the door off its hinges as he slammed it shut.

He trudged down the steps, his face hot with rage, barely able to see straight. The sheer audacity to fuck him and leave him, the night before the ascension, stung. If Aludrien ever saw the bastard again, he would kill him on sight. A voice of delusion argued that Fenris was hurt or incapacitated somewhere, taken against his will. But he knew the truth. The Tal'Rach had left of his own volition.

"Looking for Fenris?"

Aludrien hadn't realized he had reached the ship's main salon. He spun toward the voice. Nim. Standing in the doorway, their skin pale and their eyes glassy. But they were alive.

Aludrien rushed over, clasping them by the shoulder,

leading them to a nearby couch.

"I'm glad to see you have recovered, Nim," Aludrien said. "I shouldn't have placed you in such a perilous position."

"Oh, no worries. My Graciousness," Nim said wistfully, their mind clouded, not yet fully present.

"What did you say about Fenris?"

"Oh, yes," Nim said. "What a fine young man. And handsome. We chatted not too long ago."

"What did he say?" Aludrien asked.

"He talked about renting a boat," Nim said. "I warned him that the lake would take his life if he dared venture out in the darkness. But he was insistent on seeing the sunrise above the ruins. Foolish, if you ask me."

Aludrien paled. He had been a fool. Of course, Fenris hadn't fled. He was going to the site of the ascension. He would only have one reason to leave without Aludrien.

"Did he say anything else at all? Anything about me?"

"Oh, yes, that's right. I asked Fenris why he was leaving without you, which, in my opinion, seemed rude. He said you had a big day ahead and wanted you to rest. And that he was sorry. Added something about the realm, an odd bird, that one."

Aludrien sighed. He needed his chamberlain now, more than ever. But Nim was not yet lucid enough to be of any help. They would have to stay.

He thought briefly about flying his airship directly to the ruins, but reconsidered. The Imperial forces would surely bombard any airship traveling toward the ascension. Only one option remained.

The wharf.

Aludrien groaned. He did not have much time. Hastily, he

changed into nondescript travel clothes, perfect for blending in with the rabble of New Arachovia. He led Nim to their bed and ordered them to rest. Hopefully, nearby brigands wouldn't be bold enough to commandeer the ship in his absence; they had given them a wide berth thus far. Besides, by the end of the day, he would either be dead or have the power to hunt them to the ends of the earth.

Aludrien left the ship, storming down the beach toward New Arachovia's wharf, anger boiling over, threatening to consume him.

The reason was apparent: Fenris had left to kill Ignatius. That was why he had journeyed across the Imperium, not for Aludrien's sake, but to enact vengeance upon those who formed the Meridian. The altruistic freedom fighter who only killed as a last resort was a facade. It had always been about revenge; Aludrien had been a fool to think otherwise.

The ascension required the Pontifex and a dozen cardinals. The creation of a Tal'Rach was no small feat. If Fenris killed Ignatius, then the ascension would be postponed until the surviving cardinals could arrange the ceremony without their leader. The chances of Aludrien surviving that long were slim at best.

Moreover, the court would blame Aludrien for Ignatius's death. Murdering a rival was one matter, including an emperor or chancellor. But killing the Pontifex? The surviving cardinals would refuse to perform the ascension, and Aludrien would never achieve his destiny. And he had thought his aunt would be the primary source of his worries today.

The wharf wasn't far from the airship. Aludrien emptied his coin purse at the nearest dock, bewildering a filthy captain.

With the amount he presented, she could buy a third of the ships in the wharf. But all he needed was one boat.

Thankfully, this one included an insignis engine, though the device was bulky and covered in rust. But soon Aludrien was skimming across the lake, water spraying his face. The outlines of the ruins grew sharper as he sped forward, emerging from the dusty air. The mid-morning sun beat down upon him; the ceremony would commence exactly at midday, as was tradition.

If he did not reach the ancient amphitheater before Fenris, then all would be lost.

Beaching the boat along the rocky shore, Aludrien jumped out, not bothering to tie the vessel. It could float to the ends of the earth, for all he cared. He set his eyes on the ruins before him.

The ancient city of Arachovia was a marvel of engineering and architecture, though most of its majesty had crumbled under the cruel passage of time. Desert scrub overran the cobblestone streets. Caved-in roofs and weather-worn walls were all that remained of Aludrien's ancient homeland. Historians reported that the city once sat atop a mesa, overlooking the vast valley it claimed as its dominion. According to legend, the fabled generals Matthias Helianth and Rain Cassian led a group of early Animancers against the occupying forces of Kyriak. They harnessed the rach to level the mesa, bringing the city low so Empress Aleksandra could reclaim it.

The birth of his empire.

Unbeknownst to the conquering heroes of old, the reshaping of the land also forced a latent, underground lake to surface, gradually flooding the city over the span of a century. The empire expanded westward, covering half the continent. So Aludrien's ancestors built the new capital along the Cellicean Sea.

Aludrien walked along the shore unimpeded, admiring the sunken structures. A few still rose above the surface, their submerged bases covered in coral and algae. The ancient city was unguarded, as most citizens were either too superstitious, reverent, or wise enough to enter the ruins uninvited. Aludrien possessed none of those traits as he strode toward the hulking amphitheater, towering over the water's edge.

The great domed roof had long since collapsed, as had the southern wall; large sections rose from the lake's surface where they had fallen centuries earlier. What remained was an impressive semicircular wall of weathered granite, a giant horseshoe hugging the rocky shore. A cliff had formed directly to its south, saving it from further erosion. Aludrien had only entered the ancient amphitheater of Arachovia once before, when Claude ascended and named him as heir.

He had dreamed of that lakeside theater every night since. His hands shaking with anticipation, he walked along the towering wall toward the main entrance on the northern side. The dull sound of hundreds of voices echoed off the granite. The sun was nearing its zenith.

The ceremony would start imminently.

As far as he could tell, the voices were excited and anxious, without a hint of terror. Fenris must not have struck yet. The assassin had departed hours before Aludrien, so he must be skulking in the shadows, waiting for the ceremony to enact his revenge on Ignatius and the cardinals.

Aludrien quickened his pace, eager to arrive before disaster struck.

The entrance remained mostly intact; a section of the arch had fallen before Aludrien's lifetime, but the grand stairs remained whole. A group of nobles disappeared under the arch as he turned the corner. He still had time.

He rushed up the stairs, heart quickening.

"Halt!" a gruff voice shouted from above.

A dozen heavily armored soldiers stood at the top of the stairs, crossbows aimed at Aludrien.

"Imperial law prohibits provincials from entering such hallowed ground," the nearest soldier, clearly the captain, said. "The consequence is death."

The crossbows charged.

Aludrien groaned; he did not blame the guard, for his hair was disheveled and his clothes rough and plain. It wasn't how he'd envisioned his grand entrance, but it couldn't be helped now.

"Fortunately, I am not a provincial," Aludrien said. "And I would ask you to kindly get the fuck out of my way. I am late to my ascension."

"Excuse me?"

"I am Aludrien Aleksandran, son of the late Claude Aleksandran XLV, the heir to the Xandrian Empire. Move."

"And I'm the Pontifex," the captain said. His subordinates chuckled. "Do us a favor and leave, boy. I'd rather not waste crossbow bolts on scum like you."

"Move," Aludrien commanded, pulling back his sleeve to reveal his insignis tattoos. "I will not repeat myself a third time."

The guards faltered, but their crossbows remained high. Although these soldiers did not recognize him by his face, his tattoos were proof enough that, despite his appearance, he belonged in that auditorium. Regardless, the soldiers seemed cagey and stubborn. He reached out with his mind, searching for nearby spirits. To his surprise, the largest host he had ever sensed floated above him, billowing over the stadium like an invisible umbrella. They were the rach intended for his ascension. The spirits that would elevate him to Tal'Rach. A few were close enough to harness in case he needed them.

"Well, fuck me," the captain said. "It's my lucky day. My superiors gave me explicit instructions to capture the rogue heir and bring him to Grand Marshal Hestraea. If you're lying, I'll have your head. If you're not, the Grand Marshal will have yours. Seize him."

Before a single soldier moved, Aludrien struck. Invoking the power of the spirits above, he summoned a violent gust of wind. The explosive gale tossed the guards like pebbles, throwing them against the great wall. Aludrien ran past them into the archway before they hit the ground.

Releasing the spirits, he called upon his tattoos, which roiled and poured forth, covering his body and hiding his grubby clothes in steel plating. He would enter his ascension not as a peasant, but in the armor of a conquering king. His pair of swords extended, he charged into the amphitheater.

The great stadium was vast enough to hold thousands, but the upper echelons of the court barely filled half the space. They milled about the weathered stone pews, eagerly awaiting the ceremony.

An illustrious contingent occupied the stage, the lake serving as a dazzling backdrop. Pontifex Ignatius stood at its center in full regalia. Two dozen cardinals gathered around him, calmly chatting among themselves. A golden palanquin sat at their feet, its top adorned with plush, crimson cushions:

the renowned altar where the heir would receive the blessings of the rach.

Where Aludrien would become a Tal'Rach.

The first to notice his arrival were the soldiers stationed in the rear. Instinctively, they raised their crossbows but disengaged when they beheld his insignis armor. Aludrien cursed his earlier foolishness, realizing he should have summoned his armor the instant he set foot in the ancient city. He would have been able to enter as easily as he descended the steps.

The courtiers gawked and gasped. Aludrien smiled, chin held high, striding forward to his destiny.

The royal family sat in the front row. Hestraea in her armor, Basil and Jareth in robes of maroon and gold, and little Magdolina in an exquisite dress of periwinkle. He scoured the shadowy recesses of the giant stadium, but Fenris was nowhere to be seen, probably cloaked in invisibility. Aludrien found it odd. If Fenris was waiting to strike until after the ceremony, then why did he leave him at all?

A sword flowed into Hestraea's hand, her face filled with indignation and rage.

"Silence," a voice boomed. Ignatius held his arms high, his cohort shifting into a tight formation behind him. "Please be seated, the heir to the Xandrian Empire, High Lord Aludrien Aleksandran, has arrived. The ceremony shall commence."

Ignatius. The man who had ordered his father's death. The man who had corrupted a soul as pure as Fenris. The man who was about to make Aludrien the most powerful being alive. The Pontifex looked upon him with a smile. Unlike the rest of the crowd, Ignatius seemed pleased at his arrival.

Ignoring the muffled cries of objection and the resentful glares, Aludrien marched confidently to the stage, taking his rightful place next to the ascension altar.

Ignatius began the ceremony with a lengthy, prepared speech on the continuation of the realm and introduced the rightful heir to the throne. Aludrien didn't hear a word, scanning the perimeter. Aludrien searched for any sign of Fenris, hoping the assassin would hold off in his vengeance for a short while longer. His attention shifted toward the crowd before him, who stared back with hatred and disgust; several jeered in contempt. His heart sank. The court's support had long abandoned him. However, they could do little, short of challenging Aludrien to a fight to the death.

On cue, Ignatius concluded his liturgy and stepped forward, beckoning Aludrien to join.

"The intention of Emperor Claude Aleksandran was clear, for his second-born son, High Lord Aludrien, to replace him on the throne," Ignatius said. "If anyone disagrees with the divine ruling of our late and beloved leader and believes their claim is stronger than the presumptive heir, please step forward; your silence will revoke your claim."

A hush fell over the crowd; a few whispered, but most eyes in the amphitheater fell upon Grand Marshal Hestraea.

She rose, insignis armor gleaming in the midday sun.

"I, High Lady Hestraea Aleksandran, eldest living child of Empress Derulia Aleksandran, sister to Emperor Claude Aleksandran, Grand Marshal of the First Legion, stake my claim as the next empress of the Xandrian Empire."

Aludrien paled, his worst fears finally realized.

"Are there any others who wish to come forward?" Ignatius asked tersely.

No one spoke. Aludrien sighed. At least he would only compete in a single mortal combat, rather than multiple in rapid succession.

"According to Imperial law," Ignatius said. "The plaintiff party must have a majority support from the court. Stand if you support Grand Marshal Hestraea's claim."

All the politicking over the last few months was to prevent Hestraea's claim from triggering a contest in the upcoming vote. However, due to the events at the Winter Palace, he wasn't surprised when almost every soul in the theater stood.

He tried his best not to chuckle. Whether or not he ascended, he had made history as the most reviled heir in the empire.

"High Lord Aludrien," Ignatius said. "Do you revoke your claim in support of Grand Marshal Hestraea?"

"I do not," Aludrien said.

"Then we have two valid claimants to the throne," Ignatius said. "Per Imperial law, the next ruler of the empire will be chosen through trial by combat. Claimants, please prepare yourselves."

The crowd cheered as Hestraea joined Aludrien and Ignatius on the stage. She refused to look at him. A pair of cardinals emerged from behind the altar, each carrying a heavy ceremonial broad sword. They handed them to the two combatants. Aludrien recalled his swords, holding the clunky broadsword awkwardly. He had practiced for years with such a weapon for this exact occasion, but despite his preparation, the ceremonial blade was exponentially less effective than his insignis blades.

"I shall remind the court of the laws and regulations of this trial," Ignatius said. "Combatants are prohibited from using either Animancy or their Insignis steel. Combatants are prohibited from outside help and from harming another soul during the fight. Only the use of your bodies and these holy blades is permitted. The penalty for defying these laws will result in death. The fight will conclude when one combatant slays or subdues the other. The life of a combatant who surrenders or becomes incapacitated lies with the victor. Do both combatants agree to the terms?"

"Yes." They said in unison, each recalling their armor, which writhed and roiled until they lay dormant on their skin. Underneath her armor, Hestraea wore a practical, form-fitting garment. She had come prepared to duel. Aludrien felt out of place in his dirty garb.

Ignatius retreated behind the altar, leaving the pair alone at the front of the stage. The cardinals chanted, erecting a turbulent circle of wind around them. Hestraea raised her sword effortlessly, eyeing Aludrien like a stalking lioness. Aludrien was taller, younger, and stronger, but the veteran had years of experience on him.

"Are both combatants prepared?"

"Yes."

"Commence."

Hestraea lunged forward with a savage blow aimed at Aludrien's throat. Sidestepping, he narrowly evaded the golden blade, which cut his shoulder, tearing flesh and cloth.

Hestraea had passed his defenses. With ease, she used the force behind her first attack and pivoted direction in one fluid movement. Aludrien barely raised his blade before her second swipe would have sliced his head from his shoulders. The golden weapons rang out as they collided, sending vibrations down Aludrien's arms. He almost dropped the weapon, but staggered backward to absorb the blow.

Hestraea recoiled, allowing Aludrien to retreat to the far

side of the makeshift arena. His strike radius was longer than hers; he only needed to remain out of reach and allow his aunt to wear herself out.

But Hestraea was too fast.

They clashed again and again, Hestraea maintaining the upper hand. She unleashed each blow with precision and power, placing the sword in the most inconvenient spots to force Aludrien to lower his guard. Accustomed to dual-wielding light weapons that allowed him speed and accuracy, Aludrien found himself losing ground with every strike. Within a minute, over a dozen shallow wounds riddled his body. Blood bloomed on his tattered clothes, dripping down his skin. He panted, chest heaving, arms on fire.

Hestraea, in contrast, remained unfazed. He had been foolish to assume his stamina was greater than that of the best swordsman alive.

"I do not want this," Aludrien pleaded, becoming increasingly aware that his only way to survive this battle was to appeal to his aunt's sentimentality. "I cannot kill you. I never did, please you must believe me."

"Silence," Hestraea hissed. "Of course, you wanted this. You sent that creature upon your father, then poor General Barrett, and you sent it on me this morning."

"Fenris went to you?" Aludrien asked.

"Don't insult me with feigned ignorance. But I can't imagine how you would think I would fall for the assassin's little charade. Walking into my chambers unarmed, surrendering himself to my soldiers, spouting nonsense about the Pontifex and the Meridian."

"Where is he?" Aludrien asked, gripping his sword.

"Awaiting his trial and subsequent execution," Hestraea said.

"Unlike you, I'm not a murderer. But he will soon join you in the afterlife."

Aludrien cried out in rage, charging forward. He would end this with one blow.

Sword held high, he rushed at his aunt. Right before her sword connected with his, she stepped to the side. His momentum carried him past Hestraea.

Behind Aludrien, Hestraea struck. Her sword plunged into his back, cleaving through his shoulder muscles. He howled in pain as the great sword impaled him, tearing out the front of his chest. She had meant the blow to pierce his heart, but Aludrien knew this.

He had expected this.

Throughout his entire life, he had admired his aunt, who taught him the art of the sword. This obsession allowed him to understand all of her moves. Right before she struck, he had shuffled slightly to the right, allowing the blade to bypass his heart and firmly lodge itself into his body.

Right where he wanted it. The move was inspired by the late General Barrett, who had nearly bested him in the Winter Palace.

He flipped around, tearing the sword's hilt from Hestraea's grasp. Now she faced him, completely unarmed. Without hesitation, he barreled forward, tackling his surprised aunt onto the hard marble below. Her head hit the ground with a sickening crack, stunning her. Ignoring the searing pain, he pinned her down, laying his sword against her neck until a few droplets of blood trickled down. She relaxed her body, realizing any sudden movement would lead to her immediate decapitation.

"Surrender," Aludrien commanded. Although he possessed

the advantage, his strength was rapidly fading; he could not hold her forever.

"End it," Hestraea hissed. "As you did with Claude and Barrett."

"I told you," Aludrien groaned. "I do not wish you harm, and I have never lied to you."

Hestraea spat in his face, struggling against his weight.

Grabbing her by the throat with his free hand, Aludrien raised his sword high. She glared back defiantly.

He brought the sword down.

The hilt connected with the side of her temple, knocking her unconscious.

A hush fell over the crowd, who looked on with horrified expressions.

The veil lifted, and Ignatius joined him as he struggled to his feet, a torrent of blood flowing from his chest.

"High Lady Hestraea is incapacitated and no longer able to fight. I declare High Lord Aludrien the forty-sixth emperor of Xandria."

The arena remained silent, as the entire court witnessed the most hated heir in history gain the highest title in the land. They looked on expectantly.

"And as the victor, your opponent's life is yours," Ignatius said. "What is your wish?"

A few in the crowd cried out, begging for mercy. Aludrien scowled at them, cheeks hot with rage.

"As I said before," he declared, his legs trembling weakly. "I was not involved in my father's death. General Barrett intended to murder me, so I acted in self-defense. And as I said repeatedly on this day, I do not wish harm upon my beloved aunt, whom I harbor no resentment toward. I wish her to live."

A few in the crowd cheered, but most remained too stunned to react strongly. But Aludrien paid them no mind, for the world was spinning around him.

Ignatius's words were lost to him as a pair of cardinals led him to the altar. A pair of soldiers retrieved Hestraea's limp body, clearing the stage.

Someone whispered in his ear, and a blinding pain followed as someone ripped the sword from his body. The wound was fatal, but that was the reason he had defeated his aunt. He was willing to die to achieve his destiny. And soon the hole in his chest would be healed by the thousands of rach above him.

Lying on the plush cushions, he gazed up and smiled. The world faded. Only the distant chanting remained.

The sky shimmered as the rach revealed themselves at the behest of the clergy. Ghostly apparitions in every shape, size, and hue imaginable. They swirled above him in an ethereal cyclone, then gradually descended.

The first spirit, a sapphire badger, entered his open mouth and plunged inside. His entire body warmed as it entered. His chest burned as the rach dissolved into him, and odd images of a sailor stumbling down an alley entered his mind. But they were soon replaced by memories from the second rach, a young child rolling down a hill. One after another, the spirits bound themselves to him. He sensed their every emotion, their endless memories fused to his mind. More and more. His body felt as if it were going to explode.

The world fell away as the torrent overtook him. He could no longer separate his thoughts from the rach's; his sense of self was rapidly fading like morning mist.

What was his name? Was he even a man? Where was he? Nothing made sense anymore.

Only pain existed.

Aludrien cried out. It wasn't his voice that escaped his throat, but an unearthly, beastly roar.

23

Fox and Wolf

The earth shook violently, and the cell's stone walls trembled and cracked, on the verge of collapse. The guards below fled in fright, leaving Fenris floating in a cone of compressed air, completely immobile. Horrified screams echoed through the open door from the Winter Palace outside.

He had hoped his final gambit would persuade Grand Marshal Hestraea to renounce her claim and focus her efforts on the real threat. Ignatius. But judging by her reaction, he doubted his foolish stunt had swayed her in the slightest. However, marching into the ascension alongside Aludrien would have been futile. The court despised Aludrien for his tie to Fenris, and the only way to calm the storm was to sever that bond and surrender himself. What he never expected, however, was how far Aludrien's reputation had fallen. General Barrett's death had entwined their fates.

He hung in captivity once more, in a prison disturbingly similar to the one he had occupied after the late emperor's death. Aludrien was undoubtedly fighting his aunt, and though he trusted the heir's various skills, Fenris doubted that he could best her in mortal combat.

The palace rumbled violently again, expanding the spider-web of cracks. The stone creaked and shuddered as dust and debris fell from the ceiling. A large chunk of marble gave way and crashed to the earth, followed by another. A third fell above Fenris, immediately impeded by the force field.

Sun poured in from above as more of the ceiling gave way. A massive section plummeted to the ground, obliterating the control panel below. The insignis engine that restrained him sputtered and died, dropping him to the floor far below. Landing on all fours, he bent his limbs to absorb the blow, batting away falling boulders with relative ease.

An ear-splitting roar consumed the palace, a terrible, guttural sound of fury and anguish.

Only one being in existence was capable of producing such a sound.

Crouching low, Fenris pushed off the ground, his enormous strength propelling him through the gaping hole above. His body had already transformed when his paws hit the rooftop, and he wasted no time, loping across the crumbling stone to safety.

His prison was wedged against the tall palace wall, which had luckily endured the quakes without rupturing. Seconds before the roof fully caved in, Fenris leaped onto the battlements. The narrow ledge was vacant.

The air rumbled with another roar, and Fenris turned toward its origin—the ancient amphitheater.

A new Tal'Rach was born.

Whether Hestraea or Aludrien had ascended, Fenris couldn't tell. He refused to believe Aludrien was dead, shoving the possibility away like a wanton leaf. The only fact he knew for certain was that Ignatius was in the amphitheater, standing over the newly formed Tal'Rach as he had with Fenris. The bastard still drew breath. And Fenris would change that.

Frantically leaping forward, Fenris scaled down the wall and sprinted across the narrow gap of plains separating the Winter Palace's oasis from the collapsing ruins. A gigantic maw rose above the amphitheater, rows of sharp teeth glistened in the sunlight, each roughly the size of a human. Fenris froze.

It was another Tal'Rach, a being born of the conjoining of human and spirit. But the sheer scale, the deafening roars, and the violent tremors were more than Fenris, Durian, or even the late Claude were capable of.

Dodging debris and leaping over fallen columns, Fenris desperately traversed the ancient city and arrived at the massive arena. A few dozen courtiers streamed down the grand steps, screaming and running for cover as the building shuddered. A piece of the entryway crumbled and fell, crushing a few unfortunate souls. Fenris ignored them, dashing up the steps, dodging terrified nobles and falling debris. The frantic survivors paid him little heed as he galloped into the archway.

The theater was in chaos, dozens of bodies littered the floor, and half of the western wall had collapsed. Survivors huddled along the perimeter, each protected by a barrier summoned by a brave Animancer. But the wards were thin and weak, for the cardinals had used the vast majority of the surrounding spirits for the ascension.

Soldiers scurried about in a chaotic rush, scattered around the amphitheater, useless without tangible direction. A few fired their crossbows in vain, their bolts flying into the air.

But Fenris was more concerned with the colossal beast thrashing about the stage, so large that only its hind legs rested on the dais. Its front paws crushed the stands halfway up the stadium. The gigantic creature occupied most of the great space, its golden fur blazing in the midday sun. Half a dozen thick tails whipped around, smashing stone and crushing the brave soldiers who dared to face it. Back arched, hair raised, its pointed ears flattened along a conical head.

A fox.

Eyes wild and inhuman, it flailed uncontrollably in a feral state. Fenris wasn't surprised; he had seen the great host of rach that had recently hung above the ruins earlier that morning. The great host eclipsed Fenris's spirits by at least a hundredfold. No one could handle such a force and maintain their sanity.

For the first time, Fenris hoped it wasn't Aludrien who had achieved ascension, for that sort of torment was a fate worse than death.

Along the dais, a great dome of radiant light encircled a group of robed figures. Unlike the other wards, this one was fully intact. Ignatius loomed at its center, gazing at the savage beast with a prideful expression. Not a single cardinal seemed frightened or shocked by the carnage. A diminutive swarm of rach gathered behind them.

Those within the ward were Ignatius's followers. Each one was responsible for Fenris's ascension and the creation and destruction of the Meridian.

They had planned this from the beginning.

Overcome by his anger, he harnessed the spirits within and howled. A great beam of light erupted from his jaws, searing the air and colliding with the cardinals' dome. It roiled and flickered, but held strong.

The roaring above stopped. Recoiling from his assault, Fenris looked up into the eyes of the golden fox, who regarded him with curiosity. He was much smaller and infinitely less powerful, but the beast bared its teeth regardless, considering him a threat.

Growling, he dodged a massive paw, hurling a barrage of fireballs that bounced harmlessly off the beast's back. Avoiding another stomp, Fenris raced toward Ignatius and his cabal of cardinals. Attempting a battle of strength with such a monster was pointless when more fragile ones were hiding beneath a weakening veil.

Launching himself at Ignatius, Fenris conjured lightning to pummel the veil. It fluttered violently, threatening to break. One more attack, and it would fail.

A whip-like tail crashed into him, crushing his ribs and tossing him sideways. He hurtled through the air, crashed into the far wall, and crumpled to the ground.

"Fenris!" a familiar voice screamed.

Jareth and Basil stood at the center of a wavering veil, Basil's hands raised to maintain the shield. Magdolina bawled in terror, hunched over a prone figure.

Hestraea.

Elation and sorrow rushed in simultaneously. Aludrien was alive and had achieved his lifelong goal. But that victory came with a terrible, excruciating price.

Fenris howled in rage, focused only on Ignatius. He would pay for his crimes. And Fenris would make it hurt.

The fox was preoccupied with a group of soldiers gathered near the entrance. Hopefully, he could reach Ignatius before the monstrous Tal'Rach noticed. Slowly rising on all fours,

Fenris commanded the spirits to heal his broken bones and flesh.

Aludrien had left the dais, engaging with the poor soldiers above, and their agonized cries echoed off the stone walls. Loping forward, Fenris summoned another barrage as he reached the stage.

Lightning slammed into the shield, over and over. It wavered, long enough for one bolt to slip in. The deadly beam collided with the stone with a deafening pop, tossing the cardinals like rag dolls.

Fenris howled in triumph, but was cut short by a fireball that narrowly missed him.

Unfortunately, Ignatius had survived the blast, though his gilded robes were singed and blackened. He rose to his knees, smiling at Fenris as he approached.

"Behold the final god-emperor of the Xandrian Empire," Ignatius cried, cackling in delight. "After this day, no one will dare desecrate a spirit to increase a mortal's power. You should be proud of our achievement, Fenris, for we owe this victory in part to you!"

Fenris stalked his prey, growling low. For weeks, he had dreamed of this encounter and fantasized about the words he would say to the one who had used him for so much evil.

"You are more monstrous than any Tal'Rach. Do you understand how many innocents I have slain for you? For your cause?"

"Yes, my child. Sometimes, grotesque measures are required to slay a monster. The rach are sacred creatures, and we have defiled them. For what? To subjugate the world? Claude's death was necessary. The Meridian's insurgency was necessary. As was its destruction. It all exposed the danger of ascension. It caused the world to fear the Tal'Rach. And look, your new emperor is all the world needs to renounce ascension forthright."

The more Ignatius spoke, the angrier Fenris became. The Pontifex's justification was worthless. His convoluted plan had no redeeming qualities. He had used Fenris as a weapon. And he needed to be ended.

Fenris howled and lunged forward.

A golden paw fell from the sky, slamming into the dais around Ignatius. A pitiful, high-pitched scream was cut short by the gruesome popping of crushed bones.

Leaping backward to avoid the carnage, Fenris growled. The golden fox snarled, towering over him. The fox had not only taken his lover, but his chance to bring Ignatius to justice and atone for his sins. Dodging another swipe, Fenris unleashed a firestorm on the monster that was once Aludrien.

The feral monster roared, its tails flailing about, collapsing more of the outer wall with each strike. With Ignatius gone, a stark reality set in. If its rampage persisted, the beast would kill every soul within the ruins, continuing to New Arachovia and beyond. Such a force would be difficult to destroy. Only one other Tal'Rach existed.

Summoning the spirits within, Fenris willed his body to grow, tripling in size. It was the largest he could manage, but still smaller than the fox's head. But he was faster.

Charging between the front legs, he slashed at the golden fur with his vicious claws, cutting and cutting and cutting. Blood soon fell like rain, and the fox bellowed in pain, thrashing about, its legs covered in deep gashes. The fox continued its onslaught, swiping at Fenris with its paws and tails. Fenris dodged, mustering more fire, aiming for the fresh wounds.

The struggle persisted as Fenris wove under Aludrien, gradually draining him. If he could not stop the fox, no one would.

But his stamina proved weaker than his massive opponent. Soon, he was ragged and weary, and panting hard. The fox, however, was not burdened by such weaknesses. It caught Fenris with a swipe of its paw, sending him flying.

Bones broke on impact as he hit the stone steps, bouncing upwards from the momentum. He caught himself on all fours and leaped to the side, narrowly missing a flailing tail. Fenris was losing strength and fast.

There was only one way to end this. He hesitated, realizing that this horrifying creature was Aludrien.

Was.

Past tense.

A tear streamed down his snout. Aludrien was already gone, torn apart by the millions of rach inside him. Fenris had nearly lost his humanity with the burden of a fraction of spirits. So he resigned himself to carrying out the task he had resolved upon the instant he set eyes on the heir. To kill him.

Fenris glanced at the fox's wounds, unhealed and raw. It couldn't heal itself. Unleashing a dozen lightning strikes from above, aiming for the creature's wounds, Fenris bounded forward. The fox howled in pain and rotated to avoid the onslaught.

Allowing Fenris an opening.

Flinging himself into the air, he aimed for the creature's neck. His claws were long enough to tear its flesh; he only needed to land a solid blow on the jugular. Then the monster's lifeblood would spill.

The fox twisted its head, its jaws agape.

And snapped them shut around Fenris.

Great teeth skewered his legs as the darkness enveloped him, smothered by the rough, rancid tongue. He clawed, bit, and called forth fire, but the maw only tightened further. The harder he struggled, the more the gigantic jaw clenched; soon, he was fully immobilized and completely drained.

The fight was over. Once again, Fenris had failed. And for the final time.

The great tongue flexed, pushing him further into the dank tunnel. The fox was swallowing him whole. Panicked, he thrashed about in vain. He could not fight the beast with strength alone. He was incapable of overpowering such a creature.

But he didn't want to slay it. He could not.

A ridiculous idea popped into his mind.

Closing his eyes, he lay his hands on the giant tongue, concentrating on the Belantine Plains. The world slipped away as he retreated to the mind palace.

And dragged Aludrien with him.

The transition was labored and far more difficult than his usual visits. As the plains took concrete shape around him, he understood why.

Millions of rach flooded the sky above him, screaming in confusion and agony, swirling above like a chaotic storm of ghostly light. They thrashed and flailed about, ripping and tearing at one another in a feral fight. Many fled, clawing at the edges of the mind palace. The sky and earth rippled violently, threatening to break. He hadn't only brought Aludrien, but also the great host of spirits that had recently attached themselves to his soul.

But they hadn't fully assimilated; millions of unique voices and spirits swirled above, fighting for supremacy. A figure floated in the storm's epicenter, more corporeal than the rest. The deafening gale drowned out his screams.

The great host of rach was formidable, but they were in his domain. He willed himself upward, wrapping himself in a shroud of turbulent wind, tossing the spirits aside with ease. He worked his way into the storm until he reached the man floating in its center.

Aludrien howled in pain as the spirits descended upon him, attempting to burrow into his skin. But the heir remained defiant, slashing and flailing, holding them at bay. He refused to submit, to allow a single one to embrace him.

Commanding his violent gale forward, Fenris swept the rach away like a flood, forming his gust of wind around him and Aludrien, keeping the spirits out.

Aludrien whirled around, eyes wild and teeth bared, fists raised defensively, ready to fend off another assailant.

"Fenris?"

Aludrien relaxed slightly, his hands fell to his sides, and his anger dissolved into confusion. Fenris flew into him, wrapping his arms around. The larger man immediately broke, melting into Fenris and sobbing uncontrollably.

"It's alright," Fenris said, holding him tight. "I'm here."

"Their voices…they won't stop…their pain…oh their pain…I cannot take any more of it, Fenris…I tried…I am not strong enough."

Aludrien trembled, voice hollow. Fenris knew precisely what he spoke of, for he had experienced the same horror. Strength wasn't what Aludrien needed, but the opposite.

"You need to surrender, Aludrien. Embrace them. Fighting will only increase the pain."

The request was demanding, especially for one as controlling and meticulous as the heir. His reaction was less than encouraging. Pushing away, his face contorted in horror, he glared at Fenris.

"Give in to them? And lose myself? I cannot allow that."

"You already have," Fenris said, trying his best to be gentle, though it wasn't his forte. "The rach have taken your body and have been wreaking havoc on the outside. If you do not allow them in, they will destroy you. Please."

"Fenris," Aludrien said. "It is too painful."

"I know," Fenris said, floating forward, taking Aludrien by the hands. "But I'm here."

His touch calmed Aludrien slightly, but he eyed the swarming rach outside the protective barrier warily, jaw clenched.

"I...I am not sure."

Fenris sighed.

"How about you show me your mind palace?" Fenris said.

"Mine?"

"Yes, you're a Tal'Rach," Fenris said, squeezing his hands. "Close your eyes, and imagine your favorite place. Somewhere safe, where you feel most yourself. And take us there."

"Will they join us?" Aludrien asked, glancing up at the great host swirling above.

"Yes. These rach are a part of you, though not fully yet. But you'll be in total control in your mind palace. Imagine them outside, where they cannot harm you. Then we will be safe."

Aludrien nodded eagerly and obeyed. Fenris released control and allowed the darkness to overtake him. They floated into oblivion, and flashes of a grotesque, massive maw appeared through the murk. His physical body remained inside the fox's jaws. But that didn't matter. Only he and

Aludrien existed.

The darkness faded. They emerged in the center of a conservatory, the moist air clung to their skin, and a myriad of pleasant floral fragrances delighted their noses—Aludrien's garden, similar to the one in the Emerald Pavilion, but much, much larger. Rows of exotic plants stretched out in every direction, hanging off balconies above them, a true palace, housing millions of flowers.

In the center, resting on a golden plinth, was Aludrien's prized bonsai, grown to the size of an actual tree, towering over them. The heir looked around his domain and smiled, relaxing.

"See?" Fenris said, motioning to the windows high above where the masses of rach beat against the glass in vain. "It is only you and me. You are safe here; they cannot harm you. You are in total control."

"Can we stay here forever?" Aludrien asked, almost child-ishly. He still hadn't regained himself fully.

"I'm afraid we can't," Fenris said gently. "Not until you let them inside."

Aludrien glanced above, eyes wide. The garden dimmed, in tune with his emotions. "I cannot."

"I've seen you surrender before," Fenris said, pulling himself close. "You let me inside you."

Aludrien chortled, pushing him away playfully. The green-house brightened.

"It is not the same, and you know it," Aludrien said. "The spirits do not feel as good as your cock."

"I imagine not," Fenris said, holding Aludrien tight. "But the concept is similar. Relax, surrender, and ride through the pain. It won't hurt for long, and then you'll be whole. Will you at least try? It's the only way to reach your destiny."

Cheeks flushed, Aludrien grinned.

"I do have practice in that particular area," he said.

"Then open the door," Fenris said, turning to the entrance on the far side. "Allow a rach inside and close the doors behind it. I'll be here with you."

Inhaling deeply, Aludrien turned toward the door, clutching Fenris's hand tightly. The massive doors opened, and a large, serpentine dragon slithered inside, pale and white and majestic. Other spirits attempted to claw their way inside, but Aludrien slammed the gate shut immediately after the dragon cleared the doorway.

The great beast regarded them both, winding over the plants with abundant grace. Its movements were slow, methodical, yet determined, as it approached Aludrien. The heir gripped his hand tightly.

"Relax," Fenris whispered, slowing his own breathing as an example. Aludrien followed suit.

The dragon straightened its long body and dived at Aludrien. The ghostly apparition forced its way into Aludrien's mouth.

Aludrien screamed, backing away, but Fenris held him tight.

"Embrace it. Allow its memories to wash over you. Feel every emotion. Listen to every thought. It will end."

The dragon's tail disappeared, slithering into Aludrien. He ground his teeth, breathing heavily.

"How do you feel?" Fenris asked as the heir opened his eyes.

"I...," Aludrien said. "Powerful. Strong. Endless. I feel it coursing through me."

"And that is only the beginning. Ready to try again?"

"No."

Regardless, Aludrien opened the doors once more. A violet bear trundled in before the entrance slammed shut. When it saw Aludrien, it bellowed and sprinted toward them at a breakneck speed. Bracing himself initially, Aludrien relaxed as the bear plunged inside. He made no sound, allowing the rach to dissolve into him. Once it disappeared, he smiled and faced the door.

"Again."

He repeated the process half a dozen times, receiving the rach one by one, bearing the pain with a growing fortitude. Then, he allowed a pair of spirits in at once, taking them simultaneously. Gaining confidence, he increased the group size incrementally, taking more and more. After each fusion, he appeared stronger, and the room around them brightened. Fenris held his hand throughout the grueling process.

Finally, Aludrien threw the doors open, allowing the mighty storm of rach to stream in. They dove into him eagerly, dozens at once. The river of spirits poured through the opening, illuminating the garden with a blinding light. They kept coming, more than Fenris had ever seen. After each passing second, he thought Aludrien would close the doors to recover. The swarm was more than Fenris could have ever handled. Not a single emperor or empress had ever received as many rach in the history of the empire.

Instead of losing himself, Aludrien regained his senses after each fusion, and his true nature returned. Determined. Incorrigible. Voracious. He devoured the spirits with a grit Fenris could only dream of, allowing the masses inside. It almost seemed an eternity, much longer than Fenris could have lasted.

The final rach disappeared behind Aludrien's lips, and

finally they were alone. Aludrien and Fenris. Fox and wolf. A pair of Tal'Rach.

But Aludrien radiated, his power far surpassing Fenris. He smiled jubilantly.

"It appears you were right," Aludrien said.

"So you admit you were wrong?" Fenris asked wryly. "That may be the most surprising thing I've witnessed today."

Aludrien scoffed, but leaned in and kissed him. Slow and passionate, full of yearning and desire. They continued for a while, riding the adrenaline and the ecstasy of the ascension.

"Shall we return?" Aludrien asked, pulling away.

"Do we have to?" Fenris asked, leaning in for another kiss. "Can we stay for a little while longer?"

"I believe I asked that earlier," Aludrien said. "And you refused me."

"Only because you would have died if you hadn't."

"Fair point," Aludrien said. "But I believe we have unfinished business in the waking world. Come, let us attend to it. Together."

The world melted away, replaced by the brilliant blue sky of the open-air theater. Fenris and Aludrien lay in the center of a crater, wrapped in a naked embrace. Gone were the fox and the wolf; in their place were two men, staring at each other and smiling. Fenris was precisely where he belonged: at the side of the most powerful being in existence.

24

Freedom

The Winter Palace's overstated, sumptuous, and cavernous ballroom proved suitable as a makeshift throne room. Despite the numerous cracks, the chamber had withstood the tremors from the ascension. An army of servants had swiftly cleared the debris in the three days since the disastrous ceremony.

Emperor Aludrien Aleksandran XLVI lounged upon his throne, robed in fine black silks, the ceremonial crown of Xandria resting on his head with a slight tilt. He peered down upon his subjects with aloofness and grandeur. Despite his deadly rampage, the Imperial laws were clear. He had received the rach's blessing and, therefore, was the indisputable god-emperor of Xandria. No one dared defy a creature capable of unimaginable power. Not openly, at least.

Nim flanked the throne, as resolute as ever, chin held high, glowing with unmitigated pride. The meticulous chamber showed no signs of their recent brush with death.

A modest contingent stood before the new emperor, regarding him with varying levels of trepidation, reverence, and disgust. A few were wrapped in bandages, recovering from the wounds sustained during the incident.

Five groups formed quietly below the dais, waiting with a tense nervousness. Hestraea helmed the first, still recuperating from her duel with the emperor. A handful of her generals flanked her in full insignis armor, their jaws clenched.

High Lord Basil and his husband Jareth stood beyond her, both pale as ghosts. Their daughter, Magdolina, shuffled her feet but remained poised like an elegant porcelain doll. A handful of lesser royals congregated behind them, none of whom Fenris recognized.

A gaggle of cardinals cowered near the rear of the assembly, gaping at Aludrien with terror and contempt. Most of Ignatius's co-conspirators had fallen victim to the wrath of the two Tal'Rach. However, the emperor had already launched a thorough investigation into the allegiance of every remaining church leader. Any cardinal with a hint of suspicion currently resided in the Winter Palace's dungeons.

The fourth and largest group was composed of two dozen ministers. The remnants of Vispin's government milled about in bewilderment.

Fenris stood in the center of the final group, his wrists bound by heavy chains, surrounded by two dozen heavily armed soldiers with their crossbows readied. He had awoken in the makeshift prison within the Winter Palace along with the rogue cardinals and had remained there for three excruciating days. Not a single soul had come to speak to him. This audience was the first time he had seen Aludrien since the ascension. Aludrien's silence left Fenris confused and frightened. The new emperor may have intended to use him after all and devised to publicly dispose of him in front of the upper echelons of his court.

Fenris nearly jumped when the emperor finally spoke.

"I appreciate your patience and understanding in these past days. Your presence demonstrates your loyalty and dedication to the throne of Xandria. Before we return to the capital, however, there are several important matters I would like to resolve."

Aludrien paused dramatically, gesturing to Nim, who presented a scroll.

"First and foremost, the matter of my succession. I am a man of my word, and as such, I honor my promises. With my divine power, I hereby declare Magdolina Aleksandra as my heir."

The crowd buzzed softly, though few were surprised. Basil, however, beamed brightly; his trepidation melted away. Magdolina smiled, but shifted nervously.

"With that settled, I shall move on to the matter of my heads of state. As emperor, it is my divine right to appoint the leaders of my military, my church, and my government. It will come as no surprise that my dear aunt, Hestraea Aleksandran, the greatest general our empire has ever known, will remain the Grand Marshal of my armed forces."

A few of the generals cheered, and Hestraea relaxed slightly, but her expression remained stony and suspicious. Restoring the relationship between nephew and aunt would require more than a single appointment.

"As for the leader of my government, I will refrain from appointing a chancellor today," Aludrien said. The crowd murmured, and a few of the ministers shouted in protest. The emperor clapped sharply, and silence fell upon the hall. "I spoke with the late Chancellor Vispin and listened to her request to restore the ancient apparatus of the Senate. She told me the sacred art of governance should not be reliant on a single person. No one, not even the divine emperor, can succeed in such a monumental undertaking alone. In this, she and I agree. From henceforth, you will no longer be my ministers, but senators of the reinstated Xandrian Senate. In the following weeks, I charge you with electing your own chancellor yourselves."

The room erupted with shocked and ecstatic applause. Aludrien raised his hand, commanding silence. The court obliged.

"As for my Pontifex, I appoint my dear brother Basil. As a royal, he is adept in the holy art of Animancy, and his gentle and kind demeanor will unite the church that has been mired in sedition and rot."

Basil gasped, his eyes widening. The emperor's half-brother was an outlandish choice, but the remaining cardinals seemed relatively pleased the emperor hadn't abolished their order entirely. Jareth wrapped his arm around his husband and kissed him on the cheek.

Within a few minutes, Aludrien quelled a hostile court that either hated him, feared him, or both. Few would find any of his declarations controversial or in poor taste. He simultaneously strengthened the Aleksandran line through the Pontifex and Grand Marshal appointments and reinforced the court's power by reestablishing the Senate. It would take more than a handful of safe, popular choices to diffuse the vitriol and contempt he had garnered over the past months, but it proved to be an incredible start.

"For centuries, my ancestors have governed this great empire with valor, wisdom, and divinity bestowed upon them by the rach. The ancient art of birthing a living Tal'Rach has been the foundation of our Imperium, an act that strengthens our leaders and connects them to our ancestors. And to many, it is considered an abomination. And justifiably so."

A gasp rippled through the crowd. Fenris smiled.

"In addition to plotting my father's murder, Pontifex Ignatius Lilias also conspired to sabotage the ascension by significantly increasing the amount of rach used, in an attempt to create a monster, which many of you had the misfortune to witness. His motive, I have recently discovered, was to besmirch the name of Aleksandran and prevent the future defiling of human spirits during the process of creating Tal'Rach. I will not allow anything to tarnish the glorious name of Aleksandran. However, I will honor the late Ignatius's wishes. As emperor of the glorious Xandrian Empire, I decree with my divine power that the act of ascension is hereby banned, under penalty of death. No one person will be a god above anyone else. Fenris Vale and I will be the last Tal'Rach."

The nobles gasped in delight, and a few cheered. Many had silently shared Ignatius's ideals, and now they could publicly display them. A pair of royals, however, wailed in despair, screaming slurs. Such a law was in direct opposition to centuries of Xandrian tradition and would weaken the Aleksandran bloodline. But Aludrien was steadfast in his choices, and the other nobles expressed their varying degrees of agreement. He stamped his foot on the marble, producing a shock wave that silenced the court.

Fenris swallowed hard when Aludrien's gaze fell upon him. The new emperor had primarily made popular decisions that wouldn't generate many new enemies. And now the fate of his father's murderer lay in his hands. Fenris did not like the outcome, regardless of the relationship the pair had cultivated, which would explain why Aludrien had refused to see him since the ascension.

"The final matter involves the prisoner convicted of my father's murder, an individual whom I myself captured and interrogated. After intense investigation and thorough inquiries, the truth of this tragedy has come to light. Fenris Vale did indeed kill my beloved father, Emperor Claude Aleksandran XLV. However, he did so under duress and by the explicit orders of the late Pontifex Ignatius Lilias and his cohort of treacherous cardinals, who created the Meridian as a part of their scheme. Now that the individual truly responsible for regicide has faced divine judgment, I must resolve the matter of his assassin. Due to obvious emotional and psychological abuse and manipulation, I find Fenris Vale innocent of the murder of Claude Aleksandran. As emperor of the glorious Xandrian Empire, with my divine power, I hereby absolve Fenris Vale of all of his past crimes and henceforth declare him a free man."

With a wave of Aludrien's hand, Fenris's chains disintegrated and fell to the floor in a pile of sand. Such miraculous feats were beyond even Fenris's capabilities. Outrage boiled over the courtiers, and a few shouted insults at Fenris. Aludrien stomped his foot, and the entire building shook violently. The crowd fell silent. Fenris's mouth hung agape. Aludrien had intentionally saved Fenris's sentence for last. He was placating the court, preparing them for his most unpopular decision. To save Fenris, yet again.

The court looked upon him with the same fear and apprehension as before. Despite his populist appointments, he could never hope to regain their trust fully.

"As the divine emperor, my decrees are final. You are all dismissed. I will see all of you in my capital. Safe travels." The courtiers dispersed, chatting among themselves with a mixture of joy, shock, and horror.

The emperor glanced at Fenris, signaling him to stay in place as the ballroom emptied. After a short while, the great doors slammed shut, but they were not alone.

Grand Marshal Hestraea remained, standing defiantly before her nephew.

"Are you here to lecture me, dear aunt?" Aludrien asked.

Hestraea shook her head. "No. Though if I had half a mind, I would strike you down."

"For what crime?" Aludrien asked. "I have been accused of so many, it is difficult to keep track."

"What were you thinking?" Hestraea seethed. "You have made more changes to the empire in one afternoon than Claude did during his entire reign. Stripping the throne of its power? Reviving the Senate? Outlawing ascension? Exonerating your father's murderer? The way you've acted, the empire will tear itself apart."

"That may be the case. The Imperium as we know it will not survive, but from what I have seen these past weeks, it does not deserve to."

"You have destroyed centuries of tradition and legacy, Aludrien!" Hestraea said, exasperated.

"Every emperor and empress has served a different purpose. When the realm needed a savior, Aleksandra rose and united the lands. When the realm craved guidance, Regina became a scholar and wrote her proverbs. General, savior, sage, all serve a purpose."

"And what does that make you, Aludrien?" Hestraea asked.

"Savior? You believe you know better than your predecessors, who allowed the Imperium to thrive for centuries?"

"I have seen the cost of the empire with my own eyes, in the slums not two leagues from where you stand. The empire was broken, almost beyond repair. I must destroy it to rebuild."

"And you believe pardoning your father's murderer, with whom you colluded for months, will aid in your quest to reshape the Imperium into your image?"

"I never claimed the empire needed a reformer," Aludrien said. "Everyone in this room witnessed the atrocities I committed. I will never be more than a monster to them. So I will become the one they need."

"Foolish boy. You can never properly rule subjects who fear and loathe you."

"You will be happy to discover that I do not plan to rule for long."

Hestraea gaped. "What are you saying?"

"I will serve the realm as its tyrant, while you, my brother, and Jareth train Magdolina to become the realm's savior. And when the time comes, I promise you I will abdicate and allow my successor to heal the Imperium while I disappear alongside the man who killed my father. The man I love."

"You would squander your entire legacy? For a wretch like him?"

"You are mistaken, dear aunt," Aludrien said. "I am embracing my destiny, with him by my side. And I will sacrifice a lengthy reign for the good of the realm."

Hestraea gaped, her frustration morphing into something strangely resembling respect.

"You promise to abdicate?" Hestraea asked.

"The moment Magdolina is prepared to replace me," Aludrien said.

"You are more like your father than I gave you credit for," Hestraea said. "He once spoke of the sacrifices required to rule. A virtue you seem to comprehend."

"So, do I have your support?"

Hestraea hesitated, deep in thought.

"Why did you have Barrett killed?"

"Because my spies overheard him colluding with Vispin. If he succeeded married you, he wouldn't have stopped at being the empress's consort. He would have murdered you."

Hestraea blinked.

"Although I do not agree with your methods or your actions, I now know you are doing what you believe is right. Though I may never bring myself to forgive you for Barrett's death, as thanks for sparing my life, I will support you for the rest of your reign. As long as I live, I will protect the Xandrian Empire and its throne."

"Your support is all I ever wanted," Aludrien said. "I will spend the rest of my days proving that to you."

"Aludrien," Hestraea said, her tone softening. "I want to… apologize for my words in the gardens. I understand I was misguided."

"Think nothing of it," Aludrien said. "You are dismissed, Grand Marshal."

"Your Majesty," Hestraea said, bowing low.

The Grand Marshal left without another word.

"That went better than expected," Aludrien said as the doors shut.

"We shall see how her allegiance fares after she meets with her generals. A few may want your head," Nim said.

"I have every confidence that you will not allow that to

transpire, my dear Nim," Aludrien said. "If it weren't for you, I would have died years ago."

The chamberlain blushed slightly at the praise, but swiftly regained their composure.

"I shall prepare the airship at once. We can depart at your leisure, Your Majesty," Nim said, descending from the dais. They shot Fenris a wry smile as they departed.

The ballroom was empty save for the two Tal'Rach, in the place where they had shared their first kiss.

"You're an asshole," Fenris growled. "You could've come by at least once to reveal your plan."

"I needed to appear impartial," Aludrien said.

"Bullshit. I thought you were going to kill me."

"And why would I do that?"

"Because you're an asshole."

"That is no way to speak to the man who granted your freedom."

"You did not have to pardon me," Fenris said as Aludrien rose and approached him.

"Correct," Aludrien said.

"You've marred your legacy by allowing me to live."

"Absolutely."

"And you've implicated yourself in your father's murder."

"Naturally," Aludrien said, finally reaching him. "I could not live with myself if I allowed the man who saved me to die. Even if he killed my father."

"And by doing so, you've created more enemies than you had before."

"True," Aludrien said.

"Were you serious about what you told Hestraea?" Fenris asked. "That you will abdicate when Magdolina comes of age?"

"Yes."

"And you will pose as a tyrant to strengthen her reign?"

"I meant every word," Aludrien said. "Which raises a final matter."

"And what is that?"

"Well, given that I am emperor, our contract is complete. You have fulfilled your part of the bargain, and since you no longer wish to kill me and the threats to the realm are dead, I believe I have fulfilled mine."

"What is your point, Aludrien?"

"Since you have earned your freedom, I wanted to present you with an offer. To become the head of my security. It will be long hours and challenging, given the new enemies you pointed out. But you were always better at protecting than you were at killing."

"And what of Jareth?"

"He will be busy as the husband of the new Pontifex and raising my heir. I am certain he will be thrilled to be free of my company. But it is merely an offer. You can do with your life as you will. Return to the Belantine Plains, if you see fit. You can take time—"

"I accept," Fenris interjected.

Aludrien beamed and kissed him passionately and sweetly. When they parted, Fenris regarded Aludrien carefully. He seemed different. Warmer. Calmer. More at ease. It could have been because he had achieved his goal and become the most powerful being in existence. Or because Fenris chose to stay.

"Let us away, I long for a more temperate climate," Aludrien said, taking him by the hand. Fenris followed, running across the ballroom.

The emperor chuckled with almost childlike glee. It was a side of him Fenris hadn't glimpsed before, and he was looking forward to discovering much more in the years to come.

"Of course, Your Grace," Fenris said. "Or is it Your Majesty?"

"You, my dear, can call me whatever you like," Aludrien said. "You are welcome to use that name you used the other night."

Fenris laughed, following Aludrien through the twisting halls of the Winter Palace. Soon they emerged onto a narrow courtyard. The cobblestone plaza was wide enough to hold Aludrien's private airship, though the vessel was twice as large as the farmhouse Fenris had been raised in.

They dashed inside, ascending the metal ramp into the plush interior. The compact, luxury cruiser was prepped and ready for flight, and its crew was already inside, awaiting their lord for departure.

"All went well, Your Grace?" Elzia asked.

Fenris gaped at his friend, looking at the emperor, who wore a cheeky grin.

"As well as I could have hoped for," Aludrien said. "Though they almost rioted when I pardoned our dear Fenris. Has Belessia started on dinner? All of this law-making has made me peckish."

"I'm sure she can prepare a snack for you and Mister Fenris," Elzia said, bowing to both. "Congratulations on your freedom."

"Thanks, Elzia," Fenris said as she disappeared through the far portal.

The cabin door opened, and Nim strode inside, bowing slightly.

"Ah, Nim, are we ready for departure?" Aludrien said.

"Everything is in order, Your Grace," Nim said.

Aludrien smiled and pulled Fenris through the ship upwards to the large observation deck. When they arrived, the craft had already disembarked, inching upwards into the sky. Leading him to the bow, Aludrien pressed Fenris against the railing and wrapped his arms around him. Fenris marveled at the ancient city below, which grew smaller and smaller as they rose. Although this wasn't his first time aboard an airship, he had always been stuck in steerage. He hadn't seen the world from this angle before. It seemed so tiny, so distant. The further they left the ground, the closer he felt to the man behind him.

"So you love me?" Fenris asked, smirking.

"Oh, you caught that," Aludrien said wryly.

"I found it romantic," Fenris said. "Who needs an intimate, intentional profession of love when you can hear it indirectly in front of someone's aunt?"

"At least I said it," Aludrien said, squeezing him tightly. "Some go their entire lives without hearing such a phrase. You should consider yourself lucky."

"And have you ever heard those words before?" Fenris asked.

"Not from anyone whom I desired in return," Aludrien sighed melodramatically. "Yet."

Fenris chuckled, whirling around unexpectedly to grab Aludrien forcibly, pinning him against the railing. Eyes locked, he grabbed him by the back of his neck and pulled him close for a kiss—long, hot, and wet. Their hands pawed over one another, cloyingly. Cheeks flushed, hearts throbbing, they nearly tore their clothes off there on the windswept balcony. Before they became lost in lust, Fenris pulled back, placing his hands on Aludrien's cheeks.

"You are overbearing, stubborn, and conniving, Aludrien Aleksandran."

"Some would say gregarious, determined, and clever," Aludrien interjected.

"You irritate me, confuse me, and shock me daily," Fenris continued. "I've never met someone like you in my life. And I believe I'll never meet anyone else I enjoy more. You've changed me, Aludrien, given me purpose, and saved me in more ways than one. I am by your side, forever and always."

Fenris kissed him once more, soft and sentimental and slow.

Aludrien withdrew. "And?"

"And what?" Fenris said.

"Do you have anything else to say?"

"No. I believe I said much more than you."

"But not the words."

"Those you'll have to earn."

"Such a tease."

"You can take me to your bed and earn them."

Aludrien laughed, pushing off the railing, embracing Fenris, and pulling toward the stairs. Fenris resisted playfully, though allowing the larger man to shepherd him backward.

For the first time in his life, thousands of feet above the earth, with the most hated man alive, the man that he loved fiercely, Fenris felt free.

And the voices were quiet.